Proud Riley's Daughter

Joyce Bentley was born and bred in Manchester, but now lives in an old Silk Hall high on the Lancashire moors. She is the author of several historical novels, and the first biography of Oscar Wilde's wife, entitled *The Importance Of Being Constance*. A Creative Writing lecturer in the Open College North West, she is also a historian, with special interest in the 1890s, the history of Manchester, philatelic history and music halls. Being of total Irish descent, she is for want of a better word a 'Hiberniaphile'.

Joyce Bentley's grandparents' only hope of survival was to leave Ireland in the cattle boats before the first World War. They came from Westport, County Mayo, the remote region of the Connemara mountains, and Port Rush to find work in England and become part of the Manchester-Irish scene. They brought with them a fund of folk lore and stories of grinding hardship and laughter which the author has encapsulated and brought to life.

GW00598464

JOYCE BENTLEY

Proud Riley's Daughter

PAN BOOKS
London, Sydney and Auckland

First published in Great Britain 1988 by
Sidgwick and Jackson Ltd
This edition published 1990 by Pan Books Ltd,
Cavaye Place, London SW10 9PG
9 8 7 6 5 4 3 2 1
© Joyce Bentley 1988
ISBN 0 330 31118 2

Printed and bound in Great Britain by
Richard Clay Ltd, Bungay, Suffolk

To my daughter, Jade

PROLOGUE

The Great Bog of Ennabrugh, a vast vegetable waste, possessed a life of its own to which everything about it was subservient. By very nature solitary and forbidding, it inspired in all who saw it the awe and respect due to something which had developed from the mists of time and had seen the dawn of civilisation. There was nothing friendly in this feature of the wild landscape which lay dark and sullen, resisting the advances of spring.

Great clouds distilled from the mountainy terrain surrounding the bog swept heavy shades of displeasure over the helpless valley below. But nature with her coaxing ways, gentle whims and promise of fulfilment ignored such a curmudgeonly display. The first damp airs of April brought a flurry of bright flies to caress its surface with gauzy wings, and sharp shafts of sunlight to warm its depths.

The marsh marigolds, made brave by the changes being wrought, huddled together in shy little clusters, pale yellow sphagnum and purple mosses slowly began to wander along the far edge. The rushes, stirred by an upsurge of sap, began to assert themselves. Plovers called softly and red kite hovered in pairs. A garland of buttercups, encouraged by the bravery of the others, flourished on the south side. Spring had come lightly to grace the vast waste of Ennabrugh.

The weeks that followed bore no splendour of summer or softening of aspect. The Great Bog experienced a summer of its own, of subterranean bubblings, of strange noises as the gasses below fermented and frothed to erupt like miniature fountains on the surface.

In the evening when the sun had slipped behind the mountains and darkness cloaked the earth, jack-o'-lanterns – lean phosphorous fingers of light – leapt and danced like weird sprites. It was a season of surfeit too, for in the summer the unwary and unexperienced strayed, and very few escaped the suffocating embrace of Ennabrugh. It surrendered nothing easily, from the rushes which girded its shores to the peat which lined its banks.

There it lay, hot and panting, under great bulks of brassy cloud, as it had before time began; and over the eternity of decay lay the sweet stifling odour of ripeness.

There were no trees in the autumn to scatter russet coloured leaves over its surface, no soft whinnying winds to fan the drying stacks of rushes, nothing but the ethereal glories of the mist. Strange avenues of it whirled and swirled, each full of concealed desires, hatreds and appetites. Here and there clumps of vegetation rising from the deeps took on a primordial form, their curious branches bearing fruit of a ghastly nature. The pale yellow sphagnum and purple mosses shrank back into themselves as the stumps and clumps rose up like wraiths. Neither sky nor land were distinguishable the one from the other. The plover mourned softly and withdrew like souls in trouble, the red kite hovered silent as a leaf, the only witness to the passing of autumn.

But soon the wind and rain locked together to drive away the mysterious veiling. Tempest and sleet bore down, the ever moaning winds wailed like a banshee, but the Great Bog was impervious, its face calm against these wild portents. No voice of peatcutter, no plover or kite now disturbed its solitude, only the snow-fed brooks hurrying down to pay their dues.

When the rushes became hoary with frost, and the ice tinkled in the reedbeds and the sky became heavy, there was no snow on Ennabrugh; the Bog cast it off petulantly with the warmth created within its depths. There was to be no whiteness, no purity, nothing of beauty here, only death and decay. For was it not made up of these very things? Did it not depend on this process for its continuation?

CHAPTER ONE

Ennan was a settlement of cabins and shacks, huts and hovels scattered across the valley, forgotten by civilisation. Before the Great Famine the community had thrived on the philanthropic gestures of its English landlord, but now the small stone chapel and the English which had taken the place of Gaelic were the only enduring legacies. Their isolation was disturbed only by the visiting priest, tinkers on the march, and poachers on the make.

It was situated in desolate mountainy country where only the strong survived. The valley was broad and the sides steep, and at the head of it, on elevated ground, lay the Great Bog of Ennabrugh from which the community took its name.

The Bog provided the crofters with their essentials: peat and rushes. Yet only the most knowledgeable of peatcutters ventured there, for the black, brooding mass was a sight so threatening that it was reckoned to sober the inebriate immediately. It was weird, wild, treacherous and unpredictable.

Every year two outside events made an impact on this insular peasant society: the tinkers marching east on St Patrick's Day, and the ancient custom of the Long Dance.

It was the spring of 1880, the year in which Riley, at the age of thirty, gained the dubious distinction of being the only man – of sound mind and limb – to remain unmarried. He was a tough, stocky man. His eyes, dark brown in a pleasant weather-beaten face, lit up with a rare twinkle at the chatter of his friend. He wore his thick hair shortish and allowed sidewhiskers to grow along a jawline which showed no particular strength. In truth, Riley was redeemed from the unremarkable simply by remaining unmarried.

He stood now, hands deep in his pockets, with his friend O'Malley. The two men were watching the untidy cavalcade of tinkers wind its way noisily down the hillside.

'God save us!' declared O'Malley. ' 'Tis Clancy and his crew! You

9

can wait six months for them, six bloody months, and it turns out to be Clancy!'

'Just so long as his money's good,' reflected Riley.

'Ah, but is it?'

'It'll be good enough for my turf, boyo.'

'Ay, 'tis a winner you're on, Riley, old son, they can't be doing without their peat – You've done well out of the old Bog – not to mention a bit of poaching on the side!'

'The best thing I ever got out of the Bog was when I dug up that silver flute. There it was on the spade, like a gift from God.'

'I reckon it owed you that for the years you've kept it company. You'll be playing at the Fair?'

'I will so.'

'Ye know, Riley, every Fair and Long Dance I try to get you fixed up with a woman . . . there were the Hanratty girls, Duggan's sisters. Oh,' he raised his hands, 'and God knows how many more I've had lined up for you, but you won't play!'

Only O'Malley could talk to Riley like this, for he was his only friend.

'Ach, leave off, will you, some fellas are just not the marrying kind.'

'Leave off! I've not started yet. I mean, you're not bad looking and you don't lack money – but you don't talk!' He hunched his thin shoulders as though the subject was beyond his comprehension. 'That's your trouble, Riley. I blame it all on that bloody flute, and the hours ye spend on it. That flute is to you what words is to me, and it won't be doing, ye know. The women like a fella who can crack a joke and tell a good tale!'

'Like yeself, O'Malley! Honest, you can talk the hind legs off a donkey. 'Tis jealous y'are of me freedom. Sure, I've heard 'em say as I've passed by, "There goes Riley," they say, "without a care in the world." And 'tis right they are. I've only me own belly to fill and I intend to keep it that way!'

There was a pause while both men eyed the progress of the tinkers. Sure, it could be worse, thought O'Malley, at least the flute's kept him from being dour and taciturn. A talker he was not, but Riley on the flute was as enchanting a sound as ever flooded the glen. It got him mixing too, for any hooley without Riley's flute was no hooley at all!

Because O'Malley was his only friend, it did not mean that Riley was disliked, but the others had neither patience nor time for his quiet ways. Aloysius O'Malley always had time. He was never short of money, yet he did not dig turf, till the ground, keep pigs or seem to be employed in any kind of labour. He fancied himself as a man of the world, and because he had been the ten miles to the nearest town of Rohira several times 'on a little matter of business', he was Ennan's authority on the ways of civilisation.

His schemes and plans seemed to pay off. What they were no one really knew and, being the man he was, no one asked. He had been taught to read and write by the Christian Brothers and had become a kind of head-man of the community. No one said as much, but if the gamekeepers or the steward from Lord Fitzcarron's estate needed to talk with anyone in the valley, it was always O'Malley. He had married at the age of twenty, and his handsome, thin, industrious wife had ever since been in a perpetual state of pregnancy.

Clancy and his crew had arrived. With a lot of shouting, swearing and laughter the wagons were unloaded and shelters rigged. Swarms of grubby children were dispatched to find kindling to light the camp fire.

'I'm off,' declared Riley. 'Or they'll lay their thieving hands on all the timber I've salvaged over the years. See ye later!'

He mounted guard in the compound surrounding his hut until the tinkers' fire was well ablaze and they had no need of kindling. He then rapidly sold off his stack of dried peat.

Whilst Riley was always their first call, their second was to Pat Feeney the schoolmaster. Not that they went with any intention of obtaining tuition for their young during their stay, but rather for a good supply of poteen, that illicit and potent blend of whisky which was taken in large quantities to keep out the dank atmosphere of the valley.

Pat, now florid of face and corpulent of figure, had as a younger man come up to Ennan filled with a missionary zeal for the education of peasant children. Six months later he was a disappointed and disillusioned man. Whatever applied in the Board schools in the town did not apply in Ennan. The parents of these ragamuffin children did, however, prove their appreciation of his efforts by steering Feeney's scientific knowledge to the distillation of the finest poteen this side of the Connemara mountains. It was rumoured he

11

had more stills than slates for scholars, and as a consequence his popularity grew.

Having warmed and fortified themselves, the tinkers settled into groups to haggle over prices and argue over quality. Others got out their hammers and anvils to repair kettles, pails and cooking pots. The lads and girls, for whom this was their only real social occasion, wanted to dance.

'C'mon, Riley!' they yelled. 'On yer flute, man! It's spring – time for dancing and music!'

'And by all the saints, you shall have it!' he answered, reaching into his pocket for the black and silver flute.

Soon the nimble feet of the young, eager to cast off the restraints of the winter months, darted and dipped in jig and reel. Looking over and beyond the dancers, Riley was startled to see a young woman looking right at him. She was beautiful beyond any of the mountainy women, and although wearing a tattered skirt and a man's ragged shirt with a bit of a shawl about her shoulders, was obviously not tinker bred. What worried Riley was the strong air of melancholy which hung about her. She looked as though all the cares of the world were hovering over her neatly plaited head. She sat apart from the rest on a fallen boulder, and stared as if mesmerised by the music.

His first thought was to ask O'Malley about her, or even Clancy himself, but he quickly retreated from such a plan of action and, with great, thumping heart beats in his ears, realised he was afraid to draw anyone's attention to her lest they took her away. She has an air of mystery about her, he thought, and half expected her not to be there next time he looked. But she was there. The woman sat in a tall and stately manner, her knees together beneath the torn skirts and not splayed out in the manner of the mountainy women. She was slender, fair-skinned and fair-haired – totally different from any other woman he had seen, but although she looked at him, he wasn't sure whether it was him she saw. No woman had looked his way for so long a time and with such intensity. It isn't me, he thought with a mixture of disappointment and relief, it's the flute, the music. Then his spirit soared, taking off like a skylark at having so appreciative an audience. Suddenly he wanted to change the tempo, to stop all the frenzy and to offer her a softer melody which would soothe away and dispel the mists of her melancholy.

So great was his absorption with her, and hers with him, that he

12

played on and on; his fingers were not weary nor his lips sore. For the first time in his life he was experiencing the total pleasure of a rapport with another person, and not just any person, but a beautiful woman.

He turned almost savagely on the Muldoon brothers who came to relieve him. Big, boisterous with poteen, and full of high humour, they set to scraping their fiddles, entirely ignoring Riley's mood. When he dared to look her way again she was gone. After the dancing, the talking, drinking and games of dice, Riley returned to his hut and sat until dawn thinking about the lonely lady at the Fair.

The following day he spent strolling about, or just sitting outside, hoping to see her. Anxiety began to gnaw at him because she did not appear. When night fell and the fire was huge, and everyone, having got into the spirit of the Fair, was afoot, he felt cheated and wondered if she had been a figment of his imagination brought on by O'Malley's talk of women. He found no joy in the flute, the dance, the dice, the talk, and nothing but despair as he lay in indecision and torment on his bed.

The Fair was already three days gone and Riley, in a ferment of emotion, wandered up and down wondering what to do. No one bothered about him, for Riley was a loner, kept himself to himself, and it was only when they needed Riley on the flute that his neighbours concerned themselves as to his whereabouts. Then, suddenly, she was there, sitting on a boulder. He had found her again! He had the oddest sense of having reached the end of some amazing quest.

Teresa Donnelly knew she would see the flute player again. She had to, for it was his music which had drawn and coaxed her back to life. It had dispelled the dark cloud which had threatened to engulf her. She had come out of the mist into which her mind had retreated, but with the lifting cloud had come the horrifying sharpness of reality.

'Would ye mind telling me your name?' Riley had spoken.

'Teresa Donnelly,' she replied simply, and added, 'It's the music of the angels you play . . .'

'Can I, can I stay with you, talk to you?' Talk! his mind echoed. Riley, talk! His deep-set eyes met the restless shifting of the amber ones and held them until she nodded her assent. 'What is it you're afraid of?' he asked, his eyes narrowing. 'Is it Clancy? C'mon, Teresa Donnelly, time's running out, and you must tell me what

13

you're doing here, for sure as God's in his heaven, you're none of Clancy's crew.'

Animated by his perception she spoke rapidly, apprehension in her eyes. 'They found me wandering about. I'd lost me memory, I think, with the shock of . . . the funeral.' She sighed, and if there had been a stone weight on her chest the sigh could not have been heavier. 'Y'see, I don't remember whether it was one week ago or two that I stood at the graveside of Timothy . . . Timothy Thomas. We should've been married that day. And would you know, I buried him instead. He caught a chill.' She looked beyond Riley, bleakly. 'Who'd a thought a big fine fella like him would have taken a chill? It turned to pneumonia, and he was dead in five days.'

'Have you no people, no family?'

She shook her head. 'They died with the cholera. Him and me lived in the same street.' She smiled wanly. 'Childhood sweethearts as they say . . . Fate kept us together. We were brought up in the workhouse and farmed out as servants to the same house. Timothy went from boots to coachman, and I went from scullery to housemaid. We got lodgings in town and lived out, but when he was ill they wouldn't give me time off to nurse him, and with pneumonia the doctor said he needed me day and night. So I left me position. When he died they were going to bury him in a pauper's grave, but I used our wedding money . . . and the rent for the lodgings to bury him with dignity in the proper churchyard. It was St. Joseph's . . . yes, I remember that. And the next thing I knew I was getting warm by Clancy's fire.'

'Ay, he would take you in, with an eye to the mâin chance. They'll work you till you drop, Teresa.' He let her name fall from his lips as though he had always spoken it. 'You know what they think of goys, don't ye? Goys, is what they call us, and we call them knackers. It's no life for a goy woman.' He surveyed the ragged skirts and torn shirt. 'Did they take the clothes off your back and all?'

She nodded and felt a first twinge of embarrassment at the sight she must look. Her heart warmed, recognising the twinge as a return to normality. 'Me shoes . . . everything, except this belt.'

Riley looked down to the belt, his eyes catching the long graceful arch of her throat, the swell of her bosom, the tiny waist. By the grace of God, she was like an elf, he thought, so dainty and delicate.

'This was Timothy's belt. I let them take everything else, but I

14

fought tooth and nail to keep this.' She was pensive for a moment and then addressed him quietly. 'On account of all you've said, would there be room for me here? Could I stay behind when they're gone?' The awfulness of a future with Clancy's crew gaped before her, and this man, the flute player, seemed her only chance of salvation.

Something of the same gaped before Riley. She must not go. He would not let her. The boldness of this sudden emotion made him shrink into himself with bewilderment. He had always been too shy to risk asking anyone's hand in marriage, for any refusal would have been utterly humiliating, a most fearful blow to his natural pride – enough to finish him. But now he must ask, he had to risk a refusal. And what a name she'd got, he thought, what a blessed name.

'Would ye be for marrying a fella like me, Teresa Donnelly? Sure, I know the dear man ye buried is close to your heart, it's only natural. And sure as Riley's me name, you couldn't go with Clancy. But if you stayed here, what would you do? You've no money and nowhere to live, and you being from the town, sure you'd never survive up here alone. I'd look after you, and build you a fine cabin, up there, away from the rest. What d'you say Teresa? Will you marry me?'

She pulled the ragged shawl closer about her shoulders and regarded him solemnly. 'There's something you ought to know. I'm three months gone with child. The priest said that getting married would sanctify the sins of the flesh and make it all right for the little 'un . . .' Her voice trailed away at the look of overwhelming tenderness and pride which infused the weather-beaten face before her. If she had been carrying the heir to a fortune he could not have looked more proud.

'Marry me, Teresa Donnelly,' he pleaded. 'I'll be your protector, you and the little 'un, and sure to God Himself, I'll work me fingers to the bloody bone for you both.'

She continued to look at him in the same solemn-eyed manner. With no money, no position to go back to in the town – for she'd hardly get a reference after walking out like that – and Timothy dead, what did it matter now whom she married? Her lover would forgive her, indeed he'd be pleased to know their child would not be a workhouse-born bastard. Surely, St Teresa had guided her steps this way? 'I've got to tell you,' she stammered on, determined to be honest with the flute player. 'I don't think I could ever love you, if

15

that's what you're wanting. I've left all my love in the churchyard with Timothy.' She lifted her bleak eyes. 'There's nothing left.'

He nodded his understanding. ''Tis all right,' he said. 'It's as it should be, and him the father of your child, and all. There's only one thing I ask of you.' He watched her through narrowed eyes. 'It's that you'll not go away. You're a lady from the town; you'd not leave me and go back to civilisation, would you? I couldn't bear it. I'd put a gun to me heart, I would. Will you swear to me, Teresa Donnelly, that you'll not leave me?'

'Won't I swear to the priest in church?' she answered. 'Will I not swear before God? Besides, what would there be in civilisation for me now?'

A shadow fell between them. It was Clancy. Beyond him had gathered both tinkers and members of the community, the latter gazing in silent speculation at the sight of Riley talking to what they thought was a knacker's woman. He glared at Riley, and took Teresa roughly by the arm, jerking her off the boulder. 'Leave off yer talking with one of my women,' he snarled, pulling her away. Riley, who had never known anger in his life, felt it coursing through his veins like Feeney's poteen. He sprang at the tinker, who, unprepared for the attack, let go of Teresa's arm. He and Riley fell to the ground, thrashing about, rolling over and over, dealing blows, trying to get up and being pulled down, fists smashing against jaws and heads. Others came running at the sound of all the shouting.

'God save us!' yelled O'Malley, arriving on the scene. ''Tis Riley rolling about with a knacker! It's Clancy! What's up?' he demanded. No one knew. O'Malley threw off his coat. The Muldoon brothers threw off theirs. O'Malley then held up his hands. 'Back off, fellas. It's not a punch up,' he told them above the noise. 'We don't want any trouble with Clancy – he's mean,' he added to his neighbours. 'He'd like as not set fire to us all while we slept.' O'Malley knew he would have to act quickly, for if Clancy called his men into the affray, the Ennan lads would soon be in and God alone knew where it would all end. His lithe, tall figure, with its fair hair commanded attention; his very looks gained everybody's respect. He pulled the two swearing, sweating men apart.

'Riley?' he questioned mildly. 'Has the divil himself got into ye? Sure you've never turned your hand against anyone in all your thirty years.'

Riley blinked a rapidly swelling eye. Despite his bruises and aching ribs, he felt a thrill of pleasure at his achievement, for Clancy had clearly got the worst of the encounter. Having drawn blood in a punch up, he began to feel like a proper man. 'What did you do it for?' demanded O'Malley. 'Be sharp now, before it develops into a free-for-all. What set you on him?'

Teresa ran forward and grabbed O'Malley's shirt sleeve, but before she could say anything, Clancy, smeared in blood from a burst nose, made a dash for her.

'She belongs to us!' he yelled. 'She's one of us!'

'I'm not!' shouted Teresa. All eyes were upon her, for she had spoken for the first time.

'I say you are! Who found you wandering, eh? Who's given you food and shelter? Ay, and you've not done a hand's turn since we got you. As for him!' He spat in Riley's direction. 'He was after her, I could tell by the look of him. I was only pulling her away from him and he went for me.'

Aloysius O'Malley's eyes widened at the very idea of Riley being 'after' anyone. He looked at the woman still holding onto his sleeve, obviously in distress, and questioned his friend with a glance. 'C'mon, Riley, we don't want trouble. Is it true what he says about you?'

'May God have mercy on him! The lady by your sleeve, O'Malley, is Teresa Donnelly, from Rohira, and I was asking her to marry me.' Riley stopped short, suddenly realising that she had not actually agreed to marry him, for at the end of the proposal she had told him about the child . . . What was happening? Here he was, a man noted for his quiet ways, brawling and awaiting a woman's answer to a now public proposal! His mouth went dry. He felt faint. O'Malley had turned to Teresa. Every eye was on her. Oh Mother of God, moaned Riley, what would she say? His heart seemed to be outside his body waiting . . . waiting . . . Already the prospect of humiliation was eroding his confidence, already it all seemed to be happening to someone else.

'C'mon, then, Teresa Donnelly,' encouraged O'Malley, putting an arm about her thin shoulders. 'Will you lighten us as to the truth of the matter? Then Clancy can be getting on his way.'

'Sure, Riley wouldn't be telling a word of a lie.' The air was silent; not a dog barked, not a child wailed. Teresa looked at Riley, her

17

restless eyes still. 'He has asked me to marry him,' she said with more confidence than she felt. 'And I have agreed. His intentions were nothing if not honourable – which is more than can be said for Clancy!' The tone and diction of her voice, and the dignity with which she stood, raised some eyebrows and pursed some lips. What was this? Riley's neighbours openly wondered. After a brief speculation, and seeing that O'Malley was clearly on their side, Teresa seized the moment to address Clancy. 'I'd be pleased if you'd return the clothes you took off me back.'

'You can forget that,' he growled. 'You've had drink and vittles and we're out of pocket already.'

Riley stepped forward. 'I'll buy 'em off you.' Seeing hesitation, he added, 'Give you a better price than you'll get next stop. The girleen wants her own clothes.'

Clancy nodded a grudging assent, which sent two of his women scurrying for the clothes. Teresa followed, for she needed to get out of her rags and feel the familiarity of her own clothes, the comfort of hanging on to what was now her past.

Seeing that calmness and civility had returned, the gathering dispersed, their thoughts and tongues busy over the strange event of Riley's folly, for that was what they were calling it. After all, what was a man well set in his ways and as quiet as an old shoe thinking of, suddenly to air all his private life to public view? Presently Teresa, dressed in her neat town clothes and holding a wide hat, watched alongside O'Malley and a few others the tinkers hitching their wagons and taking down their tarpaulin rigs. After loading, and much swearing, the procession began the long straggle out of the valley.

The ebullient Duggan brothers – when not referred to collectively they were known as Young Duggan and Old, there being a ten-year gap and eight sisters between them – chivvied the remaining few to Young Duggan's cabin to drink Teresa's health in poteen and tea.

Even in her rags she had had a set-apart look, but her tall figure, shapely in a close-fitting coat, the skirts gently swinging as she walked, was to the mountain folk such a majestic sight as was only to be seen when folk came up to the Long Dance. Perched on the only solid chair in the Duggan household Teresa remained aloof, feeling overwhelmed and swamped. Everyone seemed to be talking at once, and being used to the orderly existence and quiet life of the housemaid, she found the contrast too much to absorb. She realised that her stay with Clancy's crew must have been similar, but it had not penetrated her dazed condition. The talk, for it could not be called conversation, was loud and given to laughter and much calling on God's name to witness this or that, to condemn or save. If it was not God, it was Christ's name which prefixed many a statement, and Teresa had never heard the Blessed Virgin or the saints called upon so frequently in so short a time.

Sensing Teresa's unease, and indeed himself not being keen on company, Riley noted the encroaching darkness and used it as an excuse to get away. The shared relief made light of their walking together for the first time, it gave them a conspiratorial feeling which overrode any self-consciousness.

'Have you always lived up here?' she asked.

'I have so. Was born in the very place I now live.' He thought over his words for a short while and told her. 'You'll find I'm a quiet sort of a fella, not much in the way of talk, y'know. You get that way when you've spent a lifetime digging and stacking turf up at the Great Bog, there. It drains a man of his talk. There are some, like O'Malley, who can talk the hind legs off a donkey!' He shot her a sideways glance. 'D'you not mind me being . . . quiet, like?'

'I'd rather have it than the other way. What about your family?'

'They've all gone. I was the only survivor of all me mother's children.'

'Did they spoil you?'

'Spoil?'

'Y'know . . .' she sought the right word, 'took extra care . . . a favourite?'

'No one does anything like that up here. Let me tell ye that my earliest memories – I must have been about six or seven – are me da putting a peat-cutter in me hand and marching me up to Ennabrugh in all weathers!'

'It's a wonder you've lived to tell the tale!'

'So, you see how hard a life it is up here, Teresa.' He gave a short laugh. 'To make it worse, me da scared the daylights out of me by saying the Bog would swallow me up if I put a foot wrong! But I had to stay, for if I went back home he used to thrash me.'

'Sounds like the workhouse! And what about your ma?'

'Ran off with a tinker. Me da went after 'em, and neither came back!'

'Didn't anyone take you in?' Her voice was sonorous with concern.

'Ach, they would have done, but only for the strength of me arm, and how much turf they could get out of me. No . . .' he sighed. 'Better the divil you know, as they say. I'd always had to look to meself, so I wasn't changing a thing.'

He stopped at the door of the hut in which his parents quarrelled and bred, in which he had been born, and in which his brothers and sisters had died. He pushed open the door with his boot, and Teresa halted at the threshold, staring in dismay and unbelief. Although a workhouse child, and having been in some way prepared by Riley's information, the sight of the one-roomed hut with its floor of bare earth took her aback. She had been in service since the age of ten and such service had lifted her far above the primitive. Why, they kept shovels and household rubbish in better huts than this at the big house where she had worked!

He, as though for the first time, looked on his ramshackle dwelling with shame and disgust. 'Sure I'll build you the finest cabin in Ennan,' he said fiercely. 'And God help me, I'll start in the morning.' He indicated the broken down bed by the wall. 'Lie yourself down there, Teresa, I'll be fine on the chair.'

'Your body'll be stiff enough on the morrow after all that fighting, and there's room for the two of us.' Her lips parted in the first trace of a smile. 'If you don't get your proper rest you'll not be fit to start on the cabin.'

'You'll be safe with me,' he murmured, bending to take off his boots and to cover the embarrassment which flooded his face. 'Ay . . . I won't say I'm not glad to be stretching out me bones.' He lay down. Teresa placed her hat on the chair and, not removing even her boots, straightened the skirts of her coat and lay beside him, her eyes wet with tears. He felt the bed sink with her weight and, although weary, lay for a while staring wide-eyed into the darkness, unable to believe that so beautiful a woman was at his side, and would always be there.

The community, having sobered itself from the overall euphoric effects of the Fair and the drink, was amazed to discover it had all been true, that a lovely young woman had moved in with Riley, and would be married when the priest next came up.

Riley was as good as his word. Refusing any offer of assistance, apart from the loan of a donkey and cart for transport up the hillside, he began to build. Unwilling to be left behind as an object of

20

speculation Teresa followed him. She could have stayed with Mrs O'Malley, but she would not have felt easy, for the O'Malleys' door was always open to everyone: women who had been beaten by their husbands; drunken husbands who had been thrown out by their wives; lovers who had quarrelled – anyone passing always called in for a cup of tea and a talk. Children, dogs, cats, all were welcome, and to Teresa Donnelly's natural reserve, it was too overwhelming.

All the spars, planks and rough wood, and eventually the old hut itself, were dismantled with demonic haste and carted up the hill. Once up, Teresa stayed in residence even before it was finished, not that it took long. She fussed like a bird seeking the best nesting place for its young, and he tirelessly fetched and carried until it should be so.

At times like this, the small community was bonded together by a common curiosity. All differences and bickering were submerged to this end.

'Just upped his sticks and went, he did; in two days he'd taken the whole bloody lot!'

'The old shack wasn't good enough for my lady! Too good for the likes of us.'

'Ach, she'll not be lasting long; town folk aren't tough enough.'

'He's always been a bit of a mystery, has Riley.'

'And what about the woman? Where's she from, eh? An' what the divil does she see in Riley? More to that than meets the eye, an' O'Malley's not for telling.'

'Did ye ever see her talk to anyone except the O'Malleys?'

Heads shook solemnly.

'Not a word has she said to a soul.'

'It'll suit Riley well, that will!'

'Getting married next week ye know, when the priest comes up.'

'Marry in haste repent at leisure, that's what I say.'

'Unless there's some other reason.'

'What! Ye don't mean . . . ?'

'She wouldn't be the first now, would she?'

'Ye mean she's taking Riley for a ride?'

'God love us, woman, I didn't mean anything. I'm just . . .'

'Anyways,' put in Young Duggan, 'it's the finest cabin I've ever clapped eyes on. There'll be no holding him now. With a lady for a wife an' the best cabin this side of the Connemara mountains, he's got something to be real proud of.'

And so Proud Riley got his name.

The night before the wedding, Proud Riley, sitting back from the best supper he had ever tasted, was somehow touched to pity at the driving desire Teresa had to make herself useful. Her town ways of doing with plates, pots and cooking, and indeed the running of the croft, were all new to him, as they would have been to the rest of the community. He did nothing to curb this flurry of expertise, nor did he speak much, but his eyes were never away from her when she was near to him. He could not believe his luck.

Teresa had a small mirror in the purse he had bought back off Clancy and Riley had taken to looking at himself in it, to shaving and washing on a regular basis. He considered himself not bad looking, and expressed his satisfaction in the playing of the flute.

On this night, he pushed back his plate and surveyed her sitting opposite him. He formed his question with care, feeling that in all fairness it should be asked. 'Are you still for getting married on the morrow?'

She clasped her hands together. He reached out to touch them. They were cold. Her restless eyes wavered a little. Fearing to offend, he took his hands from hers and placed them on his knees.

'I told you,' she said hesitantly. 'I've no love left in me. It's meself should be asking you if you've repented of the offer.'

'But you'll not be leaving me, Teresa?'

'Am I not going to swear to God? 'Tis the kind man you are, and I wouldn't bring shame upon you.' She unfastened the leather belt from about her waist, and laid it on the table. 'It's all I've got by way of possessions. Will you take it, Riley, as a wedding gift from meself. Sure it'll keep your back warm while you're up at that godforsaken Bog.'

'But it was Timothy Thomas's, the only thing you've got of his . . .'

She shook her head, her lips parted in a wistful smile. 'The child, remember?'

'Ay, but I meant – '

'I know what you meant, and I want you to have it. It's a good belt for a good man.'

Filled with an emotion he had never experienced before, for no one had given him anything in his life, he stood up and untied the rope with which he kept his trousers up. He threw it to one side, and having fastened the belt, stood with a thumb in it. He saw the buckle gleam in the firelight and inhaled deeply.

'It's a right swell that I am.' He smiled. It was a rare thing, and she was pleased.

'Y'know they're calling you Proud Riley, down there, don't you?'

'Only because I've built this cabin, and because I'm going to marry a lady and live away from all of 'em.' He paused and then added reflectively, 'Before the Fair, they took no notice of me, unless they wanted me on the flute. If they're calling me Proud Riley it's because of you, Teresa Donnelly.'

And so the matter concluded. There was no mention of happiness or love, only fidelity. Teresa stayed up by the fire for a long time after Riley had gone to bed. She stayed to shed her tears: tears silent and heavy; tears which must be shed and he must not see . . . Timothy, oh, Timothy . . . Most of the time her emotions were numbed, dried up and spent, but memory would suddenly leap out at her. Memories of herself and Timothy so vivid and bright that she imagined herself back in Rohira – he in his boots and livery, she in her little white cap and fancy apron – until his death seemed all a bad dream. So vivid were these memories that she would get up, full of purpose and joy, lifting her eyes and expecting to see him. But all she saw were the four walls of the cabin, the landscape bleak with the shadow of the Great Bog, the distance down to the valley below, and Riley's boots steaming by the turf-fire.

The tiny chapel was in the centre of the valley and boasted the privilege of being the only place built of stone, with a cross on its sod roof where the others had a tin chimney. The rain had ceased to fall and the wind had gentled itself. The bride and groom looked an odd pair as they walked together down the hillside, he in his shirt sleeves, jerkin and big boots, and she some three inches taller and looking every inch the lady. The skirts of her black coat swung gently as she walked, and her face was shaded by the wide-brimmed hat. Once on the level he drew himself up, walking very proudly with her arm through his, nodding to this one and that as they passed the boulder on which she had sat and the place where Clancy had camped. The ice into which her emotions had frozen began to thaw a little with thankfulness. If it hadn't been for Riley and his blessed flute she would have been subjected to no end of humiliations with Clancy's crew, who when her pregnancy became obvious would have thrown her out to wander. She shuddered. Riley caught the vibration and looked at her suddenly. She smiled at him with such warmth that he walked on prouder than ever.

O'Malley and his wife, having agreed to be witnesses, came out of their long-cabin and fell into step behind the couple. At first, no one realised what was about to take place, but now that the O'Malleys were on the scene, some children trooped behind, and old man Duggan shouted 'Proud Riley's getting wed!'

The priest was waiting for them and all at once the little chapel was filled. For Riley, it was like a dream come true; not that he had had any aspirations to marriage, but now it seemed as though he had achieved his life's ambition. So when he stood before his neighbours and took Teresa Donnelly to be his wife, the austere grey stones seemed ablaze with glory. Trembling and pale, Teresa heard nothing of the ceremony. She repeated her vows after the priest in a low voice and received Riley's kiss on a cold, unresisting mouth. As they turned to pass down the short aisle to the door, she realised she had promised, for better or worse, to be not Timothy's wife, but Proud Riley's.

Outside more people had gathered, from curiosity rather than well-wishing. O'Malley took her hand. 'God bless you,' he smiled. 'And may you want for nothing, Teresa . . . Riley! The wife's laid a bit on for you both,' he added. 'Say you'll come?'

Knowing his wife cared as little for company as himself, Riley left the decision to her and was surprised when she nodded. Even though the long-cabin was soon filled to overflowing with people she did not know, Teresa drank the tea and poteen gratefully, and ate currant bread, a rare delicacy in Ennan.

Feeney the schoolmaster filled the cups from the flagon of his best and passed the fiery stuff around. Teresa, flushed with the warmth and the drink, seemed as radiantly happy as any bride. Even Riley paused from his flute in amazement. Yet, it was not the wedding which had brought the colour into her cheeks, but her baby. She had felt it move within her for the first time, her child and Timothy's. The movement of its tiny body thrilled her. It seemed like a good omen. Everything was going to be right for Timothy's child. It was her charge, her trust, part of his life within her.

Teresa laughed at the priest's jokes, and answered Mrs O'Malley's questions about the cabin, and even went so far as to invite them up whenever they felt like stretching their legs.

'The sky's beginning to darken,' she observed later. 'Hadn't we better be getting back before we lose our legs, and get soaked to the skin?'

Proud Riley, never a talker, and tired of playing his flute against the bawdy jokes and good-natured shouting, was only too ready to leave.

Although they had lived under the same roof for three weeks in the unfinished cabin with an air of complete friendliness, this, their wedding night, was different. From the moment they crossed the threshold, the atmosphere had changed. Teresa, guided by the light of the fire, lit the lamp, and stood looking at him. She felt resigned to whatever was to follow, and something was to follow, she knew it.

'Sure, y'know I'm not a one for the words, but you did well at O'Malley's. It's proud of you, I am.' He stood forward and clumsily put his arms about her unresisting figure. She felt the bristles of his whiskers against her face as he kissed her gently on the mouth.

'I've never done anything like that before,' he muttered shyly. 'I didn't know how lonely I was, and I see now that a fella needs someone to look after, to work for. I'm grateful to you.' He suddenly looked up to ask, 'You'll not go? You'll not leave me?'

She looked him full in the face, and lifted a hand to stroke his cheek. 'I told you before, Riley, that my only love was for Timothy and when he died I died too. I'm a dead woman. I care for you, I feel sorry for you, but I don't love you. So long as you understand all that, I'm willing to be your wife in the accepted sense – y'know, sleeping and all. As for leaving you, have I not promised before God?'

'It's a good soul you are,' he answered, leaning forward to kiss her again. He had never sampled the pleasure of kissing before, and now they were alone, and married, he was totally unprepared for the desire it kindled in him. He had always been detached from such emotions, but now they came out of the muddle of half-understood ideas, hot and clamorous. His thought galloped. He dragged at the reins, intuitively feeling such thoughts to be shameful in Teresa's presence.

But they would not be stopped. He looked swiftly at her. She turned her head away, for the look in his eyes was like a strong clasp.

She was still looking toward the fire and still standing by the lamp when he began to unbutton her coat. This being his first experience of intimacy it bothered him not at all that she just stood there. Very tenderly, yet with trembling hands, he undressed her, folding her clothes so as not to seem too eager.

She held her head high, apart from what was happening. The caress of his warm hands did nothing to thaw her, not that he, in his ignorance, expected her to be other than she was. While slipping the high-necked blouse over her head, the buttons became entangled with her hair. Fumbling to no avail, he decided to take the pins out, and for the first time saw her long hair cascade onto her shoulders, brown against the white skin. He put out his hand to stroke the tresses, fearful at first to touch her body. He was ashamed of his brown hands, gnarled and calloused against her flesh. His knuckles grazed her breast and, fascinated by his own boldness, he fondled the softness of it. Teresa, still aloof from his passion, saw the years ahead whilst the past echoed in her brain like distant thunder. Only the present she could not realise.

Riley, tearing off his shirt and trousers, picked her up and carried her to the bed, smoothing a place for her head and laying her down as if she were a child. At last, he had found an altar. He knelt down beside her. 'I've years left, Teresa,' he said softly. 'It's strong I am. There's nothing too hard for me now I've got you, and I swear to God, no harm will come to you, or the little 'un, ever.'

It was neither his love nor his passion which struck a chord in her, but his kindness. 'I could wish,' she said in an awed voice, 'that you didn't care so much about me. You've shown me more kindness than anyone else except Timothy, but I'll do my best to please you. Indeed I will.'

His arms were about her and, eager in his latent passion, he held her fast, as though afraid the darkness would spirit her away. Later, fulfilled and gloriously replete, he realised her body was icily cold. Cuddling her to his side, she began to cry without a sound, but he could feel the tears wet against his arms. She wept for a long time, and he lay, not knowing what to do, but gently stroking her tumbled hair.

As Teresa's pregnancy advanced, so did Riley's care of her. He waited on her with a goodness and gentleness, a kindness and courtesy that almost brought tears. 'If I live to be a hundred,' she told him, 'I couldn't repay you for all this,' and he merely smiled, happy that his attention gave her pleasure. She was anxious, too, when he was away poaching on Lord Fitzcarron's estate, frightened lest he got caught, either by the gamekeeper or in one of the crippling mantraps.

'I'm glad you're back,' she always said, relief in her smile. 'I'll wet ye some tay.' It was worth the risk, he often thought, to see her concern for him.

After they had eaten in the evening, he would play softly on the flute, altering the tone of the music to suit her mood. Teresa was at her happiest at such times because they were friends, companions. He would forget his passion and just be her friend, and she would feel so kindly toward him that she thought herself on the border of loving him.

When she went into labour he ran all the way down the hillside, scrambling and scrabbling to fetch Mrs O'Malley to come and attend her. He was sick with horror at her suffering, and during the pains he stood by the bed searching for some kind of comfort to give her, finding none. And when Mrs O'Malley sent him outside, he prowled round and round the cabin, watching the moon rise, the clouds scud across the heavens. He was beside himself with fear lest she die until with the early dawn a cock crowed in the valley, and alongside it another sound came through the clear air.

''Tis the child!' he murmured to himself. 'God bless it, it's Teresa's child!'

Mrs O'Malley's news when she returned to the valley told how the Rileys were besotted at the birth of a daughter. All the chins in Ennan started to wag again, for it was obvious the birth was too soon after the wedding.

'He's calling it Teresa, after her, but she calls it Tessa – nice for a little 'un, isn't it?'

'A right fool Riley is to be so taken with it.'

'And what about the father? It'll be no one we know.'

'Just so long as she knows!'

And two weeks later the christening gave them more to talk about.

'Oh no, they didn't wait for the priest to come up and christen it.

The chapel isn't good enough. D'you know what, and God strike me dead if I tell a word of a lie, they took the child down to St Joseph's with her riding on a donkey like the Virgin Mary herself!'

''Twas the first time Proud Riley's been down the town, and God save us you ought to have heard him going on to the Duggans about the roads being so narrow, horses pulling tram loads o' folk, houses built of brick, and gas lights – '

'It's a wonder she came back.'

'Lord bless us, she couldn't get back quick enough it seems.'

Riley had seen how eager his wife was to return to Ennan, but he was not misled. He had observed while they were in the town just how different she had been, how confident and laughing and knowledgeable; it was as though she had suddenly come to life. Her delicate face had glowed with pleasure as she showed him about and explained the complexities of civilisation to his bewildered senses, but he was just as confused by the fact of himself walking along the streets with so tall and fine a lady on his arm.

The only cloud to cross her radiance was when she had pointed to a high-walled house on the road out of the town. The workhouse she said it was, and if it had not been for Riley her baby would have been born there, a charity bastard. She had to tell him this, to point it out so he would know and understand the depth of her gratitude.

He had not resented the little pilgrimage to her lover's grave. She stood by it with the child in her arms, and he had waited by the railings. She seemed so much a part of it all that he suggested taking a lodging for the night so she need not hurry to make the return journey. When she refused, insisting they return before darkness fell, he was pleased; yet he saw only too well how she had fled from temptation.

Teresa, having reached the safety of her nest again, returned to the spinning wheel, caring for the cabin, and nursing her daughter. Sometimes she looked at the child and wondered that she did not feel more joy. Life had given her this gift, for which she had not asked, and yet had denied her the gift she had asked and prayed for over and over again: Timothy's recovery. In her heart she knew that if it were Timothy's head bent over the cradle instead of Riley's, the little sleeping face would fill her with joy immeasurable.

As the weeks passed into months, Teresa began to miss all the belowstairs gossip of her time in service. She found herself dredging up old memories of what the cook had said, and how outrageous the new housemaid had been. She gradually became less and less talkative, so that Mrs O'Malley ceased to call. Teresa did not mind; she wanted company, but of her own kind. So she worked and spun and became as silent as Riley himself. The difference between them being that, whereas Riley did not know how to communicate, Teresa was fast losing the inclination.

The Long Dance was an ancient custom for the folk of Ennan, an annual event to which people came in droves. Making a day of it, they poured into the glen on foot, horseback, wagon or carriage. The Dance, accompanied by flute and fiddle, took the form of a competition and anyone and everyone entered in a spirit of great hilarity, the winner being the person or couple who were still dancing when the others were exhausted. All the trappings of civilisation came up with the dancers and were a constant source of temptation to the mountainy people, many of whom followed the townsfolk down in search of a better life.

Each summer after Tessa's birth, Riley was asked to play the flute for the Long Dance and refused. He was afraid to go down, for Teresa would accompany him and might follow them back to town as she had followed Clancy's crew. He dared not take the risk. But all the time the Dance was on she was restless. 'Play your flute, Riley,' she would sigh. 'The little one likes it . . .' And so he played her into a calmer frame of mind until the dancers had gone. Then the danger was past and he could breathe freely again.

As the baby grew older, Teresa looked on a younger version of Timothy Thomas. She had the same changeable blue-grey eyes, the same wide forehead and dark brown hair, and the same confident nature of her father. Thankfully, Riley could see none of this; he saw only her mother's features, the shape of her face, wide across the eyes, cheekbones set high and tapering to an elfin chin. If she had been his own he could not have loved her more.

Riley expected the birth of the child to strengthen the bond between them, and in a way it did, but it bound them both to the little one, instead of to each other. He knew she still mourned for her lover, for she called out his name in her sleep. Although he had married her knowing she could never love him – 'I'm a dead woman,' she had said – he never thought it would trouble him so much. She gave him her body, her care, and shared his life. But it was not enough. She lay in his arms, but was not there; he touched her, and it meant nothing to her. He yearned for a sign, a touch, a breath, a word, just one word that was meant for him alone. She had warned him, but he had hoped, still hoped.

Distance and the inability to be sociable almost cut the Rileys off from the rest of the community. They lived alone, supporting themselves and the child in a solitary kind of peasant grandeur. They were saved from absolute silence by Tessa, who, as she grew out of babyhood, demanded more verbal attention. Her childish prattle, her need of a story, her wanting to know this and that, raised the level of communication for Riley, and Teresa was pleased that it should be so for it gave her more time to retreat into her memories. Yet life in the cabin, now that her daughter had gravitated towards Riley, took on a more melancholy aspect.

Riley marked the passage of time not by Tessa's birthdays, but by the Long Dance, always fearful that Teresa would one day follow the dancers. She would look down at them gathering together into groups for the descent into Rohira, as though poised for flight, but her soul was too laden, too heavy to take off. For days after, she wandered from one window to the other, then out into the compound and back into the cabin again, like a bird beating its wings against the cage which holds it.

Soon even music failed to keep her melancholy at bay, and the flute lay on the table, a silent reminder to both of their equally silent predicament.

'Will I play you a bit of something?' he often asked, hopefully.

'No,' came the answer. 'Not just yet.'

Riley would wake up at night sweating and struggling from dreams in which she had gone, just disappeared. His relief to feel her figure still there beside him sent up a prayer of thankfulness. He was troubled to see her restlessness, and yet he could not let her go – not that she had asked, nor would she. She could not now bring shame on him whom they called Proud Riley. So out of gratitude she let him love her, and washed and cooked and spun. Starved of conversation, of company – not that she considered the community, even Mrs O'Malley, company – her intellect stifled and she felt trapped, condemned.

30

Soon after Tessa's fourth birthday, Riley woke to find her, still asleep yet standing by the door. She began to beat on it with her fists and cried out in a frenzied voice, 'Timothy! Timothy! Take me away! Timothy, I can't get out!'

He brought her shivering body back to the bed and lay beside her, gathering her to him to warm her icy limbs. Smoothing the damp hair away from her burning forehead, he was consumed with pity at the appeal in her restless eyes.

'Teresa,' he said gruffly. 'I won't hold you to your promise, girleen, not if it makes you feel badly. Listen, I'll take you down to civilisation, I'll find somewhere for you and the little 'un . . .' Tears filled his eyes, the loss already clutching at his heart. What was pride, he thought, compared to Teresa. He had had four years and was thankful. 'Do you hear me, Teresa?' he whispered urgently. 'Do you hear what I'm saying? I'll take you down, girl. Teresa?' He stared down in disbelief. Her restless eyes were still. The offer had come too late. Weary of beating its wings in vain, her spirit had flown with the dawn. Timothy Thomas had come for her; he had answered her plea. For the first time in his life, Proud Riley knew what it was to feel jealous.

All Ennan turned out to watch Proud Riley walking at the donkey's head, a coffin roped to the cart behind. Before making his way down to Rohira, Riley had noticed the silver and black flute lying on the table. He would never play it again, somehow the music had gone out of his soul. He put the flute in its case, carefully wrapped it, and took it up to Ennabrugh, to a place which yielded no turf. He stood still for a moment, his small, stocky figure insignificant against the savage landscape. Stooping, he laid the flute reverently on the dark suface. Slowly it had sunk.

The neighbours watched the donkey and cart out of sight before taking breath and launching into speculation.

'Nothing up here was ever good enough for that one, God rest her soul. Fancy being buried where no one can see you.'

'Was he grieving much?'

'Ach, you never can tell with the likes of him. Always a mystery that fella, and no one, not even O'Malley, could guess how they got on.'

'Laid her out and washed her himself, he did though that's women's work. It's morbid I tell you, for a fella to be washing a corpse, still less his own wife.'

'Do you remember how he got stuck into Clancy? God love us, he was real taken with her.'

'And sure it lasted longer than I thought; not that I ever thought she'd go down in a coffin!'

'What ailed her? 'Tis awful pale she was, white as Dooley's ghost at her wedding, and she died without waiting for the priest, she did.'

'Well, whatever ailed her then won't be troubling her now!'

'Where's the little 'un?'

'With O'Malley's lot.'

'What will he be doing with her, do you think?'

'She'll end up with the Little Sisters, or the workhouse.'

'No, she won't. I just heard Mrs O'Malley say Riley's bringing her up on his own.'

'What, up there on that godforsaken hillside?'

'If she's anything like her ma, she'll not be spending much time down here, he'll see to that.'

Heedless of the gossip and conjecture, Riley plodded the ten miles to Rohira. He plodded with purpose and found a great comfort in that purpose, for although unable to comprehend what his wife had wanted when she was alive, he knew exactly what she wanted at her death. He buried her in the same grave as Timothy Thomas. Standing at the graveside, cap in hand, he felt the tears spring up and wend their way warmly down his face. He did not hear a word the priest said, nor heeded the comforting hand laid on his shoulder in a token of farewell. After a while, he knelt by the open grave and swore to both on the name of St Teresa herself that their daughter, Proud Riley's daughter, would want for nothing. Like her mother she would be a cut above the rest. He saw no future for a dying community like Ennan, and when the time came their daughter would make a good marriage which would take her out of it, to a better life.

On his way back, his heart was heavy with memories of the baby's baptism, of how Teresa had explained the sights and ways of civilisation to him. But now he took no pleasure in the town and would never come again.

Yet he did come to Rohira for a third time. After the burial, not

32

wanting their grave to remain unmarked, he ordered a simple headstone and left the erection of it to the mason. But as the weeks passed, he could not settle himself until he had seen the gravestone. And so he came to Rohira for the third and last time.

He hurried into the churchyard. Yes, there is was, he could see it from the gates! Light of step and proud of heart he reached it. He stood by it for a moment, and then his emotions plummeted. Black despair welled up within him. What did it say? He could not read. Nothing made sense. He looked about wildly and ran to the iron railings which encompassed the churchyard. He clutched at them with both his hands. A man and a woman were walking together along the street. 'Please!' he shouted. 'Will you come and read me the headstone.'

The couple exchanged glances. 'Certainly,' replied the man, saying to the woman, 'Wait here, my dear.'

Proud Riley ran to the gates, anxious to escort his benefactor to the grave.

'Will ye read it?' he panted. 'For the love of God, read what it says!'

'Here lies,' began the man, 'Timothy Thomas, died 1880 aged 27, and Teresa Riley, died 1884 aged 25.' He read it twice and Proud Riley repeated it. He was still repeating it when the man left. The mason had wanted to put 'dearly loved wife' but Riley had shaken his head. Suffice it that she had borne his name. Posterity must make of it what they would.

CHAPTER TWO

In the desolate, mountainy region of Ennan only the strong survived, and Tessa Riley was strong. Her tall, well-shaped figure, shawl around shoulders, and a shepherd's crook in her hand, was an impressive sight. She strode across the sombre terrain like a Celtic goddess, taking her father's small herd of goats for a fresh lick of grass.

Ennan had undergone a change in the years since Tessa Riley's mother had died. Many of the younger folk, becoming intolerant of the ceaseless grind and hardship and hearing of a better way of life in the town, went down in search of it.

The exodus had now left the community in two parts. The primitives, known as 'the shiftless', lived at one side in shacks and hovels, and had little to do with their more industrious neighbours, the O'Malleys, the Kellys, Riley, young Collins, the Jarveys and the Muldoons.

The priest still came up with a missionary zeal for the welfare of souls. The tinkers every year grew more organised and businesslike, and now the Gaelic League, anxious to preserve ancient customs, expressed concern at the exodus and wondered whether this year of 1898 would be Ennan's last Long Dance.

Only the Great Bog of Ennabrugh remained changeless, and Tessa always approached its shores with a prickling sense of apprehension. She never liked coming up here, and no matter how cheerful she tried to feel, memories of the lives it had claimed, and the weird stories told about it, came to haunt her. Even Lord Fitzcarron's shooting parties treated it with the greatest respect. Gamekeepers, beaters, poachers, all were wary of it.

The wind, cold for February, flattened Tessa's skirts against the creamy smoothness of her bare legs and tore through her hair. Yet she was thankful that the wind blew, much preferring it to the quieter days when the surface bubbled and made strange sighing noises, which the old people said were the lost souls trying to get out.

Usually wild horses could not have dragged her to so desolate a place, especially at this time of year, but she had come in search of their male goat, necessary for the breeding of Proud Riley's small herd. He had broken free from his tethering and had bolted, as if drawn by some invisible power to the very edge of the Bog.

There he was. A horned silhouette in the afternoon light, submerged to his haunches. The old folk said it was a sulphur bog, and that when an animal had a yen for sulphur nothing, not even the devil himself, could stop them. The goat sensed her approach and bleated softly in muted terror.

'Oh, Billy, it's the divil's own beast you are,' she admonished. 'But don't fret yourself, sure I'll have you out o' there or me name isn't Riley!' She tested the depth near the edge with her crook and inched her way forward. Her boots began to squelch as she advanced so, stepping back, she took them off. 'The last thing I need,' she muttered into the wind, 'is the Bog in me boots, or on me skirts.' She hitched them to the level of her knees and tied the coarse material into a great beefy knot, for the homespun cloth would soak up the filth like a sponge and never come clean again. She wrinkled her nose at the stench of the disturbed slime and shivered as it oozed up the whiteness of her legs. Not daring to move beyond the firm ground she had found, she surveyed the endless surface, with eyes as round as plates. Ay, folk said it drew the eyes and 'ticed you into it. Fascinating they called it, a brooding fearful place – the only place that sobered the inebriated instantly.

'Mother o' God,' she said through chattering teeth. 'I mustn't look at it, 'tis a terrible sight.' And because her upbringing, in common with the rest of the community, had had few refinements, she began to swear. 'In all me seventeen years, sure to God Almighty, I've never been so scared, and if it wasn't for that bloody billy goat I wouldn't be here now!' She stood there, barelegged, up to the knees in bog, crook in hand, skin blue and eyes stinging with the wind. The Great Bog of Ennabrugh had already taken the Celtic goddess image and disposed of it. She was now very much mortal, weak and fallible in the face of nature's monstrosity. And having disposed of the image, Ennabrugh now began to erode her self-assurance and hope. She heard herself yelling and swearing at the immobile creature in front of her. With a surge of panic she saw he had gone a little deeper and realised that once he sank beyond his legs it would be too late. Tessa lifted her eyes to heaven, seeking help . . . calm . . . strength; but the sight of the little clouds being lured by the brisk wind to be broken on the fangs of the high rocks did nothing to comfort her.

'C'mon, Billy,' she urged. 'Oh, Billy, Billy. Sure you've had your fill of sulphur, enough to last you a lifetime if you never have another drop. I don't want to leave you here, but the Lord knows I can't stay much longer . . .' She held out her hand and stretched forward, murmuring more endearments. The goat bleated miserably, the forlorn cry echoing like a banshee. 'I'll get you out somehow, I will. Don't drown. Don't give in.' Resolve hardened. The goat represented milk and cheese and, eventually, meat. It was part of their frugal livelihood. They sold the produce to their neighbours, tinkers and folks who came up to the Long Dance. They could not afford to buy another goat. Her father was debtor to no one, and too proud to borrow. No, if Billy went down, they too would go down.

Putting aside all panic and speculation, Tessa took stock of the rescue operation. The crook was six feet in length. Dare she lean further forward? But even if the crook did reach the goat's horns, the short distance between gave her no pulling power, and what Billy needed was a good pull. What if she fell in? The goat pricked up its ears. He had heard something. Tessa turned her head, and just below the level of the wind she heard them. As sure as she was Proud Riley's daughter, as sure as God was in heaven and the devil in hell, she heard hoofbeats. Transfixed with terror, she crossed herself and dared not look in their direction. Fear trickled through her. Was it the ghosts of drowned horsemen haunting the place of their death, seeking their souls' peace? The hoofbeats stopped, and after a short pause the dull thud of footsteps came nearer.

'What the hell are you doing here?' It was a voice. A human voice. A loud voice. She sucked in her breath, still paralysed with terror.

'Well, if it isn't me good fortune to meet so fair an apparition on this blasted, bloody waste of the damned. But it's no fit place for a young woman now, to be standing with her legs bare and up to the hocks in the filth of Ennabrugh.'

Tessa continued to stare at him and felt like a rabbit held in the awful gaze of a stoat. Slowly her taut muscles began to relax; the fear of the supernatural dissolved and her senses quickly reassembled themselves in anticipation of trouble of a different kind. He walked towards her. Who was he? Strangers were few and far between, she thought, and strangers were not to be trusted. He wore gaiters with big buckles and straps up the legs, a satchel was slung over his shoulder and a shotgun on his arm.

'Mother of God,' she breathed in relief. 'I thought you were the divil himself!'

He laughed loudly, showing strong white teeth. 'Do I look like the devil?' He nodded towards the goat. 'Want it shot?' Without waiting for an answer he cocked the gun. 'Stand aside, then.'

'No!' she cried. 'I don't want it shot. I've been stood here in this perishing cold Bog for hours trying to get it out!'

'You aren't getting very far, are you? What are you going to do, then?' he demanded. 'Stand there until it sinks? Good God, girl, if it's shot you can at least eat it. I'll give you a hand with the carcase to wherever you live.'

While talking he had warmed to the unexpected sight of this attractive young woman who, despite her boldness of manner and spirited outlook, was defenceless against so inhospitable a landscape. Such a mixture of qualities appealed to him.

'I am the head keeper from the Fitzcarron estate . . .'

As he volunteered the information her eyes flashed to where the horse was standing: dangling from the saddle were two hares and a pheasant which the keeper had taken from a poacher. The sight of the pheasant immediately took her back to being a little girl.

Once, when still in pinafores, Tessa had accompanied her father on a long survey of the peat, and he had promised – as an incentive to progress – to show her Fitzcarron House. They had tramped some eight miles along the furthest end of Ennabrugh and up to the ridge.

'There,' he had announced in triumph. 'What did I tell you, now? Is it not the finest place in the green of Ireland? And this view is only the back of it, girleen! All the grand folk drive up from Rohira in their carriages to the front – though I've never seen that – and as far as your eyes can see all this belongs to his lordship. Anyone trespassing will be up before the magistrate, if they've not lost their leg in a trap already! But we're all right up here, girleen,' he assured. 'No one bothers about this side. You're the luckiest girl, for there's only you and me has ever seen Fitzcarron House – tell 'em that at Pat Feeney's school, eh?'

She stared in wonderment at the handsome parkland, the square stone-built house, the huge iron gates painted black, their long narrow spikes tipped with gold. The family crest was so boldly emblazoned she could see it even from this distance. Ownership was something new to her childish mind, and while she was grappling both with the concept and the grandeur, a great burst of shouting and shrieking filled her ears.

'The beaters!' yelled Riley. 'God save us, Teresa, it's a shoot! Of all the days there are, I choose this and walk right into a bloody shoot!'

The beaters below were fanning out, shouting and beating the air and the ground with long bamboo sticks. She eyed their approach with wide-eyed horror.

'A shoot, Da, what's that? What are the beaters and why are they shouting?'

'They're scaring the birds from their cover. See, some are taking to the air.'

'Why are they scaring them?'

'Lord Almighty, Teresa, the questions! To shoot 'em, that's why it's called a "shoot", it's sport . . .' His words were cut short by a sharp burst of guns. The wood below was alive with figures. Tessa heard the whirring of wings and the rush of feathers as the birds rose together in the air. Shots rang out. Men ran, jerking spent cartridges and reloading. A hare panicked and ran for cover. She saw its ears, just the tips as it sped by. Another shot and the hare dropped. Her father flung her to the gound; shots could go wide and he wasn't taking any chances.

'Keep down!' he yelled above the noise.

Tessa lay still, heart hammering, body stiffening, trying to crush down something in her consciousness that cried out for this shooting to stop. She plunged her fingers into her ears and screwed up her eyes.

'Good shot!' yelled a voice from the distance.

'Oh, bloody good shot, sir!'

A startled scream rose in her throat. Something brushed against her bare arm. A great copper-breasted pheasant landed with a soft thudding noise just beside her arm. She could feel the warmth of the feathers, and had never seen anything so beautiful as the gold and brown plumage. A stream of blood began to seep out of the glossy head, the bright eyes filmed over. Her heart constricted with a dull pain.

Riley, with the alacrity of poaching days, reached out, grabbed the bird and stuffed it inside his coat. It wasn't often a fat cock pheasant dropped from heaven. A gift from his lordship, you could say!

After a brief silence, the barking of retrievers cut into her consciousness. Voices rose. Tessa opened her eyes to see Lord Fitzcarron's guests below, strutting about, drinking great cups of port, jesting, throwing back their heads in laughter and appreciation of a good day's sport.

Riley had not comprehended, nor did he ever, the amount of distress experienced by the child, and she, not having been brought up to the relief of tears and not knowing how to communicate the depth of the experience, kept it locked up within herself. Much later, at school, she had recounted it to Marie Jane, but she had been more impressed with the doings of the gentry than Tessa's feelings about the shoot, the horror of which was still vivid to her.

'I am the keeper,' he said again. 'The head keeper. Where do you live and what's your name?'

With an instinct for self-protection she refused to tell him her name or where she lived. He frowned at her silence. He had been over to one of his lordship's tenant farmers, the business had gone well and it was his wish that this affair which Fate had put in his way should also go well.

Tessa eyed the gun warily. 'Put it down, mister. I don't want the goat killed, either by that stinking great Bog, or your shotgun. I won't have any bloodshed, do you hear?'

Up to now his eyes had been focusing on her good looks, the wind-whipped cheeks, the large eyes set wide apart, full-lashed and of a blue that reflected the grey of the landscape. Tendrils of dark brown hair blew about her ears and throat. Handsome rather than pretty, he thought, and she's only young; God only knew what beauty the years ahead would bring. But now his eyes roamed over the heavy shawl which protected her breast from the wind, stopping at the big, beefy knot of skirts hanging over the top of her knees like an untidy sporran. He was a man of flesh. He liked it warm with blood running through it, or cold with blood running out of it. The sight of her bare knees and a little of the blue mottled flesh above made him want to touch them, to warm them with his hands. He regretted revealing his status and was piqued that she, a mere peasant, had not given her name. Tessa caught the way of his gaze and clutched her crook more firmly.

'So,' he answered her comment with a smirk, 'you won't have bloodshed, and yes, I hear you.' His sharp eyes scanned the scowling landscape. 'What will you have then? Will you stand there till you catch your death? Till the sun and the goat sink?'

'Bread,' she cut in tersely. 'I'll have some bread if you've got any.' Surprised and encouraged by the request, he stepped forward and she saw him properly now that he stood in the light, and now that she wanted something from him. His face was that of a hunter, hawk-like, and his hazel eyes, too, were in keeping with his profession, sharp and clear, missing nothing. His thick, dark coppery hair showed from beneath the deerstalker he wore. She watched, as though her life depended on it, the lean fingers ferret eagerly in the satchel. He produced a heel of a loaf and, still with the gun crooked on his arm, brought it to her as though it were a votive offering.

'Thanks, mister.' She took it at once.

As a gamekeeper he was used to assessment, but her next move went beyond any estimation he could have made. Her cold fingers struggled to unfasten the knot above her knees.

'Me skirts are very wide and strong; I spun 'em meself, so I know. I'm going to coax Billy with the bread. He likes it – it's a treat for him – so I want you to hold on to me skirts so I can go nearer, lean forward and put me crook about his horns; it'll give me more pulling power. Besides, he'll have more confidence to move when he knows I've hold of him. If you stay just behind me the ground is firm enough.' Strengthened by the keeper's presence, and with the knowledge that he'd rescue her if the Bog gave way, Tessa thrust the edge of her skirts into his freckled hands.

The keeper was at once dismayed and elated. Dismayed that the bread was not for herself, and elated at the prospect of holding her skirts. So taken up was he by the sudden sight of the upsweep of her thigh as she leaned forward, he was nearly pulled off balance and only regained his footing by shifting his weight backward. All this,

40

for a bloody goat, he thought; she must be mad. Not that he was bothered. It was some time since he had lifted a woman's skirts, not that he lacked for female companionship. He was a hunter by nature, fancying himself as the first man pursuing a mate in a world that gave way to the strong and powerful. The reason for his present pleasure was her reluctance to be friendly. Once she got the creature free, if that were possible, she'd have no truck with him. Oh yes, he could see that coming, so, like a green youth on his first venturings, he lowered his eyes to the curve above her knees.

The creamy skin was now goosepimpled, her thighs swelled to become encased in grey calico drawers! He could not imagine anything more ugly than grey calico; and yet, at the same time, he found the sight of it positively alluring. The drawers fitted her rump closely, a firm, rounded rump, and as smooth and warm, he had no doubt, as a deer's flank. Each leg was gathered into a frill and held together by a piece of red ribbon. Red ribbon and grey calico! God Almighty! He almost laughed. It was so utterly, stupidly ridiculous! The skirts moved again as she ventured further still. She was game, he'd give her that. He took up the slack as commanded and cursed the job for being a two-handed one.

Because any advance on his part was denied under the circumstances, his imagination began to take over. What if he had a free hand? What if circumstances were different? What could she say, he wondered, if he were to insert a finger inside the leg of her drawers, inside the tightly tied frill, sliding his finger round and round, slowly expanding the frill, opening the ribbon a little more, and a little further still, coaxing it open . . . apart . . .

His lustful meanderings were not prepared for the sudden release of the goat. With an excited yell of joy and triumph Tessa leapt backward. The tension on her skirt was suddenly released, sending the gamekeeper sprawling.

The momentum of his own weight sent him into the Bog; he flailed his arms, trying to save his gun from going under. Too late. Ennabrugh received it with a gurgle of gratitude. Swearing and shocked, he struggled to his feet, covered from head to foot in malodorous slime. Wiping the filth from his eyes with the back of his hand, he saw that Tessa was no longer there.

'God help me!' he exclaimed. She was covering the ground fast, pulled by the terrified goat anxious to get back to its pen. Skirts blowing, crook in hand, hair streaming in the strong wind, he watched her through narrowed eyes. 'So,' he muttered. 'You've won that round, whoever you are, but, by heaven, just you wait until next time – and be in no doubt that there will be a next time!'

That there would be a next time, the keeper had no doubt. Change was coming to Ennan and he, Frank Kildare, was to be the catalyst. Only the day before, Lord Fitzcarron had outlined his plans for this wild outpost of his empire, an outpost which was no longer an asset but increasingly a burden. Worn down by years of neglect, the peasant farmers of Ennan rarely paid their rent; but the wider consequences of their simple hand-to-mouth existence were lost to them. His lordship, a distant figure, was regarded in the same way as God; although no one had seen him, everyone knew he was there, directing affairs from the big house as God did from heaven. His lordship's name too, like that of God, was frequently on everyone's lips. Stories of his doings filtered through by various avenues, and so long as a Fitzcarron was in residence, the crofters believed that all was well with their world.

The present Lord Fitzcarron, however, was not softened by the philanthropy which had characterised his forebears. The day before the keeper had come across Tessa in the Bog, he had been summoned to the lord's study.

'Sheep,' Lord Fitzcarron had explained. 'There's money to be made with sheep, and the estate needs it. Damn it, the valley's worth is being destroyed by the peasants in Ennan; they've not the least idea how to farm the land. The valley must be cleared.'

'But the ground, sir; the state of it. There's very little grazing, except on the steep sides. It's too wet and lifeless. Everything's been taken out of it; even the potatoes won't grow in the valley. With respect, m'lord, there's not enough grazing for sheep.'

'Good God, Kildare, I realise the state of the land. That's why those poaching, thieving crofters must go! The level ground will be treated and allowed to rest and recover itself. The hillside will be enough for the first sheep. I want it cleared before winter sets in, but it has to be done with great . . .' Lord Fitzcarron paused for a second before continuing, '. . . delicacy. We don't want trouble – no riots or Land Leaguers, Kildare! They're not paying their rent, and that would be reason enough, but I want this done as quickly and quietly as possible. I don't want charges of inhumanity flung at my head by the Church, and I don't want the press full of stories about the workhouse bulging at the walls with peasants evicted from the Fitzcarron estate!'

Kildare had nodded his understanding, still unsure of how he, as head keeper, was to be involved with this. As if answering the questioning look in his employee's eyes, Fitzcarron had continued. 'I want you to co-ordinate this, Kildare. Not only is Jackson too old – and I've discussed this with him – but if he as estate manager was to be involved, my intentions would be made clear in a flash. Will you take it on, and be well rewarded for your pains?'

Kildare was silent for a moment before replying to Lord Fitzcarron's question, knowing that beneath the controlled exterior the landlord urgently needed and vehemently desired these changes to his property. 'It would have to look as though they were moving of their own accord, sir, and I'd need time to work on a plan. But I can assure you, Ennan will be cleared by winter.'

Proud Riley stood outside his cabin waiting for his daughter's return. He wished he had gone in search of the goat himself, but as she had pointed out, it was her goat and responded only to her voice; and so he waited, a solitary figure in the darkening afternoon. He wore a goatskin jerkin over a collarless shirt, and holding up his baggy trousers was the broad black belt which had once belonged to Timothy Thomas. Teresa had said it would keep his back warm and indeed it had, becoming a necessity of life.

'Oh, it's a sad man that has no belt to keep his kidneys warm,' he often said. 'By all the saints, Teresa, if I left me belt off, me back would never be the same again. This was your real da's belt,' he had told her, hooking his thumb in it and standing proud. 'And your mother gave it to me, you know.'

'So you keep telling me,' she always replied with patience. 'But, you're me da, real and alive. I don't want to think about a ghost of someone who died before I was born.'

Her way with words pleased him. He still had his swarthy looks, but his smile was now so rare as to be non-existent. Beneath the flat cap which he wore both indoors and out, his hair had turned grey.

His side whiskers had crept down to his chin where they fluffed out into wispy tufts, adding width to the now anxious face.

Time was not wasted while waiting for a sight of his daughter. He was never tired of surveying the cabin he had built for his wife, and he never regretted building it here on the sheltered side of the valley wall, at a distance from the others. Shiftless lot, he thought; none o' them, not even O'Malley, could boast a loft for their daughter to sleep in, and was he not the only man in Ennan to own a piece of furniture as fine as they had in the town? The tinkers had brought it up five years ago, and God alone knew where their thieving hands had got it from for not one of them, down there, had money enough to buy it from the knackers. But what a dresser: black oak and polished with beeswax until it gleamed. It had a cupboard and three shelves on which Teresa – he always called his daughter by her full name – put the cups, plates and her hairbrush. The Sacred Heart had the top shelf to itself. It had been awarded to Teresa by the Christian Brothers for reciting her catechism. What with that, the five goats and his fine daughter, they don't, he reflected, call me Proud Riley for nothing!

Moments of uncertainty like this justified the way he had brought her up. O'Malley used to say it was no life for a child to be trailing after him on peat surveys, spending hours by Ennabrugh while he dug or stacked the turf. But Tessa had played about and seemed contented and interested in the plant and wild life, for although the Bog seemed empty and desolate, it was teeming with a life of its own of which Tessa was aware. Besides, it was the only life he had known as a child and he had taken no harm from it; neither had she. They would never be tolling the chapel bell because she was lost; Teresa Riley knew every inch of Ennabrugh.

But for all his faith, his heart lifted when he saw her distant figure descend the hillside. He unhitched his thumb from his belt and pushed the door open. Outside the wind whimpered and wailed like a lost dog; inside the peat-fire glowed red on the hearthstones. He hurried to set the kettle. She'd be cold. God help him, he knew how numbing the cold could be up there. And did he not know she would find the goat? His heart expanded with pride.

'Did you know, Da, we've got a hole in the kettle the size of a pig's eye?' Tessa observed a few days later. She had not told her father of

44

the incident with the gamekeeper. There was no particular reason, except that she never told him anything concerning herself. From an early age, she realised that he saw danger when there was none and she knew that in his anxiety he would curb her freedom and put a stop to her wanderings with the goats.

'We've got a pot to set on, haven't we?'

'That's nearing to thin as well. 'Tis a good thing the tinkers are coming up soon, or we'd be wetting the tay in a bucket!'

Although Clancy's crew had never returned, the coming of any tribe filled Proud Riley with a complexity of emotions he could not unravel, and memories he strove to keep alive. The tinkers were now as necessary to their livelihood as the Great Bog. They bought up as much butter and cheese as Teresa could make, and as many spuds as he could spare, and yet he wished they could survive without them.

A thrill of anticipatory pleasure ran through Tessa. The tinkers' coming and the Long Dance were the only two events in the year which brought everyone together. With the talking, drinking, dancing, singing, buying, selling, the boxing and the wrestling, the Fair went on for days. Big camp fires lit up the valley at night, replacing the dank mists with warmth, and bathing the landscape in a red and yellow glow which transformed the cabins and hovels into enchanted grottoes.

'I suppose I'd better go and see if O'Malley has something – the pot's full of broth for supper, anyways.' Tessa kept the eagerness out of her voice and tried to make it sound like a chore, for if he thought she'd take any pleasure in a visit to the valley, he would go himself and she'd be sat alone in the ashes, feeling sorry for herself. In any case, 'twas a waste for Da to go down, for he didn't stop to talk, exchange gossip or catch a joke. Besides, when it came to borrowing, even from his old friend O'Malley, he was a poor one to do the asking. 'Neither a lender nor a borrower be,' he often quoted, and it irked him to have to eat his own words.

'Take your shawl, for the chill, and don't be letting O'Malley keep you. When he gets going he'd talk the hind leg off a donkey. I'd go meself, girleen, if me boots had dried out.'

Tessa's heart lifted, taking with it any tiredness from the day's work. And work hard they both did, he digging the turf, setting spuds, earthing up, going to and fro with buckets, ash buckets, goat buckets, water buckets, hen droppings, seeing to repairs to the roof.

When not out with the goats, Tessa was cleaning their pens, milking, making cheese and churning butter, washing, weaving, carding, spinning, praying, cursing and setting big fires to boil potatoes. She had purposely waited until Riley's boots had become soaked, for although the hole in the kettle had appeared days ago, the boots had only now reached the point of being waterlogged. With a show of reluctance she reached for the shawl.

'Have you seen to the goats?' he asked, hoping to keep her longer and cut down on the time she spent away.

'Have you ever known me not to see to them?'

He was silent. Her reprimand put him in mind of her mother. He regretted the question, for it conjured up his secret dread of the cabin becoming a cage, as it had for her mother. She's growing apace, he thought, and realised that his wife had been only two years older when he married her . . . Proud Riley sighed heavily; he did not care for her mixing too much. They were all flighty girls and randy lads down there. He had better plans for his daughter. Plans of a good marriage. With whom he did not yet know, but he was working on it, and wouldn't the blessed Saint Teresa herself send the likeliest fella, and wouldn't his girl be married in style?

'Take your crook!' he yelled.

'Do I not always?'

'And mind what I said about talking.'

'Da,' she protested. ''Tis awful to go just for the borrowing. I'll have to pass the time o' day with Mrs O'Malley, and play with the children, and help Marie Jane with her reading . . . but I'll be back before dark.'

'Make sure you are, then.'

Her fingers closed about the gnarled stem of her crook and she set off at a good pace. Once out of sight she laid the crook behind a big boulder. Whoever heard of a crook with no creatures to go with it, she thought; besides, they'd laugh at me down there. It was more of a hindrance than help, for she needed to descend the hillside sharpish. The sooner she got to O'Malley's, the more time she would have with her friend, Marie Jane. She could scarcely wait to tell her about the keeper. He had been in her thoughts often, and induced strange feelings and apprehension. Of course, all the girls, herself included, had fooled about, being chased for kisses and fighting the lads off at Fair and Long Dance times, and there were always some who couldn't keep their hands to themselves. Tessa knew all about those things, but somehow the incident with the keeper lacked the innocent spontaneity which she was used to, and it worried her.

Clutching at her skirts she slithered down. A few skeletal trees, stark and spectral against the slight mist rising from the valley, told her she had reached the halfway mark. Down mounds and over tussocks she went, over swampy ground, stony ground and smooth, until she at last reached the broad floor of the valley.

She liked the way cabins clustered together, their tall tin chimneys sticking out of roofs thatched with reeds. Lean cows foraged, brown hens scratched, and grubby children, looking up from their play, recognised her and raced each other to meet her first.

Tessa's heart always warmed when she set foot in the valley, and the excitement of it all brightened her good looks with a sparkle of anticipation, so that when the O'Malleys saw her they thought her wondrously vital and beautiful. Like her mother had once been, she was a sociable creature and loved to be involved with others, yet despite her natural charm there were those who, seeing her from their windows, turned to say, 'Now, what the divil's brought Proud Riley's daughter down here?'

'It's Tessa Riley, Da! Tessa, Tessa?' Marie Jane O'Malley ran through the door which was always opened, for, if neighbours were not calling in, the children were running out, babies crawled on the steps and hens wandered across the threshold. Marie Jane, pretty, precocious and a much slighter build than Tessa, greeted her with affectionate delight and, holding hands, both laughing and talking at once, they went inside the cabin.

The O'Malleys' dwelling was long and low; the earthen floor was strewn with rushes, and a peat-fire, set on a hearth of stones, faced the door. To the left, known simply as 'the end', was a square wooden table and several stools. Hooks adorned the rafters and walls and boasted a motley suspension of fowl, coats, pannier bags and tools. Cooking pots, flour bins, salt and rows of bread decorated rough shelves.

On the other side were the beds into which the children dropped fully clothed when tired, and on which O'Malley and his wife stretched when all was silent and dark. Marie Jane, having seen the loft which Proud Riley had built for his daughter, decided that privacy was just what a growing girl needed. She curtained off her

47

bed with a travelling rug bought from the tinkers last year, and referred to it as 'my room'. A lamp hung from the rafters and rush lights in tin containers were fixed to the walls.

In the compound surrounding the cabin were two sheds: one was a privy with limewashed walls, the contents of which O'Malley had to bury every week, and the other contained a bench with two zinc bowls let into the top and four buckets of water beneath. Here, the O'Malleys washed their hair, their bodies, their clothes and their pots.

Tessa could remember staying with them while her father had been in town at her mother's funeral, and the girls had been friends ever since. The O'Malleys' eldest surviving child had been named after Lord Fitzcarron's English wife. Had anyone else named their child after her ladyship it would have been considered presumptuous, but somehow with the O'Malleys it was all right.

They had both attended Pat Feeney's school together until the dreadful day the excise man came up and marched him off to prison. No one really knew how they had got wind of the poteen. It was blamed on either the tinkers or the new magistrate, for both had been up prior to the arrest, and both were mean enough to betray him.

That spring the tinkers had been in an ugly mood towards the end of the Fair, and Pat, for the safety and order of the community, had refused to sell them another drop. They had gone off threatening revenge, but tinkers always threatened or cursed if crossed, so no one took any notice. The magistrate's horse, a big chestnut beast, had a nose for poteen, it was said, but how the animal divulged the information to its master was a subject for infinite curiosity.

Whoever it was betrayed poor Pat, O'Malley had said, would surely still be roasting slowly in hell. The sight of his portly figure dragged off, face as red as a turkey cock's, handcuffs on his wrists, was only superseded by the still more heart-rending sight of a uniformed heathen actually pouring gallons and gallons of the pure and lovely water of life into the earth, into the throats of the waiting worms.

Every living person swore they never wanted to see such a thing again. If it was a criminal offence to distil whisky without licence,

48

sure it seemed a mortal sin to pour it away. As if that was not terrible enough, the uniformed heathen then set about destroying the stills and crocks. The sound echoed mournfully against the valley walls, and the delicious aroma of the poteen itself sweetened the dank mountain air for many a day. It had without a doubt been Ennan's darkest hour.

Fortunately, Tessa, an attentive pupil, had learned to read, write, draw and comprehend basic arithmetic before the schoolmaster's arrest. Such an ability set her a little apart from the others, and Mrs O'Malley used this as a pretext to persuade Proud Riley to let his daughter come down to them one afternoon a week, ostensibly to help Marie Jane with her letters. Not that she was interested in her letters, and no one knew that better than her mother, but it gave Tessa the opportunity to meet with girls of her own age to talk of lads, clothes and, by degrees, of their pubescent maturity with each development enshrining the owner with a kind of shy pride as the others regarded her jealously.

To be developing breasts was a sure sign of growing up, bodices and blouses were blushingly let out at the seams 'to make room', and the onset of menstruation – whisperingly referred to as 'the curse' – was awaited with a tremulous anxiety.

'What does it feel like?' they enquired of Peggy Jams. Peggy hesitated, regarding them with a superior air, her little pink face pleased and proud to be the possessor of such vital information.

'How long does it last?'

'Does it hurt?'

'What did your ma tell you?'

Peggy let out her breath with a long satisfying sigh.

'Ach, she's telling lies,' accused Mona Donal. 'She's making it all up, she's not started at all.'

'I have so!'

'C'mon on then, tell us what it's like?'

They gathered round the back of O'Malleys' cabin, Mona Donal, Connie and Nora Duggan, Maureen Connor, and the gypsy-looking Una Kelly.

'Go on, then, what did your ma tell you?'

'Well, she showed me how to make things to soak it up, and said I'd not to talk about it to me brothers or me da . . . keep it private, like.'

'And what else?'

Peggy searched her mind. 'Things like I've not to wash me hair or get me feet wet when it's on . . .' Her round face beamed. 'She said I'm a young woman now, and that I've got to behave like one.'

'Did she tell you anything about babies?'

'Peg could have a baby now she's started,' said Mona, knowingly.

Peggy's newly acquired triumph crumpled to a look of sheer fright. That was something her mother had not told her – and you could die having a baby!

'No she could not,' said Tessa, a ring of authority in her voice. 'She'd have to go with a fella first. It can't happen on your own. I know because of us keeping goats. Me da says our Billy's "randy" when he's ready to mate.'

'You think you know everything, Tessa Riley!' declared Nora Duggan. 'We have pigs, so we know.'

'Don't be fretting, Peg,' said Maureen Connor, who belonged to the shiftless but had aspirations. 'You can't have babies without fellas.'

'And to go with fellas without being married is a mortal sin,' said Marie Jane piously. 'Me ma's always telling me that, and I've not even started the curse yet!'

'Oh, it's crazy you all are!' laughed the black-haired, black-eyed Una. Every eye turned on her, anxious for another viewpoint.

'Why do you say that?'

'It isn't the same for us as it is with the animals.'

'Course it is, stupid.'

'People's different,' pointed out Una. 'Goats and pigs don't kiss and start sweethearting.'

Six pair of eyes conceded she had a point. 'Kissing,' explained Una, 'is something to do with it. That's why everyone's scared of a kiss, in case they get a baby . . .'

And so, through all the discussions at the back of O'Malley's cabin, the young girls of the community shrugged off the shrivelling chrysalis of childhood. As Tessa grew up, Proud Riley found it difficult to come to terms with his daughter's sexuality, and reacted by trying to isolate her. He forbade Marie Jane to visit on account of Martin Jarvey and Keven Connor, full of high spirits, following the girls up the hillside. He considered Marie Jane too flighty for her own good and not to be encouraged where his daughter was concerned.

'Oh, for the love of Almighty God, 'tis glad I am to see you!' confided Marie Jane when they were indoors. 'It's plucking day and the place is full of feathers and carcases. Me ma will let me off now you've come. Ugh,' she shivered, 'I hate plucking, when the flesh is still warm . . . C'mon, we can sit at the end and talk.'

'So,' teased O'Malley, his eyes twinkling behind the rolled gold spectacles he now wore, 'your da's boots are waterlogged, are they?'

'They are, too,' replied Tessa, laughing and blushing, for he was well aware of her excuses to get away. He was fond of Tessa and did all he could to enhance her social life.

'Tell him I've got the finest mixture of pig's fat and paraffin, but he's got to come down for it himself. A regular recluse is your old da. He always was on the quiet side, always kept himself to himself . . .'

'Will you stop your chinwagging, O'Malley! And you, Marie Jane, will ye wet the tay!' Out of some fourteen children, only six had survived, and out of determination to see they stayed that way, Mrs O'Malley became permanently harassed. Every cough was checked for croup, every fever for cholera. Through measles, earache and toothache she had stayed up all night by the fire, nursing, soothing, poulticing, patting and crooning softly until eyelids gently closed and grizzling little sobs subsided. These gifts and the motherliness of her nature were extended to Tessa, whom she had come to love as a daughter. She looked up from the fowl she was plucking to add sharply, 'Tessa could do with a cup of tay after her long walk, and I could meself, for these feathers make a body powerful dry.'

The younger children, engaged in a game of chasing the feathers which blew about in the draught from the door, became quiet as they crouched, eyes watchful for the nimble fingers to start again. Marie Jane, making a wry face behind her mother's back, spooned tea into a chipped enamel teapot. Her father, still slim and agile, and with a permanent smile creasing his face, picked up a chicken's claw, all the while strutting and making a noise like a cockerel. Tessa's first startled gasp dissolved at once into peals of laughter; he then turned

51

on the younger children who ran shrieking with delighted terror into the compound.

'There's your tay, Ma. Me and Tessa, we're going to the end.' She juggled two large cups of tea in one hand, and with the other pulled her friend to the further end of the cabin out of the way.

'You're coming to the Fair, Tessa?'

'You can bet your drawers I am! Me da wouldn't miss the chance of selling the butter and cheese, even though it means struggling down with it. He won't have the knackers call to the cabin, you know.'

'Because of yer ma, d'ye think?'

Tessa nodded. 'Not that he ever talks about her, or Clancy's crew. I've heard more of it from you than him.'

'It's marvellous romantic, Tess, don't you think, your da lashing into Clancy to rescure your ma?'

'It isn't marvellous romantic when he thinks every knacker's after me body! Do you remember how he tried to stop me going to school when the knackers' lads were in?'

'He had reason when you think of it. Dirty little knackers, full o' fleas an' scabs, always threatened to curse us if we didn't do as they wanted.'

'It's the only thing I'm scared of, Marie Jane, the knackers putting a curse on me da because of me.'

'You think a lot of him, don't you, and him not being your real da, an' all?'

'He's realer to me than the fella that's dead. I only wish me da was more like yours though, you know, talking and playing the fool.'

'But me da's your godfather – it's the next best thing.'

O'Malley, on account of his good nature, was godfather to most of the children. There was some speculation that the relationship was in some cases much closer, but the gossip was kept low and the speculation went unchallenged. The girls knew none of this, and Tessa was pleased at having so nice a man for a godfather.

'I don't know how you stand it, all alone up there with your da being so quiet.' Full of tremors and flushes, disturbed and excited at the cycle of life going on around her, Marie Jane could imagine herself in hell rather than isolation. She sipped her tea, feeling, as she always did, flattered at being a friend of Proud Riley's daughter.

'I'm used to it, I suppose. And there's only two of us to do all the work, so there's not time to think about it till I come down here.' Tessa, who never noticed the squalor of their life compared to her own, gazed at Marie Jane with open admiration. She wished her own skin was as pink and white, her lips as rosy red, or that she possessed some engaging mannerism, such as Marie Jane's habit of forming her mouth into an 'O' which prefixed almost every statement. In the forming of this her red mouth pouted in a way which drew the eyes of all the lads. And her clothes; no homespun stuff for her, for did not O'Malley trade in town every now and then, and did he not buy skirts and blouses for his womenfolk from an old Jew who went with a cart?

'Who d'you think your da will get to marry you?' Marie Jane finished her tea and settled to her favourite subject of love. 'Everyone knows he's out for a good catch, though in this place the blessed God knows where he's likely to find one. If anything's going to happen in Ennan, Tessa, it happens either at the Fair or the Long Dance. It's like going to meet your fate, isn't it?'

'It is so,' agreed Tessa, entering into the excitement of the subject. 'But I don't want to get married yet. Do you?'

The dark ringlets shook emphatically. 'Oh, I want to enjoy meself, like you've read to me in books, and like me da's seen in town. You get married, Tessa, and what happens? You get round-bellied every year . . .' She paused. 'When I think of the weddings I've danced at, and not twelve months later they've took to their grave with childbed fever – ugh, it makes me shiver. I don't want to get ugly and sick for the sake of a lot o' brats I don't want. What's the good of that?' She looked around, suddenly despairing. 'I want to get out of all this, and yet me da says the only way to start is in service. But, how do you get into it? Dacent service, that is.' She drew up her slim shoulders indignantly. 'I'm not skivvying up here for the rest of me life, scheming and scraping, to end up like me poor old ma.'

After casting a quick glance at Marie Jane's 'poor old ma', who was chopping up a fowl and tossing it into the cooking pot, Tessa lowered her voice.

'Listen, Marie Jane, I've been dying to tell you what happened to me when our Billy got loose, but swear to Almighty God and all the angels not to tell a soul, for if me da gets to know he'll never let me out of his sight again.'

'Oh, I do swear,' answered Marie Jane, readily. 'May I burn in hell if I utter a single word.'

Tessa had so looked forward to this moment for it was usually her friend who had adventures, yet despite the golden opportunity to brag she could not relate the incident in the light-hearted way of Marie Jane's eye-fluttering yarns.

'Oh,' was the awed response. 'Oh, Tessa, and you asked him to hold up your skirts! Oh, Tessa Riley, sure to God, he'd see right up your legs! You did have drawers on?'

'Grey calico,' came the modest reply. 'Drawn in above me knees. You don't think I'm that daft!'

'Were you not scared out of your very wits, being up there on your own?'

'I was so, at first, because it was the darkest day, and didn't I remember every tale that was ever told? But me mind was on our Billy and getting him out.'

'Oh, I wish I'd been lucky enough to meet a stranger, but I wouldn't fancy meeting him up there! You're sure it wasn't Old Nick? I mean it, now. One of them man . . . manifestations.'

'It's the gift of a colourful imagination you've got, Marie Jane. But, you'll never believe me when I tell you who it was.'

'Go on, who was it? Wait a minute – whoever it was, did you really leave him sprawling in the Bog?'

Tessa nodded, eyes shining, lips parted in a mischievous smile.

'Sweet Jasus, oh, you fixed him good and proper. C'mon, who was he?'

'The keeper from Lord Fitzcarron's estate.' She had deliberately left the identity until the last for full effect, and effect it had. Marie Jane's eyes rounded to their fullest, darkest extent.

'Which one?' came the unexpected question. 'Was it the young one with the black teeth or the older one with a limp?'

Tessa recalled the strong white teeth. 'It wasn't either of them,' she replied in triumph.

'Then it wasn't the keeper,' said Marie Jane flatly. 'I ought to know because me da gets to hear things in town about the big house. There's Mrs Quail the housekeeper, and Mr Flavell the steward, Mr Jackson the elderly manager who's been in charge for years, and – oh, he must have been having you on, it'd be one of the stable-lads out with a gun.'

54

'What! A stable-lad finding his way over the ridge and round the top end of the Bog? Besides, would I trust my body and skirts to the puny strength of a stable-lad?'

'C'mon, then, for the love of God,' Marie Jane fretted. 'You can be a rare tease when you've got it in you. Who the divil was it?'

'The head keeper.'

'The what? You mean Frank Kildare?'

'It must be.'

'Oh, fancy you having all the luck. He's a good looking fella, Tessa, and I'm a fair judge,' she added archly. 'He only used to come to warn the tinkers about poaching, but he's about more often now.'

'I didn't know him from Dooley's ghost. And I didn't care for him at all . . .' Her wide forehead gathered into a frown. 'He had a dead pheasant dangling from his saddle and it reminded me of that shoot me da and me walked into when I was little – '

'When your da stuffed a pheasant into his pocket!'

'It's all very well to make light of it, Marie Jane. You weren't there with the guns blazing over your head and the beaters yelling like madmen. I bet he was one of 'em.'

'Gamekeepers don't lower themselves as beaters. Honest, Tessa, you know nothing! Anyways, all that was a long time ago and you can't go bearing grudges for years.'

'I'm not bearing grudges, just telling you why the sight of the keeper with his gun aimed at our Billy didn't do anything for me! Anyways, it's all over and done with. He's probably fogotten about me by now.'

'Forgotten! Would you forget someone who'd left you sprawling in the Bog? He'd have to go back to the estate, stinking like a privy, and without his gun – they cost a fortune, you know. He'll not forget that little escapade in a hurry, no matter how much he was taken with your grey calico drawers! Besides, fellas don't like the brushoff. I should know! But, honestly Tessa, if you'd played your cards right you could have worked on him, got round him, been nice to him and,' she giggled, 'you never know, he could put a word in to get us into service.'

'Where?'

'In the big house, where else?'

The magnitude of the concept overawed Tessa. She flashed a sudden look at her friend. 'Did you say get "us" into service?'

'I did so.'

'Oh, you do get some fearful ideas, Marie Jane, but you can leave me out of that little scheme. And as for the gamekeeper, I don't know how you can be so taken with him when he's so old.'

'Heard me da say he was thirty. But isn't it better to be an old man's darling than a young fella's slave? That's all women are in this godforsaken glen!' Marie Jane thrust her stool back from the table, suddenly tired of the conversation and anxious to start on another. 'Are you game for a bit of fun?' she asked mischievously.

'What kind?' came the suspicious demand.

'How about us two going to call on the Aunt Hanratty, to borrow a kettle, like?'

'But your da's already loaned me one.'

'She doesn't know that.'

'I don't see what you're getting at. I don't want to call on the Aunt Hanratty; they say she's crazy.'

'It's not the Aunt, Tessa, 'tis the nephew I want you to cast your eyes on.'

'What for?'

'Oh, honestly Teresa Riley, sometimes I think you've not got the cradle marks off your arse! He's a lad, isn't he? A young man, more like, turned twenty-one he is, and as much kept under his aunt's thumb as you're kept under your da's.'

'I'm not kept under his thumb. Look at the times I get down here! I'm wondrous good with me excuses!'

'Come on then, let's be away.' Marie Jane pulled her friend to the door.

'Not going yet, Tessa?' called out Mrs O'Malley.

'Not yet, Ma, just going for a walk,' said Marie Jane.

'I'd a thought Tessa'd done enough walking...' But the girls were through the door, walking arm in arm to where the valley floor narrowed and a solitary limewashed cabin was perched on one side of it. They peered over the compound wall. A tall young man in corduroy trousers, split boots and a leather apron was scrubbing a huge grey and pink pig. Catching sight of the two faces, he came to the wall wiping his hands.

'An' what can I do for two of the finest young ladies in the glen?' he said with an air of bravado. His wide mouth lifted in a tantalising smile.

'Oh, isn't he bold?' giggled Marie Jane. 'Wants to know if he can do anything for us! Shall we tell him?'

His deep blue eyes looked at Tessa with such frank admiration that her face went into a crimson blush.

'I'm Tessa Riley,' she said, fidgeting with the cuff of her sleeve.

'I know.' All the bravado was gone out of him. His tone was lowered almost to a whisper. 'It's a name I'll never forget.'

'Oh,' Tessa wished her lips would pout on the word.

'He watches you walk the ridge when he's supposed to be tending his aunt's pigs! Honestly, he does so!' Marie Jane giggled at his obvious embarrassment.

'There's nothing wrong with that, is there?' he appealed to Tessa.

'No . . .' she murmured, laughing to cover a further blush. 'No, nothing wrong. But, how do you know me name?'

'Went to Pat Feeney's school. Didn't learn anything because I wasn't there long before the Aunt set me to work. I don't suppose you remember me?'

He looked so crestfallen when she didn't that she wished she had! And fancy ever forgetting so handsome a mop of peat-black curls!

'I always think of you as Tess,' he said earnestly. 'Not Teresa like your da, and not Tessa like everyone else. Don't I, Marie Jane, always call her Tess?'

Tessa caught Finn's conspiratorial glance to her friend and burst out with mock indignation. ''Tis crafty as a cartload of monkeys y'are, the pair of yes! You've arranged all this between you!'

'Would you have come if I'd have said he wanted to meet you? No, you wouldn't, in case your da found out you were dallying.'

'And you're so right! If he was to see me now he'd never let me out of his sight again.'

'Besides,' added Marie Jane, with arch candour, 'Finn and me made a deal. I said that if he fixed it up with Martin Jarvey to take me to the Fair, I would fix him up with you. Now, that's an honest deal isn't it?'

A sudden sharp rattle from the cabin behind them caused three pairs of eyes to swivel guiltily. A figure stood behind the small window and a hand beckoned like an agitated spider. A sign of invitation, yet scarcely an inviting one.

'God help us,' muttered Marie Jane, 'that's the Aunt.'

Finn dropped to his knees at once and resumed his scrubbing of the pink flanks.

'Why are you looking so scared?' whispered Marie Jane. 'You only want to borrow a kettle.'

'No, I don't,' flashed Tessa, in a panic. 'It was your daft idea. Why can't we just run off?'

'Because if she thinks he was dallying with us she'll give him hell! C'mon, she might curse us if we run off!'

Marie Jane at once opened the door and propelled her friend inside the shadowy room. All the fragments of the weird love story which surrounded the Aunt's name suddenly came together, and there seemed more shadows than ever.

Finn remained outside. He did not want to complicate matters by his presence. People suspected his aunt of being a witch. She had put the mockers on many an unfortunate soul, and sure the terrible bad luck had overtaken them. His growing up seemed to be scattered with dark incidents, and snatches of low-toned conversations which all pointed to his aunt having powers.

He remembered vividly one family whom she had roundly cursed, for what he could not recall. The Mullaneys had been a family of fine boys and buxom girls, and look at them now. One was in a decline, another in the madhouse at Cork, one across the seas in prison, Mullaney himself taken by the gamekeeper, and Mrs Mullaney in her grave.

Then there was Flynn the tinker last year – and if anyone can lay curses it's a tinker. His aunt laid one across him from which he never recovered. Yes, people did not avoid his aunt for nothing, and under no circumstances would they confront her or arouse her anger.

He was fearful of crossing her himself, of being cursed. He was even afraid of the word and always used the euphemism 'mockers' instead. The most humiliating aspect of it for him was that she knew he was afraid, and his fear put him firmly in her power.

His nature was so open and guileless that every passing thought was mirrored in his eyes. He did not want his aunt even to suspect he had an interest in Proud Riley's daughter, so he stayed outside in the compound, close to the pig and within earshot of the open door.

58

CHAPTER THREE

Marie Jane had seen Shena Hanratty before, either through the window or standing in the doorway, but Tessa never had, so she was quite unprepared for the strange sight that met her eyes. The angular figure sat upright in a high-backed rocking chair; her face was pale and gaunt, not a trace remaining of the beauty she had once possessed. Two grey ringlets hung on either side of her ears like tassels, a red flannel bonnet covered the top of her head, and beneath it her close-set eyes, dark and hostile, surveyed the two young women standing by the door.

The red glow of the peat-fire added to the sombre spectacle, and her black draperies made her look like a huge bird of prey. In the silence, the chair on which she perched rocked, but not to and fro with the gentle action associated with rocking. There was nothing soothing about Shena Hanratty's chair. The rockers were hard and stiff and, as though bearing a grudge against the good earth on which it stood, the chair went back and forth with a remorseless crack-and-grind . . . crack-and-grind.

Shena Hanratty paused from her eternal contemplation of the injustices of life, and saw in the two young women an almost forgotten image of herself and her sister Molly.

In that instant the years fell away. She felt herself growing younger. She was a young woman again. Shena and her sister Moll used to stand by the door, arrested by their father's voice at Fairtime warning them of the dangers of being flighty. They were two of the prettiest girls in Ennan. 'Surpassingly lovely', O'Malley always said. Moll, with her long black hair which tossed like the mane of a wild horse, and the greatest, most beautiful eyes that ever beheld a daybreak. She was small, slim and vivacious. A flirt, some said, for she only had to blink her great eyes and the men came running, with the exception of Riley and her sister's sweetheart.

It happened about four years before Tessa's mother had wandered up with Clancy's crew. Shena's auburn ringlets, creamy skin, tiny waist and captivating ways had caught the attention of Tony Collins. She was steadier, more reliable than Moll, and when she fell in love with Tony, it was deeply, and for ever. He was a charmer, a big man with bristling black hair and huge hands stained brown with digging turf. He possessed so infectious a laugh that all who heard it wished they had been in on the joke.

It was the talking point of the community for many a week that it was Shena and not Moll who had landed Tony Collins. Opposites attract, they said, and so it seemed, for when the priest came up in a few weeks they were to be married.

Their settling down was no kind of example for Moll, and she continued to flirt with all the men, married or single, happy in her own way and fluttering about like a gorgeous butterfly. The Duggan boys fought over her, the Jarvey men besieged her with little gifts from the Fair, and Pat Feeney declared – less romantically – that he would give his eyeteeth for her. O'Malley and the others worshipped from afar, or as near as they could without discovery.

The only man whom she avoided like the cholera was Tony Collins, and the refusal to acknowledge Tony irked Shena, even though her father had warned her, from the very chair in which she now sat, to 'let things be'. She could not, and the more Moll refused even to speak to Tony, the more adamant Shena became.

Moll, all too aware of her rampant partiality for a nice man, did not want to spoil her sister's chances; she could take her pick, but Shena was made of deeper, quieter stuff, and despite her beauty not as many chances would come her way. She could not take the chance of being friendly with Tony, because he would, Moll thought, probably make a fool of himself over her and where would that leave Shena? Especially since it would be all over in a few weeks. Moll could not stay the course like Shena.

'I just don't want to bother with him,' she would say, and with a wink, add, 'Don't be too anxious to spread him about.'

'I'm not. But, you're my sister, and I'm going to marry him, and it's only natural I want you to at least be on talking terms.'

'It's because I am your sister . . . Tell you what, when you've married him, I'll dance with him at your wedding!' He'll be safe then, she thought.

Deep in Shena's heart lay a stubborn streak; she was convinced her love for Tony could not be complete until Moll acknowledged her good fortune. She wanted Moll to dance, to talk with Tony, and only when she'd tasted his attraction would she realise what a fine prize her sister had landed.

But still Moll refused to have anything to do with the man who in a few days would be her brother-in-law. Refused, that is, until the Fair came up. The glow of the tinkers' huge fire provided lighting for one of the strangest scenes that had ever taken place in Ennan. Some said it was the drink and high spirits, others that it was the devil. But the idea suddenly leapt into Shena's head as Moll whirled by with Pat Feeney. Why wouldn't Moll dance with Tony like that? People would begin to think there was something wrong with him. And when the pause came between the dances, Shena grabbed her sister by the arm. I'll challenge her before everyone, she thought with a twinge of triumph; she'll have to dance with him then!

'Why will you not dance with me fella?' she demanded. 'Is he not good enough for ye?'

'Sure and haven't I told you before,' replied Moll patiently, 'I've not time for him.'

'It's jealous you are, our Moll, bloody jealous!' There, it was out, and before them all.

'Jealous! Me, jealous? Of that great clod!'

'Dance with him, then.'

The sisters glared at each other. 'You don't know what you're doing, Shena. Why in the blessed God's name can't you leave it? I don't know what's got into you.'

'Tony,' Shena's auburn ringlets tossed impatiently, her colour had risen. 'Dance with her.'

'Why? For God Almighty's sake, Shena, she doesn't want to.'

'Oh, she doesn't want to!' mimicked one of the tinkers, giving Moll a push which sent her flying into Tony's arms. 'Go and dance with her, or you'll have the sun up before we've got going!'

To cover the shock, Riley set up a tune quicker than he'd ever done in his life before. And, with a laugh that echoed against the valley side, Tony seized Moll by the waist, and the frenzy of the reel became the frenzy of their two hearts. Dancing together it was instantly obvious that they were a perfect pair, to the exclusion of all else.

Aloysius O'Malley, the first to see this intense and fatal attraction, dropped out of the dance and stood as though turned to stone. Others, following his astounded gaze, also stopped. Soon everyone,

61

tinkers included, stood and stared in shock, dismay and sheer unbelief.

Now that the stamp of feet had ceased, the shouts and laughter faded, only Riley's flute filled the air. The scene was so awful that Riley, imperceptive by nature, felt he must play on. To keep playing added a semblance of normality, yet normality was not there. Moll and Tony were still dancing, stepping it out like phantoms in a world of their own. Now together, now separate, side-stepping back and forth. They looked unreal, ethereal.

O'Malley forced himself to look in Shena's direction and wished he had not. Her eyes were fixed uncomprehendingly on the two figures. Her face was immobile, blank, her eyes like holes in a winding sheet. Her body was stiff, frozen, rigid, and Riley's flute suddenly sounded ghostly, weird and unnatural.

O'Malley jerked his head to the others and, grabbing the nearest woman, began to dance. He did not know which was worse, the previous scene or the present. There was no life in it, no joy or emotion. The community and tinkers alike were moving like matchstick people, like puppets jerked by the strings of chance, acting out a terrible melodrama. Even the light of the fire had turned lurid. Riley kept the flute going until folk dropped out and wandered off.

'Ye shouldn't have done it, Shena!' cried Moll when the music had stopped. Her long hair was blown across her face, she was panting from the exertion and great tears were gathering. 'Oh, didn't I tell ye to let it be! Oh, God and His merciful Mother, did I not tell you!'

'I'll come and see you in the morning, Shena,' said Tony gruffly. 'It's all over between us, girl. Sure, I'll explain to your da.'

Moll wanted to put her arms about her sister, to weep with her, to beg her forgiveness; but Shena had no tears, no words. At home in their father's cabin, she neither went to bed nor changed her clothes, not eating or drinking but sitting upright in the old rocking chair; not a word passed her lips, not a sigh escaped.

As though disembodied, Shena heard Tony's voice the following day, his broken voice . . . sorrow . . . regrets . . . she shouldn't have . . . And she silently cursed his bent head and shoulders.

Moll tried to explain, couldn't explain the overwhelming suddenness of their love. 'Why did you not wait? I would've danced at your wedding. It's married you would have been . . .' Shena cursed the mane of long black hair.

She heard the neighbours moving about, walking round, looking at her, talking softly about her in hushed tones as if she were dead.

'Do you think it's a stroke?'

'If she doesn't eat or drink soon, it's a wake we'll be having and not a wedding!'

'She tempted providence you know, Mr Hanratty . . .'

'Better if Moll moves out to her uncle's . . .'

Then they were discussing the wedding – Moll's wedding.

'As Collins said, sure there's no point in wasting time. The priest will be up in three or four days, and he may as well marry one as the other!'

'I feel sorry for Shena . . . It's a terrible shame, but why didn't she let things be?'

On Moll's wedding day it rained. The little procession left her uncle's cabin for the chapel, thankful not to have to pass Hanratty's place. They were almost there when a subdued yet audible commotion made Moll turn swiftly. On the tail end of the wedding party she saw Shena, dressed in mourning, in black from head to foot.

'Take no heed of her, Moll. Moll, it's our wedding day.' Tony held her arm tighter, and added with a wink, 'And you did wish she'd come!'

'But not like that. Oh, Tony, Tony, what have we done to her?'

'It's what she pushed us into. The God Almighty knows neither of us wanted it to happen.'

Shena refused to take shelter in the chapel. The doors closed. The ceremony began. And from outside the closed doors came a wailing and keening that set everyone crossing themselves. Shena Hanratty was returning to life. The extreme bitterness in her soul had urged her feet to move, her voice to return, her clothes to change. What would never come to life again were the things of the heart, warmth, emotions, a song, a smile. If a heart could die yet still beat, it was Shena's.

She followed them to her uncle's house, her black a sombre contrast to their gay wedding clothes.

'Ach, I wish she'd stop that keening and wailing' said Mrs Duggan. 'It's fair making my flesh creep.'

'More than that, it's terrible bad luck at a wedding. Oh, dear God, save and bless us; I never heard such in all my days.'

'You go and have a word will you, O'Malley? Sure, young as you are you've got a way wid ye.'

His 'word' made no difference. He returned crossing himself against the curses which fell from her lips. Never had he seen a person change so much. And still she went on, wailing like a banshee, competing with Riley's flute and Duggan's fiddle until her throat cracked into a rough rasping noise.

The following day Moll and Tony were encouraged to put as much distance as possible between Shena and themselves, and this they did by inhabiting a shack near Ennabrugh. When they had gone people saw that Shena's auburn ringlets had turned completely grey.

No one spoke of Tony and Moll in Shena's hearing, but she knew of their happiness and called the bad luck down on it with all the vehemence of her broken heart. She had forgotten her own part, that it was her own doing which had brought it on; all she could, or cared to, recall was the stab of pain and the shame of being jilted. The desolation of losing the only man she had ever really loved, and the dreadful perfidy of her own sister . . . her own fella.

The birth of a son took old Mr Hanratty up to their shack. Others went up, for the Collins's were not bringing their baby within earshot of a curse. Some two years later the community was shocked when Moll's nearest neighbour brought news that both Moll and Tony, in search of a fresh cutting on Ennabrugh, had drowned. No one knew how or where. Their spades were on the shore but no bodies had been found, which was nothing strange, for very few were.

Their little son, whom they had called Finn, having been left with the neighbour was brought down to the valley. They sat him on a compound wall and stood round, like tinkers weighing up the form of a donkey.

'What's to be done with the little fella?'

No one could afford another mouth to feed, yet no one could frame the word 'workhouse', at least not while the little boy looked at them with his mother's great eyes, and his father's crop of peat-black hair. One or two nudged each other, for along the valley floor came a tall figure in black. People shifted their feet uneasily and recalled all the curses.

'The Aunt Hanratty will have him,' she croaked.

They stared open-mouthed and round-eyed. This was the last thing anyone expected.

'Is he not me nephew?'

And, of course, there's room now, thought O'Malley, for her father died last year. Clearly the idea was not a popular one, but after all she was his aunt. He was lifted from the wall, and trailed behind the gaunt figure like a lost puppy. From that moment no one called her by name. Shena was dead. She was now the Aunt Hanratty.

As the Aunt Hanratty, she reared the boy well enough and set him to work as soon as he could carry a spade or wash a pig, but she took it all out on the growing child who so much resembled his parents. By subjugating and subduing him, despising and depriving him, she worked out her own revenge.

The memory began to fragment, it shattered into a thousand pieces and slowly reformed itself into the present, into the reality of the two young women by the door, O'Malley's girl and Proud Riley's daughter.

Tessa and Marie Jane guessed what she was thinking and were petrified by the starkness of her gaze, the silence, the atmosphere. They both wanted to get out, to step to the door and be gone, but neither seemed able to move a foot.

'What brings Proud Riley's daughter to this door?'

Tessa could not have answered if she had wanted to. The recollection of this woman's story, coupled with the atmosphere and the hoarse, croaking voice, robbed her of speech.

'She's come to see if you've got a spare kettle . . . to lend . . .' Marie Jane shrank from the gimlet eyes, and added lamely, 'Just till the knackers have been up.'

'Ha! By all the saints that ever lived, sure I never thought I'd live to see the day when Proud Riley would send his daughter begging off the Aunt Hanratty.' She, too, always referred to herself as the Aunt.

If me da gets to know about this, thought Tessa, there'll be trouble the like of which I've never seen. It took him all his time to borrow off his old friend O'Malley – and he had only done that twice in fifteen years. He was not called Proud Riley for nothing.

The close-set eyes now turned from the shrinking Marie Jane to Tessa. 'Stand forward, girl. And what are you staring at? Have ye never seen an old woman before? You'll be old yerself one day.'

Tessa met the hostility with as much candour as she had faced the gamekeeper. It was on her tongue to tell the Aunt the truth, that it was all a prank to look her nephew over, but her mind suddenly centred on Finn Collins . . . his long, corduroy-covered legs, his shy smile, the fact that his aunt 'put on him'. An act of defiance would rebound onto him and she could not add to his troubles.

'Don't bother about the kettle,' said Tessa, calmly. 'It's all right, me da will manage.'

'Your da will do no such thing. He will not manage. He shall have my tay kettle with all the compliments of the Aunt Hanratty! Be sure to tell him that, girl! And be sure to let me have it back, but then Riley's so proud he won't rest; it'll be on his mind for weeks that he's in the debt of the Aunt. Take it, girl, it's there by the pail.'

Marie Jane being nearest, seized the kettle and turned toward the door. But Tessa reached out and grabbed it from her. It dropped, striking the side of the pail, metal against metal. The clanging sounded like a warning to Tessa. To walk out of this cabin with the kettle would spell trouble. She realised the old woman wanted her to take it so she could crow over her da, and no one was going to crow over Proud Riley through any act of his daughter's. One thing was certain, the old woman could not force her to take it. This certainty brought confidence. She lifted her head slowly, with a gracious upsweep of her chin, and braced herself.

'I thank you for your kindness, but Marie Jane was only trying to help and got it all wrong. Proud Riley isn't for borrowing a kettle, ye see.' On that final note of triumph, she turned to the door; Marie Jane had already gone and Tessa followed quickly.

'Oh,' panted Marie Jane when they had reached the safety of her father's cabin. 'It's a brave girl y'are, standing up to the old witch like that. Holy Mother! When you dropped the bloody kettle I nearly died!'

'What a terrible mess you nearly landed me in! You and your adventures! If me da gets wind of this, he'll kill me.'

'Christ Almighty, Tessa, take your mind off your da!' Then in a softer tone, 'Is it settled then? That you'll go to the Fair with Finn Collins?'

'Wouldn't dream of going with anyone else!'

'There,' Marie Jane was delighted. 'What did I tell ye!'

Aloysius O'Malley paused before he rapped at the Hanratty's door. 'Are you in there?' he yelled, knowing full well she was never anywhere else.

'And where d'ye think an old woman of my infirmities would be?'

Finn sprang to welcome O'Malley, who had pushed the door open.

'God love us,' she croaked. 'It's honoured I am. But you can't fool me, O'Malley, you're wanting something are you not?' It was almost an accusation. She did not mention the visit of his daughter. If O'Malley was thinking to have her nephew for his daughter, he had another think coming. Her nephew was not for anyone, she would see to that.

The chair began to creak with its crack-and-grind motion. Finn was apprehensive, he knew all the signs of displeasure. Visitors, though few, were unsettling to the Aunt, especially this man with his smooth-talking ways. She would never forgive his conciliatory role regarding Moll and Tony. It was he who had poured oil on troubled waters. They would have been drummed out of the valley and left to live with their own perfidy if it had not been for him. Even now, after all these years, she thought, they treat me as if I were the guilty one.

'I need the strength of the lad's arm,' he said, with a glance at Finn. 'Since the miller dropped dead it's fallen on me to go down for the flour, and if I don't go soon we'll all be famine short. Ay, and what will you do for griddle bread then, Aunt Hanratty? No one will lend any because no one'll have any until I take the donkeys down, and a strong young fella.'

The nervousness which Finn had felt was now quite gone. He tried to conceal his delight and excitement from the gimlet eyes of his aunt and busied himself with trimming wicks for the lamp. He had always admired O'Malley's capacity for dealing with the ways of civilisation, and hoped it extended to dealing with his aunt. He was inwardly trembling and flattered that he had been chosen to go down with the donkeys.

'God love us, O'Malley, you're not telling me the nephew's the only young fella that's strong in the arm and weak in the head?'

'You see, it's like this, Aunt Hanratty, there's not a lot o' choice when it comes to a job like this. The Muldoon brothers have seven lads between them, but they'd never last out the ten miles to Rohira, still less coming back with the load. And it has to be one of the young 'uns; they need to see there's another world down there. Now, where the divil was I up to?'

'The Muldoons,' put in Finn.

'Ach, 'tis so,' nodded O'Malley, and went on with his summary. 'There's young Jarvey, but he's a fool. Me own two aren't strong enough. And there's Gypo Kelly,' he announced brightly. 'But sure to God, he's light-fingered and could land me in jug. Jams' got two.' He shook his head sadly. 'But one's too little and the other's too fat. There's a few married fellas that'd fit the bill, but the wives won't let 'em down in case they don't come back!' He laughed at his little joke, but the Aunt remained fierce. 'The shiftless are always fighting, and Eddie Byrne has six but they're all a bit short upstairs, if you get my meaning.'

'I get your meaning all right. What you really mean is you're divil-bent on taking him! Will you cast your eyes now on that leaking roof and the bucket that's been beneath it these six months? That lazy spalpeen of a nephew is always going to fix it, but he says he has no time. And, if he's no time to fix that roof, he's no time to go gallivanting with a fancy fella the likes of yeself!'

'I'll go down, Mr O'Malley.' Finn, startled at the sound of his own voice, looked up from trimming the wicks; he would never have dared to open his mouth if it hadn't been for Tessa Riley's example yesterday, and the presence of O'Malley. 'The roof's been waiting six months already, another day or two will make no odds.'

'It's settled then, lad. I'll give you a call at sun-up.' He turned to the Aunt. 'It's proud you should be that he's going to save us from starvation; there's not above fifty of us, but we still need a crust in our bellies. I'll bid you a good night.' Then he added unctuously, 'May the Holy Mother of God be with you!'

'Good night!' yelled Finn, starting forward. ' 'Twas good of you to think of me!'

'Good of him!' spat the Aunt. 'No good will come of him filling your stupid head with fancy ideas!'

'Every young fella should see the ways of civilisation,' said O'Malley as they walked, each with a donkey and cart. 'That godforsaken valley can't support life much longer, you know.'

Finn nodded. 'It scarce supports the pigs. I blame it on the ground being worn out, but when the pigs die, the Aunt says it's all my doing!' He began to relate to the listening O'Malley much of what the older man had already guessed about the Aunt's domination. Finn felt free to talk for the first time in his life. The visit of the girls was not mentioned, and he enjoyed the thrill of conspiracy. His whole being seemed to be coming alive, as if awakening to the touch of spring.

'You ought to be clearing out of there, boy. Break free from the Aunt before she breaks you. She's after keeping hold on you to get her revenge on your da. She's settling old scores at your expense. And you,' he put a slim hand on the muscled shoulder, 'being a bit soft on the sentiments, like, are no match for the scheming ways of the Aunt.' Later, when St Joseph's steeple was in sight, he delivered his most daring advice. 'You've started to make a stand by coming down here; go one further and wrestle at the Fair. Knock hell out of the knackers! Never mind the Aunt, get a bit of money in your pocket, works wonders for the confidence. Gives you something to aim for.'

Finn instantly felt the lack of an 'aim' in his life. He had known something was missing and felt there was more to living than the eternal round of drudgery.

'Don't let her keep you down, boy.'

No, thought Finn, his mind embroiled with the story of his parents ill-fated love. No, not any more. I owe it to me dead ma and da to break free.

O'Malley smiled indulgently as the small market town of Rohira unfolded itself to Finn's bewildered gaze. He did not know where to look first. He stared down at the cobbled street and up at the two-storeyed houses which lined either side. His chest expanded with a great intake of breath as he surveyed the wonders of civilisation for the first time.

Where were all the people going pushing and bustling? And so many horse-drawn carts and pony traps. They stopped at the drinking fountain on the corner, and Finn, with child-like amazement, pressed the button again and again, laughing as the water spurted up to quench his thirst and refresh his face. It was like another world. This was, he realised, the proper world where people were not dependent upon the whims of a bog for their living. While O'Malley talked to the miller at the granary, Finn loaded the sacks of flour. He eyed the mechanism of the great millstones with something like awe, and marvelled that O'Malley was so much at ease with it all!

And later when he was introduced to froth-edged glasses of Guinness in the brightly lit parlour of a public house which was warm with fires, he felt the world was indeed a marvellous place.

O'Malley tipped back his hat and heaved a great sigh of satisfaction.

'Come on, Finn boy, we'd best be getting back. It's no joke with loaded carts and those donkeys after dark – I'll swear those beasts are man's natural enemies!'

Walking at the donkey's head, Finn absorbed everything he saw. The dress of the women, the hats and jackets of the men. Shops with all manner of things in the windows that he never knew existed, still less knew the names of. He turned his astonished eyes in the direction of a barrel organ.

'God save us!' he breathed. 'It's a bloody miracle.'

'And that church is where Proud Riley's wife is buried, and the girleen was christened – no valley chapel was good enough for him.'

'So he's been down, then?'

'Three times, all told.'

'How could he bear to go back up? How can you come down, time after time like you do and see all this, and then go back up?'

'It's a matter of economics, Finn boy. To pay rent for houses with an upstairs and windows like they have, you've got to be in work. Now, I have six children, that makes a total of eight of us to keep. And once you come down here there's a style of living and rules to be kept. But I'm working on it, Finn boy, I'm working on the idea. As for Proud Riley, in Ennan he's known as a proud fella because he has goats and a dresser and a loft for his daughter to sleep in. Up there, he's cock o' the walk, but down here, you've got to face it, down here they call us peasants. It's just like us feeling superior to those thieving knackers, so the town folk feel superior to us. You've got to know their ways.'

'And is that what you're doing, Mr O'Malley?'

''Tis so, Finn boy, 'tis exactly so.'

The lamp was already lit when Finn, after unloading the sacks of flour, turned the donkeys loose and entered his aunt's cabin. Peasants . . . peasants . . . the new word rolled round and round in his head. Up to now he had known of no comparisons, but the gulf between him and the people in the town seemed a lot wider than between him and the tinkers.

His aunt was sitting silently in her chair. He knew she was watching him as he stood in the shadows removing his boots. He threw his coat down by the hearthstone to dry and watched it steaming, wishing he could join it, that he could squat by the glowing turf, for the mist had dampened him to the skin.

The fragments and fingers of light did their utmost to infiltrate the shadows, as though in apology for having created them. Finn did not mind the shadows tonight, he never minded them at any time, for they were his refuge from his aunt's searching eyes. She always said she could read his soul and that his mind was written all over his face, so when he had anything to hide he kept to the shadows. His aunt knew this but could do nothing about it.

Neither made any reference to the town. He had dumped their supply of flour inside the door and flung himself on the bed by the wall, well out of his aunt's sight. He had made the decision to wrestle, and he knew full well that even a glance from those burning eyes would erode his newly found courage. Yet he recognised that a source of strength had sprung up within him. The first seeds had been sown when he had heard Tessa, and she a mere girleen, refuse to take the kettle the Aunt was trying to foist onto her, and those seeds had been nurtured by his long talk with O'Malley.

'I'm going to the Fair,' he said firmly.

'Who says you are?' demanded the peevish voice.

'I say I am.'

'Brave words coming from a fool! We'll see about that, ye lazy good-for-nothing crayture! Have you not enough to do with the pigs and the peat?'

'I'm over twenty-one, Aunt, and it's time I made up me own mind.'

'Mind! Is that what you're calling it! Just let me be telling you this, you've never made your mind up on anything. It's O'Malley putting all these fancy notions to you. Well let me put another. You didn't go to the Fair last year, or the year before, and you're not going this year.'

He tried to shut out her goblin mirth, clutching all the while the little crucifix in his pocket. He had known it would not be easy, this standing up to the Aunt. She was right of course, he was a fool. Marie Jane would have left it until the daytime, or even not say anything at all. He should just have gone off to the Fair. It was O'Malley who had given him courage and made him feel brave. That was it, he must make it clear that O'Malley and others were involved. She couldn't curse them all, or could she?

'O'Malley's got me down to wrestle with the tinkers. It'll put money in me pocket.'

'Then you're a bigger fool than I thought. It'll put money in his pocket, ten times more than in yours. He'll be running a book, taking bets, while some big bruiser of a knacker is nailing you to the ground. Now you just listen to me . . .' The chair stopped its grinding and Finn did not know which was worse, that or the silence.

Outside the wind moaned softly, inside the lamp flickered. Finn lay stretched out, inert and sweating, wondering where his newly found confidence had got to. To stave off his fear of the mockers he thought of Tessa and Marie Jane, and all the words he'd had with her father, and what had been revealed about his aunt.

'Where would you have been, you ungrateful young devil, if I'd not taken you in? You would have ended up at the workhouse, or worse . . .' As the Aunt continued, her words pushed the images of his dead parents into his head, and he recalled how only earlier this very day he had sworn to break free.

'And so you keep telling me,' he declared bravely. 'And it's thankful I am, but you just listen to me, Aunt.' He heard the sound of his own voice and scarcely recognised the strength of it. 'I've been digging, stacking, and drying turf for you all me life. Not to mention the little still, and the pigs. I work from dawn to dark – and for what? Sweet Jasus, for what?' he repeated. 'I've never had any money to call me own and jingle in me pocket. Martin Jarvey and the others have money for tobacco, and Jarvey's even got himself a jacket – and none of them work like I do.'

'No good'll come of this going to town. I told you, didn't I, and see, your head's full of fancy ideas already. Go and get your head split open and your eyes blacked! That'll teach ye! You'll be the laughing stock o' the valley.'

Finn took a great breath of relief. He'd got the best of that round. He could hear the thin rasp of her voice. If she only knew the half, he smiled to himself. He conjured up a vision of Tessa Riley, and of him escorting her to the Fair. He had been wondering what they would talk about, but now he could tell her all about Rohira, the pubs and street lamps . . . There'd be no shortage of words! He might even sound knowledgeable like O'Malley. He felt good. He had learned more this one day than in his entire life.

'Da,' cried Tessa, looking through the tiny window. 'The tinkers are coming! They're on their way. I'm sure I can see 'em in the distance, coming along the far ridge. It's a sure sign of spring when the tinkers are on the march.' Not waiting for any comment, for she expected none, Tessa continued to look out of the window, leaning forward, hands on the narrow ledge. 'It gets into ye, Da, doesn't it? Spring . . . The air's softer, and up by the Great Bog the saxifrage is just beginning to show, creeping along the edge as though to cheer it up. And by all that's holy, Da, it needs it. The only birds you hear up there are those with a mournful cry.'

On and on she chattered, sometimes pausing for thought, and all the while amazing her silent father with her knowledge and perception. He had spent a lifetime at Ennabrugh and not seen anything she had described. Sometimes he wondered if it was the same place she was referring to; and sure enough when he went up for the turf he would look for what she had described, and see that it was so.

Sometimes this talk of hers bothered him. It seemed she was going ahead too fast. He wanted somehow to stop her progress so he could catch a breathing space to think and take stock. But each day almost, especially in spring, there was something new and different . . . ideas, views, longing, wishes; things he could not comprehend.

Tessa turned from the window and looked across to where her father was sitting cross-legged on the rushes, mending one of her shoes. The front of his homespun shirt hung open, revealing a dirty woollen vest; the buckle of Timothy Thomas's belt shone, and the smell of sweat and newly tanned leather beamed across the short distance.

'Oh, Da!' she exclaimed, suddenly impatient. 'It's the tinkers coming, are you not glad? I'll swear to God that if the very roof fell in on your head, it'd make no impression!'

'I've told you before, and I'll tell you again,' he muttered through a mouthful of shoe tacks. 'Knackers are not to be trusted. They're a thieving lot of vagabonds. I'd hang and draw the lot of 'em!' He extricated a tack from between his teeth and hammered it in with feeling. 'The only good and dacent thing about them coming at all is that O'Malley can have his kettle back!'

He had mentioned the borrowing about a dozen times, and Tessa had thanked St Teresa fervently that she'd had the guts to refuse the kettle the Aunt Hanratty had tried to foist on to her. She gave an immense sigh of exquisite relief every time she thought of it.

'But, Da, we can't do without 'em. Think of the things our people buy off them, things that they need. Think of the fixing and mending they do, not to mention our produce which they give good money for. And don't I sell lengths of me homespun cloth?'

Proud Riley was not impressed. 'We'd survive.'

'But who wants to just survive? Oh, if only you could read, Da, you'd realise – '

'Have I not been down to the town three times? Have I not seen it all?'

Tessa closed her mind against the same old rhetoric. Sometimes she wondered about him, even despaired of him. He was so unbending, so set in his ways. True, he had been to the town and she had not, but what were visits to the town compared with reading? The priest brought up old newspapers and the odd magazine for O'Malley, and he passed them on to her. Each page was like a window onto the world. She gave a sharp sigh. It would never do to argue too much or go against him, especially now.

'Da,' she said hesitantly. 'You did tell Mr O'Malley I could go down and watch the tinkers set up camp with him and Marie Jane?'

'Did I now? More fool me. Aloysius O'Malley could persuade a fella that the Great Bog of Ennabrugh was the Garden of Paradise!'

'I can go?' she persisted. Her voice was small against the four

74

walls, and there was a plaintive note in it, an edge that was not lost on him. It reminded him of caged birds.

'You may as well have put her in a convent,' O'Malley had said in that soft, easy way of his. 'Give the girleen a bit of interest, let her loose a little.'

'Sure, I can't feel me way to do it,' he had replied. 'You see, if anything was to happen, if she was put in the family way, it would ruin any chance of a dacent marriage. And I swore over her mother's grave – I could never live with meself if any trouble befell Teresa!'

'It won't,' O'Malley had urged. 'Not if you loosen the reins. She's got to develop a bit of social charm – '

'Social charm! If you mean flighty like that eldest girl of yours, then Teresa can manage without it.'

'Oh, that's just Marie Jane's way. It's all talk and daydreams. And by social charm, I mean she's got to know how to mix in, to talk, to hold her own in company. You must admit, Riley old son, you're the last fella on God's earth to know anything about that! Tessa will be all right with me. Did not Mrs O'Malley bring her into the world for you? And instruct her in the ways of womanhood? May God have mercy on us,' O'Malley had sighed in exasperation. 'We're only talking about her coming down for a few hours to watch the tinkers set up their camp! The greatest social occasion after a winter of nothing and you're twittering and dithering like Jams and his missus! Besides, there'll be no trouble with the knackers this year. It's Spider Murphy's lot, and you know how strict his wife is, having five daughters.'

He had winked at Riley, easing away the worried frown. 'You can just picture Mrs Murphy can't you, standing with full audience and arms folded, and saying with all seriousness, "There'll be no fornicating in Murphy's camp, got it?"' Riley thawed further at his friend's mimicry of the tinker woman. 'As for the Fair itself,' continued O'Malley, 'I've got Tessa the best and most reliable escort. Young Collins, you know, the lad Shena Hanratty brought up.'

'And to think you tried to fix me up with her once!' Riley gave one of his rare smiles.

'Ay, but she was a beauty then . . .' O'Malley had paused to give a deep sigh. 'Her and Moll . . . and Tony. Ay, the world was younger and you could have had your choice. Well, what do you say about Tessa coming down, old son?'

It appeared he had said yes.

CHAPTER FOUR

Tessa had risen early to complete her tasks so Riley would have no cause for future complaint, and after an anxious morning she now scrambled down the hillside toward the valley. Although she was awed by the Great Bog, there were times when Tessa could understand its moods. Like today, when great clouds distilled from the mountain terrain surrounding the Bog were sweeping, heavy with displeasure over the valley below – just like her da. But spring was in the air, as she had been telling him, and with its coaxing ways and promise of fulfilment, Tessa felt closer to the sprites and mischief of spring than the brooding presence of the Bog.

Treats such as this expedition rarely came Tessa's way and they needed a lot of thought and preparation. Indeed, because of her father's strictness, deceit and even downright cunning were now a matter-of-course. Riley did not mind 'titivating', as he called it, if she were going down with him, for he liked to think of them as a well-set-up pair, liked to see heads turn, eyes appraise. But on an occasion like this it would never do to appear excited to go, eager to change her clothes, to wash or even brush her hair. So, under cover of scrubbing down Billy's flanks, she had used the bucket of water to wash herself. On getting up that morning, she had had the foresight to wear her blue gingham blouse with long sleeves and high-buttoned neck, and she wore her wide homespun skirt to tend and milk the goats – the same skirt which the gamekeeper had held on to – it being wide and accommodating enough to secret another one beneath, although it had to be pinned up so the hem wouldn't trail in the goat's urine. Tessa did not have a great many skirts apart from the homespun, just another two. A white cotton affair which O'Malley had bought for a present, and the fine black woollen skirt she was now wearing, which she had found after the last Long Dance had gone down. How the owner had come to lose it, and how she had contrived to go home without it, had been the subject of much hilarity between herself, Marie Jane and the six elder Duggan girls. It bore a label with a tailor's name sewn into the waistband, and had been the envy of all until O'Malley had been instructed by his daughter that her next garment from the old Jew's cart must bear a label.

As she scrambled down the hillside, toward the valley, toward the descent of the tinkers, to Marie Jane, and Finn Collins . . . all negative thoughts dissipated. Once out of sight, she stopped behind the few skeletal trees to take off and fold up her thick skirt. Smiling, enjoying the delicious sensation of titivating, she stood brushing her hair, feeling the wind cool the nape of her neck. She touched her face, feeling the smoothness of her skin, for hadn't she taken a little of the cream from the milk and rubbed it into her cheeks to counteract the effect of wind and weather? The long sleeves were unbuttoned and turned back to show a length of shapely forearm, and then puffed and pulled out above the elbow to give an attractive fullness. A little shawl with tassels had also been smuggled out beneath the homespun canopy, for when it became chilly. Lastly, she tied her hair back with a black ribbon, knowing it did marvellous things for her profile – at least, Marie Jane said it did.

Feeling suitably preened and ready to set off she glanced down. Mother of God, she thought, I can't believe it! For beneath the graceful fold of the beautifully cut black skirt stuck out two muck-stained shoes. I had all the time in the world, she admonished herself, and I forgot to bring me pumps! She continued to stare at the clumping leather shoes her father had made, and likened them to elephants' feet. But forlornness soon passed. She'd been lucky to get the rest out. Still, the pumps wouldn't have taken much room, she could have hidden them in her drawers, one at the side of each leg! With a philosophical shrug, a mental note for future strategy, and no further time for regrets, Tessa negotiated the mounds and tussocks, the swampy ground, stony ground, and eventually the smooth track that widened into the valley floor. She noticed the grass, the growing greenness of it; and yet, out there in the valley, it was all so worn out, so badly looked after.

As she speculated Tessa kept her eyes on the raggle-taggle procession descending the ridge, and tried to keep her thumping heart under control. She could see everybody swirling about or standing in groups, heard voices floating up. Thank God I managed to smuggle me clothes out, she thought. What would Marie Jane have thought of me smelly goat clothes! Besides, she was not the only one on which a good impression had to be made. Surely Finn Collins would be there?

'Tessa! It's Tessa Riley!' Marie Jane, catching sight of her friend swinging along, paused as always in admiration and then, leaving Finn and Martin Jarvey, she ran to meet her. Slipping her arm through Tessa's she tossed her gleaming ringlets in the direction of the young men. 'He was terrible anxious in case you didn't make it! Oh,' her lips pouted. 'Me da said he had an awful job talking yours round, I thought you'd not be coming after all.'

'So did I at one time, but your da has such a way with words, Marie Jane. But I've to be back before dark.' Tessa gave her friend's arm a squeeze. 'I don't know what I'd do without you and your family. It's nervous I am now, though. What the divil am I to talk about all day?'

'You'll find something, or he will!' They exchanged glances of excitement.

'We'll keep together, Marie Jane? Don't go off and leave me with him,' she begged. 'I hardly know him except for that few minutes at his aunt's.'

'He'll not be short on the words. He went to town with me da for the flour and can't wait to impress you with it all!'

Little confidences exchanged and their relationship re-established, the girls, now hand in hand, ran toward the two young men, one tall and dark, the other a little shorter and fair.

'Here she is, Finn. I told you she'd make it.'

'Isn't it exciting?' Tessa said. She spoke with genuine pleasure, and then she smiled. It illuminated her face, making it bright with anticipation, and her eyes, blue-grey beneath the thick lashes, seemed to be darting everywhere until arrested and held by the openly admiring gaze of Finn Collins.

Why, he thought, momentarily staggered by her radiance, she's different. Not that he'd had the opportunity to get to know many of the young women; but he'd known this one, or seen her, been aware of her, since the few times he had attended Pat Feeney's school. There was something about her. A certain indefinable quality. The usual phrases to describe the attractions of women did not apply to her. Pretty . . . beautiful . . . lovely? She was something above all these. The proud way she walked, held herself, the tilt of her head to show off so graceful a neck. The way she strode the hills . . . He struggled with these thoughts in the greatest wonderment. Then a soft sigh escaped his lips. Ah, 'tis like a woman regal born she is . . . His heart seemed to shift with the impact of sudden emotion. They continued to gaze at each other as if held in a world apart. The others had disappeared. Silence had fallen.

Tessa felt herself becoming weak in the grip of a new feeling – a sense of dependency, a disturbance of poise. A light flush began to colour her neck and cheeks. She wanted to pull away, to gather herself, to gain some kind of control. Holy Mother, she thought desperately, it wasn't like this when I saw him before. And although she wanted so badly to regain normality, she held onto the magic of the moment, for it was only a moment.

Marie Jane rescued her from panic with a nudge. Startled, Tessa smiled to cover her embarrassment and Finn thrust his hands deep into his pockets.

'Enough of that,' she teased. 'If her da knows you're giving her the once-over, he'll not let her out again!'

'I'm glad you made it,' said Finn in an exaggeratedly matter-of-fact tone, and as she did not answer, added, 'It's Spider Murphy's camp.'

'Yes, I know. Hasn't he got a caravan, or something? I saw it from the distance.' She turned to watch the first of the tinkers enter the end of the valley, and saw O'Malley and some of the other men approaching.

'Hello to ye, Tessa. It's fine you're looking this day.'

She blushed. Nodding towards the tinkers, she struggled for something commonplace to say, to restore her shattered heart. 'Have they got a caravan, Mr O'Malley?'

He held back a smile. Just look at them, he thought, glancing from Finn to Tessa, faces as red as turkey cocks and as flustered as a pair of old hens. What the devil have they been talking about!

'That's what it looks like to me, but,' he raised an eyebrow, 'how did you know it was so? Sure, 'tis the first to come to Ennan.'

'There was a picture in the magazine that the priest brought up – you passed it on to me.'

'Ah,' he brightened. 'So I did. It proves that you do read them, then!'

'Oh, Mr O'Malley, 'course I do! Do you think I feed them to the goats!'

79

The elder Duggan stopped to talk. 'Do you reckon Spider must be in the money?'

'If he hasn't bought it, he must have borrowed it!'

Duggan nodded his red head. Red hair and bad teeth seemed the only failing in so large a family. 'Ay, they've a clean way of putting it. Borrowing sounds a lot better than stealing!'

'It'll be peaceful. They're a dacent lot.'

'So long as we don't cross 'em.'

Murphy's band was travelling in a group of six families. The Murphys were principally tinsmiths, the others were chimney sweeps, marching east to sweep the chimneys of the big houses for the spring clean. There were horse dealers, castrators of pigs and cattle, and metal runners, too.

The orderly parade entered the valley like a circus. Spider Murphy, tall, thin and gangly-limbed, bedecked with gold chains, led them in with all the panache of a ring master. The barrel-shaped caravan swayed pompously from side to side, drawn by a piebald pony with a long tail.

Marie Jane treated Tessa to another nudge, indicating a young woman sitting on the box, reins held loosely in her hand. 'Hope it's not his wife,' she commented in horror. 'She's only our age.'

'Eldest daughter,' informed her father. 'Weak in the lungs, had the wheezes from a girleen.'

'You know everything, Da!' She threw him an affectionate glance.

For all the grand entrance, no smiles, cheers or greetings were exchanged. The tinkers' children ran alongside their elders, dirty, sullen and tired. As a race they were naturally taciturn, and even the dogs walked in an uninterested manner, tails held still as if reserving judgement. The cavalcade halted. Spider Murphy left the bridle of the pony and stood to address the camp in their own language of Shelta. His face was fierce, eyes permanently narrowed and constantly alert; his long black hair was knotted into a pigtail and he was afflicted with a facial twitch. When startled or caught off guard the twitch was so violent it set his large gold earring ajog.

Murmurs broke out among the tinkers and rapidly escalated into a heated discussion as to the best sites to occupy. Marie Jane, alarmed at the ferocious tones, took the opportunity to move closer to Martin Jarvey. Tessa cast a worried glance at Finn; if there was any trouble before the Fair even started she'd not be allowed down on the morrow. He closed one eye in a confident wink. She smiled at the unexpectedness of it and looked away, her fears dissolving.

The ringmaster quickly calmed his circus, striding about and allocating places with staccato precision. He then turned his attention to the audience. He knew the tinkers were looked upon with suspicion, as a kind of necessary evil. Knowing they were despised as itinerants, Murphy took a perverse pleasure in providing necessities with an exaggerated tolerance. It was up to him to woo these people of Ennan, and this he did.

The silence which had greeted their arrival was a ritual which was followed by the pitching of camp, and the address of the chief. This was Murphy's way, his accepted way. The ritual over, normality returned. People moved and talked, watching with hands in pockets the antics of the travellers, the erecting of their rigs, the assembling of the fire, and gazing with more excitement and anticipation at the big bundles and sacks. None of these would be opened until the Fair started, which left plenty of time for speculation.

Tessa and Finn, Martin and Marie Jane, wandered toward the caravan.

'Do you think they'll let us look inside it?' asked Tessa, inhaling a great breath of satisfaction. 'Sure, it's a marvellous thing.'

The others began to crowd around, among them the Duggan girls, with their red ringlets, fringes, curls, plaits, and one shaven for head lice but wearing a pretty cap. The Jams family, the Kellys, and even a few of the shiftless, had stirred themselves to look upon this painted wonder.

The chief's wife, as swarthy and sinewy as her husband, and wearing a bright red spotted scarf to tie back her hair, emerged from the barrel-shaped caravan with arms folded and exuding an air of hostility. Two deep furrows running from eye to lip on either side of her nose added a sinister expression. Gold teeth gleamed in the cavern of her mouth as brightly as the gold rings looped through her ears.

'Spider Murphy's camp is a good one,' she announced. 'We're not out for trouble. It's a strict camp and all who travel with Murphy obey Murphy's rules. Got it?'

Tessa nodded wide-eyed; some smirked in unbelief; O'Malley and those who had heard it all before raised their eyes to heaven. Others murmured, feeling they had to say something to prove their comprehension.

'There'll be no lying, cheating, stealing, or fornication in Murphy's camp. Got it?' Tessa, not knowing what the last word meant, nodded again. 'I'll tell you straight, I've as much liking for goys as you have for us. You remember your place and we'll remember ours.'

'It's fair enough,' remarked Mrs Jams, as everybody started talking, and to her progeny she added, 'And don't you lot be forgetting what she said!'

'This is as bad as watching the shiftless,' declared Marie Jane. 'We wouldn't stand about watching them fix their shelters. Let's go. C'mon, Tessa, it's safe, we've got the fellas in tow.' She laughingly looked up at Martin and Finn who, eager to please, would agree to anything.

'Look,' said Martin. 'There's the girl from the caravan.'

'So,' replied Marie Jane, 'What of it?'

He shifted uncomfortably. 'Nothing. I thought you were curious, that's all.'

'Me? Why should I be curious about a knacker?'

'Well,' he floundered, feeling he was not making a good impression and wondering why Marie Jane was giving him a rough ride. 'With her being the chief's daughter and all . . . Eh look, she's got a tent.'

They stopped where the tinker girl was trying to get the tent up.

'It's a fine thing ye have there,' said Martin.

'Ach, it would be if I could get the bloody thing up!'

'Sure, I don't know what to do,' put in Finn charging forward, 'or I'd give you a hand.'

Martin, close on his heels, took over. 'I've seen them before – leave it to us. What's your name?'

'Kate.'

'Right, you leave it to us, Kate.' He swelled and swaggered with importance. 'Here, Finn, you hold these two poles while I see to the ropes.'

'Ah, it's thankful I am. 'Tis me brathing, you see. I get the asthma something terrible.'

'Little Jams use to wheeze like an old squeeze-box,' put in Marie Jane, annoyed at Martin for being so handy.

'It catches you badly,' Kate went on. 'Can't dance, or work much, or walk far.'

'Is that why you were in the caravan?' asked Tessa.

The tinker girl nodded. 'Me brother is usually here, but I try to do things for meself. The tent keeps the chill from the air.'

Marie Jane grudgingly acknowledged to herself that Kate Murphy was the most beautiful tinker girl she had ever seen. Her dark skin was smooth, her almond-shaped eyes brown and soulful. Never had straight hair looked so good on anyone: it fell heavily, like black velvet curtains on either side of her thin face.

Twice Kate's long hair brushed Martin's cheek as she leaned forward to offer advice. To make sure it did not happen a third time Marie Jane was stung to ask, 'And where's your brother, then? What does he do?' She ignored a warning look from Tessa and went on. 'Is he a metal runner or a tinsmith?'

'He's called Mick . . .' she inhaled with an effort, finding it difficult to carry on a conversation. 'He . . . works the boxing booths . . . on the fairs.'

'Oh.'

Tessa recognised the signs. Martin was going to get his come-uppance for being attentive to Kate. Whatever happened they must not split up their foursome; her da would go mad if they paired off.

'Seeing the lads have nearly fixed your tent, will you not ask your brother if we can have a look at your da's caravan?'

Her voice trailed away as one of the tinkers suddenly disengaged himself from a group and strode beligerently towards them.

'What the divil are you doing with me sister's tent?' he demanded.

'Hold on, hold on a minute,' cried Finn. 'Can't you see we're fixing it for her?'

'Well don't. I'm here to do that.'

'Y'are now, but you weren't when she wanted it up.'

'Take your thievin' hands off it!'

'Look who's talking!' laughed Finn. 'Besides, what would I want with a tent?'

Tessa grew more uneasy. Years of warnings about the tinkers made her apprehensive. She could see her chances of attending the Fair tomorrow rapidly disappearing.

'Mick?' wheezed Kate. 'It's all right, really it is. Sure, they've helped me and they meant well; and anyways it's up now.'

'You could have waited till I came,' he muttered petulantly.

Marie Jane eyed his figure, compact in breeches and black gaiters, his rounded buttocks spreading to muscular thighs. He was jaunty, swaggering, strong, and proud of his position as the chief's son, his only son. He soon realised that Marie Jane was looking him over, and stood enjoying it, basking in the obvious pleasure she derived from it.

'Your sister was just saying,' Marie Jane rearranged the truth a little, 'that we might be allowed to look in the marvellous van your da's got.' She rounded her mouth and set her eyes on him. 'Oh, d'ye think we might? Could you fix it?'

Such tactics never failed to shock Tessa, not priggishly – for she had done a lot of rearranging of the truth herself – but with a giggly kind of shock. Poor Martin, he was really in for the cold shoulder! As if to make up for Marie Jane's attitude, Tessa slipped her arm in Finn's. The pressure immediately conferred upon both a closeness, a kind of pride in the safety of their companionship, for even Finn, not used to the vagaries of male and female relationships, could see something had gone wrong between the other two.

'Maybe . . .' drawled Mick. His eyes, like holes in his tight rosy face, surveyed the quartet of faces before him with a mixture of arrogance and suspicion. Goy faces, pale and wearing the all too well-known expression of superiority. They put him in mind of Aunt Sallys at the fairground. If I'd a coconut, he thought, I'd spoil their beauty for 'em! Then, thrusting his hands deeply into his pockets, he said airily, 'To be sure they'll not mind if I show it to you.'

He turned and Marie Jane stepped forward first, with Martin awkwardly behind. He was mystified by the subtleties of feminine behaviour and quite unaware of the nature of his offence. Tessa hung back and, heedless of the countless warnings, smiled at Kate. 'Are you not coming with us?' Her invitation was not altogether altruistic. She felt that Kate's presence would be a safeguard should anything troublesome occur.

The caravan stood aloof from the rigs and shelters. The shafts, from which the pony had been removed, stuck out like rigid limbs, and the driver's box now let down into a step.

'You're sure the chief won't mind?' asked Tessa.

Mick shook his dark, cropped head. 'How can he?' he replied insolently. 'There's Kate on the outside and me on the inside as a check on any light-fingered goy.' Then in a better tone, 'Sure, it's proud of it he is. He'd show it to Lord Fitzcarron given half the chance! C'mon now, one at a time, or you fellas won't be able to turn round in it!'

Feeling better now that an air of levity had been displayed, Tessa admired the gaily painted exterior. There were scrolls in yellow, red and two shades of green. And the shine on it! Or at least at the top; the lower half was mud-stained and scratched.

Mick disappeared into the van, and both Martin and Finn, not wanting to show the tinker how impressed they were, merely put their heads inside, chins level with the top step. Mick resisted the temptation to apply his boot, especially in view of what his mother had said.

The girls, all three, exchanged glances and stood together while Martin lit a pipe and, ignoring the caravan, began to extol the virtues of tobacco to his friend. Mick, angry at the snub, was watchful. Into the silence came Kate's breath, softly wheezing. Finn and Martin maintained their disinterested air as the girls mounted the step.

'One at a time,' said Mick, 'or you'll be squashed.'

'We'll be squashed then,' said Marie Jane pertly. 'Catch me alone with a fella in there – especially a prize fighter!' Kate followed them and sat on the step, head inside.

The interior was cosy with red velvet drapes and white crochet work; horse brasses gleamed and a lamp hung on the roof in a corner.

''Tis marvellous,' breathed Tessa. 'Like one of the wonders of civilisation.' She glanced round. 'Where do they sleep? On the floor?'

'Not Spider Murphy,' boasted Mick, and with a flourish let down a broad shelf, which served as both bunk and table. The girls gasped in surprise at the novelty of it, and were immediately aware of the shortage of space. Mick had engineered himself between the two girls and, still smouldering from the attitude of their escorts, proceeded to make the most of the situation.

He spread himself blatantly, widening his knees to touch the skirts of the young women on either side of him. Kate giggled, looking to the lads outside and then back to the others.

'God love us, Mick, if it won't go back you'll all be wedged in!'

'I can think of worse things!' He gave a tight little laugh and licked his lips like an animal about to enjoy a feast.

Marie Jane, pleasantly conscious of her good looks, settled back to await developments. Always ready to explore the thrill of physical contact, she was determined to play the game. There was a further bonus, too. She was most partial to any display of strength or muscle, two things which Martin Jarvey lacked but a prizefighter would have in abundance.

Feeling safe with Tessa on the other side of Mick, the escorts outside, and Kate on the step getting the best of both worlds, she waited with breathless delight for the first move. It came in the form of a hefty muscled thigh, so close to her own as to seem positively too daring. She was right at the end of the shelf and against the wall, so really, she told herself, there was nothing much to be done. After a few moments, and having got into the mood of the game, she pressed her leg against his gaiters until she could feel the buckles digging into her.

She was afraid that one day things would go too far in these intimate skirmishes. But the eternal quest for a spine-tingling, cheek-warming contact, overrode all her hesitations and made her take the risk. After all, it was only for a lark.

Mick's round cheeks fired scarlet as he lingered in his explanation of the intricacies of joinery. He leaned toward Marie Jane, his sleeve brushing her arm as he reached to indicate a secret cupboard in the panelwork. He was taking a perverse delight in pressing his attentions on these two goys, and wondered how far he dare go with the owner of the pretty ringlets.

Turning to Tessa, he frowned. She had moved. There was only a few inches between them, but there she was, hunched to the back wall of the van, withdrawn and aloof. Annoyance crept over him like a shadow. The game had ended and was about to take a more serious turn. There was something about her attitude that stirred his memory and set up a new area of mistrust. Tessa, mindful of her father's warnings, did not want to antagonise the chief's son, but was not for flirting with him either.

Mick Murphy could accept many thing in life, but he could not tolerate rejection and defeat. His eyes strayed from her hair to her skirt, the black softness fanning out over her hips, the shawl with its provocative little tassles, and beneath it, the swell of her bodice.

He heard the two outside bragging and boasting, making up to Kate. He heard their muted laughter and wondered if they were laughing at him. He took a sharp look at Tessa and the floodgate of memory burst open. It all came back, pouring into his mind, filling it, drowning him in a rising tide of anger and jealousy.

It was obvious that neither she nor the big fella recognised him. But, they wouldn't, would they? For at Pat Feeney's school he had been just 'tinker scum'. Fat, florid Feeney! Sure, what a sight he had been with his purple nose and bloodshot eyes!

That school, he recalled, was the source and cause of every misfortune for him. To begin with, he reflected, he didn't want to go, but the priest had persuaded his da to make him attend any school near the camp, and Feeney's school, he said, was a good one. Didn't they say education was a fine thing, and wasn't his da impressed? God Almighty, how he'd expected him to learn all that, Mick would never know. He thought it was as easy as picking a pocket! He had been forced to attend one hated school after another, but none were so bad as here at Ennan, where he was treated as an outcast. Even then he had hated the smug valley people in their smug white cabins, with their pink and grey pigs – and especially this girl who had known how to read and write.

His own inability to grasp the basic principles irked him, goading him on to call Tessa Riley names behind her back, names he could not now recall. They had said he was 'rude' and threatened to tell Feeney. He had run at the big lad with the black curls and got floored for his pains. Even now Mick could feel again the humiliation of defeat, made worse by his father's anger at his lack of literacy . . . Without a word Mick slammed up the shelf. The van shook with his displeasure.

Marie Jane, startled out of her daydreams, sat upright, pulled her knees together and brushed a ringlet from her scarlet cheeks. She too was not keen on rejection, and to show it said in a cold voice, 'I'd consider it very cramped to have to live in here!'

She purposely trod on his foot as she got up from the shelf, but his boots were proof against anything lighter than the hoof of a donkey. While his arm was extended she gave him a dig in the ribs with a practised elbow but, being a fighter, his toughened rib cage did not feel a thing. With an angry toss of her head she scrambled out with as much dignity as she could muster. The smiling welcome she gave Martin as he stood forward gallantly to assist her down the step bathed him in sunshine for the rest of the afternoon.

'What's up with our Mick?' asked Kate as he stalked off without a word.

'Who knows,' answered Marie Jane witheringly. 'He's a fella, isn't he?' Although it was no answer, it sufficed.

Tessa drew in her breath deeply. She had guessed the cause of Mick's annoyance had been the distance she set between them. It had only been a few inches and she thought he might not have noticed. But he had, and he was mad about it. And so am I! Who does he think he is? God's gift to women! Damn him! she thought. They're all as randy as goats, these tinker lads. She'd never liked them, even at the school. And if he thought she was easy, he could think again!

'Will we see you at the Fair?' Tessa turned her attention to Kate. She looked much better for having been in their company, her face more lively, her eyes filled with interest.

'Come on Tessa,' yelled Marie Jane above the noise of the dogs, children and donkeys. 'I'll take root if I stand here much longer!' And, as Tessa had not moved she added on an even shriller note. 'You'd better be starting up or you'll have your da after you!'

'There's no need to be sharp with her,' protested Finn.

'You don't know her da,' admonished Marie Jane. 'And don't think to be walking her back either. She won't allow it in case he sees you. Even I'm not allowed up there, still less you!'

'What a shame for her, having to go back alone,' declared Finn solemnly. His eyes followed the departing figure and he felt forlorn and deprived; aimless and lost.

By nightfall the tinkers' fire lit up the valley. A bold, blazing symbol of their intrusion, of their presence, their settling in. Tessa's eyes were drawn to the transforming glow, and as the sparks shot up she felt herself tingling with excitement, yet at the same time angry that a knacker, chief's son or not, had taken liberties. She threw off the mood and became philosophical about it. It would all be different tomorrow. The Fair would be started, the tinkers rested from their travels and full of good humour. There would a lot of counting on fingers, and bargains sealed, not with a handshake but with the slapping of palms.

She thought it wiser not to mention Murphy's caravan to her father. Thank heaven he would be bartering or selling, it would keep his mind off her. And she regretted there had been so little time spent with Finn. It had all been taken up with Marie Jane's interest in the van – and Mick! Apart from the sensational beginning she had scarcely spoken to him. Still, looking down onto the fire, she hugged to herself the memory of Finn's conspiratorial wink . . . He must be interested or he wouldn't have chided Marie Jane not to be sharp with her. Yes, things had made progress.

While Tessa was leaning on the window-ledge, going over her thoughts of the day, down in the valley Mick Murphy sat hunched up with his chin resting on drawn-up knees. Only half his attention was on the sweeps, who, being paid so much per pint of soot collected, were noisily calculating their season's expectations. The rest of his attention was taken up with Tessa Riley. Who would have thought that little know-all with the white pinafore and bright, perky face would grow into so attractive a creature? He saw again the soft folds of the black woollen skirt as she had stood on the top step to enter the caravan and, through the weave of it, the shapely outline of her thighs. He had flirted with the pretty one, but he had been saving the best to the last. His throat tightened. He ran his tongue slowly round lips suddenly gone dry, and it seemed to take an age before the vision passed from his memory.

CHAPTER FIVE

The following day Proud Riley fumed with impatience. 'It's only a knacker's fair we're going to, girleen,' he grumbled while waiting for her to get ready, 'not the Long Dance!'

He felt very uneasy when she wore a ribbon in her hair or leather pumps on her feet. When dressed in her finery, he thought, she looked as grand as a lady, and as sound as a well-grown spud. Her mother would be proud of her. Sometimes he felt physically ill because, up to now, he had not found a man for her. Those who had anything about them left the valley to work in the town and never returned, and could you blame them? He wanted her to marry someone with position, to take her away from this bog-infested place. He had surveyed the eligible young men and none were suitable; they could not read or write, and on the whole they were a feckless lot. His hopes were beginning to gather about the Long Dance; many a girl had been courted and whisked away to a better life through meeting a young man up from the town. Only when she was safely married would he be able to rest, for he had sworn on her mother's grave that no misfortune would befall her daughter, and that Tessa would not spend her young life beating her wings against the cage he had built. The older he got the more onerous became the responsibility, and he longed to be relieved of it – to the right man. But, until that man put in an appearance, he would fight tooth and claw to preserve his daughter's honour. At least, he concluded, she'll be taken care of at the Fair, not that he knew the Collins fella that well, but if O'Malley had arranged the escorts it was bound to be safe, for had he not females of his own?

Tessa, hearing the impatience in his voice, struggled into her gown, the only one she possessed. Dressing required precise movements, for the loft lacked height. Riley's cabin was not a long-cabin like the O'Malleys'; it had been built as one square, spacious room, large enough for a hearth, square table, two chairs, two stools, a spinning wheel and the black oak dresser. To give his growing daughter some privacy Riley had built what he called a loft, but was in reality a wide shelf, a kind of balcony over the side of the room facing the door. It stretched the length of the wall, some nine feet, and when she sat up Tessa's head only just cleared the slanting roof at its widest point.

From a sitting position, then, it was not an easy task to get into a gown. Skirts and blouses, being separate garments, posed no problem. But she was happy with her little domain; it was here she kept her treasures, keepsakes of her mother's, like the little mirror and reticule, and a muff which she never wore. At the end of the loft she kept every magazine which O'Malley or the priest passed on. A wicker basket contained ribbons, precious writing paper and her pencils.

The heat from the fire rose to keep her warm and the shadows added seclusion. Here, she moved about on all fours or sat with knees hugged to her chin, planning her strategies and hatching her schemes.

'C'mon,' shouted her father. 'You'll have it dark!'

'Coming, Da. 'Tis the impatient fella you are today.' The swish of her skirts on the top rung of the ladder convinced him of her descent, and only then did he move to open the door. As her feet touched the floor Tessa adjusted her gown. She had made it herself, copying one of her mother's, from a length of peacock-blue twilled fabric bought off Mrs O'Malley. Having sewed every painstaking stitch herself, it fitted her figure superbly. The deep colour added maturity to her seventeen years and gave a subtle shading to eyes that were now a summer blue, now a misty grey.

'Your shawl, girl,' said her father roughly. He never commented on her looks and she did not expect it. 'And the cheeses.'

'Yes, yes, I know, Da, and the bag.' She slung the canvas bag containing rounds of goat's milk cheese over her shoulder and together they set off down the hillside.

Proud Riley had washed, and wore a clean shirt beneath his jerkin. His 'other' cap, a tweed one left on the grass after the Long Dance some five years since, graced his head and crowned the tufty sidewhiskers. Hanging from Timothy Thomas's belt were two kettles, his own to be repaired and O'Malley's to be returned. With his big hobnailed boots, moleskin trousers wrinkling at his ankles and a sack of potatoes on his back, he looked, as he leaned forward beneath the weight, every inch like an overgrown goblin.

It took a little while to come within reach of the valley floor, not that time was important. No one in Ennan boasted a clock, the day being measured by sunrise, high noon and sunset. They rounded the skeletal clump of trees, the scene of Tessa's clandestine transformations, and she passed with a secret little smile. She clutched her skirts up as best she could with her free hand, and swore softly when her pumps sank into soft pockets of peat. Her mind was not on the load she carried or the money it would bring, but upon Finn Collins, and whether their first looks would have the same unnerving effect as before.

The valley floor had never looked so colourful. All the disorder and confusion of yesterday had disappeared. Yesterday . . . her heart lurched with apprehension as she thought of Kate Murphy and her brother. Kate, to be sure, was the sweetest of creatures, but the brother – a lecherous swine he was! As they continued downhill she considered that Marie Jane was right when she'd said that going to the Fair was like going to meet your fate.

Thick tendrils of smoke from the huge fire crawled about the valley as if seeking an escape, but there was no wind and so they hung, suspended, the silent spectators on the foibles and follies of Ennan Fair.

Even Proud Riley cast a curious eye as they almost completed the descent on the community below. A multitude of noises rose on the still air, shouts, curses, cries, braying donkeys, barking dogs, screeching hens, wailing babies, and laughter, yells of it, loud outbursts and then a higher pitch of the giggles. And beneath all these lay the more earnest undertones, the persuading, cajoling, resisting, the wearing down and the final capitulation.

He saw plump Mrs Jams, followed eagerly by her offspring, pushing and shoving to see what the tinkers had to offer. The Duggan girls – well, some were grown women now – there they were, you could still tell 'em by their red hair, all eight of 'em. And Gypo Kelly; you could tell Gypo and his family a mile off, with their swarthy looks. His eyes narrowed to see Spider Murphy with three gold chains across his embroidered waistcoat racing up and down, holding a dappled pony by the bridle to show off its points. He'll be lucky to sell that thought Riley, reflecting on the financial state of his neighbours. God help him, he'll be lucky! He then turned his acrimony onto the tinker children. A scabby lot, ragged and barefooted, sprawling and fighting, getting under people's feet – just let 'em get under mine and won't they feel me boot!

He stopped suddenly. 'Teresa,' he pointed a finger. 'Will you be telling me what the colourful wagon over there is?'

'Spider Murphy's got a caravan, got it from a place called Wales he did, across the water somewhere.'

His eyes narrowed again. 'And you never told me?'

'Sure, you didn't ask, Da. You're never curious about what goes on down here, and with getting the cheeses ready an' all . . .' She breathed a sigh of relief as he resumed his steps again.

'Come an' have your fortune told, dearie?' called a woman in a bright headscarf. She had her foot on a cradle and her hand on a crystal. 'Sure, I've raised fourteen of 'em on this.'

'C'mon, Teresa.' Her father's voice, brisk and matter-of-fact, cut short any temptation. She looked about for Kate Murphy, hoping to see her in the jostle of women who had opened their great canvas bags to reveal a cascade of braids, toys, basketwork, and a jumble of musty clothes begged in the name of charity. All the goods were laid out on the ground and the purveyors sat, stood, or squatted by them. But Kate was not there.

Men, stripped to the waist, heated and hammered out metal repairs. Their skin gleaming with sweat, they applied the bellows for more heat, while a fascinated audience watched them melt down a lead pipe and set it into a mould. They all drew back, suitably impressed, as other moulds were plunged into barrels of water which bubbled, hissed and spat with the venom of a hundred snakes. Others, rough, tough and scrawny, plied their separate trades or crouched on their heels supervising a cock fight.

Tessa stood enthralled at this emergence of life. At any other time the number of people out at once, apart from children, could be numbered on ten fingers. But now they were pushing past, some running, others strolling, the elderly shuffling, and all were talking, laughing and speculating. She saw O'Malley and waved. He wore a grey stetson procured from the old Jew in Rohira and his rolled gold glasses gleamed as he greeted them.

'Ah, Riley old son, 'tis glad I am to see you – what?' He was quite unprepared to have the kettle thrust hurriedly into his hands. 'You'll never change!' he laughed. 'And where is Tessa going to lay out her cheeses?'

'Here,' she replied. 'The sooner I'm sold up, the sooner I can find Marie Jane.'

'You'll have no bother selling up, girleen. The knackers are as keen for their dairy produce as your goat was for a lick of sulphur.' As Tessa eased the bag off her shoulder, he glanced at his friend's expression. 'Now, you're not to be worrying and fretting about her. I've told you, on me solemn oath, and may God strike me dead if I lie, that Collins is a good lad. The four of 'em will stick together. I've told Marie Jane, I have, that if they don't her mother will tan her arse, no matter how big she is!' He touched Riley's arm. 'Wait till ye clap eyes on Murphy's caravan! But, come and get your kettle done first, while they can still see straight!' So, carefully but firmly O'Malley eased his friend away.

Tessa quickly shook out the cloth and spread it on the ground. She had seen people do this for picnics when the Long Dance was on and thought it provided a pretty background. As she laid out the cheeses a shadow crept across the cloth. She looked up. It was Mick Murphy. Her cheeks flamed at the sight of him.

'Will you sell me three of your cheeses?'

Tessa paused on an intake of breath. She had not expected this. 'Yes,' she answered warily. 'Take your pick.'

'I will so, but they all look as good as each other.'

'It's money I take, not kind,' she put in quickly, catching sight of a dead cockerel in his other hand, obviously for barter.

Mick dropped the bird and thrust his hand into his breeches pocket. He had been watching her for some moments, indeed he had seen the conversation with O'Malley and watched the two men walk away. She looked different in her gown, he thought, as if she could be a lady. She'd had that superior look as a child, but why was he finding it so attractive now? Why think about this goy at all? Why not, he chivvied himself. There's not much else in this godforsaken valley. He hadn't wanted to come. But Spider wouldn't listen . . . He returned to his former thoughts. Seeing that Kate was quite taken with Tessa, he had decided to be in his sister's company more often.

'An' how is Kate today?' asked Tessa, not for any desire to stimulate conversation, but to cover the embarrassment she hoped was not evident. She would have felt easier if he had continued to be angry after she had snubbed him yesterday, or if he had never crossed her path again – indeed, why had he taken the trouble to seek her out? To see him standing there, a smirk on his tight, rosy face, and money in his hand, enough to pay for a quarter of her stock, put her at a disadvantage.

'Her breathing's wheezy. Why don't you go and see her after? Take your friend.'

Tessa extended her hand for the money. He did not drop it into her palm but left it on his own, as though offering an enticement to a timid animal. It was the most natural thing in the world to take money in payment for goods, an action performed many times before without even thinking, but now she hesitated. There the shillings lay, waiting on the dirty, calloused skin. Never had two people concentrated such energy on the position of their hands. Tessa wished the sleeves of her peacock-blue gown had been wrist length instead of just below the elbow. She was conscious of her naked forearm as if it had been her legs or shoulders. And he, too, was conscious of the smoothness of the skin, and the pulse beating heavily at her wrist. Tessa knew it, and determined to end the confrontation immediately. Her fingers, strong, clean and supple, closed swiftly on the payment. Her finger ends brushed against his palm. The money was still warm from his breeches pocket. She shuddered and dropped it quickly into her pocket. His quick eyes missed nothing. He saw the shudder of distaste and remembered Pat Feeney's school. The moment of intensity was at an end, and Tessa indicated as much by saying she would call on Kate. Then, as an afterthought, she added, 'But only yesterday you were tellin' Kate that your ma didn't like her mixing with us goys.'

'That was yesterday. Me sister's frail; me ma makes exceptions for her. She would be pleased for you to call, and Kate always seems more set-up after company.'

'What about her sisters and the other young women?'

'They've all got work to do, and the other women have men and families to see to. That's why me ma sent me, partly so you'd feel free with Kate, and for the cheese of course; she needs the dairy produce, her being delicate an' all. Anyways,' he shrugged his compact shoulders, 'suit yourself.'

'It's a good thing you came early,' she called after his departing figure, anxious to make him aware she was under no obligation, 'Or you'd be out o' luck. I'm one of the first to sell out.'

As if in corroboration of her statement, she was immediately surrounded by the slovenly figures of the elderly tinker women, the grandmothers and great aunts. These crow-like women seemed to shrink into their black shawls, as if hiding from a world they had once adorned with bright headscarves and embroidered blouses.

Having sold the last of the muslin-wrapped cheeses, Tessa stopped to talk with first one and then another, before finally seeking her father to leave the money with him. And, because he was late in setting out his potatoes, on account of having his kettle mended, she stayed with him awhile to assuage any anxiety about her rushing off. She also felt the need of her father's reassuring presence to counteract the shadow Mick Murphy had cast.

It was as well she delayed, for Marie Jane had been charged with the responsibility of fixing up the three younger children of the family with whatever second-hand clothes would fit, or could be made to fit.

She had resented the burden from the start, for the tinker women were full of an aggressive persuasiveness which intimidated her. Tim, sensing his sister's resentment, took it personally and rebelled by being difficult. He would not stand still or try on any clothing, and when Marie Jane found a white pinafore for eight-year-old Bridget, he whispered hoarsely, 'Don't touch it! Some scabby knacker's girl died in it!' Bridget, who had been quite taken with it, now backed away in fright.

'Shut your mouth, Tim,' Marie Jane hissed from between her teeth. She cast an alarmed glance at the gaunt tinker woman who stood with folded arms. 'If she hears you, she'll curse us all!' Then to Bridget, 'Take no notice of him. Just look at the lace. Now how could anything as pretty as that have belonged to a tinker? Have you ever seen a tinker in a white pinafore, Bridget, have you, now?' She modified her tone and bent down to her little sister. 'It's come from some grand house, like Lord Fitzcarron's.' Oh, if I can just get her fixed up with something, thought Marie Jane wearily, it'd be worth all the bother and ma would be pleased.

'Don't believe her Bridget. She's making it up. Sure, she only wants to get back and get out with Martin Jarvey.'

Marie Jane turned swiftly to cuff Tim's head, but he ducked and the blow caught Little Annie, the baby of the family. She was a frail, inoffensive four-year-old who suffered from a slight curvature of the spine. She was a docile, fragile and very loving child. To be dealt a blow for having done nothing at all drew floods of tears and great woebegone sobs which seemed to be torn from her soul.

'That's done it!' yelled Marie Jane. 'Come on the lot of yous!' With ringlets tossed, colour high and temper at breaking point, she pushed Tim in front of her with a jerk. 'You just wait till Ma hears about this. God help you, Tim, she'll tan your arse till it's black and blue! Such a dacent pinafore! And its through you that Little Annie got clouted!' She turned. 'Oh, Annie, Annie, love, sure Marie Jane wouldn't hurt her little sister, would she now? It was meant for him, that spalpeen of a brother. There, there, c'mon now, stop your tears.' She gathered the pale little thing to her arms, soothing and kissing the one, swearing at the other, and entirely ignoring Bridget, who gazed at her brother with adoring thankfulness, for hadn't Tim saved her from the pinafore? Everyone knew what queer things might happen . . . Look at Gypo Kelly, Una's da; everyone said he'd been a changeling . . . With every grotesque bit of gossip whirling about her head, Bridget clung to the folds of her big sister's skirts, sensing that although Marie Jane was angry with her, there lay safety.

And Marie Jane, smartingly conscious of failure, heedless of scenes and shouts, marched grimly back to the cabin. Tim, a tough little figure, trotted sturdily behind, confident of his ability to charm away any wrath aroused by his sister's version of events. In his own way he was punishing his mother for having packed him off with Marie Jane instead of his two older brothers, and in pursuance of this policy he warded off the unwelcome truth that Pat and Dion, aged fourteen and twelve, did not want him tagging along and telling tales of their exploits. It was his ma's fault, he reasoned blithely, that they were returning empty-handed.

Tim was correct in his reasoning. Mrs O'Malley knew that even Marie Jane could not talk or flirt with young men while the younger children were about her skirts. She worried about her eldest daughter, despite her husband's dismissive talk of 'daydreams'.

'Sure, an' were you never like that yourself?' he had asked only once.

'Was I ever like that meself!' she had echoed. 'Did I ever have the chance? Was I not wed to yourself in me sixteenth summer, and brought to bed with her in me seventeenth! And have I not been conceiving, carrying and burying ever since!' That had shut him up, she reflected. He never came that one again!

Mrs O'Malley's love for Marie Jane was sharply protective, yet hedged with a kind of jealousy. She was glad her daughter was pretty, but at the same time she couldn't help but envy the girl her freedom, for had not her birth put an end to her own youth? She often resented the bond between father and daughter. Marie Jane could do no wrong. She scarce did a hand's turn about the place without such an argument – in which her da usually came down on his daughter's side – that it was not worth the shillyshallying. Both were full of charm and as crafty as a cartload of monkeys. She often wished her daughter was more like Tessa Riley. Marie Jane had wanted to go out with her da this morning but, knowing he would be with the men to set up the wrestling, Mrs O'Malley had decided to ward off any complications. Martin Jarvey, she reckoned, was a 'nice young fella'; he was 'safe', and that was how Mrs O'Malley wanted to keep it. If there was any folly in Ennan it always came about through the Fair or the Long Dance. More candles were lit in the chapel then by the parents of precocious offspring than at any other time of the year.

By the time Tessa had left her father, Marie Jane, having weathered the storm at home and emerged with a haughty composure and wearing a black-and-white checked skirt, retraced her steps to the centre of the valley. They had arranged to meet by the chapel, but Marie Jane had been urged by Tessa to 'look out for me, I don't want to get there first!'

'Tessa,' she called out above the noise of the Fair. 'Oh, by all the blessed saints, am I glad to see you. It's the awful time I've had, barneying with me ma and yelling at the children. If there's anything I hate in this world of sin and deceit it's being sent out with them. Me ma knows I don't like it, they know I don't like it, and yet she keeps on doing it! One of these days, I'll turn round and tell her straight, I will!'

Having got rid of the last of her bad humour she linked her arm through Tessa's. 'Oh, you look really something in that gown. I knew you'd wear it today.' She cast her eyes down to Tessa's feet. 'I see you've got your pumps on. Sure, the sight o' those great clodhopping shoes beneath your fine wool yesterday was enough to make a pig laugh! Like boats they were! Not that anyone noticed,' she added more kindly.

'Guess who came to buy cheese?'

'I'm not in the mood for guessing, Tessa.'

'Mick Murphy.'

Marie Jane's lips pouted, her eyes widened as Mick's invitation for them to call on his sister was related.

'Shall we go before we meet the lads?'

'Yes,' answered Marie Jane thoughtfully. She had not cared for Martin's attentions to the tinker girl yesterday, but those attentions had opened her eyes to Martin's good points. She liked, for instance, his self-assurance; he had a kind of worldliness, a bit like her da. He was nice-looking, really. Not as tall as Finn Collins, but not many were. She liked the way his brown hair would not part in any direction but flopped becomingly over his forehead. He had luminous eyes and an air of impertinence which extended to his clothes. She also liked his vague but growing conviction that his fortune and future lay with the donkey trade in which his father and uncle dabbled. 'But why you want to go and see her at all, I don't know. Your da wouldn't like it.'

'I feel sorry for her, not being able to brathe easily. No dancing or walking must be terrible.'

'And no rescuing goats stuck in a stinking Bog! Sure, Tessa, she's not missing all that much. If she was as fit as us they'd have her going out in all weathers for rushes, and going round the houses in towns selling bags and pegs, and she'd probably be landed with a baby slung over her back!'

'I don't know about all that, Marie Jane, but no one seems to bother with her, and you must admit she was a lot brighter for our company yesterday.'

Marie Jane conceded that was the case. But when they reached the tent there was no sign of the beautiful tinker girl. Conscious of being watched from a distance they quickly turned their steps towards the chapel.

'Brathing being bad or not,' muttered Marie Jane, 'she's certainly off somewhere. They can put it on, these knackers, you know. The craftiest beggars this side of the Connemara mountains. Me da said he recognised Clancy years ago passing himself off as a blind beggar with one leg. Making a fortune he was, sitting in the road outside St Joseph's!'

Tessa nudged her friend to silence. 'Look, the lads are there, already!' She drew a deep breath and felt the need to smooth her hair, or adjust her sleeves, do something, for she felt it was impossible to look as fresh and composed as Marie Jane. Despite the urge, she resisted the temptation to do anything and began to feel the overwhelming emotion of yesterday, the weakness, and yet the wildness of it. Did her friend feel like this every time she saw Martin?

And suddenly he was there, standing by the chapel gate. If it had been St Peter himself she could not have beheld him with more wonder. Not daring to throw herself into the exquisite excitement of looking on his face straight away, her eyes, directed to the ground, admired his long legs – 'dancing legs' they were, and the corduroys could have been velvet, so taken was she. They weren't tight to the skin like Mick Murphy's breeches, nor encased in leather gaiters like the gamekeeper's. She almost stopped in mid-step, slightly alarmed at having her thoughts occupied by so alarming a figure. But her sight was already on the wide shoulders, the strong chest covered by a striped shirt, its collarless neck open to reveal his sinewy throat. His black curls gleamed from the soapiest wash they'd ever had.

Finn could not, even now, believe he was waiting for Proud Riley's daughter. His mind had not been on the conversation with Martin Jarvey. It was not on the sinister threats of his aunt, nor on O'Malley's trip to the town, nor even on the Fair. His mind, thoughts, beliefs, his very life, it seemed, were suspended, waiting, empty – ready to be occupied and filled by Proud Riley's daughter. He was standing free of his aunt today; free from servitude; free from fear. Today he was his own man and his recent sense of growing self-awareness added a touch of princeliness.

None of this did anything for Martin, who despite his pipe and newly acquired jacket, looked insignificant.

'For the love of God!' exclaimed Marie Jane, slowing her pace. 'Is that Finn Collins? I don't believe it!'

'You didn't think he'd come in his pig-apron, did ye?'

Full of senseless little jealousies, Marie Jane, glanced sideways at her friend and saw her as she had never yet seen her, dissolving in the first breathless moments of overwhelming attraction. Well, she thought, Lord love us, Tessa Riley's taken with a fella, after all!

It was the blush which Finn saw first, the lowering of the dark lashes, the little smile touching the corners of her mouth. His apprehension vanished. He had wondered if he looked dull compared to Martin, but Tessa had not even given him a glance. He had felt lost and deprived after she had gone yesterday, but now he felt complete and fulfilled again.

'I'm glad you could come,' Tessa said by way of starting the conversation. 'You know, with your aunt and all.' She lifted her head, preparing herself for the confusion of meeting the look in his eyes.

'And you with your da, and all!'

They smiled broadly, eagerly, and were at once plunged into awe at having mentioned the domestic tie which bound them both. He wanted to tell her how lovely she looked in so colourful a gown. She looks, he thought, like a lady, not that he'd ever seen one. Then he heard a voice. 'Shall we get round the Fair, then?' The voice was his own. The very asking surprised him, for he was not used to taking the initiative, merely orders from his aunt.

'Oh,' Marie Jane pouted her lips deliberately for him, but he was still looking at Tessa as though she was about to disappear for ever. 'Yes,' she said tartly. 'We'd better go. Best enjoy the freedom, both of yous, while you have it.'

Martin, seeing something had gone slightly askew and recalling the incident of yesterday's displeasure, thrust his hands into his pockets and jingled the coins.

'Shall I buy you something, Marie Jane? I'd like to!'

Her attention was his. Putting her small hand on his sleeve, she guided him to where a fat tinker woman was selling silver rings. The four kept together, as bidden by their elders, and joined their neighbours, looking with curiosity on the tinkers, their wares and ways. They revelled in the exhilarating bonhomie, exchanging views and news, and scandal.

The other young men were crowded around O'Malley to talk about the boxing and wrestling, weighing up form, discussing tactics, speculating on the betting possibilities. And later, with each other, they bragged about last year's exploits with the girls and what they hoped for this year.

The girls also talked about boxing and wrestling, but from a different point of view. Who had the best legs? The widest shoulders, the neatest rump, and wasn't young Duggan just too hairy? They speculated on the tinkers too, their litheness and well-set-up bodies. And those young men who were jaunty enough to ignore Mrs Murphy's commands winked and leered wickedly at the clusters of young girls, who ran to their friends letting out little screams of delighted terror. As for last year's escorts, no one would be seen dead with them! And how about Mona Donal finding herself in the family way after last year's Fair? No, she didn't want to marry Kevin Connor because he was one of the 'shiftless' and his father, when maudlin drunk, moaned about what a useless beggar he was and how if he had a grain o' dacency in him he'd put an end to himself. Mona was terrified of finding her father-in-law 'hanging, drowned, or just dead'. But the priest had insisted on her marrying Kevin to absolve the sins of the flesh.

When the gossip was exhausted and the young people, bored with the company of their own sex, drifted together again, a kind of madness reigned. Games once childish, now provocative, broke out spontaneously. Hide and Seek, Blind Man's Buff; games too silly for young men and women, but being short of social intercourse they were entered into with all the enthusiasm of childhood.

The tinkers, a race apart, occasionally paused to watch. Mrs Murphy patrolled the camp, while Spider boasted of his son's prowess as a wrestler over mugs of poteen. No one gave a thought to the invalid Kate.

Unlike the other girls, Tessa was never caught for a kiss or a forfeit in any of the games. 'Go on, you great ninny,' urged Marie Jane. 'Let Finn catch you. You do want a kiss don't you?'

Tessa put a hand to her throat and to save herself from having to answer burst out laughing as Young Duggan of the hairy arms scooped Una Kelly up and pretended to make off with her. Under cover of this Tessa wondered whether she wanted a kiss. Her father had warned her about the dangers of 'dallying' and 'larking'. He was always giving mysterious advice, such as 'Don't give till you're asked. Ay, and be asked many and many times – and then give only once you've a gold ring.' She had intended to ask Mrs O'Malley to interpret but could never remember it at the right time.

On her visits to the O'Malley cabin none of the young men ever called after her as they did the others and she wished she could be like Marie Jane who tormented them something awful, led them on and then slapped their faces for being bold. Her envious mood made her feel a measure of resentment at having to live so much apart from the others. Tessa sometimes felt herself quite unable to cast aside a reserve of which she was not even aware until occasions such as this. So, Tessa was not caught for a kiss because the other young men were not sure how Proud Riley would react if he was watching.

Finn, sensing her reticence, did not make a serious attempt. It was not that he did not desire a kiss; he did, badly – he had never kissed anyone before – but not with everyone looking. So, instead, he told her about his visit to the town. 'And I saw the church where your ma's buried and you were christened.'

'Did you, now?'

'Ay, and 'twas a blessed place. That and the pubs, Tess. It was like magic. Listen, when I go down again, sure I'll bring you back a bottle of Guinness. Oh, the taste, Tess, it's like drinking black velvet. And one day, you'll go down to the town.'

'God have mercy on us, I never shall!' But Tessa was impressed by the vividness of his talk, and how different he was when away from his aunt.

'Will you all come and watch me the day after tomorrow, cheer me on, when the wrestling's set up?' Finn asked a little later. The wrestling took place when all the wares were sold. It served as a release for emotions hitherto held in check, and was also a final means of extracting money from those with an urge to back their favourite. He had addressed his remark to all, but his eyes were on Tessa.

'Sure we will,' piped up Marie Jane, 'We wouldn't miss it for a gold ring, would we girls? That show of bare flesh, an' you fellas in your drawers!'

Above the giggles and levity Finn had seen his answer in Tessa's expression. He would wrestle now, not merely for the money, but because Tessa Riley had turned her fine eyes on him.

'Tessa? Tessa?' called Peggy Jams. 'Your da's here. He's ready, so he is, and asked me to tell you he's on his way up and ye've to follow.'

'Will I see you tomorrow?' Finn asked quickly.

'Yes. Yes.' She answered, thrilled with the conspiratorial whispers. 'I've got some cloth to sell yet, and me da some spuds. We'll be down.'

'Promise?'

Tessa was wary of tempting Providence. 'I'll try.' She gathered the folds of the peacock-coloured gown and fled.

The following day, Tessa with the lengths of cloth in a canvas sling, and Riley again looking like an overgrown gnome, made their way down to the valley. Tessa's cloth took longer to sell than the cheeses, but the last length went to the fortune-teller who had raised fourteen children on the crystal.

'C'mon, now,' urged Marie Jane, who had waited patiently with her friend. 'Let's go and find the fellas. Oh, Mother of God, will you look what the wind's blown our way?' Before the shadow fell, Tessa knew it was Mick Murphy again. She brightened to see his sister with him.

'We came to look for you yesterday, Kate,' accused Marie Jane. 'But you weren't in the tent, nor anywheres we could see. And that despite him,' she jerked a thumb at Mick, 'telling us your brathing was bad.'

'I went up to Ennabrugh,' came the simple explanation. 'After Tessa told me about it. I felt I had to see it, see all those things.'

'You went where?' Tessa could not believe her ears.

'I told you, to Ennabrugh.'

'You shouldn't be going up there alone. Why didn't you wait for Mick to go with you?'

'Mick's always doing something or other, me ma and da's the same, so I wandered off. I took me time, I had to. When I got there I was fairly pegging out, but oh, the air was so wondrous bracing –'

'Bloody cold, I call it,' cut in Marie Jane.

'I was telling Mick the rushes are good, too.' Kate's eyes flashed and her skirts rustled as she turned with enthusiasm. 'We should gather lots; they'd keep us going for months.'

'Oh, you shouldn't go up there on your own, Kate.' Tessa's voice was heavy with concern. 'What if you were taken badly and couldn't get down, and no one knew where you were? The Bog's firm near the edges, and some of the paths into it look safe, but it isn't always so. It's treacherous, Kate. Many a one's perished in it; people who knew it well have gone down, been drowned, suffocated with slime.'

'Were you not scared?' asked Marie Jane. 'People see things up there, ghosts, and in the summer jack-o'-lanterns leap about like spirits from hell. And the bubbles, they pop and splutter. And in the autumn the mist covers it like a web.' She crossed herself soberly. 'I'd never go there alone. Tessa goes, but she knows it like the back of her hand, don't you, Tessa?'

Tessa nodded. 'Don't be tempted to go for rushes on your own. Ennabrugh has a kind of fascination, you know. If you keep looking at it, it draws your eyes, and before you realise you've lost your way and can't get out. The air might be good for your brathing, but it'll do you no good if you're dead!'

While Mick was contemplating his boots, the changing tones of the female voices began to irritate him; the lightness, the sheer femininity seemed to exclude him.

'Can you stay for a while, Kate?' Tessa asked, directing the question to the tinker girl and by implication excluding her brother.

'Sure, and why not,' came the answer on a bold intake of breath. 'There's precious little else for me to do.'

'You're mixing too much with the goys, Kate,' said Mick, who was not for being excluded. 'C'mon, stay with your own people.'

'But you're mixing with them as well,' protested Kate. 'It was you – '

'Come away, I tell you.' He took her arm and uttered something of a threatening nature in Shelta. Kate had been waiting anxiously for this invitation to join the two girls. She had longed for the moment as the righteous long for a sight of heaven. But with her brother's words, she felt that heaven was closed, locked and barred against her. She could see golden hours of companionship which made her forget she was an invalid; she could feel the stimulation of their company and the stirrings of unknown delights – these bright illusions of her fancy had been within reach. And now it was not to be.

Tessa and Marie Jane exchanged sympathetic glances with the tinker girl as her brother pulled her roughly away.

'I think you've started something there, Tessa Riley.'

'Me?' echoed Tessa. 'Who was it set her eyes on the caravan and couldn't get into it fast enough, and with Mick? If it comes to that, Martin started it off with all that boasting and bragging about putting tents up – '

'Anyways,' interrupted Marie Jane in her best coaxing tones, 'let's not squabble, not in Fairtime. There's plenty of time to squabble after!'

Tucking her arm in Tessa's they approached the chapel. Finn stepped forward to meet them, a relieved smile on his eager face. 'Sure,' he breathed. 'I thought you'd changed your minds.'

Tessa was about to reassure him when Marie Jane rounded her mouth. 'Oh, ye might well say that! We're a bit late because we were wondering if there was anything better to do!'

'I'm glad to God there wasn't,' gasped Finn, immediately prey to the uncertainties of love. He shot a quick look at his friend, hoping to share the sudden anxiety, but Martin was lighting his pipe nonchalantly. He was more used to the teasing ways of the girls and tried to play Marie Jane at her own game by feigning unconcern.

'Did you sell your cloth?' asked Finn to cover his bewilderment.

'It took longer than I thought, and then Mick Murphy and his sister came . . .'

Finn fell into step beside her as she related the incident, occasionally turning to Marie Jane for confirmation of some detail.

'You're not scared of the knackers, are you?' he asked with sudden insight.

'I'm awful suspicious of 'em, Finn, especially that Mick. I'd not trust him as far as I could throw him!' Looking up, she smiled mischievously, and Finn felt as if he did not want to remove his eyes or look elsewhere in case she never ever looked that particular way again.

Marie Jane and Martin exchanged indulgent smiles. Martin coughed. 'Sure, I'm the last fella to spoil a bit of sweethearting, but if you two don't get a move on the Fair will be over and gone!'

Almost at once the four of them were sucked into the last vital fling of Ennan Fair. Bets were taken on runners and Martin, feeling himself to be a man of the world, placed a bet on Pat O'Malley who was fourteen and the fastest runner. How they cheered as his long thin legs covered the hillside, leaving the others far behind. They roared with laughter at those fool enough to ride the greasy pig and the mad donkey. As the last of the wares ran out, cockfights and dogfights came in, and finally for that day, the shooting.

Tessa, not liking guns, yet not wanting to break up their foursome by leaving, watched O'Malley, his wide hat tipped to the back of his head, fixing the range of targets.

'By all that's holy,' muttered Marie Jane. 'Look who's over there?'

Stretching her neck and thinking it to be another young man who had taken her friend's fancy, Tessa saw the gamekeeper. 'God Almighty,' she breathed. 'What's he doing here?'

'Checking me da's targets, I suppose, and warning the knackers against poaching. This is their best time, you know. While we're occupied they'll have a few catching trout and one or two after the game and then they're off; by the time the keepers have caught on it's too late!'

Tessa immediately lowered her head and shrank into the company of the escorts. She fidgeted uncertainly for a few minutes, her fingers plucking at the skirts of her gown. 'I'm not stopping Marie Jane,' she leaned forward to whisper into her friend's ear. 'God knows I live in mortal fear of the guns, but him! Tell me da I've started on me way back.'

Turning quickly, Tessa ran off before Finn realised what had happened.

'Where's she gone?' he demanded. 'Sure, she never said a word about leaving. Eh,' he called, 'Tess! Tess Riley, come back!'

He was about to go after her when Marie Jane laid a firm hand on his bare forearm. 'Don't go after her, you'll only make it worse. If her da sees you chasing her he'll get the wrong idea, and if Proud Riley gets the wrong idea Tessa's done for. Be easy, now.'

'Be easy!'

'Sshh. Don't raise your voice. She'll be down tomorrow for the last day and to watch you wrestle. She did promise, and if anyone keeps her word, it's Tessa Riley.'

'But she left without saying anything.' His voice was gruff with hurt. 'Not even goodbye.'

Marie Jane sought to console. 'Well, if ye must know, it's the guns. She's terrified out of her very life at the sight of a gun, but she didn't want to spoil your enjoyment.'

'As though I care about bloody guns! Ach, the poor girleen, if only she'd said.' He gazed helplessly after her retreating figure. Once again she had fled, leaving him morose. Interest in everything else plummeted, and great waves of frustration at not being able to go after her, not to be able to do anything, flooded his soul. And thus he stood, bereft and forlorn.

CHAPTER SIX

Tessa had passed the clump of trees before the shots filled the air and echoed with a dull ricochet off the valley walls. As if pursued she ran on, scrabbling up the hillside clutching the hem of her gown, more to ease her speed than from fear of spoiling it. She swore as the stones bit into her feet and all the time she hurried, not daring to pause or consider the cause of her flight. Time for that once safe within the soft warmth of her loft. Her father could move more swiftly than herself and she needed to be in the cabin first. Once in the loft he always assumed she was asleep and never called her unless something was wrong, such as when Billy broke from his tethering.

At last, she reached the cabin, pushed open the wooden door, closed it and stood with her back against it, panting. The cold mountain air outside had kept her cool, but once indoors she started to sweat. She hurriedly took the gown off and carefully hung it over a line by the dresser, then, going outside, she doused herself with water from the barrel, plunging both arms into it above the elbows, splashing her heated face with great handfuls. The cold water soaked her cotton shift, until gasping with the chill, she hurried back inside and up the loft ladder. Drying the front of her hair and face on a piece of hessian which did duty as a towel, she leaned with her back to the end wall of the cabin, her chin on her knees.

Only now did she allow herself to reflect on so uncharacteristic an action. What, she wondered, had got into her? Never in her life had she fled with such fear from anything or anyone. Her racing thoughts stopped to admit that one incident when she had left the gamekeeper sprawling and swearing in Ennabrugh, his arms flailing in search of his rapidly sinking shotgun. Following this came the picture of him holding up her wide skirts. At the time so urgent was the rescue of Billy, it seemed the only thing to do; but in the clear light of reason it had been a blatant immodesty of which no one – especially not her da – would approve. Yes, she had fled from that scene as filled with panic as today. The first time it was a natural enough reaction, she conceded to herself. But why the panic now, over something past and gone? She could and had been willing enough to put up with her dislike of guns for the sake of Finn and the others, for after all, it was only target shooting. But it had been the sight of the gamekeeper that had prompted the immediate flight. What had Marie Jane said he was called? Frank? Frank Kildare, that was it. But the thought persisted: why had she taken to her heels?

Sitting here in the loft it was easy to be amazed that she, Proud Riley's daughter, could have been so scared. Into her mind's eye flashed a sight of the dead creature on his saddle. The crooked gun. Cold darting eyes, the eyes of a hunter? She hurriedly crossed herself. All the time, deep down inside her, she had been afraid of him hunting her down, demanding recompense of her da for the loss of his precious gun. Her da could never afford money for a gun, and if her da could not offer recompense, what would the gamekeeper do? Her mind went back a few years, and her heart thumped to recall one of the shiftless who had somehow destroyed a mantrap of Lord Fitzcarron's. The magistrate had ordered him to meet the cost. Of course he couldn't, so the bailiff had taken his pig, sticks of furniture and stock of turf, and that was how the Byrnes became 'shiftless'. Would the bailiff take their goats, the dresser, her da's peat-cutter, the spinning wheel? She broke out into a fresh burst of sweat. Her da, Proud Riley, would never live down such a disgrace. Oh, God help me, she moaned, why didn't I tell him right away? It would have sounded better at the time, besides, if it all came out now he would accuse her of being deceitful . . .

She began to think about Frank Kildare, going over what she knew of him, what Marie Jane had told her. If he was going on thirty he was at least ten years older than she. That was the daunting bit; young fellas she might be able to handle, older ones she didn't understand at all. All the girls reckoned the elder Duggan was old and he wasn't yet thirty. Older people, she mused, didn't care to be taken advantage of by anyone younger – a seventeen-year-old in her case. Him having a position in life, too, didn't help. It would take a lot of living down! A little smile curved her mouth. Had anyone seen him returning covered in slime? She imagined that prowling walk, as though he were stalking and tracking. What excuse would he make to the others? That he'd been thrown off his horse, lost his way? And surely they would laugh and hold their noses. All of that, she thought, does not bode well for me.

Hearing her father's familiar grunts of relief as he finished the climb, she lay down on her bed. Her father entered, saw her gown over the line, the pumps drying by the hearth, and closed the door. He stopped by the ladder.

'May God and the Holy Mother herself bless you, Teresa.'

She did not answer. He never expected her to. He had repeated these words every night since she could remember. They served as a blessing, a benediction, and summed up all the love he felt for her. She listened to the familiar sounds below. The soft thud of him backing the fire up with turf, the opening of the cupboard for his final cup of poteen, the clinking of the cup, the closing of the door. Darkness was not complete when he took to his bed, sinking noisily onto it with a deep sigh of contentment. There was silence. Tessa lay for some time staring up into the rafters, waiting for the heavy breathing of her da to turn into deep growling snores. She envied him. Usually, sleep did not escape her, but it did this night, as surely as she had escaped from the Fair.

Of course, she need not go down tomorrow; that was the simple answer. Her da would want to know why, but she could think up something by way of a satisfying explanation. But no! It was the wrestling tomorrow! Her fearful speculations had sent it clean out of her mind. Oh, dear God, what should she do? Dare she run the risk of meeting the keeper? What if he's still there? What if, having liked the shooting, he stayed to the wrestling? She imagined him standing there, the buckles of his gaiters all up his legs and the terrible gun crooked easily over his arm. What if he recognised her, or worse, spoke to her? Sure to God, she'd die on the spot!

Another figure superimposed itself on that of the keeper, tall and straight, with black curls, an eager smile and a lovely pair of dancing legs. Finn and Ennan Fair would ever be linked in her mind. The past days were unforgettable. She relived the warmth and strength of him, his big rough hands touching hers as they danced, and how she had to look up to him and how his eyes were always on her first – such blue eyes, a deep blue, haunted by shades of uncertainty – and the vulnerable honesty of his open face. And his manner had so much to commend him. He had told her of the wonders of Rohira, but had not boasted like Martin Jarvey. He seemed to want to know her opinions on everything, on aspects of the Fair, life in Ennan. He was impressed by her ability to read and write and Tessa, having lived the quiet life with her father, felt flattered that anyone should be interested in her opinions. They had talked vaguely about the future, a subject about which she thought little; it had never occurred to her that she could influence her own future.

But above all, she had enjoyed the freedom to mix with the others, even the shiftless; to go about with a young man and her da not mind. And it was all because of the Fair. Her spirits sank a little. What would happen after the tinkers had packed up and gone? There'd be no excuse for seeing Finn. Tomorrow was the last, the very last day. The wrestling day. I must go, she thought urgently. It might be the last time I'll see him for weeks and weeks. The prospect of those empty weeks stretching endlessly ahead, grey and heavy as the clouds over Ennabrugh, charged her with courage to run the risk of meeting the gamekeeper. Her mood turned militant. Why should she be afraid of him? Out there on the shores of the Bog she had been his equal, standing her ground, stopping him from shooting Billy. If she'd faced Frank Kildare once, she could do it again.

Determined to make the most of the last day's freedom, Tessa went down into the valley with her father. She had put on her peacock-blue gown, tied her hair with a blue ribbon and, swinging her shawl in one hand, sauntered towards the O'Malleys' cabin, where Aloysius stood outside waiting for his old friend, and Marie Jane, fretting with impatience, sat inside. At a call from her father, she ran out and took Tessa's hand.

'Fancy running off like that yesterday,' she accused. 'Took all me powers to stop Collins going after you, still less explain.'

'Never mind about that now, Marie Jane. Do you think the gamekeeper will be here, at the wrestling? Sure to God, I could scarce sleep for thinking of it all!'

'And did not the angels answer your very prayers?'

'What do you mean? Is he not coming down?'

The dark ringlets shook vigorously from side to side.

'It's a relief, honest, I can't tell you!'

'I don't see why you don't call him by his name. He's got one, you know. Just because he offered to shoot your Billy, you can't hold it against him forever!'

Tessa stared at the blushing face. 'And what's all this? Why are you defending him?' She recalled how her friend had thought the gamekeeper handsome and had admired his gaitered legs: 'I thought you were struck with Martin and now you're taking the cudgel up for a fella you hardly know, and who's pushing thirty if he's a day!'

'I'm still gone on Martin, but Frank's got his good points when you give him a chance to talk.'

'Frank?' echoed Tessa, alarmed at the familiarity. 'You've talked with him? God preserve me, I'd rather talk with the divil!' Tessa stopped walking and faced her friend. 'When did all this happen?'

The rosy red lips parted in a teasing smile. 'We talked for some time, and all. He looked at his watch from his pocket and said it was best part of an hour.'

'When? When? Oh, God save us, Marie Jane; you didn't mention me, did you?'

'Now,' her eyes twinkled boldly, 'why should I be spoiling my own chances by bringing yourself into it?'

'You mean – '

'No, I don't mean. Sure I was only teasing. Oh, you should have seen the look on your face! He came talking to me da in the cabin, something about Lord Fitzcarron or his manager coming to look over the valley some time. But I managed to get round him.'

'Get round him? You mean you pouted your lips and made yourself agreeable. Oh, Marie Jane, I'd never have thought it of you – '

'Oh, I don't know about you, Tessa Riley. Sometimes I despair of you. You're a real looker, you've a way with you, and you'll not use any of it to better yourself. I told you, Tessa, I'm after going into service in a proper place, and if you've any sense you'll fall in with me, or you'll still be milking your da's goats when you're forty!'

'You asked about service?' The shocks seemed never-ending.

'I did so. Oh, come on. We want to watch the wrestling from the front.' She put her arm through Tessa's. 'Don't let's squabble,' she said as they set off walking again.

After a brief silence, Tessa's curiosity got the better of her. 'What did he say, about going into service?'

'Said he'd see what he could do; and he was nice about it. A bit of a wandering eye, but with me da there he couldn't let it wander as far as he did with you!'

Tessa ignored the last remark and Marie Jane, having enjoyed delivering her piece of astounding news, remained deliberately silent, enjoying the effect it was having on her friend.

Tessa's thoughts whirled. The implication of Marie Jane going into service, and 'getting round' the gamekeeper for such an end, astounded her. Far from being relieved that her name had not been mentioned, Tessa was filled with anxiety. Had he not asked because he already knew about her from someone else? Mr O'Malley perhaps? Anyone at the shooting could have told him that Proud Riley kept goats, indeed was the only one who did.

They were approaching the 'ring', a section roped off to keep supporters at bay. After a final look to be sure the keeper was not about, they pushed their way through.

The young women at the front of the ring had watched the earlier bouts, following all the throws and holds. They had cheered and jeered, clapped their hands in delight, and bitten their nails in suspense. Now they waited for the final fight.

'Can we get to the front, Mrs Jams?

'Ye can so; squeeze in there. It's only the early bouts you've missed. You're supporting young Collins, are you?'

Tessa responded with her spontaneous smile. 'Now, who else, Mrs Jams! And I hope you've followed your faith with a coin or two.'

While the young women settled themselves at the front, Finn, who was getting ready behind the wagons where the bouts were organised, was suffering from a slight shock. The opponent the tinkers had put forward was none other than the chief's son. On hearing this Finn instantly recalled all Spider's boasting of his son's prowess. Never in his wildest dreams did he expect to be pitted against Mick.

'I've not had much experience, you know, Mr O'Malley,' he said, slowly unfastening his shirt.

'You've got muscle, lad, and you're a big fella. Would I have asked you if I'd no faith in your capabilities? Besides, Mick insisted on wrestling with you, or no one.'

'Don't tell me any more,' grinned Finn. 'It gets worse! Jarvey and me took him down a peg or two over his da's van; made him lose face with the girls. I expect he wants to crucify me.'

113

'If there's any crucifying to be done, just be sure you're the one that does it. Nail him, good and proper, Finn boy; I've got a lot o' money on you, and so have the others. We want to fleece this knacker scum; take 'em for every penny. Now, you'll not let us down, will you?'

If the name of his opponent had come as a slight shock to Finn, the announcement made by O'Malley in his blandest tones sent a shiver of cold apprehension down Tessa's spine. She and Marie Jane looked at each other, one with pursed lips, the other with raised eyebrows.

Tessa was suddenly afraid for Finn, and this she had not been prepared for. At previous Fairs she had watched the wrestling with enjoyment, and during the final bout, when everyone was thoroughly into the mood of it all, she had yelled with excitement, cheered until she was hoarse, fully entering into the spirit of the contest. But now, before the bout had started, it was clear that for her it was not going to be a source of amusement.

O'Malley charged up and down, shouting the odds and taking last minute bets. Then the moment arrived that they had all been waiting for. The fight was about to begin. Finn was the first to appear, leaping easily over the ropes to great cheers from his neighbours.

'Here comes the talent!' shouted Young Duggan.

'He's not got any!' came the reply from a tinker. They were all assembled on the far side of the ropes.

'He'd better have, by God,' yelled Muldoon. 'Half Ennan's got its shirt on him.'

'Mick's done the boxing booths and he's toured the fairs; he'll knock hell out of any goy.'

The tinkers cheered for Mick as he dodged smartly beneath the rope. The two faced each other, and Mick began to prance about like a circus horse. Peggy Jams drew the attention of the young women at the front to his thighs and buttocks, tightly moulded in black drawers.

'Just cast your eyes on Collins,' breathed Moira Muldoon, her pale and freckled face flushed, her eyes glazed with juvenile lust. 'Did you ever see such a lovely pair of haunches?'

'Indeed, I have not,' replied Tessa, with more feeling than she had intended to show.

114

She had seen wrestlers before, and although knowing herself to be not indifferent to male beauty, the sight of their half-naked bodies had never affected her like this. The sheer physical grace of him set her heart racing and her mind alive with a million fantasies. He was not a hairy man, and she blushed at the relief she felt in knowing this. His chest looked broader without the covering of a shirt, his muscles were firm and stomach flat. He moved about a little, muscles rippling as he flexed his arms, waiting for the signal. His whole body seemed sharp with youth and brilliant with . . . was it hope? she wondered. His new experiences, or something else?

She wanted him to see her, to know she was there and had been able to fulfil the promise she had not been able to make.

He caught her glance with an intense look. He did not smile or relax his face, just captured her gaze and held it. When he let go it seemed like a caress, as though he had been holding her hand, and it left her happily bewildered. The exchange was just their own; if he had smiled others would have noticed it, others would have partaken of it and she would have felt cheated.

'They do say that crazy aunt of his raised him on spuds and brawn.'

'He's got brawn enough for me,' said one of the shiftless.

'Where's he been all the time?' demanded another.

'Did ye ever see such a lovely fella?'

'And the nicest dancing legs this side of Connemara!'

Silence wrapped itself about the spectators as the two barefooted figures faced each other. The bout had began. Although smaller in height than Finn, Mick Murphy seemed possessed of a pugilistic prowess which, even as he stood there, bordered on evil. Tessa urged Finn on to win, and yet was afraid to see him hurt. Confused, she didn't know what to make of her feelings and regretted the outlay of fourpence to see him bruised and battered.

'Bloody goy!' snarled Mick Murphy, as they closed for the first clinch. 'I'm not afraid of no long-legged mountainy bastard. Come on!'

Spider Murphy, on the far side of the ropes, gold chains about his neck, boasted that the fella wasn't born who could floor his son. He was proud of Mick's reputation as both a wrestler and a boxer. He had been disappointed at the lad's inability, or disinclination more like, to read a little and learn to sign his name. Now that would have been prowess. All his life he, Spider Murphy, had had to put a cross where his name should be. He had wanted something different for his heir.

Mrs Murphy's narrow face looked more sinister than ever. Her four younger daughters were arrayed in front of her. Where, Tessa wondered, was Kate? Surely she would want to see her brother fight? She looked about the assembled people and Kate was neither lined up with her own people nor with the goys. Had she stayed away because she was angry with him for dragging her away from their company? Deciding to pay her a visit later, in case she was ill again, Tessa set herself to watch the contest.

Without any limbering up, horseplay or testing of strength, the two young men closed up against each other, breast to breast, their bodies as one, clinging like limpets in grim and silent combat, each striving to unbalance the other.

A great cheer went up from the crofters as Finn, with a quick thrust of his hip, propelled the tinker backward.

'Good for ye, lad!'

'Throw him over here!'

'Will ye wipe the floor wid him!'

Mick swore, and in the manner of fairground sparring leaned forward, extended both his arms sideways and charged. With an unerring accuracy, born of experience, he floored his opponent. The tinkers cheered. The two now rolled over and over on the ground, one snapping and yelling, the other silent and serious. The crowd loved wrestling theatricals and each side shouted encouragement. Finn had now begun to realise very quickly that Mick was not offering sport, nor was he wrestling just for show.

Suddenly the rolling had stopped. Murphy was on top of him, squeezing out his breath, rendering him inactive by gouging his fingers into a shoulder nerve. The cheers and shouting had dwindled into silence, an ominous silence.

What was happening? Tessa frowned anxiously. Her searching eyes widened in horror, for just beside Finn's head a small piece of rock jutted from the bare earth. With a savage movement the tinker released his hold on Finn's shoulders and seized him by the throat.

With a swift glance Mick lined up the back of his opponent's head with the jutting rock. An audible gasp at such deadly ferocity went up from both sides. Finn's head was jerked up. Mick set his aim. Alerted by the horrified gasp, Finn jolted his head to one side. He felt a searing pain as the rock cut into the side of his face. A surge of anger pumped painfully through his veins, enabling him to throw off the tinker. He leapt to his feet. Mick now danced about in thwarted rage, his little round eyes filled with a rare venom. He bent his knees, spread his arms sideways again, leaned forward and advanced with menace. But if Mick was furious, so was Finn.

'So, ye'd stove a fella's head in would ye! That's not wrestling,' he panted. 'And no one, least of all tinker scum, is going to get away with that!'

A murmur of agreement from O'Malley's crowd backed him up. 'It's right y'are, lad. Give him hell!'

'Dirty! Dirty!'

'Wipe the floor with him!'

'Twist his arm! Twist it off and throw it to us!'

Once again they closed in. Wrestling and striving, they pulled and pushed, pummelled and punched. The supporters became deadly silent again. All realised this was no ordinary bout, but there was nothing they could do about it. Whatever it was, it had to run its course.

Tessa watched as if mesmerised. She didn't want to, yet could not help herself. Thick fingers were now about Finn's neck in a steel grasp. He did not know how they had got there, how they had slipped his guard, but of course Mick had gone the rounds of the boxing booths in fairs for years. Finn began to feel helpless. He heaved and twisted, tried to elbow the tinker's arms away, but still Mick held on with the tenacity of a terrier. His fingers would not be dislodged from Finn's throat, nor his feet from the ground, sway as they might.

Morale-sapping thoughts began to seep into Finn's mind, curling round his courage like the fingers at his throat. What if he were to lose? He heard the thin rasp of his aunt's voice. 'Go and get your head split open, and your eyes blacked . . . you'll be the laughing stock o' the glen . . . what do you know about fighting . . . about anything . . .' Had she put the mockers on him?

He heard O'Malley's persuasive voice, his silvery tones. 'If there's any crucifying to be done, just be sure you're the one that does it . . . I've got a lot of money on you . . .' O'Malley would lose a small

117

fortune if he went down. Marie Jane and the other girls would never let him forget defeat. And what about Tess? So brave and fearless a girleen wouldn't want to know a loser. Life would not be worth living.

He became breathless with anxiety. He was in a stranglehold and he knew it. He could not move, and miracles did not happen anymore. His eyes bulged from their sockets. The hills, the ridge, the sides of the valley, rocked and dipped. His knees began to sag and the ground came up to meet him like the deck of a heaving ship. The tinker's battered face came curiously close to him, jeering grotesquely.

'Oh, God Almighty, help me.' Finn heard his strangled grasp.

Tessa saw him, glistening with sweat, sinking down, eyes half-closed.

'Stop the fight!' She heard her own voice echo in the still air. At a sharp word from Marie Jane, she suddenly clasped her hand to her mouth. But it would not still the cry from her heart. 'Stop the fight!' she burst out. 'For God's sake, stop it. He'll kill him!'

Her voice reached Finn, cutting through the mass of cloud which was threatening him. Her voice, her concern, touched off a reserve of strength he never knew he had. He had thought he was finished. Thought the mockers had got him, Murphy had got him. He had all but given up and was prepared to collapse.

'Finn! Finn! C'mon! C'mon!' He heard their voices . . . Tess, Marie Jane, Jarvey, Kevin Connor . . . Others joined, all the neighbours; and the valley itself stopped its rocking and dipping to echo encouragement.

Mick Murphy laughed in derision. He momentarily turned to his father, seeking approval, recognition. He turned to the goys, to Tessa and Marie Jane, his little eyes gleaming with malicious triumph. That momentary lapse, that gleam, that glimpse of victory, proved Finn's salvation. He only needed a slight relaxation of his opponent's guard, a minute opening in the chink of his armour. Having found it, Finn's body forced itself up from sagging knees with superhuman power, and with a sudden upward thrust he wrenched the tinker's hands free of his throat. Filling his lungs with great gulps of air, the clouds dispersed from his head. He could see again. The world was clear. Finn seized his suddenly bewildered opponent, grabbed him in a body-hold, and with a mighty straining of muscle raised him slowly until he was above his head. It was a marvellous sight. Everyone held their breath in admiration. He stood tall, every muscle rippling and straining, from his shoulders to the curve of his thigh and the calf of his legs. He stood like Atlas holding the world above his head; indeed, at that moment, Mick Murphy was the world.

On a great intake of breath Finn hurled the tinker. The compact body sailed through the air. Every eye widened in astonishment. Such strength was rare, such a turning of tables totally unexpected. With a tremendous thud Mick Murphy touched ground by a wagon. He slumped down against the wheel, dazed, head to one side, looking for all the world like a puppet thrown onto a rubbish tip. A ripple of relief rather than of cheering escaped the lips of the onlookers who, like Finn, had been stunned by the ferocity of the contest.

Everyone seemed to come alive at once. The tinkers surged about their chief's son, gathering around him in hushed discussion, some sympathetic, others angry at having lost their money to the goys. O'Malley was surrounded by his neighbours anxious to collect their winnings. Others crowded to discuss the bout, to speculate, to congratulate. Finn stood free and jubilant, his grazed and bruised face abeam with the first intoxicating taste of triumph.

As a sign of respect Martin Jarvey took off his new jacket and draped it over the champion's shoulders, leading him behind the wagons to get into his patched corduroys and collarless shirt. But not before Finn had thrown a wild, grateful look at Tessa.

'I thought he'd have done for me, Tess. I was all but gone when I heard your voice . . . I don't know what you said, but it got me going – '

'Time enough for talking when your face is fixed and you've got some of that mud off yourself. C'mon,' urged Martin, anxious to fulfil his self-appointed role of looking after the champion.

A few moments later, dressed and with some salve rubbed on his injured cheekbone, he emerged to fresh peals of praise. The young people swarmed around him. The girls saw him with fresh eyes and were jostling to touch him, on the shoulders, on his back, to grab his arms; and Mona Donal, not wanting to be left out, clutched the baby to her body with one hand, and ruffled Finn's curls with the other.

Only Tessa did not touch him. She stood apart from the general euphoria, pleased to be witness to his popularity. The young men, eager to say their piece, gathered round offering playful punches and friendly digs.

'It's a dark horse you are, Finn; never thought you'd got it in you!'

'You should have seen Murphy going through the air – what a blessed sight!'

'And the way he tried to stove your head in, the dirty swine!'

'Did he not do well, Mr O'Malley?' shouted Young Duggan at the approach of the older man.

'Ay, he did so.' And with a wink especially for Finn, 'And what will the Aunt say now, eh?' He thrust a canvas bag at Finn's chest. 'Here's your share of the winnings. It all adds up to three pounds; I've checked it well.' He smiled at the flushed face, touched at the air of innocent pride. 'It's money of your own, Finn boy. Money to jingle in your pocket; you've earned it.'

Finn felt the weight of the money bag and imagined himself turning the money over in his pocket like Martin Jarvey did – but, he had another thought. 'Will you hang on to it, Mr O'Malley, until we next go down into the town, and for the Long Dance, too? For if me aunt gets her grasping hands on it, I'll never see the colour of me money again.'

'I will so, Finn boy. C'mon, now,' he urged everyone. 'Let's drink to your health, for it's the last day of the Fair, and a long time to the next!'

CHAPTER SEVEN

The Duggan brothers, inspired by the victory, struck up their fiddles for Kelly's Reel. The young people, anxious to make the most of this last opportunity, grabbed partners for the dance and the soft thudding of feet on the dank turf, like sheep stamping, began to grow in volume until even the shyest were drawn into the revelry.

The old men stood about in groups, smoking, drinking, occasionally spitting and discussing the deterioration of life. Tinkers were not what they were; Lord Fitzcarron's estate was going to the dogs . . . Why, at one time ye could live well from it: pheasant, partridge, salmon, the odd trout or two; but now it was bristling with bloody keepers and mantraps.

The women sat about on stools, legs apart beneath their skirts, elbows resting on thighs as they leaned forward in earnest gossip, or arms folded across skinny bosoms as they leaned back to discuss more general issues. The shiftless mingled unobtrusively with the industrious, for on so convivial an occasion discrimination was out of place.

Proud Riley stood with O'Malley, one foot placed before the other, his thumb hitched into Timothy Thomas's belt, his eyes on his daughter who, along with the others, was dancing with intense concentration. Each touch of the hand as they partnered, reeled, formed a chain or a circle, was precious.

Finn, in the elation of victory, forgot his bruised body. His grasp of Tessa's hand grew bolder as the desperate moments passed. And as she thought back on the games, she regretted not being caught or having to give a kiss as a forfeit. With each whirl he held her closer than he had ever dared, and was already entertaining thoughts of the Long Dance. How he could deceive his aunt, how she could persuade her father . . . How well they were suited as partners, and that's what mattered in the Long Dance. The line of her body seemed to flow with his, her steps complemented his; there was no jerkiness, no uncertainty, no hesitation.

Suddenly, the scraping of fiddles stopped. Feet halted in mid-step.

Heads jerked up. Spider Murphy was standing like a ringmaster, holding up his hands.

'Will you listen?' he yelled, as the garrulous continued to talk and the young to shout for the Duggans to strike up again.

Mrs Murphy, arms stiffly at the sides of her thin body, approached and stood beside her husband.

'They're out for trouble!'

'Rotten losers! It was a fair fight, Murphy!'

'Is it a punch-up you're after?'

Spider Murphy twitched and his earring jangled. Mick swaggered forward; despite the pain, he put on a jaunty show. He wanted to assert himself, to make up for his defeat by being his father's right-hand man. He glanced out of bleared and bloodshot eyes at the goys assembled. Goy faces, smug, pale, superior. It was obvious Collins had been dancing . . . Mick groaned inwardly, and every bone in his body echoed with it. The memory of being thrown like a bale of hay, of landing on the stony ground, and his head striking the big wooden wheel of the cart, sent him wild with fury. He was out to make these goys smart.

'Will ye listen!' He had none of the commanding presence of either of his parents. He lacked their height and made up for it with belligerence. 'I know what you're up to!' Then to his father, 'Leave this to me, Da. For God's sake, leave it to me!' He turned on the others. 'Spider Murphy's daughter's missing. But I don't have to tell you that. Because one of you's got her. Kidnapped her. Whatever you want to call it. You could all be sheltering her!'

A great derisory yell went up.

'She's gone off with a sweep!'

'Who'd have her, anyway!'

'I told you, they're after a punch-up.'

'And we'll have one if that's what it comes to!' yelled Mick, his round cheeks puce with anger. 'We're not leaving this godforsaken glen without her, even if I've got to tear the thatch off your stuffy little cabins with me bare hands! God help me, I'll do it! There'll not be a stone unturned till we find our Kate –' He caught a look of panic cross Tessa's face. 'They've got her!' he pointed, shouting vehemently. 'They've got her, Dad, I'll swear. Her and the others were making up to Kate, getting friendly, and she was taken with 'em. It was like they'd put a spell on her. All she could talk about was them, the goys. Did I not warn her, told her what our mother said? But she wouldn't listen, would she?'

Proud Riley, who only once before had felt anger coursing through his veins like Feeney's poteen, was quick off the mark. No one, least of all tinker scum, was going to point a finger at his daughter. A vision of Clancy passed before his eyes and he would have sprung at young Murphy's throat if an insult had not suddenly occurred to him. Not a one for words, he spoke this one with a satisfying relish and all the contempt he could muster.

'Stand back, will ye. Sure, I'll talk to the organ-grinder, not the monkey!'

As if stung, Mick catapulted forward, only to suffer the indignity of his father's hand on his shoulder. Spider Murphy's fingers, like all his limbs, were long and thin, but the grip was of steel and Mick's shoulders were very tender. With a low moan of pain he turned, and, swearing savagely, ran into the ranks grouped behind the chief.

A murmur of approval and surprise went up for Proud Riley. 'We've not got your girl,' he said with simple authority. 'If anything, it's the other way round. It's the tinkers that are well known for spiriting folk away.'

'I think I know where she is, though.' Every eye turned on Tessa. Marie Jane, knowing the direction her friend's thoughts were taking, left Martin and stood beside her. Lifting her head, her face flushed with dancing, Tessa related to the Murphys how Kate had seemed fascinated by the Great Bog of Ennabrugh, how she had been up once and found the air good and the rushes of the finest quality. She also related the warning she had given, with Marie Jane nodding her black ringlets in confirmation. 'Sure, may God strike me dead this very minute,' said Tessa, 'if it isn't the truth.'

A sense of awe swept tinkers and crofters alike. All eyes looked skyward, taking note of the clouds, of the light, judging how much would be left, now that it was spring and the evenings were longer. The shadow of the Great Bog was already creeping over them, evoking past memories of neighbours lost. No one was ever found, and every search ended with the solemn tolling of the chapel bell.

O'Malley stepped forward and took Proud Riley's place before the chief. They stood facing each other as Finn and Mick had done only a couple of hours before. All of Ennan knew that the immediate thought in the chief's mind was to get up a search party to look for

123

his daughter, but that without local knowledge it would be impossible. It had been on O'Malley's lips to offer this knowledge as soon as he realised Kate was lost, but he had bitten back the words. Why make it easy for the knacker? It was his daughter, let him ask the goys, even if his son's defeat was still rankling.

Yet the chief still did not speak. His face twitched and his black eyes held the silver-grey of O'Malley's steadily. And meanwhile, thought O'Malley, your daughter could be sinking slowly in Ennabrugh, but he kept his lips closed. Tinkers and crofters watched. Who would give way first? That's what they all wanted to see – a knacker eat humble pie! They might have stood there until sunset if Mrs Murphy had not pushed past her husband.

'Just look at the two of yous! Standing there like a pair o' fighting cocks weighing each other up. Considering your pride and place, while Murphy's daughter's in danger of her death!' She had no difficulty in jettisoning her pride. Anxiety softened the sinister lines of her narrow face, and the bright scarf which tied up her hair seemed to mock her misery. 'We're travellers; we know nothing of your Great Bog. To be sure, we've seen it from the ridge, and a terrible place it is. To think of a slip of a girl like our Kate being caught in its toils with night coming on. But I've a blaggard of a son, who's venting his own spleen, and you stand there, Murphy, on your dignity, while your own flesh and blood's in danger of her mortal life. And her with her brathing bad and only a bit of a shawl!'

Then Mrs Murphy turned and appealed to the gathered community, to the old women in black shawls, to the old men with their pipes and caps, to the younger people standing about in groups. 'For the love of God himself, will you help us? Only God's own chosen can walk that terrible place. I'm asking you, not as Spider Murphy's wife, not as a tinker, but as a mother. Have you not daughters yourselves? Would you stand by and let mine perish? Would you have such a sin on your immortal souls? I ask you in the name of the Holy Mother herself – ' Her voice broke into a sob. Spider looked awkward, wanting to comfort his wife, but not in front of the goys. He remained dignified and aloof.

Always touched by sorrow, O'Malley's heart went out to her. Had it been anyone else he would have put an arm round her shoulder and held her until the tears stopped, but with Murphy he would no doubt get his throat cut!

124

'Sure, I'll go, Mrs Murphy!' shouted Tessa, with a sudden recollection of Kate's shining black hair, of the newly acquired light in her dark eyes. She remembered with a pang Kate's face glowing with anticipation at the thought of spending the afternoon wandering about the Fair with herself and Marie Jane, and how the anticipation had dwindled as Mick hustled her off, swearing at her in Shelta. 'I know Ennabrugh like the back of me hand, and me da, he knows it too, don't you, Da?'

O'Malley suddenly came to life and his organising ability took over. His neighbours, and even some of the tinkers, recognised the subtle tone of authority as he calmed the flurries of alarm and issued instructions for his search. There were not above half a dozen in the glen who knew the Bog in its entirety and were capable of leading a party. Apart from Tessa and her father, there was Old Duggan, Martin Jarvey's uncle, Gypo Kelly, and Kevin Connor's father, and their knowledge gave the crofters a sense of community pride.

The tinkers were given the task of searching the edges of the Bog, under supervision, and with all grace they accepted their subservient role. In the subsequent commotion of forming groups, the shiftless sidled off behind the tinker wagons and rigs, making for the safety of their own.

By fanning out over the area, O'Malley explained, there would be a better chance of finding Kate, if she was out there. Of course, everyone knew the Bog had strange powers and a fascination for some folk – many had felt it 'draw their eyes' – and maybe it had affected Kate that way.

'By all the angels in God's heaven,' averred O'Malley, 'if she's alive at all, we'll find her.' And under his breath he added, 'But pray to God we're not too late.'

O'Malley was not one of those who knew the Bog, nor did he go out searching. As co-ordinator he felt his place to be in the valley, and as such, he sent the rest of the tinkers off searching the nooks and corners, the walls and rocks, in case she had been overcome with faintness and was resting somewhere.

Purpose and dedication now filled the air as the parties moved off. Marie Jane, terrified of the Great Bog, and more than a little annoyed with Kate for putting an end to the last of the dances, stayed behind with the other young women. She wished she was braver, for

Tessa's name was on everyone's lips; they were all praising her presence, her ability.

'Wish I had a shilling for every time I've seen her striding out, crook in hand and shawl across her shoulders . . .'

'Ay, it's a fine young woman she's made. Who'd have thought it?'

'Do ye remember her ma?'

So the talk ran on among those that were left.

'And Riley and Clancy, all those years ago?'

'He wasn't Proud Riley then; he lived in the hut he was born in and scarce had a shirt to his back . . .'

The rambling conversations trailed to a halt. All eyes turned on the forgotten Mick Murphy.

'If you think you're keeping me from going up there, you're mistaken! I've no fear in me soul of anything, still less a Bog! C'mon, Da!' he shouted to the chief. His father did not move, and after a moment Mick burst out in exasperated fury. 'Da, ye're not going to take orders from a goy, are you?'

'These people know the lie of the land. We should trust that they know best. Your mother doesn't want to lose her only son as well . . .'

The tenderness which choked Spider's voice was lost on Mick. His young hot head and hasty heart had suffered enough defeat and he could not take any more. To one used to strutting and swaggering, the last few days had been bitter indeed. Ever since he had set foot in Ennan his emotions had suffered terrible things and he felt desperate. As yet he could not see what could be done, or how his cause could be furthered; but one thing was certain, he was not staying behind while the goys went searching for his sister. That was all he needed, for one of them to find her; that it should be Finn Collins or Tessa did not even cross his mind. Lightning, he thought, never struck the same place twice.

Support came from one of the tinsmiths who hustled his burly figure into everyone's view and raised a hand in a brandishing gesture. 'What in the name o' God has come over ye, Spider? Sure, and I never thought I'd live to see the day when Spider Murphy stepped down to the goys!'

'When it's Spider Murphy's daughter whose life's at stake, sure I'd back down to the divil himself,' yelled the chief's wife. 'And, 'tis a blaggard of a son who'll turn his mother's hair white with worry!'

'I'm with ye,' said the tinsmith hurriedly to Mick. But Mick

126

shrugged him off; a companion was not what he had in mind. If he was not to share victory with his da, he didn't want to share it with anyone. In order to redeem his standing with the tribe and raise his own self-esteem he had to search alone.

Mick turned abruptly and began to ascend the valley, anxious to get away from curious eyes. The climb jarred his aching bones. There had been no celebratory drinking for him and his mouth was dry; his belly was empty but his pride urged him on. Kate, he thought, will I tell ye now what a bloody nuisance y'are! If you had to get lost, why do it here?

The ridge loomed menacingly as the sun took its course, casting a long shadow on the vast waste of Ennabrugh. The searchers converged like animals on a watering hole, but hesitantly, carefully, as though approaching a power of which they stood in awe. In the afternoon light the colour of the Bog was diffused; it was neither black, nor grey, nor purple, but a mixture of each. Far into the distance it spread, mournful and threatening, surrounded by mountains and the fissured rock of the ridge. Here and there clumps of vegetation rose from the deeps like the remains of a prehistoric forest, their curiously shaped branches thick and muffled with moss.

Mick Murphy, who had only seen the Bog from the ridge, shivered, not with cold or fright, but with a feeling of helplessness, of being completely alone in so hostile a place. He could hear the goys shouting to each other, their voices covering the distance easily in the still air. He felt a stab of jealousy at their comradeship and wished he had allowed the tinsmith to accompany him. Surveying the desolate scene before him, he did not know where to go or what to do.

There was no obvious path, no track he could follow. He stepped forward gingerly and drew back. The blackish earth was soft and it was hard to tell the difference between solid earth and bog. His gaze picked out a line of bracken, all gnarled and brown, which trailed between stumps of decayed growth. He followed it, only to find that it had petered out. Not wanting to add the indignity of getting lost to the long list of recent failures, Mick gave up the idea of a search and sank into the long grass to rest his aching bones . . . to sleep.

Tessa, too, had mixed feelings. On her way up she had mused happily on the warm pleasure which Finn's glance gave her, and

127

marvelled that a look from a fella could cause such a sensation. He was proud of her. She had seen that special kind of light in his eyes, the eager, embracing depth of it. Or had she imagined it all? Was her imagination, like Marie Jane's, overwrought? If I can feel like this with just a look, she wondered, what would a kiss feel like? What if he put his arms round me?

Her thoughts nervously backed away and swung with a sense of urgency to Kate. Anxiety now began to pluck. There were other dangers up here beside the Bog. Lord Fitzcarron's keepers had laid mantraps, great steel things with cruel jaws that could bite a poacher's leg to the bone. Sometimes savage dogs escaped – sometimes the keepers allowed them to escape. With a sense of shock Tessa recognised the place where Billy had strayed. She looked up, alert and anxious, half expecting to see a horseman with a loud voice and strong white teeth, with sharp clear eyes, and lean fingers ferreting about the crook of a gun. She sighed with relief at the barren horizon and the desolate terrain.

Anyway, the cold winds had gone. Spring had come to Enna-brugh. Tessa inhaled the damp air of April with a sudden gratitude, and observed the flurry of bright flies, their gauzy wings caressing the surface, hovering over little clusters of marsh marigolds. She noticed the pale yellow sphagnum, how being sheltered from the wind had brought it out. She bent down to look more closely and saw little fronds of purple moss, obviously dropped from a larger clump . . . Someone had been gathering it. Her heart quickened. Had Kate been this way? Of course, she would be gathering the moss for dye! She looked out over the expanse. Nothing moved. But, she encouraged herself, that did not mean Kate wasn't there. What if she had sat down to rest, perhaps fallen ill, or worse? What if she had been caught in one of those bloody traps? She began to run. 'Kate! Kate Murphy, where in God's name are you!'

Finn Collins, accompanied by Jams, Young Duggan, Martin Grady and O'Malley's eldest, Pat – who at fourteen felt wonderfully grown up to be included with the men – searched the far side of the Bog. Finn knew every inch of this bank for this was where he dug his aunt's turf. Not that it was very good turf – it was brown and fibrous and did not hold together like the black stuff – but not everyone knew or could reach the best, only those with special knowledge like Proud Riley.

Full of energy, Finn led the way, sweeping back the fringe of rushes, using his bare forearm as though it was a scythe. On and on they searched, hoping to find a clue – a handkerchief, a scarf, a shoe, her shawl. Finn and Martin were almost sure she would not have come this way, for this was the bleakest, most barren shore, shaded by the ridge from the sun. The rushes had not yet asserted themselves here, the upsurge of sap which had stirred those on the sunnier shore was slow to rise here. No, he felt sure Kate would not have come this way, but still they to search everywhere while the light was good. Come darkness she would perish in the cold mountainy air. And so they continued.

Proud Riley, eyes narrowed, thumbs thrust into Timothy Thomas's belt, cap on head and body leaning forward, tramped Ennabrugh with a patient, purposeful stride. Even thought he had no regard for tinkers his heart went out to the Murphys. To lose your child . . . he shuddered. God forbid anything should happen to his Teresa; and in the light of this terrible thought he brought a lifetime of knowledge to bear upon his part of the search.

He was not worried about Teresa, for had he not brought her up to be tough and hardy? He was immensely proud of her, of her knowledge, her bravery, and how striking she had looked when everyone's attention was on her. Ach, God save us all, his daughter was no ordinary colleen. He wondered uneasily about the friendship with Kate Murphy. He was suspicious of tinkers, all of 'em, but as they would be gone when Kate was found perhaps it did not matter. But what, he asked himself, if Kate was not found?

Down in the valley the Aunt Hanratty sat in her rocking chair, brooding. A change in the distant sounds disturbed her dark thoughts about the perfidy of those around her past and present. The fiddles had stopped. The dancing, the noise. Was it ended so soon? She sat for a little while longer, the chair rocking with its remorseless crack-and-grind motion. Voices were raised. Curiosity moved her. The Aunt Hanratty, gaunt and grey, her black skirt and shawl

129

accentuating her height, stood in the doorway of the cabin. She blinked in the spring sunshine like an owl, taking in the anxious flurry of activity as the entire community searched and looked for Kate, gathered to speculate, then to search again.

The speculations fell to silence when the searchers saw the Aunt Hanratty standing in the cabin doorway. They drew together, uneasy at the sight. The gimlet eyes roved over the crowd. None met her gaze but looked away quickly. At last Una Kelly, made brave by being part of the crowd, asked cheekily, 'I don't suppose you've got Murphy's daughter in there?'

'Una,' whispered Marie Jane, recalling her recent experience with the Aunt. 'Just be careful. Don't go tormenting her.'

'Listen who's talking. Surely to God, I've heard you doing it often enough.'

'But not to her face – '

'How can you torment anyone if not to their face?' Una was losing patience. 'Honestly, Marie Jane O'Malley, you've done nothing but moan and groan since the dancing broke up – '

A rasping voice cut across their heated whispers. 'And what if I have got her?'

'There,' breathed Una, her dark eyes wide with terror. 'Did I not tell ye.'

'Did ye hell!'

'Where's Mr O'Malley?'

'Mr O'Malley! Come quick! Come on . . .' The cry reached his cabin. He finished his tea, put down the cup and hurried out.

'We've found her! Kate Murphy's found!'

'And God be praised for that! Where is she?' he demanded of Una, who had run to meet him.

'With the Aunt Hanratty, where else.'

'And what in the name of God Almighty is she doing there?' He saw the crowd and passing through it, walked up to the Aunt.

'They say Kate Murphy's with yourself?'

'They can say anything they like. All I said was "what if she is?"'

'Does that mean she's not with you after all?'

'To be sure. You see, O'Malley, I was doing what you're always doing, playing with words. And how they do get swallowed and taken up! What in God's name would I do with Murphy's girl?'

The little crowd had drawn nearer, for it wasn't every day they got a chance to see O'Malley and the Aunt, or more to the point, to hear O'Malley and the Aunt. The tinkers who had run to the scene now wandered aimlessly away.

'Pity about that,' commented O'Malley, looking at the sky and the encroaching evening. 'They're searching the Bog. Reckon she went up for rushes and lost her way.'

'Won't be the first – or the last.'

'If you can't be helping us then, we'll be on our ways. Oh,' he turned back on his steps. 'Your nephew's got a fine bit o' muscle there. He knocked the living daylights out o' Mick Murphy, wiped the floor with him, he did.' The silver-grey eyes did not flinch before the sudden blaze of venom. He had wanted her to know before Finn returned, and yet he wondered whether it might not have been better for the lad to have surprised her with the news. She would now have time to brood over it.

'And where is he now, then? At the poteen 'till he's flat on his back?'

'Searching the near shore for the girl.'

'More fool him. It's a poor bloody fool he is, Aloysius O'Malley, and none o' your meddling will cure him!' Then, in a lower tone, 'And what was the money like? For was he not boasting there'd be money for him to jingle in his pocket like Martin Jarvey does?'

'About that,' he lied sweetly, 'I wouldn't know.'

'You think you're clever, O'Malley, setting a nephew agin the Aunt that took him in.'

'Wouldn't you say it was a case of the Aunt against the nephew from the very start, from the moment he sat on that stone wall as a two-year-old? So, I'll bid you good day, Shena Hanratty.' No one but he ever dared call her by her first name, and he used it only to invoke the past she could not forget.

The sun was beginning to slip slowly down the sky. All those who had scoured the valley were now sitting disconsolately by the tinkers' fire. Spider Murphy paced up and down, occasionally striding off to the caravan where his wife sat with her apron over her head, rocking to and fro in misery. While she rocked, he would circle the caravan several times before returning to the fire to begin all over again.

Murphy's younger girls, estranged from their parents because of the grief and anxiety, allied themselves with the tinsmith's family.

Conversation hung in the air as if muffled by a blanket. Marie Jane sat or stood with equal impatience, giving Martin the rough edge of her tongue. He in turn smoked and speculated on the outcome. Most of the young people spoke in low tones and eyed each other as solemnly as they did on Good Friday and Ash Wednesday.

Finn and his party made their way back to the camp and reported having seen not even a dog all day. The elder Duggan, Kevin's father, and Martin's uncle had already arrived. Then Gypo Kelly returned, his long-eared, lantern-jawed face drooping even longer. It was superfluous to ask how their search had gone. It was written on their faces and in their steps.

Finn sat with Martin and three of the Duggan girls. Everyone, tinkers and crofters alike, was crowded about the fire, drawing comfort and a measure of solace from its warmth and brightness. The women were making griddle bread on the hot turves, and there was plenty for everyone. Finn ate hungrily. He was always hungry. The Aunt was frugal, to say the least, and often withheld bread and spuds as a punishment. He dared not tell anyone, or ask anyone, even for a crust, in case they would think him soft in the head. 'Ach, a big fella like yerself,' they would say, 'feared of an old woman.' They would not understand the fear was not of his aunt but of the underlying darkness, the superstition, on which he'd been reared. Physical things he could cope with. Tinkers, pigs, bullies, dogs. No task was too difficult to undertake; it was the unseen, the unknown, which were a threat.

'What are you thinking Gypo?'

'I'm thinking there's only three to come down: the Rileys and young Murphy. And I hope to God nothing overtakes him, for his ma's sake, you understand.'

Finn nodded. 'And what a sorrowful end to the Fair. This'll be talked about for many a year.'

'Unless we've all gone down to Rohira, like O'Malley keeps on about.'

Finn recalled his talk on the subject. 'There's got to be something to go down to, Gypo. Work, a place to live. Sure, there's no shanties and shacks down there – 'tis a different set of rules . . .'

He pushed a piece of the smouldering turf with the toe of his split

132

boot. He'd felt knowledgeable explaining about the town. He felt warm with the poteen and the fire, and his belly was full. He had won the day; everything was right – except Tess was not there to share it.

The buzz of conversation suddenly became quieter. Everyone looked up. It was Proud Riley – alone. God help us, they all thought, if he can't find her, it looks bad . . .

Riley's eyes narrowed. 'Is Teresa not down yet?'

'Neither's young Murphy.'

Gypo passed the older man a chipped enamel mug. 'Get this down ye, Riley, and remember, your girl knows Ennabrugh like the back of her own fair hand.'

'Ach, but I hope to God she'll not stay up after dark! She's never been up there in the dark before.' He frowned. 'I'll kill Spider Murphy if anything befalls Teresa, for didn't I swear on her mother's very grave? All me life I've had no truck with knackers, especially since Clancy – ' He tossed down the fiery liquid in the enamel mug and smacked his lips appreciatively. 'I'm going back. I'm going to find her. O'Malley might have to toll the chapel bell for Murphy's girl, but by Christ and His Blessed Mother, he'll not toll the bell for mine.'

'I'll come with you,' volunteered Finn.

'You'll do no such thing. I'll have me work cut out to find her in the dark, and I'm not for being hampered. Besides, Ennabrugh's already got your ma and da; you don't want to join them, do ye?'

Finn did not answer. No answer was needed.

'He's right,' said Gypo, holding on to Finn's sleeve. 'He's better off alone.'

Finn hesitated and sat down. Martin Jarvey offered him tobacco and a pipe.

'I've never had one before. Never had the money.'

'Now's the time to start. It'll take your mind off things and by the time you've finished choking and coughing she'll be down!' He lit the pipe and watched Finn take his first tentative puff. 'What old Riley just said, about the bell tolling, has got O'Malley anxious, you know.'

'What d'you mean?'

'Just suppose Kate isn't found. That hot-headed Mick – if he ever comes down – has only got to whip them up, about us harbouring

133

her, and taking revenge and all that. It won't be the first time the knackers have fired the cabins before they've left.'

'Not Spider Murphy,' pointed out Finn. He mimicked Mrs Murphy's intonation. 'Anyone who travels with Murphy abides by the rules.'

'Even to fornication!'

'Specially to fornication!' Finn spluttered on the pipe.

While the two were making fun of the Murphys' ideals, Gypo had stopped Proud Riley from going back to Ennabrugh. 'Let it be, Riley. She'll be down soon, and if you're up there she'll insist on going back to find you and might get into rale trouble. She'd want ye to stay and wait for her. No purpose'd be served. Listen, if she's not back by the time darkness is upon us, we'll all come up wid ye. Now rest man, sit and take your ease.'

As the light faded, Mick Murphy woke up. He was cold and his limbs were stiff. He got to his feet, slowly, painfully. A ripple of alarm went through him. Thank God he'd had the sense not to go wandering off, for he could just about find his way down. Or could he? One track, in this light, looked very much like another. In fact, they weren't tracks at all, he discovered, but rabbit runs, he realised when he found himself at a dead end. The humiliation of not having found Kate, and of getting lost himself proved too much. He sank back onto the ground, too frightened to move lest he got stuck in a bog-hole. The thought of having to spend the night alone in so dreadful a place filled him with terror – he, who could take on all comers, who feared nothing.

'Mother of God!' he exclaimed. 'Oh, Christ Almighty save and preserve me from . . .' His trembling voice trailed. There was a noise, a soft, trailing noise like an animal nosing its way through the bog-grass. Heart thumping in his head, prayer and profanity frozen on his lips, he crouched lower. The sound passed a little away from him, ahead of him. Cautiously he raised himself. In the twilight he saw a figure. A human figure. Tessa Riley! He almost cried out in relief. The trailing noise had been her hand sweeping the long dry grasses as she walked. He recalled seeing her swinging that tasselled shoulder shawl, a basket, a scarf, and in the absence of anything else she trailed her hand. She, too, had not found Kate! This was indeed a stroke of the blessed luck – it hadn't forsaken him altogether. He eyed the widening gap between them and decided to risk bounding over the grass, and if he fell into a hole there'd be help to get him out. She wouldn't stand by and see him drown. Elated, he made short work of the gap and fell into step some way behind her.

Tessa's sharp ears picked up his movements. Now it was her turn to be alarmed. Oh, not the gamekeeper, she prayed. Please God, not him, not now when I'm alone and the darkness is almost . . .

'Tessa Riley! Will ye wait for us?'

Recognising the voice she turned, relieved. Oh, it was only Mick Murphy! Under different circumstances meeting him would have given her a twinge of alarm, but not here, not at Ennabrugh where she was mistress of the situation. It was obvious he had no news of his sister, or he would be yelling it out at the top of his voice, boasting, bragging.

In a way she was glad of his presence, for her spirits had been flagging and she was very tired. Earlier on anxiety, and the hope the little fronds of purple moss inspired, had kept her searching, but since turning back, having failed to find Kate, she could not get down to the valley fast enough. Not that she had gone as far as the Fitzcarron estate, because Kate would never, even if she had been strong and well, have got that far.

The valley, with food, fire and poteen, seemed a long way off, and Tessa's legs were uncomfortably chaffed by the wet hem of the peacock-blue gown. The hem, and indeed some eight inches up the skirt, were soaked with peaty water. The gown was ruined but she did not care. Terrible thoughts of the tinker girl dying, drowning up here alone, crowded in on her. Tears blinded her and sobs rose in her throat. The wind, since the sun had gone, was cold. It had torn at her hair-ribbon, reminding her of the day when Billy was slowly sinking. She saw again the terror in his mild brown eyes, heard the pitiful bleating . . . The image fused with that of Kate, her long velvety-black hair falling straight on either side of her face, dredged with the fibrous ooze of Ennabrugh, the clammy coldness of its grasp inching up and up, taking her breath . . .

Poor Kate, she'd wanted so little out of life, just to go round the Fair with herself and Marie Jane, and that swine of a brother would not let her. And there he was behind her now, not even asking if there was news. If he had wanted to talk about his sister, to grieve for her,

135

she would have forgiven him and waited for him to catch her up to share their common sadness. She heard him lunging and lurching over the uneven terrain and guessed he was frightened of getting lost and losing face yet again.

On and on she pushed, leaving him to struggle as best he could to catch up. She breasted the wind, head high, a tall, perfect figure, majestic on the skyline. Proud Riley's daughter was not one to bow her head to the elements, to shrink or cower from the rain; and so she strode on, swearing softly as a stone pressed against her sore feet, for her pumps were soaked almost to a pulp and offered little protection.

Mick made a special effort – as far as his stiffened ribs would allow – to catch up with her. Not yet aware of her increased speed, he was considering himself lucky. If she'd not appeared God knows where he'd be now. He, the chief's son, losing his way! No, he couldn't bear that, especially after losing the wrestling to Collins. Was it, had it only been earlier on today that it had happened? Jasus, it seemed years ago . . .

By the time a stitch was developing beneath his ribs he realised her pace was not slackening, in fact if anything it was quickening. Bitch! Bloody goy bitch! And him struggling along at the back of her! He eyed the slim shoulders, square and resolute. The swing of her hips, the sway of her skirts. Her vitality made him angry. She wouldn't be so jaunty if she'd been hurled through the air like a rag doll. He felt sick at the memory. The unexpected thud of his body, the excruciating jarring of his bones, his teeth biting into his tongue. Oh, and the stars when his head had landed against the wheel! Jasus, it was like the universe being split into a cascade of shimmering particles which had refused to come together until someone had forced poteen between his lips.

By the time Mick Murphy had decided on a strength for strength policy, Tessa, having rounded the hill, could see the crimson glow of the peat-fires below and the sparks flying as the wind gusted down like huge bellows. She heard the murmur of voices, the shouts and excitement as those by the fire noticed the two figures; and then the excitement and hope dwindled as the figure accompanying Tessa was recognised. Mick had returned without his sister.

Tessa hurried down and he trailed after, just in time to see the rapturous return with which she was greeted; a heroine's return,

136

even without Kate. He felt this welcome for the goy to be somehow more condemnatory than the faces of his stricken parents. His father, strained and white-faced, his mother tear-smudged and drawn to gauntness, and the wide-eyed disappointment of his younger sisters, all struck him like a blow, and all the more because he had not even lifted a finger to search. He thanked God Tessa Riley had not come across him asleep.

The crowd about the fire made way, pushed the poteen into his hand and gave him griddle bread, and all the while the hushed talk was about Kate.

'Ach, come on, Mick, ye poor fella,' said the tinker woman who had raised fourteen on the crystal. 'Get something inside of you. You must have walked a terrible way.'

'I have so, on the hoof all the time. It's a wonder me boots aren't worn to the sole. It's a terrible place, full of bog-holes and awful soft the ground.'

Everyone looked down at his boots, at Gypo Kelly's, Proud Riley's, Jarvey's and Old Duggan's and at Tessa's worn and shredded pumps: all four pairs were wet and peat-stained, steaming by the fire. Mick's boots were dry; there was no soft earth sticking to the soles, and no peat stains on the leather. No comment was made, out of respect for his grief-stricken parents, but everyone knew that wherever Mick Murphy had been, he had not been searching for his sister.

It was dark now and people still stood and sat about in clusters, talking in hushed voices, waiting for O'Malley to toll the chapel bell.

'Don't go for the bell tonight, Da,' said Marie Jane.

'And why d'you say that, my girleen?'

Marie Jane nodded her head in the direction of the Murphys. Mrs Murphy sat on the ground, keening, rocking to and fro, her apron covering her face. Spider sat by her side, immobile, forehead resting on his pulled up knees. Even his gold earrings seemed dejected, and the chains hung about his neck like a weight.

'Give it till daylight, Da. What do you say, Tessa?'

'It'll make them feel worse to hear that terrible din; it's bad enough in daylight. Besides, who knows, the angels may be with her, guiding her back. She could be here tomorrow, you never know,' she ended lamely.

'God Almighty!' put in Mick. 'Go on, toll the bloody bell. You

137

make me sick, you goys. If Kate's gone, she's gone. Spider Murphy can take his grief like the rest of ye. Go on. Toll it, and be done!'

That was all O'Malley needed to make his mind up. 'It's not yourself I'm thinking about,' said O'Malley. 'It's your ma.' And then to his daughter, 'It's right you are, Marie Jane; we'll give it till morning.'

Some of the tinkers turned slowly away to their rigs; others sat by the chief and his wife, the women moaning in low tones some sad song of their own language. Most of the crofters stayed by the fire, some keeping an eye on the tinkers to be sure they did not embark on a rampage of revenge.

'Can I stay down the night, Da?' asked Tessa. 'Mr O'Malley and Dion and Pat and Marie Jane are staying by the fire, an' I've got no shoes to me feet, and sure they're sore, Da, to be going up home – '

'Ach, you've done well, girleen,' he cut across her words with an unexpected softness. 'Rest yerself now, and I hope that Spider Murphy's thankful for your efforts!'

'He'd be a thankful fella, Da, if I'd brought her back!'

'Maybe so, but – '

'Will ye milk the goats?' she asked with sudden concern. 'They're terrible late.'

'If the divils'll let me!'

He looked towards O'Malley who, perceiving the thought behind it, said. 'She'll be safe with us.' And in this sombre atmosphere of grief, Riley felt it would be so.

Rushes had been cut and piled in sheaves. Marie Jane and Tessa gathered armfuls, helped by Finn and Martin, and piled them a little distance from the fire, to sit or sleep on. There was a conspiratorial mood between the young women, for it was a long time since they had spent a night together, and although the circumstances took the edge off the treat, it offered comfort to Tessa, and compensation to Marie Jane for the loss of the dancing.

As soon as Proud Riley was out of sight Finn came to their pile of rushes.

'Are you not stopping?' asked Marie Jane. 'Sure, after the search and all you're not going all that ways back to the Aunt?'

He pulled a wry face and looked at Tessa. 'Some folks have a da to milk their goats.'

'So? Does that mean you've to go and see to the pigs?'

'There's no one else.'

'Will ye not be back for first light?' Tessa could not keep the eagerness out of her voice. 'Before me da comes down?'

Finn nodded his dark head. Oh, God help me, he thought, gazing at Tessa's shining eyes and windblown hair. Her face flushed with fire, poteen and pleasure. What wouldn't I give to stay here all night, to take Marie Jane's place on the rushes beside her, and sit and talk and dream of what might be? But superimposed on that lovely image was the dark figure of the Aunt Hanratty. Now that the excitement of the Fair was fizzling out, normality was staring him in the face. He had to go and tend the pigs, stupid bloody animals that they were. He knew that if anything happened to them she would curse him sure as hell – it was a threat which always brought him to heel.

Across the fire, Mick Murphy sat hunched up. Only part of his attention was on the subdued wailing and keening for his missing sister; otherwise he was concerned in taking surreptitious glances at Tessa. At the cloud of brown hair in attractive disarray, at the neat ankles, and every now and then at the creamy smoothness of bare legs as she held up the ruined hem of the peacock-blue gown to steam before the fire. Her face in repose, now that Finn had gone, was solemn; dark smudges of fatigue made her eyes appear dark and mysterious. He had caught the radiance directed toward Finn and wondered about it. At one moment of looking in her direction, the fire sparked up in a blaze of flames, and his little eyes almost started out of their sockets, for at that same moment Tessa had stood forward to lay more rushes, and in the movement he saw clearly the outline of her breasts, taut against the fabric of her gown. She repeated the action by getting rushes for Marie Jane. His throat tightened; he ran his tongue slowly over lips which had suddenly gone dry. He found himself wanting her to do it again, to repeat the tantalising movement, and was angry when she sat down. Who did she think she was, flaunting her handsome body? And it was handsome, not scraggy and scrawny like the travelling women, who had scarcely a pick on 'em. Soft, her whole body would be, soft and smooth.

CHAPTER EIGHT

Dawn was upon them by the time Tessa and Marie Jane opened their eyes. Tessa jerked upright at once to see if Kate had by any miraculous chance returned. The camp seemed grey and dirty, the fire almost burned out. Mrs Murphy was still sitting with her back to the wagon, her apron still over her head, and Spider was sprawled stiffly beside her. The Murphys were unwilling to face the day. Marie Jane and Tessa were of the same mind, but for different reasons. O'Malley was already apace, hat on head, grey eyes thoughtful behind spectacles. Mrs Jams and some of the Duggan girls were darting about like early morning birds, making tea and pouring it into the discarded poteen mugs of last night, then distributing it to the outstretched hands. Conversation was muted. The business of the day was slow to come together; questions hung in the air. What was to be done about Spider Murphy's daughter? Would the Murphys take to the road without knowing her fate?

It was at this stage that Tessa confidentially told O'Malley about the trail of purple moss which she was sure Kate had gathered. 'She's been up there, I'll swear she has, Mr O'Malley. It's just like they said about Tony Collins and Moll; she seems to have disappeared without trace. I didn't tell you last night because Mrs Murphy was badly enough. People can take bad news better in the daytime.'

'Can they, now? And how would such a young colleen as yourself know that?

'Oh, sure, you're teasing me! It stands to reason. Everything's worse in the dark.'

'Ach, I'd better get on then and toll the bell, get it done with. I've sent young Pat off for the priest to say mass for her poor lost soul,' he sighed. 'It's a terrible day, Tessa, and this is a terrible place to live. You know, sure it seems to me that Ennabrugh demands payment for the turf it yields and the rushes it produces. How many more people have to be drowned, I wonder, before the Jams, the Connors, the Jarveys, the Kellys and all the rest are convinced that any place is better than here . . .' But he was talking to himself, for Tessa had caught a sight of Finn's athletic figure, running easily despite being half asleep and his stomach as empty as a drum.

When he had reached his aunt's cabin last night, after locking the pigs up and feeding them, she had been waiting for him, sitting tight-lipped beyond the circle of the lamp.

'Just look at the sight of ye, you big, long-legged idiot! No brains in your head! Making a fool of yourself for O'Malley! Leaving the Aunt that took you in. O'Malley didn't take you in, did he? Oh, no, he's too sly, that one! All mouth, all talk, and you, bloody fool that y'are, take it all in! You see where you'll end up . . . And what about that money? Do you hear me?'

But Finn did not hear, for he had thrown himself down on his bed and was so deeply asleep that had she cursed him to his face he would not have heard.

Finn woke to the crack-and-grind of her chair. He lay for a few moments gathering himself together. She was waiting for him, just waiting till he got up. Thank God he slept soundly, for even she could never wake him. He lay there, trying to figure out what to say. This was his morning ritual and it always ended negatively; he was no match for the Aunt. He wished he had set his jug of cold tea nearby the night before; lack of it was a disadvantage. He eyed the distance to the door. He could be out through it in three strides; she wouldn't have time to breathe, still less say anything, and even he knew that you had to hear a curse before it could take effect; besides she wouldn't waste a curse for a little occasion like this, she would be saving it . . . He noted with some surprise that he had not even taken off his boots. He leapt up quickly and was through the door before she even drew breath. The pigs, unused to such turbulence, eyed him through baleful pink eyes, their long white lashes blinking in disapproval. Not staying to wash them down – he could do that later – he vaulted over the compound wall and was off. Just so long as he saw Tessa before she went back up with her da, that was all he wanted. As he ran he wondered if Kate had miraculously turned up. But then he heard the bell tolling.

He slowed his pace on arrival at the camp and stood before Tessa, not sure whether to laugh with happiness at seeing her, or go all over solemn on account of the bell. He stood there, panting, smiling, unwashed, still with yesterday's peat on him, clothes crumpled and check shirt open almost to the waist. He looked vulnerable and hunted, and Tessa's heart went out to him. They stood there, equally helpless, wanting to say something, everything, and yet saying nothing, nothing that mattered.

Mrs Jams thrust tea into his hand, and after three cups he was listening to Tessa's story of the purple moss as though they were old friends who met and talked every day.

Spider Murphy had taken to pacing round and round his caravan, and Mrs Murphy had taken the apron from her face to announce she was not leaving Ennan without either her daughter or confirmation of her death. Mrs Jams pointed out as kindly as she could that the Great Bog of Ennabrugh issued no such confirmation.

On hearing this O'Malley was troubled. The last thing the resources of the valley could tolerate was a longer stay or a permanent influx of tinkers. Indecision was everywhere. The sweeps had their chimneys waiting to be swept before the big houses had their spring cleaning. There were horse fairs to attend and other numerous engagements which could not wait. None of these families was willing to linger, and yet out of respect for the Murphys' trouble they did not want to move off in indecent haste. The balance of life was upset. At the end of every Fair the tinkers should depart and their not having done so was already an anticlimax; the likelihood of their not moving off at all presented real problems.

'They can't stay,' declared Jams. He had run to the chapel to divest himself of this news, and now looked helplessly to O'Malley, who had taken off his coat and, in his shirtsleeves, was pulling on a solitary bell rope. The noise echoed all around the valley walls, a dull, ringing monotone. 'Nothing'll be safe. They'll be fightin' and drinkin' all the hours God sends. An' that Mick'd cut our throats soon as look, after the luck he's had – '

'Will ye hold on a minute, Jams, for the love of God! Give them a couple of days to get used to their trouble and I'm sure they'll move on.'

'But what if they don't, O'Malley?'

'If no one sells them any flour for bread, if we guard our turf stocks so they'll have no fire, sure they'll go. As for poaching, you know what the Fitzcarron estate's like, now. Sure they'll get neither fish nor fowl without a shotgun in the arse.'

'Ach, O'Malley, 'tis green y'are! Somone'll sell 'em flour. Those

142

shiftless buggers in the shacks, sure they'd sell their grandmother – anything for an easy penny, that lot!' His brown eyes had grown as mournful as a spaniel's. 'If she was found dead they could have a funeral, and that'd be the end; they'd go.'

'Jams, you get as flustered as that little woman of yours. Sure to God, there's nothing to choose between you! No, Jams, the question we've got to ask ourselves is what is Mick doing? He's the fella we've got to watch.'

'If I'd thought my two lads would turn out like him, I'd a drowned them at birth. Drunk as a lord last night. A trouble maker he is. As though the Murphys haven't enough on their plate.'

O'Malley pictured the Jams boys, wide-faced and constantly open-mouthed; those lads hadn't even the backbone to be worthless!

'C'mon, Jams, get your coat off and do your stint on the rope. I'll send Gypo to give you a hand later on.'

Father and aunt forgotten, Tessa and Finn, along with Marie Jane and Martin, gathered with most of the other crofters to talk and speculate.

'There's something I can't understand,' said Tessa. 'Can anyone think why she didn't come down after she'd got the moss to dye the rushes with?'

Martin Jarvey's air of impertinence had deserted him entirely. Nor was he wearing his new jacket, but a thick navy blue jersey with holes in the sleeves. 'It's sorry I am now that we didn't take more notice of her.'

'Don't be blaming yourself on that score,' put in Marie Jane tartly. 'You couldn't get her tent up fast enough, remember?'

'I mean, she wanted to be friendly,' he went on, as though Marie Jane had not spoken. 'And if we'd put ourselves out a bit and made more of an effort she'd not have gone wandering on her own.'

'Ye don't mean – '

'I do so,' he said, boldly speaking what had been on his mind all night. 'She could've deliberately waded into the Bog and let it take her because she was ill and lonely and no one bothered about her. You were saying, Tessa, that it must be hard not to be able to work and dance and be like everyone else.'

'People don't do that,' said Marie Jane. 'Look at Kevin Connor's

143

da, always talking of making away with himself, but he never does. It's all talk.'

'It's those who are always on about it, like him,' answered Martin, 'that never do it. My uncle says it's the quiet ones that suddenly decide they've had enough.'

'I don't see,' went on Marie Jane, who did not like this line of talk, 'why we should blame ourselves. She's got sisters, a brother and a couple o' parents. What were they doing about her?'

'Ach, I know all that, but it doesn't alter the fact of us knowing and not doing anything.'

'What about the moss?' said Finn. 'Sure, if she had her mind fixed on dying rushes, she's hardly likely to wade into Ennabrugh deliberately, is she?'

'Another thing,' Tessa lowered her voice. 'It's too terrible up there to . . .' She could scarcely bring herself to say the words, 'to knowingly walk into all that cold, black . . . It isn't like walking into the river or the sea where it's all over so quick – '

'Tessa, it's your da!' whispered Marie Jane frantically.

The two sprang apart and looked at each other with the guilty air of children caught in mischief.

'Jasus!' Marie Jane grabbed her friend's arm. 'Look who's with him?'

Tessa looked and wished she hadn't.

'Tess, are you alright?' questioned Finn in alarm. She nodded.

'Just surprised that's all. The gamekeeper's the last person I expected to see with me da.'

Everyone else thought so too. The sight of the two set tongues wagging on a different tack.

'What the divil does Frank Kildare want?'

'What's he doing here again?'

'He'll be after the knackers.'

'But it's Proud Riley he came down with.'

'What's he want with Riley, then?'

'God Almighty knows – and neither He nor Riley'll tell a word of it.'

'It'll be the bell will have bothered him; you can hear the bloody thing for miles.'

Tessa's thought whirled. She could hear Finn talking, Marie Jane answering, Martin's voice rambling on. Someone was whistling a tune, but she could not name it. Her mind would take in nothing for the rush of thoughts. It had happened. The day she most dreaded and had begun to think would never come to pass. After all, if she'd lived seventeen years in Ennan without ever seeing the gamekeeper, it seemed only reasonable to hope she could manage a few more years without seeing him. Fate had a lot to answer for.

The gamekeeper had obviously been to see her da about the loss of the gun. But why wait so long? Had he only discovered where she had lived after the shooting contest, and thinking the knackers had gone by now, decided to tackle her da about 'compensation'? She had heard Mr O'Malley use the word and it had remained in her head, lurking, waiting for just this occasion.

In those few first seconds her father and the gamekeeper seemed to stand out from all the rest. How tired and small her father looked against the restless hunter-like energy of the younger man. Her father's face seemed to have shrunk into his sidewhiskers as he stood there, gnome-like in wrinkled trousers, hobnailed boots, and goatskin jerkin, with the big silver buckle of Timothy Thomas's belt the focal point of his appearance.

The gamekeeper took stock of everything and everyone. Tess could not bear her father to be Kildare's victim. If there was any blame for the loss of the gun, she was going to take it upon herself. She recalled the rabbits dangling from the gamekeeper's saddle that day, and the headless pheasant. A shiver brought back reality. She moved forward, stepping over those still sleeping by the fire; through a cluster of tinkers talking excitedly in Shelta; past the Jarvey men arguing about donkeys; around the women making tea, and the playing children.

'Da!' she exclaimed, not daring to look at the man beside him. There's still no news of Kate Murphy – oh, you've brought me shoes.' Her gaze went to the shawl on his arm. 'But I don't want that, or me crook.'

'You will, Teresa. Mr Kildare wants you to go with him.' A note of pride infiltrated the statement, and those who heard pursed their lips, raised their eyebrows, and thought, ach, fancy that now!

If her father had said she was to go with the devil himself Tessa could not have been filled with a more astonished terror. But before she could gather her thoughts together in any coherent form, the keeper took off his hat, wiped his forehead with the back of his hand and yelled, 'Mr O'Malley, have we got to listen to that blasted bell?'

O'Malley called his second son, Dion, who, hands thrust deep into cut-down trouser pockets, was watching a game of jacks. 'Dion, will you run and tell Jams to stop the bell?' The lad sprinted off instantly, as fast as his spindly white legs could carry him.

No sooner had he gone than people made way for Mrs Murphy, who, looking more gaunt than ever in her grief, approached the gamekeeper, followed by Spider. God save us, thought Kildare, what now?

'Have ye no Christian charity in that heart of yours, Frank Kildare? Will ye not leave the bell to toll, to mourn with us for Murphy's eldest daughter, his beautiful Kate?'

The tinkers, including the recently awakened Mick, began murmuring their agreement; the tinker women set up a fresh bout of wailing, and over all the bell tolled monotonously.

'Will you stop your noise!' Kildare held up his hands. 'Stop it! Will you listen while I tell you I've got someone in the lockup who calls herself Kate Murphy – '

'Lockup?' echoed Mrs Murphy, who in the space of one delirious second had risen from the depths of grief to the heights of indignation. 'And why in the name of God Almighty have ye taken Murphy's daughter to the lockup? And she as innocent and as good a girl as ever set foot in this godforsaken glen. Will ye tell me before God and all these people why you've laid hands on Murphy's daughter?'

'For trespassing on Lord Fitzcarron's property. Did I not,' he inhaled deeply, 'Have I not, warned the lot of you about trespassing and poaching on the estate?'

'Kate is not a poacher,' declared Tessa. 'She's innocent; I'll swear it on oath, mister.'

Kildare's dark coppery head swung round from the Murphys to stare at her.

'Yes, she said you would . . .' He tapped the top of his boot thoughtfully with the peak of his deerstalker.

So, she's alive, thought Tessa. Kate's not drowned or lost but alive and well – at least, as well as anyone could be in the lockup. The implication of the news had only just seeped into her mind. The gamekeeper had not come to arrest either her da or herself over the loss of the gun!

Martin, too, was laughing in a relieved kind of manner, while Finn was talking earnestly about the charge against Kate. Marie Jane's eyes were fixed on Frank Kildare's authoritarian figure.

Oh, she rounded her lips, he was a man, a proper man. Look at his clothes, how well they fitted, all buttoned and buckled neatly. His jacket didn't hang open and loose like Martin Jarvey's, and you couldn't see the waist of the trousers where the braces fitted on to buttons. Gentlemen did not display their braces.

She liked the magnificent dark eyebrows that curved so neatly, the straight nose. True there was a hardness about the mouth, but she preferred to call it firmness. Suddenly, she was consumed with jealousy, not so much of Tessa, but of the opportunity which had come her way and which she knew very well that Tessa would not want! Fate had something to answer for.

All these scrutinies and assessments were brought to an end by the sudden cessation of the bell. O'Malley had begun to think Dion had forgotten, but then, as if prompted by the thought, the bell had stopped. The world suddenly became still. But not for long. Questions. Questions from the Murphys, to the Murphys, echoing back and forth among the ranks of excited tinkers, for poaching carried a sentence of imprisonment.

Then the questions turned to Tessa. 'Your father tells me your name is Teresa?'

Tessa recalled her former instinct of self-preservation up at Ennabrugh which had withheld this information . . . and now her da had just spilled it out! After a moment's reflection she lifted her head slowly, and with that lifting of her chin which Finn thought of as 'her regal manner', answered, 'Only me da calls me Teresa, mister; everyone else calls me Tessa.' Except Finn, she thought. He was the only one to ever call her just 'Tess', and she liked it that way.

'Very well, Tessa Riley, get your shoes on. Take your shawl and crook and we'll be away.'

'Away?' Her father's words came back to her. 'Where to?'

'Why, to the Resident Magistrate, of course. This Kate insisted you would be able to convince the RM she was not a poacher.' He glanced at the Murphys and added drily, 'Her parents could scarce do that! Naturally, your father was not hellbent on the idea of his only child being witness for a tinker. We spent some time discussing it. Did we not, Mr Riley? Of course the alternative, if you decide not

147

to be a witness, is for Kate to stay in the lockup until Monday week and to come before the Magistrate with the other miscreants.'

Hearing this, Mrs Murphy's indignation turned at once to wheedling and pleading with Tessa. 'And she with her brathing bad! Mother o' God, if ye don't do what he says, Tessa, the brave and wonderful girl that you are, the chapel bell will toll again. It's a wonder one night in the lockup hasn't already brought her to her death.' She pointed out that she and Spider would crawl there on their knees if it would do any good, despite the fact that the very sight of a magistrate brought on her excruciating palpitations, and Murphy, God help him, his face would twitch for a week!

As for Mick, he quailed inwardly and pressed himself back to avoid notice; yet at the same time his soul smarted at the prospect of more goy interference in their lives. What were his parents thinking of to allow the name of Spider Murphy – known to every traveller in the land – to be in debt to the goys? Had all the family pride gone? He smouldered in angry resentment that once again Tessa Riley was heaping up for herself glory that should have been his.

'C'mon, girl,' Kildare said briskly. 'Sure, I haven't all the day.'

Finn sensed Tessa's anxiety. It was on his tongue to offer to accompany them and bring Kate back, but such an offer would arouse her father's suspicions, and above all things he didn't want that. He knew that she wanted it that way, too, so he remained unhappily silent.

Martin Jarvey offered a donkey for the return journey, but the gamekeeper gave a short laugh. 'A donkey! What do you think this is, a bloody cavalcade?'

'But Kate's delicate, Mr Kildare,' he answered, his face flushing slightly.

'As delicate as my arse, Jarvey! She was strong enough to find her way onto his lordship's land, she'll be strong enough to get back.'

Tessa stooped to put on her shoes and winced slightly at the impact of the hard leather on feet tender from yesterday's search. She smiled wryly; these were the clodhoppers which Marie Jane had said looked like boats! The hem of her once lovely peacock-blue gown was crusted with dried mud, the skirt stained brown with splashes of peaty water and bits of rush stalk were caught in the weave. Her hands and face were besmirched, and as for her hair . . . After the search she had been too weary to wash, and this morning since waking everything had happened so quickly. Marie Jane was the only one to look fresh and clean and pretty and Tessa longed to look the same. What would the Magistrate reckon to Proud Riley's daughter?

'Mr Kildare?' Her father's voice cut into the silence which surrounded their departure. 'You'll remember what I said?'

'I will so, Mr Riley.'

As they left the camp O'Malley, relieved that the tinkers would be away when Kate returned, crossed to where his friend was standing, and looked at him keenly from behind the rims of his gold spectacles.

'Is it all right, Riley, old son?'

'Surely, Aloysius, surely everything's fine. Thank ye, now.'

And so O'Malley had to be content.

While still within earshot of the camp, the gamekeeper whistled for his horse, which had been grazing on the hill. 'You don't think I walked?' he answered Tessa's look of surprise. 'C'mon, put your foot in the stirrup, and get up.'

Tessa cast a fraught look back at all that was familiar, then eyed the big horse and thought of the immodest display of skirts involved; this brought a sudden blush.

'I can't get up there, I've only ridden one of Jarvey's donkeys before. We don't have saddles and fancy things up here.'

'Either that, or you walk and I ride.'

'I'll walk,' she announced.

Her father was immediately proud of her independent spirit. Finn and Martin admired her courage. And Marie Jane thought her a fool – why, if only Tessa would play her cards right and be sociably inclined, it might put Frank Kildare in a mind to getting them both good places in service in the big house. And me, she privately railed, me, who would lap up any such opportunity never even gets a chance. Look at Tessa, setting off in front of the horse, shawl about her shoulders and that bloody crook in her hand. Oh, she's as much idea as me foot!

Tessa's hand curled round the comforting stem of the crook, the smooth wood warming at once to her touch like an old friend. She felt the need of comfort, for every step took her further away from home and safety and nearer to Ennabrugh – as though she'd not seen enough of it! There was nothing that could erode confidence more effectively than the wide expanse of primaeval nature, with its avenues of whirls and swirls, of strange shapes and weird tricks of light. And, as if this was not enough, Tessa was made more uneasy still by the figure on horseback. Why was he putting himself out to save a knacker from prosecution? It was well known that the keepers of the Fitzcarron estates had it in for the tinkers even worse than her da – and that was saying something! And there was another thing; why had her da let her go off with this fella to vouch for Kate? Sure, it wasn't out of love for Murphy!

A wry smile occasionally curved Frank Kildare's thin lips. He had to give it to her, she was a good pacer! He had thought she would not be able to keep it up and had looked forward to offering her the saddle. She'd guts, all right. Mother of Jesus, he thought, they were tough, these crofters.

But his lips assumed their firmness of line as he remembered the Bog oozing up his sleeves, down his collar. He had stunk like a privy. His gun had gone down and his clothes had been fit for nothing but burning. 'Just you wait till next time,' he had muttered. He had not forgotten either, and when calling to talk to O'Malley and to warn the tinkers against poaching, he had been curious enough to ascertain her name and where she lived. This information he had stored away for future use, never thinking the future would come so soon.

It was only yesterday, to be exact, that the steward, Flavell, had sent a message that he had caught a young tinker woman on the estate. Flavell was sure she was up to something but could not get a word out of her and had put her in the outhouse they called a 'lockup'. Kildare had ridden over this morning and found her cowering and trembling in a corner. He recognised her by her wheezing as Spider Murphy's daughter. She had poured out a tale of how she had been collecting mosses and had seen some yellow ochre growing just inside the wall of the estate.

'See?' she had cried, pulling purple and yellow moss out of her pocket. 'Sure your honour I'd already got the purple . . .' She had blathered on about Spider's daughter being an honest girl. 'And if ye don't believe me, send word to the valley, to Tessa Riley – her da is Proud Riley . . .'

His blood had quickened with sudden interest. 'I don't believe you,' he had said. 'I've heard too many tinker's tales to fall for that one. You've been caught trespassing, and everyone knows what happens to those trespassing with intent. It's the Magistrate for you.'

Kildare had known Kate Murphy would be terrified at the mention of the Resident Magistrate, and he was right. She set off invoking God and numerous angels to strike her dead if she spoke a word of a lie, and 'The Almighty will surely keep your soul from purgatory if ye'll only go and ask Tessa Riley to be a witness that I'm innocent, that I wasn't out for poaching, and the Lord Almighty knows I never knew I was trespassing.' Nor had she, but 'loitering with intent' was good enough. So, he had reason to track down Tessa Riley!

Telling Flavell to feed the prisoner and throw her a blanket pending the arrival of a witness, he had ridden off to Ennan. He had called at the cabin and was surprised at the depth of disappointment her absence caused him. On the way down to the camp the old man had explained why the bell was tolling and about the widespread search for the missing girl, and Tessa's part in it. And so they had descended together, and Kildare had come face to face with that full-lashed look from those blue-grey eyes.

He had gazed, not on her appearance, but on the tendrils of brown hair blowing about her ears and throat. As she stooped to put on her shoes he watched her as though he had never seen a pair of feet before. He could have put out a hand to touch them – yes, and made a bloody fool of himself!

But, what had he really hoped for? Had he expected a coquettish exchange of words, a bit of tomfoolery and, as a natural progression from his holding her skirts, a quick fumbling about the frayed ribbons? He admitted on an intake of breath that he had had something like that in mind when he had ridden over from Flavell's but, when he saw her by the camp fire, something told him she'd crack his skull with that damn great crook first! He was puzzled; he got on very well with O'Malley's girl, and with the Jams girls – why could he not get on the same easy footing with this one? Why in hell was he bothering at all? She was not his kind, yet he was the first to admit that his kind had not been of interest lately. They were ten a penny, too easy to capture, too willing to please.

Feeling something mysterious mingling with his lustful thoughts,

Kildare grew irritated. Mysteries and emotions were not part of his life and he shied away from these as his horse shied from Ennabrugh. The son of a gamekeeper, he had been brought up to dislike and mistrust everything that savoured of emotions or ideals, to consider such things unmanly. All the same, he felt cheated that his little scheme had not even resulted in an exchange of words. Soon they would be at Flavell's, and then she would be gone, leaving him sprawling again, not in Ennabrugh, but in his own ineptitude.

'This isn't the way to the house, mister,' shouted Tessa against the wind. He used the noise of the wind as an excuse to dismount and put the horse on a long reign behind them. He felt a sense of satisfaction at the wide-eyed look she cast at him. He had looked so big in the saddle that to see him cut down to normal size was slightly reassuring, but now she had to reckon with the prowling air, the restless virility of his walk. Tessa was sure that not a blade of grass moved without his being aware of it; a cloud did not pass without his registering its shade; and she was glad to feel the warmth of her shawl protecting her from the scrutiny of those sharp, clear eyes. 'I said this isn't the way to the house,' she repeated.

'And did I say it was?'

'You did so.'

'I said she was locked up for trespassing on Lord Fitzcarron's property, which, in this case, is steward Flavell's cottage. Will you tell me this now, Tessa Riley, what's Spider Murphy's girl to you? Knackers and crofters are almost daggers drawn, and your father made it clear he had no regard for them, yet you were out searching for her all yesterday.'

'Marie Jane and me felt sorry for her, her being bad with her brathing and all – and to think she was locked up all that time!'

'Did you not think to ask at the estate?'

'What!' she exclaimed with spirit. 'Me asking if they'd seen a tinker! They might have put me in the lockup as well! She's no poacher, mister. Kate was only after moss to dye the rushes for making into baskets.'

'I've heard those tales before.'

'It's the truth, mister, and I'm willing to swear it.'

He tossed her a keen look. It had been on his mind to say that what happened to Kate would depend on her:

'Me?' she would reply with eyes like saucers.

'Yes, Kate need never appear before a magistrate if you . . . if you'll come to my cottage and . . .'

But, he could not even think the improper suggestion in her presence, let alone utter the words. Dare he do the decent thing and ask if he could call at the cabin, with her da present, of course? No; there'd be talk. He could just hear them. 'God Almighty!' they'd say in their irreverent innocence, 'The gamekeeper's getting his feet under Proud Riley's table!' No! Lord help him, no! He could not make that kind of commitment. It was not in him.

They walked the rest of the way in silence. Tessa was relieved they were only going as far as Flavell's which was on the edge of the estate. The cottage was in sight when Frank Kildare turned towards her and said, 'Marie Jane was saying the other day about the two of you going into service with Lady Fitzcarron when a place is available?'

'Marie Jane can be very fanciful at times.'

'Don't be too sure. There's no future for places like Ennan, and the time may come when . . .' He reigned in his tongue sharply. 'When you'll be glad of a few shillings; and young women who can read and write will get on.'

Oh, will I not kill Marie Jane when I get back, thought Tessa.

'Your father told me all about you – they don't call him Proud Riley for nothing.'

Tessa was secretly elated, for obviously the gamekeeper was not going to ask her da for compensation or he wouldn't be talking like this. Praise God. Oh, Blessed Jasus and His Holy Mother be thanked! Aloud she said primly, 'Me da can get awful carried away, mister.'

'Not in this case.' He smiled at her, but her eyes were on Flavell, who was coming towards them, walking with a limp through getting caught in one of the traps.

'Will you come and look at the girl, Mr Kildare? Sure, she's wheezing like an old fella.'

'You can turn her loose, Flavell. This young woman here has satisfied me that she was not loitering or trespassing with intent.'

The steward opened the door.

'Kate!'

'Tessa, oh, Tessa,' she wheezed. 'Will you tell 'em, for the love of God – '

'Sure, it's all right now, Kate. C'mon, lean on me; we're going down to your ma – aren't we, mister?' Tessa suddenly had the wild idea that she could ask anything, and he would comply.

Kildare looked up. 'You've got away with it this time,' he said to Kate, who had shrunk back against Tessa's side. 'Mainly because of Tessa Riley. But if you're caught again on his lordship's property, you're for the RM, and that goes for all of Murphy's tribe.'

'Ach, thank you, your honour, sure God'll be merciful to you. I didn't mean no harm, and as God is me judge, I didn't know I was trespassing.'

Tessa led Kate out of the lockup. She did not know what to say by way of leavetaking, so left without a word.

'At least you've rested!' Tessa joked as they set off.

'Oh, but the wheezes . . . Can you hear 'em, Tessa? It was that horse blanket they threw in for me; I could scarce draw breath at times.' She cast a frightened look at the desolate landscape. The emptiness of it intimidated her; the distance from the camp at Ennan seemed utterly beyond her capabilities. It was so unlike yesterday, when somehow she had wandered unknowingly, her attention so set on the mosses and her ideas for their use that the distance went unnoticed. But now, after being locked up in the cold and dark with little food, she felt exhausted.

Sensing something of the kind, Tessa was apprehensive too. But Kate must be kept going, must be kept on her feet. 'You never know,' she encouraged. 'The clear air could do your lungs good, blow away the blanket dust. There's no rush so we'll walk nice and easy, like. Here, let me fasten your shawl. This'll never keep you warm! I've used better than this to wrap the cheeses in! Here, you have me own.' She removed it from her own shoulders and arranged it about the slim form of Kate. 'God help us, it nearly drowns you!'

'It's lovely and warm.' Kate snuggled into it.

'Will I tell you this, now, Kate Murphy; you're the only living soul that's ever walked back to Ennan after the bell's tolled for 'em! Oh, and the search yesterday; you couldn't see the grass for people!'

But Kate was not yet ready to be amused. Another frightening thought had occurred to her. 'Do you think me da will take his belt to me? I mean, we would've been on the road by now. And it's all my fault, holding em up.' She put a hand to her mouth with a gasp. 'Oh, Mother of God, when I think of our Mick! Sure, he'll be that mad –'

'Don't talk to me about your bloody Mick! Let me tell you now

154

how Finn Collins wiped the floor with him, and how he's disgraced himself by only pretending to search for you! And Spider and your ma have aged overnight with worry; sure he'll never take his belt to you again!' So to encourage her companion, and to keep her own spirits from flagging, Tessa related all the events in graphic and hilarious detail. But, after only an hour's walking, it was clear to Tessa that Kate, at this pace, would not reach Ennan until dark. She was pondering the wisdom of leaving Kate in a sheltered spot and hurrying on ahead for assistance when she saw two figures in the distance frantically waving and leading a donkey.

'Finn!' yelled Tessa, jumping up and down as though terrified they would pass on. 'It's Finn and Martin Jarvey! You remember Martin, the one who muscled in and got your tent up – and got your Mick all worked up!'

'Yes, I do. Oh, Tessa, sure I must look a terrible mess.'

'You! What about me!' Their giggles became laughter as the strain of effort was gone; help was on the way.

For Tessa, the peculiar heart-thumping pleasure associated with seeing Finn Collins was like a shot of poteen. It warmed her heart and flooded her limbs with a weakness that had nothing to do with lack of strength.

Finn, head and shoulders above Martin, strode vigorously towards Kate and Tessa, arms swinging, covering the terrain with the sure-footedness of a mountain goat. 'What are you standing there for?' he yelled, and laughed with sheer pleasure at the energy which flooded through him. He was off before Martin had realised what was happening.

'I'll show you!' shouted Martin to the wind, and with a high spirited whoop leapt on the donkey and urged it forward, leaving Finn to run until his breath gave out.

'Martin, am I glad to see the sight of you!' exclaimed Tessa on his arrival. 'Kate was all but pegging out.'

'I'm all right, now, but I don't know what I would've done without Tessa.'

Martin shot a quick glance at her pale face, which looked paler than ever between the long curtains of sleek hair. Her breathing was laboured, but she was trying to make light of it.

'C'mon, let's be having ye, Kate. If we get you on the donkey we can take it easy.'

Having helped her onto the donkey, Tessa took the opportunity to hurry on. She lifted her mud-caked skirts and ran. Meeting up with Finn, her exuberance melted into a kind of shyness at having hurried on so; breathlessness served to cover up the need to say much. She gasped, holding on to her side as if she'd got a stitch beneath her ribs, at the same time laughing with relief at having met up finally.

'They were getting anxious down there. Your da's been pacing about like Spider was!'

'I thought we'd never make it!'

'You should've heard your da going on at O'Malley about what he'd do if you weren't back before dark!'

'Sure I was wondering whether to leave her and come down, when I saw you both. Oh, Jasus, Mary and Joseph, sure I was never so glad to see you in me life. Well,' she smiled, blushed beneath her already flushed cheeks, and murmured, 'You know what I mean . . .' Then, having caught up with the others, they walked slowly, side by side, their bodies touching occasionally as they stumbled over stone or tussock.

As they neared the camp, Spider Murphy, twitching, came loping towards them, Proud Riley at his heels, and following closely a gaggle of tinkers and crofters, curious and anxious to be the first to hear all that had happened. Then the O'Malley boys, Dion and Pat, ran like the wind to relate the gist of it to their father and the others waiting by the fire.

Only Marie Jane stood back from the excitement. She had not been pleased at Martin's generosity of spirit in going to meet Tessa and Kate with one of his uncle's donkeys. Everyone gathered had cheered them as they set off – all except herself. It seemed that everything was happening to everyone else. Why, she wondered, why in the Almighty God's name could she never get lost and be found by Frank Kildare! She, who craved excitement, seemed to sample it only at second hand.

'Ach, don't be going into the mulligrubs, now,' Martin had said to the shiny ringlets which hid her averted face. 'The sooner the Murphys girl is back, the sooner the knackers can be off and we'll be our old selves again.'

'Yes,' she had replied, head still averted. 'But who wants to be "our old selves"? You working with the mangy donkeys, and me ma palming me off with Annie and making me feed those squaking

156

flea-ridden fowls! Kate Murphy's ruined the Fair for all of us. She broke up the dancing by getting lost, and you'd rather go off and meet her with a donkey than stay with me.'

'I'll not be gone long, and Kate's bad with her brathing – '

'Ah, but she keeps on doing it, doesn't she!' She turned abruptly towards Sean Muldoon with her most brilliant smile. He was only fifteen, pale and freckled like his sister Moira, but being the object of so ravishing a smile brought the colour to his cheeks and loosened his tongue in conversation he never knew he had.

CHAPTER NINE

Two days later O'Malley called on Riley. The tinkers had not set off, on account of Kate's condition. The slightest exertion made her breathless and the swinging of the caravan, it was feared, would not make for improvement. Kate was asking to see Tessa and Spider Murphy had sent him up to see if it was possible.

'Just in the afternoons, until she's well enough to travel,' said O'Malley. 'The days can be awful long for an invalid, and since she rescued Kate the Murphys think your Tessa is one of God's own angels.'

'She sold 'em a goat,' said Riley with a touch of pride.

'Did you now?' O'Malley smiled at Tessa. 'And how did you go about that?'

'I told them what Father Donaghue said: how he had it from a Dublin doctor's own lips that goat's milk was good for what she's got. "A boon to asthmatics," ' Tessa repeated carefully, ' "and a cure for convulsions." Have you not seen the mangy cows they trail about, Mr O'Malley?'

'I have so.'

'I told 'em to start on the goat's milk straight away. They even noticed a difference with the cheese.'

'She's surely improving,' said O'Malley. 'It's nothing short of a miracle!' He turned to his friend with a smile. 'They'd be pleased for Tessa to go down.'

'Oh, will you let me go, Da? A bit of company will liven her up, and the sooner she's on her feet the sooner the knackers'll take to the road and we can all get back to what we were.'

In the face of such logic Riley could only nod his shaggy head and agree; yet he knew it was all down to O'Malley's charm. That fella had a way of handling things beyond belief!

'Sure, you'd persuade a fella that Ennabrugh was a garden of roses. Ye can go down in the afternoons, Tessa, but I want you back before dark.'

When Tessa went down, she found the valley suffused with a different atmosphere. All the community feeling of the past few days had gone. Now the Fair was over, and the excitement concerning Kate had settled, the crofters resumed their own lives, and kept away from the uncertain tempers of the tinkers, who felt themselves to be thwarted by circumstances. The open road called; the chimneys of the big houses called; and the castration of pigs could not be left much longer. They were as impatient to get on the road as the people of Ennan were keen to see them on it.

Tessa had imagined company for Kate and herself – little gatherings of Marie Jane and the Jams girls – but she had reckoned without this invisible curtain which had slowly been drawn over the communal relationship. When taking the goat down for the first time, she had been conscious of being the only goy, the only young woman with no bright scarf on her head. The only language she heard was Shelta, and most of the tinkers ignored her, except for Spider and his wife and Kate's sisters, who could not do enough to show their appreciation, not only for their daughter's return, but also for the difference already apparent in her health.

Mick also became more attentive to his eldest sister, especially when Tessa was about. He always contrived to be either entering or leaving the caravan at the same time as Tessa, making sure his body touched hers as they jostled in the doorway. He congratulated her on the goat's milk cure and stood, hands deep in pockets, while she showed Kate how to milk the small, hardy goat. Face flushed, sleeves rolled, head bent to show the back of her white neck, Tessa explained the procedure.

'Will ye remember, now, to milk her twice a day, morning and night or she'll dry up? Otherwise, she'll keep on for three years. And you must keep 'em clean, not only the udders, but the flanks. If you don't wash 'em, the milk'll taste of goats!'

Mick reflected that this was the second day of Kate's improvement; she could walk round the van now without a wheeze. Her dark eyes sparkled and her face was no longer drawn, but infused with a kind of inner light. He wondered how much of his sister's animation was due to the new milk and how much was due to the owner of some spilt tobacco he had found on the top step of the caravan. Neither he nor his da smoked.

When Tessa went into Murphy's caravan the following afternoon, Kate was not there. She stood for a moment looking down at the neatly made covers on the shelf-bed, at the crochet work, the intricate carpentry, the lamps and brasses.

'Brought you some water.' Mick set down a pail on the bottom step and perched himself on the top.

'Oh, you shouldn't – ' Conscious of the camp's protocol, she looked beyond Mick to see if anyone was outside, and knowing how strained the balance of the tinker-crofter relationship was, added, 'Did anyone see ye?' He did not answer and she went on hurriedly. 'They won't like it – I mean, the chief's son fetching water for a goy . . .' Her voice trailed off. The water was not needed yet, and besides, he had never done it before. 'Have you no work to do?' The way he sat looking at her with unashamed interest made her stomach give a little lurch.

'Work? Not when I can pass the time of day with a heroine, a beautiful heroine like yourself.'

'You'd better go, Mick.' She tempered the request. 'Thanks for the water. You really shouldn't have bothered. Now please go away. You know how strict your ma is.'

'Fornication, and all! She'll not stand for any fornication in Murphy's camp – do you know what that means, Tessa Riley?' His little round eyes questioned her. Tessa had a hazy idea of what Mrs Murphy meant, but was not for discussing it. 'Didn't learn much at that school, did you? Nor did I for that matter. You didn't know I came to lessons, off and on, did you? I know all about the schoolmaster's house; all of them benches in the front room, and chalks and slates, and all them books, spelling, sums, poetry. Best was when the Excise got wind of his poteen, and sure, was it not like seeing the glory of heaven itself when they marched him off to jail! See, I know a lot!'

'There were only a few of us at Feeney's school. Sure, I'd have remembered you if you'd been there when I was.'

'I'm sure you would not!' He gave a bitter laugh. 'None of you ever took notice of the knackers' lads. We came and went for a few weeks here, and a few days there.' His voice sank to a harsh undertone. 'We were treated as though we'd got the scurvy; none of you at Ennan even talked to us! I heard you telling me ma, boasting you could read and write, but where's it got you, tell me that, eh? There you stand,

160

never been any place beyond this stinking great Bog where you were born, and waiting all the year for the knackers to come to give you a bit of excitement. You see,' he ended on a note of smug satisfaction, 'the wheel of fate has a way of turning hasn't it?'

'If your feelings are hurt because I didn't remember you, it's sorry I am, but it's the divil of a time ago.' She took a deep breath. 'And if you've come to make trouble, don't bother. Will you get out of that doorway and I'll get on with washing down the goat. Your ma won't like you being here, and besides, Kate will be back soon.'

'Kate'll not be back for some time.'

'Why?' Her eyes opened wide in alarm. 'Where is she?'

'Ach, you're so clever, aren't ye, Tessa Riley?'

'Oh, for God Almighty's sake, Mick, stop your blather. Where's Kate?'

'I sent one o' the tinsmith's lads with a message supposed to come from Martin Jarvey, saying that she'd to go and see him.'

'Martin Jarvey? What for?'

'What for?' he mimicked. 'What the divil do you think for? I found some tobacco here, and put two and two together.'

Tessa was momentarily stunned. She recalled Kate's long hair brushing Martin's cheek as he put the tent up. His remorse when she'd gone missing, and how he had raced up on the donkey, walked back talking to her. Yes, and all Marie Jane's little jealousies. Kate and Martin? Yes, it could be. Oh, Marie Jane will kill him. But in the meantime, she did not know what Mick was up to, and besides, what would happen if his ma, or indeed anyone, found them alone in the caravan?

Suddenly Mick turned from his sitting position, pulled the door closed and stood up.

'While Kate's away the mice will play.'

Tessa's face flooded into a sudden scarlet as she understood his meaning. 'Ah, go on with you Mick Murphy!' she exclaimed, hoping to show him she was taking his suggestion in fun. 'I must be getting on, and I think you should be doing the same . . .' Her voice trailed to a stop for, as she stooped to pick up the pail, she felt his hand, hot and moist, on her ankle. It slowly moved beneath her skirts to the bend of her knee. For a second she remained immobile with shock. Then, with a violent reflex action, she took hold of the pail and flung the water over him.

161

'You bitch!' he yelled. 'You bloody goy bitch!' Red faced, spluttering, and the words choking in his throat he seized her arm and pushed her back against the wall. The water dripped from his hair and ran in rivulets down his face. 'You shouldn't have done that,' he said thickly. 'No one's done that to me before.'

'And no one's ever laid hands on Proud Riley's daughter before! That'll teach you not to maul me!'

'I'll put me hands anywhere I like on a goy woman, and I'm going to pluck your feathers one by one.' He grinned at her as he eyed Kate's bed, with its neat covers. 'I'm going to take them off one by one, like the feathers off a fowl – and you know how one of them looks!'

'And what the divil do you think I'm going to do? Stand here and let you! And there's another thing, you know how strict your ma is. Lay one of your thieving hands on me and she'd kill you!'

He laughed in her face. 'Don't count on it. Any goy woman's fair game.'

'This one isn't!' She flung the words at him. 'And if your ma doesn't kill ye, Finn Collins will!'

'Ah, I knew it, I did,' he gloated, making a predatory move. 'I guessed there was something between the two of you.'

Tessa swore at herself, wondering what made her make such a statement. 'There's nothing between him and me,' she said quickly. 'But he's wiped the floor with you once!'

But Mick was not listening, and she knew it. He was looking at her, blatantly devouring her with his eyes, and she could do nothing. His gaze turned from her thick brown hair tied neatly back with a ribbon, to the bright spots of anger on her high, wide cheekbones. Her eyes had changed from summer blue to blaze at him like sapphires. Her body was fine in its outrage, so desirable and utterly unlike anything he had ever known.

'I'll ask you just the once. Give us a bit o' what you've been giving to the big fella – and don't try calling out or screaming! Or I'll knock those nice white teeth to the back of your lovely throat!'

The water she had thrown on him had sleekened his hair to a black skull cap, and in the half light of the van it added to her disgust. All the warnings which had accompanied her growing up came back to her now. 'Get them where it hurts most,' Mona Donal's voice echoed from hypothetical situations discussed at the back of O'Malley's cabin. Tessa lashed out, jerking up her knee. Quick as lightning Mick grabbed at her skirts, caught her off balance and pushed her down onto the neat covers of the shelf-bed.

'Let me go!' she writhed beneath his weight. 'For Almighty God's sake, get off – ' His finger and thumb dug into the flesh beneath her chin, closing her windpipe. She choked on the words; she could not breathe. He was using his strength and she thought herself dying. His face went blurred, the roof of the van began to go round and round. With a laugh Mick loosened his hold of her throat, and while she gasped for air his lustful fantasies paraded before him. He was not to be thwarted.

His hands, thick bruiser's hands, were now on her clothes. Her bosom rose and fell with as much fright as his rose with passion. She felt his fingers rummaging about her breasts, trying to find a way in, plucking at the material. The sweat on his forehead mingled with the water she had thrown as he imagined the sight beneath her bodice. He could not wait to have those shapely breasts in front of him, open to his gaze, his touch, his lips.

'Undo 'em,' he muttered harshly. 'Undo the buttons.'

'Like hell . . .' she gasped, feeling sick at the prospect of violence. Surely there'd be tinkers outside, she thought, then realised the van stood apart from the camp on Kate's account. 'You're wasting your time. They're sewn on with me da's wax thread.' Fear of her father now vied with fear for herself. Proud Riley's daughter taken by a knacker! He'd never live down the disgrace. She thought of the Sacred Heart on the black oak dresser, but her mind would not focus on prayer. 'I've made me own clothes – ' she gasped again. 'It'll take more than you to get 'em off. No knacker's going to get the better o' me!'

'We'll see about that!'

Helplessly, Tessa saw his hands fumbling, unfastening his breeches. Oh Mother of God, help me! Sickened, she turned her eyes away from the sight of such aggression.

The struggle was on again. Mick's hands, hot and moist, were up the side of her trapped legs. He swore at the unexpected barrier of calico drawers. His other conquests had worn nothing beneath their skirts, but this one had to! He laughed, an ugly belligerent sound. The sudden challenge was exhilarating. He tore at the neckline of her blouse. It didn't give. Tessa's neck jerked almost to dislocation.

He muttered something in Shelta, each phrase full of desire and frustration. He was getting nowhere. The buttons held firm in their waxen thread, their very shape, the roundness of them, mocking him. No longer were her struggles provocative. Time was running out, and a vague notion came that Tessa Riley was beginning to get the better of him. His lustful passion, which had been teased and inflamed, could contain itself no longer. He had to settle for what he could get, and thrust his body against her disarranged skirts and petticoats.

He dropped like a sack onto her, taking her breath away and making her gasp. She turned her head away in revulsion as the force of his body butted against her, snorting and grunting like one of the Aunt Hanratty's pigs. With a final shudder he rolled off the shelf-bed onto the floor. Tessa, far from lying supine beneath the nauseating experience, had gathered strength. She leapt up, leaving him snorting into the flood of his own passion, and in her panic to escape didn't even realise how she got through the door. Pushing, shoving, lifting the latch . . . stumbling up the steps . . . down the other side. Out into the air, the fresh, the beautiful air!

'Kate! Kate!' She heard a voice yelling frantically. It was her own. 'Mrs Murphy! Help! Help!'

The tinkers came running towards her. Mrs Murphy, fearing for Kate, hurried on their heels. Tessa threw a terrified glance at the caravan. Mrs Murphy went in and the others packed themselves round the door to witness the spectacle of the chief's son struggling up from the disorder of the bedcovers trailing on the floor, and at the same time trying to button his stained breeches.

News travels fast, and this particular piece of news went out on the spring wind, whispering urgently to the ears of tinkers and crofters alike, fetching them at a pace.

Kate and Martin Jarvey exchanged alarmed glances. They were sitting on upturned boxes in the corrugated shack which housed the Jarveys' donkey tackle.

'God save us, Martin. Sure, they've found the van empty and they'll think I've gone off again! I knew there was something wrong when I discovered you'd not sent the message . . .'

I hope to heaven it wasn't Marie Jane, thought Martin. Supposing she'd got wind of him and Kate and wanted to get Kate into bother with her da? But, no. Marie Jane was not vindictive; she had little jealousies, but spite wasn't in her. Besides, he'd felt for some time that she'd only been stringing him along.

'It's our Mick,' Kate was saying. 'He's found out about us. He's had it in for you ever since you put up the tent. He's told me da!'

'C'mon then, Katey, let's go and see.' He took her hand and pulled her up from the box.

'No.' She shrank back. 'You can't, you being a goy and all. No, Martin,' she begged. 'Mick will get at me da, set him going against you, and he'll make sure I'll never see you again. Oh, Martin, I couldn't stand that . . .'

Martin pushed back his floppy hair. 'Just let him try. Whatever's going on, Kate, we must face it. We'll have to sooner or later. Katey,' he lowered his voice, 'I love you, and nothing on God's earth is going to keep us apart. It's all got to come out in the open. Your da will be on the road in a couple o' days or so, now that Tessa's goat milk is doing you good. You've got to decide whether you want to stay in Ennan with me, or take to the road with me. With your da, if he'll have me, or without yer da, if he won't.'

'Ah, you make it all sound so easy, Martin Jarvey. Still, ye always did, from the puttin' up of the tent to the puttin' down of Mick!'

'Trust me, Kate. I'll never let you down, never.'

And so they came upon the gathering where Marie Jane, to whom Tessa had blurted out the whole terrifying experience in a series of dry, choking sobs, stood with her arms protectively round her friend. Tessa felt cold, and the strength which had enabled her to combat Mick Murphy now deserted her.

'Jasus, she's goin' to faint!'

'She looks just as pale as her ma used to – '

'Fetch a stool. For the love of God get her something to sit on.'

'It's the shock just settling in.'

'What the divil's happened? Is it that bloody Mick?'

Marie Jane bent down by the stool Tessa was sitting on, and with a mug in her hands tried to force some poteen between the stiff lips.

'Ach, the poor, poor girleen – '

'Mother of God, these knackers've got something to answer for.'

The comments swarmed about Tessa's head like a swarm of wild bees. Marie Jane draped a horse blanket about her shoulders and forced more poteen down her. The rough spirit made short work of Tessa's state. She inhaled deeply and the swarm of bees gradually cleared. But, as the life coursed through her veins, so did fear. Fear of Mrs Murphy. Mick had said the tinkers regarded any goy woman as fair game . . . He had said not to count on his mother . . . And where was Finn, she wondered. Oh, dear God, if only he was here, standing with the others. Just to look at him would have made all the difference. She suddenly felt angry at the Aunt Hanratty for keeping Finn at the far end of the valley. He wouldn't have heard the noise, the running feet – God Almighty, she never thought feet would be running or a crowd assembling on her account . . .

Heads turned as Spider Murphy approached. The assembled tinkers parted to let him through. Mrs Murphy, after listening to Marie Jane's account of the attack – for Tessa could not bring herself to relate any of it in public – turned her black eyes on her son. He stood in an attitude of insolence, hands in pockets, feet planted firmly apart. In that silence the full effect of Mick's conduct began to sink into the souls of the spectators.

Then Mrs Murphy let loose. 'Is this the truth that I'm hearing about Spider Murphy's only son?' She spoke with enforced calm.

'So?' answered Mick angrily, not meeting his mother's eyes. 'She's only a goy.' He removed his hand from his pocket and waved it arrogantly. 'I don't see what in the name o' God Almighty you're blathering about.'

'It's you I'm blathering about. You think you're above the rules – your mother's rules – just because you're the chief's son. You've been nothing but a disgrace to the name o' Murphy!'

'I'm telling ye, Ma, for Christ Almighty's sake, she's only a goy. Why all this?'

'All this!' she yelled, the lines in her long face narrowing even further. 'What you do on the fairground is nothing to me. But in Murphy's camp, like all the others that travel with Murphy, you abide by the rules. You've proved yerself a bad lot. You were too lazy and good-for-nothing as a lad – didn't even learn to read or write, even though you knew it would've pleased your da. And at the wrestling the other day you dishonoured your da's name by going agin the rules and hitting the goy's head on the lump o' rock. You deserved the beating you got – '

'But, Ma, for – '

'An' then you tried to bring discredit on the good people o' this valley by accusing 'em of harbouring your sister. And as for the way

166

you put yourself out to go looking for her, and then lying through your teeth about it.'

'Jasus,' breathed Mick, looking about for support. 'Jasus Christ!'

'Will ye stop your blasphemin' tongue, Mick Murphy. God alone knows you've enough sins to keep you in purgatory for ever! And as if that were not enough you've brought a terrible shame to the camp. This goy, Proud Riley's daughter, is in Murphy's debt for ever. Not only did she get your sister out o' the keeper's clutches, but she's cured her brathin' with the goat's milk – a thing I never thought to see. And now for the chief's son to rape – '

'But he didn't,' cut in Tessa, terrified of the word and its dreadful implications. 'I'll not have it put about that I've been raped – ' All heads swivelled in her direction. 'He wasn't getting the better of me! I fought him off. Look at all me skirts wet and . . . sticky. You can see the same on him.' Modesty prevented her saying more. As if on puppet strings, all the heads turned to Mick, observing his stained breeches. Those who had been first on the scene with Mrs Murphy corroborated the state they had found him in. Mick's insolent stance gave way to a sheepish shuffle.

'Rape was in your mind. It blackened your heart, and you attacked her. You coward! You insolent bloody blaggard! For the son, the only son, of Spider Murphy to bring such a foul deed to the camp is a terrible thing.'

Spider was silent, and seemed to regard the proceeding as a neutral who was not yet for taking sides. His wife, still overwhelmed, lifted her jewelled hands in an attitude of sorrow and despair. 'No one could ever point a finger at the Murphys. We've held our heads high at every fair in Ireland and beyond, and now we'll be the talk of every gathering. For when we split up and the Mahoneys settle to their chimneys, and the Duffys to their horses, will they not snigger and tell with relish of the day they caught Mick Murphy with his breeches down, and of how that young divil went agin the mother that bore him!'

'Eh, woman, don't take on so,' soothed Spider, whose face had started twitching; he was more deeply affected by his wife's sorrow than by her anger. 'Ach, what do you want to make yourself badly for? The girleen's not been harmed – '

'Only because she had the courage to fight him off! Oh, what if it was the other way round, eh? What if one o' them had attacked one of your own daughters? Sure, there'd be daggers drawn then – and rightly!'

'Ay, it would be so.' He shrugged his thin shoulders and tugged at his earring. 'But what's been done is done.'

'That's what troubles me, Spider Murphy, and how it was done and all! In our very caravan, and on his sister's bed.' Her narrow eyes took in Tessa. 'And that young woman's been good to our Kate.'

'She's not the only one,' Mick accused. 'Ask our Kate who else has been good to her! I told you we shouldn't have come to Ennan, and none of ye would listen – '

'Don't you dare to drag your sister into this! It's you, me first born, that's caused trouble like I wished I'd never lived to see! And you stand there defying me!' Fury blazing in her furrowed face, she snatched up a wheel spoke lying on the ground and flew at him. 'Get out of the camp, out of the valley, out of me sight! Get out, and never let me see your face again!' She would have struck him and he would not have resisted, but Spider came between them and dragged his son away.

'Will ye come away now, Mick? Get your stuff and go quiet, like. You've done enough damage, enough to last a lifetime.' Mick roughly shook his father's hand off his arm.

'Go, as your da bids you.' Mrs Murphy was suddenly solemn. 'And take wid ye, if you can, all the bad luck and trouble you've brought on a dacent camp with your dishonourable ways. Go on! Get off, before you earn a mother's curse!'

With an arrogant glare Mick slowly turned and ground the heel of his boot into the ground on which he stood. This grinding of the heel signified total rejection of family and tribe. Hands in pockets he strode off without even stopping to collect his stuff. They could keep it. He'd had enough. He was sick of the petty codes and restrictions. He knew of fairground proprietors who would welcome him to stand their boxing booths on a regular basis. The bright lights, the carefree life called. Sure, his luck hadn't been bad after all; it had been good, for he had got his freedom. He was banished, and relieved to be.

No one spoke. A great sense of awe came on the gathering as they watched his departure. The silence was profound, as if they were witnessing a ceremony of excommunication from the church. Solemnly, they began to drift away, the men to their tasks, the women to the children.

And, like a god of vengeance bent on retribution, Proud Riley bore down the hillside. The wind, it seemed, had brushed his ear too. Without a word, and with as solemn an aspect as Mrs Murphy, he took his daughter's arm. Still nothing was said. With a last lingering look at Marie Jane and O'Malley, at Kate, and Martin Jarvey standing at her side, Tessa went with her father. They, too, like the excommunicated, walked away in silence.

O'Malley looked towards his daughter, and they both looked beyond Martin and Kate to Spider and his wife. Not wanting to intrude on family matters, O'Malley turned and Marie Jane made to follow him home.

'Will you wait awhile, Mr O'Malley?' Spider's words halted his steps. Both he and his daughter turned back. 'Seeing this young fella is a goy, he'd better have a witness of these proceedings from his own race.'

'Oh, yes!' put in Martin, who much preferred O'Malley to witness whatever went on than his father or uncle, who, if sent for, would spoil his chances by the aggressive attitude he knew they would adopt.

'Now,' said Mrs Murphy to her daughter. 'What did the spalpeen of a brother mean about someone being good to you?'

'The truth is, if I may speak, Mrs Murphy,' Martin said easily, 'The truth is that I love your daughter and wish to marry her.'

Spider's earring moved as his face twitched. 'Is this true Kate?'

'It is so, Da. I love him so much that I'll not be parted from him.' As though afraid of having said too much, or of being snatched away, she stepped towards Martin and stood close to his side. He put a protective arm about her shoulder.

Marie Jane could scarcely believe her eyes, but Martin was not even aware of her presence. His future was at stake, his and Kate's.

'But he's a goy,' said Spider. 'Does that mean nothing to you?'

'No, Da. It does not.'

'I'll become a tinker, Mr Murphy, if you'll have me. I'll marry Kate according to your custom. I've no wish to take her from her people, but if you'll not have me – "

'I can vouch for him,' put in O'Malley, quickly adjusting to the change in Martin's affection; he had thought Martin might have made him a good son-in-law, but the Fair had obviously changed all that! 'He's an ambitious young man, he'll go far. The valley's too small for the likes of him. Will I tell you now, Murphy, he'll make the finest travellin' man; he'll be a credit to you; and your girl there will have a good husband.'

If Marie Jane could scarce believe her eyes before, she was now doubting her ears. Her father was talking about the young man who was hers but a week ago!

'You've lost a son, Mrs Murphy,' he continued, not unkindly, 'but in Martin Jarvey, you'll find another.'

'Ma,' Kate hesitated. 'Da, will you not give us your blessing? I don't want to leave you and me little sisters, but if you'll not admit Martin . . .'

'What do you say, Spider?' asked Mrs Murphy, who was not unfavourable to the arrangement. She had seen young Jarvey about and noted his kindness to Kate and the little girls.

Spider nodded. 'I've taken a liking to him already. I could do with a good right-hand man. Mick was all the time at the boxing booths. Tell me, young fella, can you read or write?'

'I can do both, and sure, I'll teach Kate.' Spider let out a contented breath. 'And you'll accept all our customs and laws, and our way of life?'

'I will. And Kate can teach me Shelta,' he said eagerly.

'And you'll marry her over the brush, as our custom is?'

'I will so – as soon as Kate names the day.'

'Is it all agreed?' Mrs Murphy smiled, showing her gold teeth. Her heart lifted; sure God never sent a trial without a blessing to follow.

'Your hand to it, young man,' The chief put out his hand and slapped Martin's palm in the manner of the tinkers.

'To signify your intention to everyone, Martin, you must give our Kate a neckerchief to tie over her hair; that means she's spoken for.'

Martin went scarlet. He reached up to his open-necked shirt. 'Mother of God! I don't wear one,' he said in a panic. 'I've not got one!'

Mrs Murphy handed him a bright scarf from her pocket.

'Oh, God bless you,' he breathed, clutching it. 'May God and Mary bless you, Mrs Murphy.' And to Kate, 'Does she carry them about, in case! Do I put it on for you?' He was so happily agitated his fingers shook. Kate stood before him as a bride stands at the altar, and with the others looking on he tied back her long black hair and sealed the tying with a kiss.

Proud Riley, always a silent man, asked no explanation from his daughter – O'Malley had supplied that – and Tessa dared not broach the subject because of its very nature. The dreadful incident had been what Riley referred to in his own mind as a 'close shave', and he was determined nothing like it would ever happen again.

That this 'close shave' had taken place at all justified all his past and future care. It cemented for all time not only his mistrust but his hatred of the tinkers. Ungrateful, dirty, thievin' beggars, he thought. Hadn't all the valley turned out to search for Murphy's girl, including Riley himself, and Teresa. And even though they knew Ennabrugh in all its seasons, that was no guarantee of safety. The Great Bog was treacherous, unpredictable and no respecter of persons. They had risked their lives, and Teresa had ruined her clothes; she'd even thought of the goat's milk cure for the asthma. And how did young Murphy show his gratitude? That the Murphys were grief-stricken at the conduct of their son, and had banished and disowned him, was no consolation to Riley.

He should never have paid heed to O'Malley's persuasive tongue. 'You may as well put her in a convent,' he had said in that soft, easy way of his. 'Give the girleen a bit of interest, let her loose a little.' And he'd still hesitated, God help him; he should have known. 'We're only talking about her coming down for a few hours to watch the knackers set up their camp. The greatest bloody event after a winter of nothin', and you're twittering and dithering like Mrs Jams!' And they had laughed at O'Malley's mimicry of Mrs Murphy. 'There'll be no fornication in Murphy's camp.'

Sure, I must be going soft in the head! The very idea of meself being talked into letting Teresa spend the afternoons with a tinker's daughter! True, they'd bought a goat. But what had got into him? he wondered. Tinkers! The only good 'un was a dead 'un! By all the saints, if Mick Murphy had had his way with Teresa's daughter, sure he'd have killed him. Perhaps it was as well that Mick had gone before he had arrived. He had set about Clancy and drawn blood all those years ago in defence of Teresa Donnelly. Yes, if Mick had been there, the story might have ended differently.

From what O'Malley had told him, Teresa had defended herself

171

well. She was a daughter any man could be proud of. And so he went on torturing himself. If I'd not let O'Malley talk me into this idea of escorts at the Fair and them going about in fours. But, with the Fair ended, her escort had gone back to his crazy aunt and her pigs. It was his own fault entirely that his daughter had been the victim of such a mean and cowardly attack. He broke out in a sweat each time he thought of the possible consequences, and yearned more than ever for some younger, stronger man to take over the responsibility. It was at times like this that he felt old.

And now, before the incident was cold, O'Malley had the devil's own nerve to ask him if Teresa could go down to some practices he was organising for the Long Dance in July!

'This could be the last year of the Long Dance,' O'Malley had said. 'The way things are going, and all. Your Tessa is a fine dancer, sure she's got the staying power. Wouldn't it be a marvellous thing now, Riley old son, if Ennan was to win the last of the Dances?'

Riley was curious. 'And why do ye think it'll be the last?' he had asked.

O'Malley had pursed his lips reflectively. 'The Long Dance has always had an unsettling effect on the community.'

'The Fair's not done too badly either.'

'But you know what I mean, Riley old son. Folk coming up from the town impress the young 'uns with their clothes and their ways, and the things they talk about. Each year more and more go down. It's like the Pied bloody Piper. Times are changing. Do you remember Pat Feeney reciting that poem when he'd had a skinful? What a sight he was with his face aflame and his stomach out before him.' He let out a sigh, long and slow, as though loathe to dismiss the memory of happier times. 'And there's another thing,' he had said at last. 'Have you noticed Lord Fitzcarron's steward and Mr Kildare out and about more than usual? You could say it was the Fair that brings 'em, but I think there's more afoot, Riley old son. So, we'll not see your Tessa at any of the practices? All the valley will be out. Do you remember now when you used to play for the Dance? Riley on his silver flute? A hooley without Riley on the flute, they'd say, isn't a hooley at all. As I was telling you, all the valley will be out; the nights will be lighter, and not a tinker in sight . . .'

His words had fallen on deaf ears.

CHAPTER TEN

Sitting in the loft, knees hugged to her chin, Tessa stared disconsolately at the ruined gown. Encrusted with mud and peat, it lay crumpled and stuffed in the corner where she had kicked it, a relic of Ennan Fair.

Blinking back hot tears, she tried to think up a plot, a scheme, but nothing would come: even her strategies seemed to have deserted her. Her mind kept coming back to the weekly visit with Marie Jane. How could she survive without the anticipation of it, the gossip, the news, and talk of Finn Collins – for Marie Jane always had an idea what he was up to.

Yesterday, she had watched the heavy clouds gathering over Ennabrugh, grouping together to flee across the heavens as though giving chase to the raggle-taggle line of tinkers making their way out of the valley. She had seen the barrel-shaped caravan, swinging seductively from side to side, pulled by the piebald pony. How thrilled she'd been to see it when they arrived. It seemed years, not days ago. If only she had known. The clouds had gathered pace, scudding after the tinkers, chivvying, hurrying, until the landscape was clear. Good riddance, as the Aunt Hanratty would say. Well, good riddance and bad cess and bad everything else to Mick!

Thank God they'd banished him. Oh, thank God they had! For apart from her da, she felt sure Finn would have gone for him. It was natural enough for a da to defend or avenge his daughter's honour, but everyone would have wondered what the divil Finn Collins had to do with it.

Wherever he was, whatever he was doing at the time, she now thanked all the saints – and St Teresa in particular – that Finn had not been present when she had shouted for help. His absence – although at the time she would have given her eyeteeth for a glance of him – had preserved the secret of their friendship. If her da had got wind of that, Almighty God alone knew what would have happened, · especially coming after Mick's attack.

173

She sat there, knees to chin, and although not aware of it, rocked slightly to and fro, silently sorrowing, bewailing her fate; it was clear she was not to be allowed down into the valley again. No more afternoons with Marie Jane at the O'Malleys' cabin. No giggles with Peggy Jams. No practising for the Long Dance – and she wouldn't put it past her da to stop her from going down to the actual event! And all because of Mick bloody Murphy!

Ach, he was a bad lot. Looking back at the various incidents, from the squashing up in the caravan onwards, she might have guessed what was going on in his head but there was such a lot happening, and all at the same time. And besides, with such a lovely fella as Finn at your side, who could waste time worrying what a jumped-up little knacker was up to?

The very phrase recalled what Mick had said about Pat Feeney's school, and, yes, she was the first to admit that none of them bothered with the dirty, scabby knacker lads. Why should they? Having been imbued over the years with some of her father's intolerence towards them, it was no wonder she and the others ignored their existence.

She stopped her rocking. Anyways, he'd met his match with her! And the water she'd thrown on him – he hadn't expected that! Nor had he expected to be caught with his breeches down or to be the recipient of his fellows' coarse jokes. She immediately cast him out of her mind; he was not worthy even of thought. She began to dwell on the good things of the Fair: it had brought her to know Kate, and for the hundredth time she wondered what had happened about Kate and Martin and Marie Jane; it had cleared up her fears of the keeper suing her da for compensation because of the gun; but above all it had brought her Finn Collins.

Tessa recognised that she always felt miserable for a few days after the Fair, but this curtailment of her liberty – especially after the recent freedom – made the outlook particularly grim. Her mood was a grey one, to match a grey day, a grey future. Future? The word came out on a long breath. She had not thought of one until recently, and now each thought was linked with Finn. Daydreams! Mother of God, she was getting as fanciful as Marie Jane.

Tessa was glad the tinkers had gone, but the silence seemed unnatural and their going had left a void, an emptiness. No longer did the hammerings, shoutings, barking of dogs and braying of donkeys echo about the hillside. Their huge camp fire, that bold blazing symbol of their intrusion and presence, no longer lit up the valley after dark; the enchanted grottoes had been changed back to hovels and huts; the wild landscape was no longer made warm by the red and yellow glow. The light had been snuffed out, and the dank mists began to rise.

While Tessa was brooding in the cabin on the hillside, in the valley Marie Jane was conspiring with her father.

'Go on, Da,' she wheedled, watching him mending a broken chair. 'Oh, go on. He'll be glad of a chinwag with his old friend – '

'Glad of a chinwag? Riley?' cut in Mrs O'Malley. She was trying not to be impatient with the delicate Little Annie whose fringe needed to be trimmed, and who would not keep still while the operation took place. Each time the scissors advanced her head shrank down into her curved spine. 'Glad of a chinwag? That fella would happily spend the rest of his life without even passing the time of day with you, and well you know that, Marie Jane. Now will you stop bothering your da and set them lily-white hands to the spuds?'

'Dealing with Riley's like flogging a dead donkey,' her father hedged, trying to keep the balance between wife and daughter. 'He'll not forget Mick Murphy's attack in a hurry, and he'll not let Tessa out of his sight for years, not down here, anyways.'

'Don't I know all that!' exclaimed Marie Jane. Eager to convince she stood up suddenly, and the stool slid from beneath her, crashing to the ground. The noise startled Annie into another bout of wailing. Ignoring the noise, Marie Jane tackled her father again. 'What I'm asking is for you to go up because you want to talk to him!'

'About what, in the name o' God?'

Marie Jane appealed to the assembled family. 'Will you listen to him!' She raised her hands in mock exasperation. 'Him who can talk the hind leg off a donkey asking me what he could talk about!'

'Proud Riley's not the easiest fella to deal with, you know, even for me.'

'So, if you want a reason for calling on him take the papers the priest left. You've passed them on to Tessa for years. Just because she can't come down here doesn't mean she's got to do without her reading stuff. So, you'll have to take them up, won't you?' He squinted up at her. She paused, rounding her mouth slowly. 'Oh, Da, surely you're teasing all this time. Have you no regard at all for the education of your eldest daughter?'

'Education!' yelled Mrs O'Malley. 'All you've ever thought about, miss, is your looks!'

'Ah, well now.' O'Malley laid down the chair. His thin face creased slowly into a smile. His eyes behind the spectacles livened up. Any display of inventiveness or downright cunning always pleased him. 'Ah, well, now,' he repeated. 'I see it all. You want me to go up there with the papers – and yourself. So while I'm talking to Riley, you can scramble into the loft where Tessa will help you with your reading! I'm to appeal to Riley's belief in education, pleading that me eldest'll be deprived of her lessons! By the Grace of God,' he chuckled, 'it's good. Sure, you're as crafty as a cartload of monkeys!' He was pleased. He was happy.

Turning to Little Annie, O'Malley took the scissors from his wife and coaxed the child. 'Will you come to your da, sweetheart? Here, let's kiss away those tears . . . that's my girleen. Come to your da and I'll tell you about the beautiful fairy who has a special pair of scissors for trimming fringes. But, she only allows them to be used on very special little girls. "And how about Annie O'Malley?" I asked. "Oh," says she. "Annie O'Malley is a very special little girl." Come on your da's knee, now. Once upon a time . . .'

Marie Jane, Pat, Dion, Bridget and Tim stopped what they were doing to listen, charmed by the silver-tongued voice, backed by the solemn hiss of the lamp and the occasional splutter of the fire. Mrs O'Malley sighed and began to peel the potatoes.

The following afternoon Tessa had just finished milking the goats when O'Malley and Marie Jane arrived. She hurriedly wiped her hands on a piece of hessian and ran out to meet them.

'Oh, praise be to God, Marie Jane!' she laughed. 'Oh, am I glad to set me eyes on you. You've not changed a bit,' she giggled. 'Oh, 'tis the wonderful, darling crature that you are! If you'd been the blessed Saint Teresa herself I'd not be more amazed!' The girls hugged each other and, stifling their amusement at Marie Jane's cunning, walked sedately after O'Malley into the croft whre Riley was sewing together a new pair of leather pumps for Tessa.

'See, Da,' she said, seeing his astonishment which if anything surpassed her own. 'Here's Mr O'Malley! He's brought me the papers from the priest. Isn't it real dacent of him? He wants to know if I can still help Marie Jane with her reading.' Turning quickly to the visitors she asked, 'Would ye care from some tay, Mr O'Malley, and you too, Marie Jane?' Without giving anyone time to reply to either question, Tessa took a deep breath and set the kettle to boil.

After the tea and a short period of talk, led mainly by O'Malley, the two young women scrambled into the loft, and O'Malley, on the pretext of interest in the spring sowing of potatoes, inveigled Riley outside.

'I still can't get over seeing you!' declared a delighted Tessa to her friend. 'You've saved my life. At least in a convent you can have a chinwag with the other nuns! You'll keep coming?' Satisfied by the emphatic nod of ringlets, Tessa jerked her head toward the valley. 'I saw them go.' She hesitated. 'Are you still going with Martin Jarvey?'

'Chance would be a fine thing,' came the cheerful reply. 'Did you not know that he's gone off with Kate Murphy?'

'What do you mean, "gone off"? Left his da and uncle?'

'He has so. Said he wanted to get on, make something of himself, but that his da and uncle had no go in 'em, no ambition.'

'But, where've they gone? Spider Murphy wouldn't let her go with a goy.'

'Ah, now,' Marie Jane wagged a finger. 'That's just were you're wrong! Spider welcomed him as a son; sure, he was that taken with him. What do you think o' that? Martin Jarvey with the knackers! Mother of God, the things that happen at Ennan Fair!'

'How do you know all this?'

'I was there. It happened before me very eyes, just after you'd gone. They asked me da to stay as witness. He brought Kate before they left – not that I wanted to see her. She was terrible sad at going without even a sight of you. Martin wanted to bring her up – Christ Almighty, I nearly died! Anyways, I soon got them off that tack – just think of what your da'd have said!' Tessa nodded. 'Kate sends her thanks. Sure, it's too small a word, she said, for all you've done for her. Do you know she's even got breath enough now to do a little jig! Martin had to stop her before she went too fast. So protective of her

177

he was, and her looking up at him through all that black hair – enough to make you sick!'

'I've seen you doing it often enough.'

'Well . . .' Marie Jane drawled on a smile, 'that's different! Oh, and they took the little goat with 'em, of course. Called it Riley, in remembrance and all o' that. But I will admit they seemed well suited. And Martin was all boastful, like, saying he'd soon have enough money for a caravan for him and Kate – no tarpaulin rigs or tents for them!'

'Don't you mind about it?' Tessa squinted up in the half light of the loft. 'Not even one little bit? You seemed really set on him.'

'I was, a bit. He's the best up here; at least he's got some ambition. He always wanted to get out of the valley and I thought that if I stayed with him it would be a way out.'

An uneasy notion had suddenly crept into Tessa's mind. She hoped her friend was not going to latch onto Finn. So awful was the thought that she just had to find out. Marie Jane had been quite smitten when she saw Finn all spruced up for the Fair; she hadn't believed it was really him. No, her friend wouldn't . . . or would she? Not that anyone could blame Finn. Tessa couldn't help envying her friend, just a little. Her delicate complexion, rosy cheeks, and her ringlets hanging in gleaming tresses looked as though they had never been disturbed by a puff of wind. She was wearing her black and white check skirt, white blouse and black shoulder shawl. She looked so dainty Tessa was sure she could detect the odour of goats rising from the folds of her own brown skirt.

'I think Finn Collins is as good looking as Martin,' Tessa hoped for a clue to her feelings, 'Especially if he'd the clothes.'

'That's just it, Tessa; if he'd the clothes! You see, me da's always made sure I had nice clothes, a choice. And to get married to someone who couldn't afford his own clothes, still less mine, isn't my idea of a good marriage. No, Tessa, I couldn't be doing with Finn Collins. God Almighty, and that crazy aunt of his sitting there like Dooley's ghost and . . .'

Tessa did not hear the rest. Who cared about clothes anyway? She could always make her own. Happy in the knowledge that Marie Jane was not going after Finn, she returned to the topic of Kate Murphy, wondering why her friend hadn't visited with her.

'To be honest, Tessa, I could have come, but I was jealous – a bit, anyway.'

'What of?'

'Oh, you and Kate . . . and I'd seen Martin sneaking off in that direction.' She parted her red lips in a quick smile. 'And I didn't fancy playing second fiddle to either of you. I knew the tinkers would soon be on the road and you and me'd be our own friendly selves again. But, honest to God, Tessa, if I'd have had any idea Mick would jump on you like that I would have been there. It's gone badly for you, hasn't it? Given your da good reason to keep you from coming to the Long Dance practices. I don't know how you put up with it. I think I'd sooner taste the fires of purgatory! Finn's just the same with that aunt.' She leaned closer. 'You could break out, Tessa, and go against your da. No one would blame you, and surely he can't keep you away from people altogether?'

'I couldn't go against him, Marie Jane; he'd probably wither away, all silent and lonely up here on his own. You see, your da's got six of yous and your ma. It's different when there's only two. I suppose it's the same with Finn and the Aunt.'

'Mother o' God! He's a fella, and he ought to have the guts to get out and leave her to the pigs. But just as you're scared of your da being left, he's terrified stupid of her laying a curse on him – not that I'd be any different. Mother o' God, what a set-up! But, me da's working on him. Anyways, I'll tell you what I was really jealous of: you going off with Frank Kildare like that! What's more, you refused to get up on the horse with him!' She leaned forward, ready for confidences. 'What did you talk about?'

'Didn't talk at all till we got near Flavell's and then it was about Kate.'

'What a waste.' She sat back in disgust. 'What a bloody waste! I don't suppose you even thought to put a word in for service in the house?'

'I did not! Honest, I've not half your nerve. The first time I clapped eyes on Kildare I was getting Billy out of Ennabrugh, and the second time I was getting Kate off the hook. And, the more I think about it, the more I wonder why he went to all that trouble to save Kate from coming up before the RM I tell you, Marie Jane, me heart nearly went out of me body when I saw him that morning with me da. I thought he'd come to take him off because he hadn't the price of the gun which sank in the Bog. But, do you know, he never said a word about it. Has he forgotten do you think?'

'Course he has. I keep telling you, Frank Kildare's the fine fella.' She glanced below, making sure their fathers had not returned, and said almost bashfully. 'I like him, really I do. Honest to God, I think I'm in love with him.'

'How can you be? You don't know anything about him.' Tessa's wide eyes were suddenly warm with concern. 'Don't get too set on him, eh? You've such a flight of fancy it amazes me. I mean, if that's what you want I hope it works out. But how can it?'

Marie Jane laughed softly and tilted her head in an attitude of pertness. 'Wait till I get me housemaid's white cap set on me ringlets, and me apron round my waist! I can see me waiting on her ladyship already! I was called Jane after Lady Fitzcarron, you know. Just imagine, Tessa, those names I've known all me life will suddenly be real people. At least you've seen the back of the big house and that shooting party.'

'I could've done without the last bit,' commented Tessa dryly. 'But I'll tell you what is magnificent: all the lands and farms as far as the eye can see. Although we never set eyes on the gentry, Lady Fitzcarron visits the other side of the estate; the farm cottages there and the sick workers and all of that.'

'I wonder if she's beautiful, and what his lordship looks like.'

'They must be as old as our fathers, or she must, for you to be called after her. If she was married when she was twenty, she'll now be going on thirty-eight, and could be even older.'

Marie Jane was not for pursuing that line of thought. She wriggled contentedly on the bed and continued. 'Of course, when I'm on the estate Frank Kildare is bound to call on his lordship for this and that, and I'll be opening the door, all graceful . . .' Her voice trailed off at the sight of Tessa's smile. 'Ah, you've no faith, Tessa; that's your trouble, no faith or ambition! Another thing, Frank's coming to the Long Dance practices. Now, he's never done that before, so it looks as though he coud be interested in me, doesn't it? And, when he calls on me da he makes the opportunity to talk to me.'

'It certainly sounds encouraging,' admitted Tessa. 'And I hope it works for you, seeing you're so keen. But sure, I don't know what you see in him at all.' She shook her head in bewilderment. 'Do you not think there are women enough of his own age and class?'

'But if he's so taken with them, why is he suddenly spending more time in this godforsaken place – even to attending the practices?'

'Yes, it does seem – oh, I don't know, Marie Jane. I'm almost glad I'm forbidden to go down, except that Finn will be there.' She lowered her voice. 'Will you try and find out about Finn for me, whether he knows about Mick? I mean, he'll not think Mick did anything, will he? I wouldn't like him to think I was . . . easy.'

'He'll not think that! Besides, I bet he doesn't even know. His aunt's cabin is set on its own, away from the rest of us.'

'But word gets round.'

'Not there it doesn't, not to her. No one calls on the Aunt for a chinwag and a cup of tay, not with her reputation! And of course, Finn doesn't want her even to suspect he fancies you!'

'What, in case she puts a curse on me? Just let her try, that's all!'

''Tis all right to be joking about it now, but I'm serious, Tessa. I can't see a future for you with Finn and the Aunt. She'd curse the pair of you like she did his ma and da before him, and you'd both end up keeping 'em company in Ennabrugh. Ach, don't look so solemn, girleen.' She brightened the loft with her smile. 'I'll find out all about him for next time I come – ' She jerked her head toward the compound where the men were. 'That's if there is a next time.'

'Oh, there must be! Sure, I'd suffocate to me death if I wasn't to see you at all.'

'There's always the Long Dance to look forward to. Set your sights on that, and make your plans: what you'll wear, and your shoes, and how you'll do your hair to last out the day – oh, and find a blouse that won't make you sweat or you'll end up as smelly as one of your old goats – '

'But, if he won't let me go to the practices, he'll not let me go to the Dance itself, will he?'

'He'll bring you down himself. He's after a good marriage for you, isn't he? And that's the only place you're likely to meet anyone worth a wedding ring, and he knows it. He'll be hawking you down to every Long Dance like the tinkers hawk their wares!'

'Thanks!' said Tessa indignantly. 'Sure, it's nice to know how you rate me charm!'

'You'd have a better chance of meeting the right fella if you came into service with me.'

Tessa's lips widened into a smile at the outrageous optimism of her friend, and on meeting Marie Jane's upturned glance, she burst out into a great fit of the giggles. 'Oh Almighty God, I'll die! Sure, I've not laughed so much in years! Oh, Marie Jane, it's a splendid imagination you have! Service you say, and you've not even been taken on! You're worse than your da!' Tears flowed, and every attempt to stifle the laughter sent them off into more paroxysms.

'Is that what ye call book learning, Teresa?' The men had returned, and Proud Riley's voice came up the ladder. The giggles choked to an immediate halt.

Tessa thought swiftly. ''Tis Marie Jane's reading, Da.' She winked at her friend. 'Sure, it's enough to make a donkey laugh! But tell Mr O'Malley she's improving and we'll be down straight away.' Then to plant the idea firmly in her father's mind, she added. 'I've given her something to study for when they come up next week.'

And so the precedent was established. Proud Riley did not like the regularity of the visits and doubted their educational purpose, especially when the Jams girls or Una Kelly accompanied them, and O'Malley's calm and benign influence only made him feel uneasy. By nature he was a solitary creature, and he felt vulnerable and unable to cope with or put up a reasonable defence against this invasion of his privacy. He had thought once of telling O'Malley to leave him and his daughter to themselves, but at the back of his mind lurked the secret dread of the cabin becoming as much a cage for Teresa as it had for her mother.

It happened one day that O'Malley was passing the Aunt Hanratty's cabin when Finn vaulted easily over the compound wall.

'So, you're still here, then? Still skivvying for the old Aunt, I see!' Finn leaned over the wall for his spade. 'Sure to God, you're not going up for turf? Riley's not started on his yet; says it's too wet.'

'I don't care if it's like water,' said Finn, solemnly. 'She doesn't know what state it's in. I want a chance to breathe, to get away from herself.'

'Could ye fancy another chance?'

'I could so.'

'Thought that'd cheer you up! I was coming to ask you, in any case: will you turn out to some practices I'm holding for the Long

Dance? I'm after a good turn out; we've got to win this year. What do you say?'

'Count me in on it, Mr O'Malley,' came the eager reply. 'Tell me, it took the knackers long enough to get away. Did Kate's illness hold 'em up?'

'Where the divil have you been putting yourself?'

Finn glanced at the cabin window. 'That's a long story.'

'So, you've not heard about Mick, then?'

'No.'

The cabin door opened and the Aunt Hanratty stepped out in to the compound. 'I might've known it'd be O'Malley wasting the nephew's time again. First ye take him down to town, then you encourage him to go against me in the wrestling. What in God's name are you up to now?' Her black eyes bored into his; it was such a look as had made him cross himself at Tony and Moll's wedding all those years back. 'You've got a lot to answer for, O'Malley. I can see you burning for ever.'

He countered the gimlet eyes steadily, thankful that his spectacles acted as a shield. 'Being convenor for the Long Dance,' he explained affably, thinking it would come better from himself than from Finn, 'I'm drumming up support, organising practices. I want everyone with a good pair of dancing legs. 'Tis only three months away and we need to build up stamina and staying power – '

'It'll take that great lazy lout three months to dig us enough turf for the winter.'

'As I was about to say,' declared O'Malley, his patience wearing thin, 'Your nephew's already pledged himself. We need a good turn out; it could well be the last held at Ennan.'

'And a good thing, an' all,' she croaked. 'We don't need town folk coming up with fancy ideas. I've warned ye.' She pointed at Finn. 'Nothing good will come of this.'

'I'll bid you good day,' put in O'Malley hastily. He did not want one of his prime dancers put off by threats. Taking Finn's arm he moved away. 'If we stand chinwagging, your nephew won't get out to the Bog, and that would be a disaster of the first order!'

Marie Jane's next visit to Riley's cabin found the two girls huddled in the loft.

183

'Did you find out about Finn?' Tessa wanted to know. 'You said you would.'

'And so I did! He didn't know you were spending the afternoons with Kate. And even if he had, he couldn't have called.'

'Why not?'

'One of the pigs died.'

'What difference does that make?' asked Tessa in astonishment. 'Did they have a wake!'

'God help us! You're sounding more cheerful. Last time you looked as miserable as sin.'

'So would you if Mick Murphy had jumped on you, and if that weren't enough, your da kept you from going out! You'd be the first to be sulking! Have you seen Finn yet?'

'I haven't, but me da has. When Finn dashed out to see you that last morning – with not a drop of tay to cross his lips – he had to dash because the Aunt was on to him. So he let out the pigs but didn't wash them down, thinking he'd do it in the afternoon. But of course he didn't get back in the afternoon because we were all waiting for you to fetch Kate from Flavell's place. Anyways, as the bad luck would have it – and sure fate deals out some rotten cards, Tessa – he vaulted over the wall as usual, right onto the carcase of a pig. Of course the Aunt was waiting; said it wouldn't have died if he had seen to it proper. Anyways, that was it.'

'What do you mean?'

'I was forgetting you don't know about pigs. Nor do I, but I've picked up a thing or two! When a pig dies, the butchering of it has to start at once, and it takes three days from the bleeding to the salting. And it has to be done at once or the flesh gets poisoned by whatever it died of. The Aunt said it had already been dead hours, so he had to bleed it at once. I bet it was a grisly sight, Tessa.' Her voice took on a dramatic tone. 'The weird figure of the Aunt standing there with a lamp, and him at the animal's throat with a knife! Of course he got blood on his clothes – it would be everywhere – so he couldn't go in company until they were washed and dried. Anyways, once it had drained, Finn had to singe the hairs on the skin and scald it with buckets and buckets of water, and you can imagine how many he'd need for a pig that size! What with quartering it, jointing it and preparing it for salting, and the brawn and tripes, he was at it three full days. And that's why he couldn't have come to the caravan to see Kate.'

'What about the Aunt? Doesn't she do anything with the pig?'

'Swore her joints had stiffened on account of the draught which has been blowing through the roof for six months or more! But they weren't, and he knew she was getting at him both ways, one for not fixing the roof and the other because he's beginning to stand up for himself like me da told him to. But she had him over a barrel because those pigs are their meat supply like the goats are yours. So, you see it was fate helping the Aunt.'

Tessa shuddered. 'At least,' she reflected, 'me da spares me the sight of slaughter when one of the goats has to go. Bad enough knowing it's going on while I'm out. But,' she cheered up, 'I know now that Finn wasn't keeping out of the way on purpose . . . Tell me, Marie Jane,' she was prompted to ask. 'Tell me honestly, do you think Finn likes me – proper, I mean?'

'Course he does. Didn't he scheme with me to be your escort at the Fair? And has he not watched you walk the ridge many times when he was supposed to be watching the pigs?'

'But what if I've not come up to his hopes of me?'

'Ach, Tessa, a blind man could see he's head over ears for ye!'

'A blind man might, but I can't! He said nothing about seeing me again. He's not even sent a message up with you.'

'How could he? I daren't go near the old Aunt. She'd take one look at me, and because of me da, she'd guess something was in the wind and winkle it out of me! Besides, though he's terrified of being cursed himself, now he's doubly terrified of your being cursed too! But don't worry; he'll get to you soon in his own time and way.'

Tessa smiled ruefully. 'I just wish he'd hurry up, that's all!'

'Did I not tell you was he coming to the Long Dance? And the practices – me da made sure of that. A complete turn out of the valley he wants, shiftless and all. Everyone,' she said pointedly. 'Everyone will be there.'

'C'mon,' urged Tessa, 'by "everyone" you mean someone you fancy. By all the saints, talk about "off with the old and on with the new"! Who'll be drawing your eyes now?'

'Frank Kildare.'

'God help us! You mean he'll be at the practices as well as the Dance?'

'What else?'

'Why is he coming this year? Sure, he's never even been to watch before.'

'Oh,' Marie Jane rounded her mouth deliberately. 'He hadn't set those lovely hazel-coloured eyes on the "perfection of me form" then!'

'You've remembered that bit at least from the magazine!' laughed Tessa.

'Oh, me studying's coming on fine!' The sudden levity brightened the atmosphere of the loft. 'Frank Kildare's not a bad mover either.' Marie Jane returned to the subject near to her heart. 'I can tell he'll be good by the way he walks.'

'As though he were stalking prey!'

'I wouldn't mind if he were stalking me – '

'It looks as though you're stalking him!'

Marie Jane let out a long, happy sigh. 'God help me, Tessa, and would I like to bring him down!'

'So you really don't mind about Martin?'

The ringlets shook emphatically. Tessa recognised the signs. Marie Jane was on the scent; she was excited, and her pretty head was astir with notions of love. But Tessa could not, no matter how hard she tried, see the gamekeeper in the shape of her friend's lover – or, indeed, anyone's lover. Frank Kildare, she felt sure, was trouble.

A few days later Tessa, returning from grazing the goats, saw a horse tethered to the gate in the compound wall – it was a brown one. Not that the colour mattered; there was only person went about the valley on horseback, and that was the gamekeeper.

Her first instinct was for flight, but what if he had already seen her arrive? What, she wondered with a panicking heart, did he want with her da? The old uneasiness about the loss of the gun came to mind. Then, for some obscure reason, she recalled the exchange of words she'd overheard when she and Kildare were about to set off for Kate Murphy.

'You'll remember what I said, Mr Kildare.'

'I will so, Mr Riley,' had been the response.

What could they possibly have in common? The door opened. Her father had seen her coming.

'Just in time for some tay, Teresa. We've got company.' He inclined his head toward the keeper.

'A bright enough day, Teresa Riley.' Kildare smiled with barely concealed amusement at her obvious annonyance.

'It was.' The words came out crisp and tart, the tone hitherto unfamiliar, even to herself.

'Cloud's coming then?' asked Riley, glancing in his innocence through the tiny window.

'You could say that.' Standing near the door, Tessa propped the shepherd's crook in the corner. She kept her shawl on, not wanting to take it off with those hazel eyes on her. She took up the big cracked cup and, holding it between both hands, raised it to her lips, eyeing Kildare over the rim.

He too held a cup.

'Why has he come?' she asked her father.

'To ask about yourself, girleen.'

Her glance shot round to Kildare. 'Why are you asking about me, mister?'

'Can you not call me by me name,' he asked, a little irritated by the distance of such a designation. 'You don't refer to O'Malley or anyone else in that manner.'

'What manner?' The devil drove her to add, 'Mister.'

'Teresa! Sure, Mr Kildare's only being neighbourly; and he's not a stranger, so you've no need to keep calling him mister. You know his name.'

Accepting the reproach, she returned to the exchange with the gamekeeper.

'What did you want to ask about me, then?'

'I heard about your nasty experience with young Murphy – '

'Did you, now?'

'Will you not take your shawl off and settle, Teresa?' Riley frowned, and in his voice Tessa recognised appeal. He had never known his daughter like this and could not understand her attitude.

'It's as well the Murphys banished him – '

'Otherwise you would have hauled him off to Flavell's?'

'I can see you're no worse for the attack,' he commented dryly. 'Most women I know would've been distraught for weeks.'

'Proud Riley's daughter is not "most women".'

'I can see that. Anyways, I heard you gave a good account of yourself.'

'I always do.'

'Yes, I'm aware of that too!' His tone distinctly recalled the scene at Ennabrugh. 'Now that I've enquired about you, I'll come to the second reason for my visit. I attended the first practice for the Long Dance and was discussing with O'Malley how we want a good turn out. Marie Jane told me why your father wouldn't let you attend, so they sent me to see what a little persuasion could do, for the good of the community, you understand. We all understand your father's concern for your welfare and reputation but seeing that I, too, am going to the practices, he's agreed to let you go on condition that I escort you there and back; in other words, guarantee your wellbeing and safety.'

Tessa could scarcely believe her ears. What could possibly have made her da change his mind? Her wide gaze went from one to the other. They were both watching her. Willing her to say something, willing her to agree! She did not know what to make of the look in her da's eyes; there was something in the brown depths she had not seen before. As for the gamekeeper, his entire stance seemed to have altered. His cup had been set down and he was perched on the edge of the square table, one gaitered leg swinging easily, triumphantly! What was behind all this? Her heart fluttered in a frenzy of panic.

'You've had a wasted journey, then,' she answered. 'I'm not going to the practices. Even if St Teresa herself guaranteed my "safety and wellbeing", as you put it, I'd still not go.' She put the cup down, and the noise echoed about the cabin. The intake of her father's breath was audible.

'God love us, Teresa; sure, I thought you'd be pleased, I thought you'd wanted to go down. Didn't O'Malley see me about the very same thing?'

'But Mr O'Malley didn't get the same answer, did he, Da?'

'He did not. Sure, did he not convince me against me very inclination that you should spend the afternoons with Murphy's girl, and look what happened there? Mr Kildare's . . . well, he's a gentleman, Teresa, he'd see no harm came upon you.'

You wouldn't say that, she thought, if you'd have seen him holding me skirts at Ennabrugh, and the lust glinting and gleaming in his eyes.

'I'm not going down, Da, and that's the end of it.' Whisking up a clean bucket from the hearth, she went out to milk the goats.

So intent was she on her whirling thoughts that Kildare's appearance at the shed door a few moments later went unnoticed. He saw the shawl hanging on a hook and stood watching her sitting on the three-legged stool, her knees splayed apart beneath the same homespun skirts, the folds of which he had held bunched up in his hands. Her sleeves were rolled, and somehow the innocence of the picture struck a chord of something . . . something to do with a side of his character he did not understand.

The profile of her bosom rose and fell with the exertion; her windswept hair brushed the nape of her neck, a few locks escaping to her ears. It was on his tongue to say farewell but he thought better of it. A few moments later she heard the sound of hoofbeats on the ground; she realised he had been standing there.

All Teresa's thoughts on the subject did not prepare her for the avalanche of opinion which poured from her friends.

'Why did ye not come down?' demanded Peggy Jams after puffing her way up the ladder to join the inquest. She and Marie Jane sat hunched in an uncomfortable silence – proof to the two men below that serious study was afoot – and were regarding Tessa with barely concealed impatience.

'Why, in the name of God Almighty,' Marie Jane whispered ferociously, 'you didn't jump at the chance, I'll never know.'

'Because I don't like Kildare.'

'Surely you can put up with him for the sake of a bit of freedom, not to mention the valley's chances of coming first in the Long Dance? Who the divil cares whether you like him or not? What's liking to do with it?' She drew breath, exasperated. 'Honest to God, Tessa Riley, sometimes you're too high and mighty for your great clodhopping boots! You're not Proud Riley's daughter for nothing!' Another breath, another ferocious whisper into the silence. 'Who the hell cares whether you like Frank Kildare or not?'

'I do.'

'No one's asking you to go and live with him! Though God Almighty knows, I'd jump at the chance – '

'Oh, Marie Jane!' exclaimed Peggy, her pink face showing intense delight. 'Oh, I never knew . . .'

Marie Jane bit her lip. God preserve me, she thought, me and me big mouth. 'It's a secret, Peg. He doesn't know. No one knows; only Tessa, and she'd never, ever tell. So if it gets about – '

'Sure, I swear before God, Marie Jane, not to say a blind word.' She was thrilled to be occasionally part of this close friendship and had always known there would be rewards. Her thoughts, no longer bound by jealousy, took flight into the rosy land of romantic love.

'Now,' Marie Jane returned to the inquest. 'Listen. It was like this. Frank – '

'Ach, it's Frank now, is it!'

Marie Jane ignored the remark. 'Frank said what a grand turnout it was, and was it a good percentage of the fit and able? Me da said it was – except for yourself.' She paused to mimic one of Mrs Murphy's phrases. 'Got it?' Peggy giggled.

'Martin's uncle then told him about the terrible thing Mick Murphy tried on you, and how his parents had banished him, and how Martin'd gone off with Kate, and how because of all this your da wouldn't let you down. Una said you were one of the best on your feet, and they all stuck up for you. Finn was there too, putting in more than a word – and, oh!' A determined expression crossed her face. 'How I angled all that talk! Then me da said he'd tried to persuade yours and how not even for Ennan's chances would he let you down. Then, I sorted it so Frank would come up. And after all that effort, you turn him down flat. It isn't dacent of you, Tessa.' In a harsher whisper she added. 'What will Frank think of me, now? I bet you've ruined me chances of a place in service in the big house. He'll think I'm one of them young women who makes a fuss for nothing; and who wants a housemaid that gets things wrong?'

'I've not ruined anything! Sure, you know full bloody well, Marie Jane O'Malley, that I don't like Frank Kildare. And it's worse than that, for he makes me scared of him. You've no right to encourage him to come up here. If anyone's got room to complain, it's me!'

'I didn't know he'd be guaranteeing your welfare too, did I?'

'Just don't discuss me with him, that's all!'

'Will you calm down, the two of yous?' whispered Peggy hastily. 'We're supposed to be learning books.'

The two protagonists eyed each other sheepishly and at once a warm air of conspiracy filled the loft. Tessa said softly. 'Let's not quarrel, eh?'

'No, we'll not quarrel. But, I did me best for you; we all did.'

The inquest was over. 'We all did.' The words echoed. Tessa sighed. Finn, Mr Jarvey, the O'Malleys, the Duggans, Una ... They had all done their best to get her to the Dance, where under other circumstances she would have given her eyeteeth to be.

'Me da's started running a book already and you were one of the first tipped to win . . .'

Tessa nodded miserably. I've put me great clodhopping foot in it again, she thought. What conclusion would Finn draw from her not taking the opportunity to go down and practise with him? What in heaven's name had she been thinking of? Why, she wondered, why had she refused? Her da had actually given his consent – Kildare seemed to have more of a way with her da than O'Malley – and she could imagine some of the gossip which would follow her refusal:

'What do you think? Tessa Riley's growing like her da.'

'Ach, and her mother was a solitary creature, shutting herself off up there.'

'It's only to be expected.'

Or, worse, they would think she was letting down the community, that she did not care about Ennan's standing – and this perhaps the last Long Dance, if O'Malley was right. And she'd once been Ennan's heroine, a figure striding across the hills, shawl across her shoulder, crook in hand. Or, still worse, perhaps they'd think that the terrible experience with Mick Murphy had scared her off going out, destroyed her confidence. God help me, she thought, it'd take more than a scabby knacker lad to scare me off! Yes, she acknowledged soberly, it had taken more than a scabby knacker lad; it had taken Lord Fitzcarron's head keeper.

Proud Riley went about his work as though the Long Dance did not exist. His arms, veins standing out like cords of rope, swung hammers and wielded spades, repairing the damage wrought by the gales of the past winter. He prayed fervently before the Sacred Heart for a spell of fine weather to drain the turf of Ennabrugh, so he could start on it properly; but each day clouds came and he had to work nearer home, carrying buckets, making bricks, mending the fowl house, roofing the shed.

These things he understood. Digging turf he understood; there was something rewarding, satisfying in seeing the firm black substance on the cutter, in digging a whole trench out, and leaving the turves lying, resting, draining, rows and rows of them. That was nature; the earth, the elements. These things he had known since he could hold a spade. It was human beings he was no good with. He did not know how to cope with their actions and felt agonisingly helpless when things did not run simply.

So Riley had been more taciturn than usual after Teresa had refused to go with the gamekeeper. Although not given to daydreams, flights of fancy or wishful thinking of any kind, he had at once sensed the keeper's interest in his daughter from the moment he had first set foot over the threshold, and it had given him a glimmering of unexpected hope for Tessa's future. He knew Kildare to be unmarried, and his position spoke for itself. He was several years older than Teresa; but Riley himself had been considerably older then her mother, and that wasn't such a bad thing. Kildare was good-looking enough for any girl, with a tidy body on him. And he was the only man hereabouts who could take Teresa away to a better life, and relieve him of his precious burden; the Almighty God knew how it grew heavier each year.

On that first visit, Kildare had asked him questions about his daughter, veiled and guarded, but even so Riley had picked up the man's interest, and in return had conveyed his own hopes and fears in an equally veiled manner. This unspoken understanding was only admitted as Kildare had set off with Teresa to redeem Kate Murphy.

'You'll remember what I said?'

And the gamekeeper's answer: 'I will so, Mr Riley.'

The civility in the title bestowed on Riley was proof enough of Kildare's honourable intentions. St Teresa had answered his prayers, it seemed, and Riley's heart had felt lighter. Something good had come out of Ennan Fair after all. But had it? He was not so sure now.

After Riley's first bewilderment had passed off, the atmosphere between father and daughter soon settled to the working routine which characterised their relationship. So, when she observed the weather and said, 'It's time the goat's went out, Da. It looks like being a fair day. I'll take them for a lick of fresh grass; it'll do 'em good,' he simply answered with his usual, 'Take your crook and shawl, girl.'

The young goats, out for the first time, trotted behind their elders cautiously, their nostrils quivering as they sniffed the spring air. The fragrances and scents borne on the wind went to their heads and set them off frisking, playing, nuzzling and butting each other, testing their newly discovered strength. The older ones looked on indulgently, content to feel the warmth of the sun on their flanks.

Tessa strode behind the goats, crook in hand, keeping up a brisk pace so as to give them more time at the pasture. She felt especially thankful for these creatures, for without them there would be no reason to go out. She inhaled deeply. Oh, spring was certainly here. Despite all the rain Ennabrugh was kindly today, and cheerful.

The bog plants, the bladderwort and red andromeda, no longer huddled together but had spread themselves; the yellow sphagnum had opened its tiny petals and the purple moss rampaged along the bank.

Purple moss . . . She would always associate it with Kate Murphy. Tessa thought of her and Martin Jarvey; how love came easily and naturally to some, not like Marie Jane, who had to search for it, or herself, who could only dream about it.

The sun was now at its height, shining across the soft, peaty surface of Ennabrugh, transforming it into an expanse of deep black velvet. Her eyes followed the bog asphodel stretching to the south like a yellow garland. Yes, spring had come lightly to grace the waste of Ennabrugh. It was in her step, in her heart. It would all look even better from the top of the ridge! Without hesitation she struck off the track, shepherding the goats with her crook.

There was a cave in the side of the ridge, a small one in which Tessa sometimes sheltered from rain or strong wind. She doubted whether anyone knew of it and regarded it as her own, for no one had reason to go up there except herself searching for decent grazing. And there was no doubt the grass was good; anywhere was an improvement on the valley floor. The years had exhausted it, O'Malley said.

Tessa hurried, it was not so much desire for the view which stirred her, but the sudden longing to see the cave again. It was hers, her very own place, and this was something which was lacking in her life,

193

for even the loft was not absolutely private. At any time her da's voice would shout from below, calling for tea, to get her up, to blow the candle out, to hurry up, to stop reading, to set the spuds on. Up here there was only the wind. She did not come this far up in the winter, so now it was like going to meet an old friend. Her step changed to the lengthened strides of a climb . . . up and up . . . she was panting, breathless and eager to get there.

Her arrival disturbed a pair of red kite who, resenting her intrusion, opened their wings haughtily and vacated the crag. The goats spread themselves as though realising they had arrived, and Tessa went into the cave.

Nothing had altered. But then, it wouldn't. Nothing had changed in hundreds of years; only the people who came here ever changed. Even the rushes which she had brought up two years ago had not been disturbed by the wind. No spider's webs adorned the grey fissured walls; no bats had wintered here.

Tessa leaned the crook against the wall and took off her shawl, laying it on the rushes. She looked about eagerly, brightly, almost with excitement. 'My little kingdom,' she breathed, then flew to the mouth of the cave to absorb the view and survey her domain. She frowned. Satisfying as the view was, it did not calm her restlessness, did not insist she sit and feast her eyes on it. Sit? She did not want to to sit. Then it came to her. She knew at once what had driven her to come up: dancing! What had Marie Jane said? 'Set your sights on the Long Dance.' She hummed a little of 'Paddy's Reel' and tried out a few tentative steps. The floor of the cave was not too uneven. That's what she would do! Practise alone in the cave, as often as she could. 'Stamina . . . staying power,' Mr O'Malley had said. No one would know, not even Marie Jane; and when the great day arrived she would go down – with or without her da – and everyone would see Proud Riley's daughter had not let them down. As though a weight had rolled off her shoulders, Tessa began to sing softly, her feet moving in time to the tune.

While Tessa was dancing her way into a new confidence on the ridge, in the valley below Finn Collins was having trouble with his. Standing on a board across the water barrel, he was mending the roof of the cabin. He hated what he was doing; hated having to work for the Aunt; hated having to live with her. And, what was worse, he recognised his hate was tainted by fear, and with the fear came a sense of his total helplessness to do anything about it.

He had thought of clearing out, as O'Malley had advocated many times, but it was easier said than done. Any 'clearing out' would have to be sudden and for ever. He would have to disappear completely to be out of range of the mockers.

He turned his head to look up the hillside. Now there was reason to stay: Tess Riley. The only sane reason for staying in Ennan. He groaned inwardly everytime he recalled O'Malley telling him of Murphy's attack on her. He had let her down. He had not been there when she had needed protection and why had he not been there? Because he was nailed down under his aunt's thumb! If he had been with Tess none of this would have happened and her da wouldn't have clamped down on her freedom. At the practices he danced under a shadow. How could he enjoy himself knowing Tess was up there with her old da? If the wind was right she would hear the strains of the fiddles . . .

Another thing O'Malley had said was that you had to have an aim, a purpose, to make sense out o' life. Martin Jarvey would laugh in his face; he was always full of purpose and always got things done. But, thought Finn, what the divil can I do? Dion had told him how Marie Jane went up there once a week for book-learning, and he had grinned to himself; Marie Jane book-learning! God help us, it was enough to make the pig laugh! He had thought of sending a message with her, but he could never be sure Marie Jane would get it right. Besides, what message could he send?

He stared at the square of turf in his hands. 'What the hell am I doing with this?' he muttered. He hurled it over the roof to the other side of the compound and jumped down from the barrel. In case the Aunt was spying, he seized the long-handled peat-cutter and vaulted over the wall.

Free of his aunt, Finn set off towards Ennabrugh. He would climb the ridge and from there would see if she was out walking the goats. If he was not lucky today there would be other days. His spirit rose urging him to hurry, not to lose a second in finding Tess.

He approached the ridge from the far side and, having seen no sign of her, was about to give up when a white goat came into view. He set off again, covering the distance swiftly and easily.

CHAPTER ELEVEN

Finn whistled softly to himself. A cave, up here? He approached it cautiously. The young goats lifted their heads and acknowledged him as part of this wonderful freedom. The older ones stood and blinked, white lashes closing over the mild, brown eyes. Having perceived that he did not represent a threat of any kind they resumed their grazing.

Above the noise of the wind he heard a sound. 'She's singing,' he muttered in astonishment and, still outside the cave, he called her name, 'Tess . . . Tess . . . Tess . . .' But the sound of the wind kept it from her ears. Not wanting to startle her he stood outside for a few moments, wanting to see her before she saw him.

His heart went out to enfold her. She's dancing, he thought; the poor girleen's up here dancing on her own. But there was nothing 'poor' about her! And she was singing! Mother of God, he never knew she could sing like that! He felt her happiness, her freshness, and wondered how he could have forgotten it. There was so much to her, it would take a lifetime to discover it all!

Her cotton skirts swung and swayed. Her feet barely touched the ground, despite her heavy shoes, and her graceful figure remained straight-backed, hands at her sides in the manner of the dedicated dancer. The activity had brought colour to her cheeks and her vitality seemed, in his enchanted eyes, to transform the cave. Finn felt like a trespasser, like a mortal catching a glimpse of a goddess. Her simple happiness pervaded him. Almighty God, he thought, she who all these years had been cooped up with that silent old fella, living so melancholy and mournful a life, she could dance like this. She had to dance like this, there was no other way. In a few seconds she had gone from poor girleen to goddess, and now she was her dear, familiar self.

Through the wind and the sound of her own voice Tessa thought she heard something; her name being called, 'Tess . . . Tess?' There was only one who called her by that name! She looked round quickly, eagerly.

'Could you be doing with a partner?' he called out, responding to her obvious pleasure and surprise at seeing him.

'I could so!'

Finn took his place in front of her, and expressed his astonishment at finding the cave. 'And this is what you do in it?' he teased.

'And don't you be telling a soul. I want to surprise them all!'

He swore God could strike him dead if he so much as whispered a word, and poured out his remorse at not seeing her while she had been nursing Kate and not being there to defend her from Mick's filthy hands. Then they talked and talked. At first about the pig that had died, and his Aunt.

'I hate the old crone,' he said with an air of simple vindictiveness. 'It was her scheme with that bloody pig that kept me from seeing you. Did you wonder why I didn't come?'

'I did so,' she answered almost shyly; and across the short distance between them, they both laughed with the sheer pleasure of each other's company. She could scarce look at him now they were on their own. Out of the corner of her eye she noticed his shirt was open to the waist, and sleeves rolled to the shoulder made her aware of his muscular arms. He was the tallest man she knew, a bit on the scrawny side but strong, and the way he danced was quite alluring. At the wrestling the other young women had commented on his 'lovely haunches', and 'the nicest dancing legs this side of Connemara'. And here she was, actually dancing with him – alone!

'Tess,' he said, a little later, after they had already discussed Kate and Martin. 'Will you tell me now why you dance up here on your own, when you could be down with us at the practices? Kildare said your da was for letting you down but you refused. I thought you might've come, if only to dance with me.'

'Now you know,' she said, glad of conversation to draw her eyes off him. 'how I felt, when *you* never came to Murphy's van, when there was I going down each afternoon hoping for a sight of you!'

'And would I not have been there – but for that bloody pig!'

'And I would have come down with anyone else except . . . Kildare.' She followed Finn's way of using the surname with a detached kind of pleasure. 'He's a man of blood, Finn; there's something threatening about him.'

'A man of blood?' he echoed.

'Yes,' she answered with feeling. 'Walking about with that great gun on his arm, shooting birds and animals.'

'Fancy thinking of him like that. It doesn't bother Marie Jane. The schemes and angles she uses to be his partner at the practices! God alone knows why he's taking part.'

'Could be he fancies her as much as she likes him.'

'There's talk of him getting her into service with Lady Fitzcarron, you know.'

'She's always on about that; she wants me to go with her.'

'It's a way out, Tess. And wasn't your ma a maid in Rohira?'

'She was so, but I've told you, Finn, I won't be doing with all the hunting, shooting and trapping they do there. No, if Marie Jane goes to the big house she goes without me.'

And so they talked quickly, eagerly, breathlessly. Tessa had called the dances and both were aware she had chosen those which did not include holding hands. They danced until she noticed the slant of the sun in the mouth of the cave.

'That's the last! It's time I was on me way. Me da gets terrible fidgety if I'm overlong.'

'Can I come again?'

'Can you get away? Without the Aunt getting suspicious, I mean.'

'I've left me peat-cutter outside.' His mouth curved into a mischievous smile and he closed his eye in a conspiratorial wink.

'She might guess it's been too wet to dig turf.'

'And she might not!' He was suddenly bold and brave; the Aunt and her curses a thousand miles away. Tessa reached for her shawl and he reached for the crook. 'Tomorrow?'

She shook her head. 'If you come up once in the week, after the practice, you can show me what they've done.'

'Have we to win the Long Dance for Ennan? The two of us?'

She nodded, catching his enthusiasm. 'Do you think we can?'

'If we can't, who in God's name can?' Now that he had an aim, he felt stronger still. 'But do you think only practising once a week will be enough?'

'Don't let's tempt providence,' she answered practically. 'You'll have a practice down there, and me another one up here, that's two each a week – more than the others.' She wiped the sweat off her forehead with the back of her hand. 'And not a word, not even to Marie Jane, mind?'

'Have I not sworn?' he reminded her. 'Who's leaving first?'

They looked at each other uncertainly. Her glance wavered towards the goats, he took it as a sign and when she looked back again he had gone.

Tessa fought down the urge to dash out and call him back. So, she breathed, this was how Marie Jane must have felt all those times. And did Marie Jane feel like this about Kildare? How grandly Finn had used the name. Kildare; that was how she would refer to him in the future, just 'Kildare' . . . no 'Mister'. He wasn't worth it. She shuddered away from the memory of buckled gaiters, and deer-stalkers, the lithe walk and the ferreting fingers; and feasted her thoughts on the boyish smile, the touchable black curls and friendly blue eyes of Finn Collins.

When Marie Jane next called at the Rileys' cabin Tessa could scarcely keep down her animation, and pretended her obvious lifting of spirits was due entirely to her friend and the news she brought.

'And it's been so wet, Tessa. Dear God, every time me da calls a practice, sure the heavens open and when we all go back to the hearth, it stops . . .' On she prattled, but Tessa was consumed with curiosity as to her friend's progress with the keeper. 'You're not listening, Tessa. I was saying if this strength of rain goes on we'll all get soaked at the Long Dance – '

'You're right, I wasn't listening. God preserve us, who wants to know about the rain! Are you any nearer getting into service, or any nearer to Frank Kildare?'

To her surprise a pink flush suffused Marie Jane's cheeks. 'Oh, Tessa, I can't bear to talk about him! Sure, he's life and death to me. Even though it rains, he comes just the same. He always ties his horse up by our compound and if the cabin's tidy me da will ask him in for a drop o' the poteen, but if the ashes haven't been cleared and Little Annie's grizzling, he goes out to meet him and I sit and watch by the window. Sometimes he sees me and raises his hand, and when me da calls me out to the dance and I walk between the two of them, I can hardly hear what they're saying for me heart thumping away in me ears! And, when I answer any questions or pass any comment, sure I sound so calm and matter-of-fact that I can't believe it's me! Tessa, I've got to make a good impression if I'm to go into service.'

Marie Jane paused and added with a tremulous sigh. 'It's all fixed, really. Me da's arranging it all.' Then picking up speed she was off again. 'There's a place for a kitchen maid, but me da wasn't having me go for a skivvy. "I want something better than that for my girl, Mr Kildare," I heard him say, and Frank replied, "You're pushing up the price, Mr O'Malley." And me da, in that persuasive voice of his said, offhand like, "Well, Mr Kildare it's like this, you can always tell his lordship to get someone else to do the deal." "Come now," says Frank, all agreeable. "You mustn't be like that. And I quite agree it wouldn't do at all to keep such a pretty young thing in the kitchen. Marie Jane would be much better above stairs." Now, what do you think of all that? Will you come and see me on me half-day?'

'Can you see me da letting me? You talk as if you're going next week!'

'I wish I was.'

'You mustn't go yet,' said Tessa, suddenly in earnest. 'You're my best friend. I don't know what I'd do without you, honest I don't. Listen, why don't you set your mind to the writing so you can send me a note? When you go, that is.'

'And why don't you set your mind to the future and come with me? Me da says it'd be a good thing for you. There's no future in the valley. And we'd have many a good laugh, you and me!'

But Tessa was not to be drawn. 'Just don't go getting your heart broken when you're alone and miles from anyone. You're not going just for him, are you?'

The glossy ringlets shook from side to side, eyes sparkled, lips pouted. 'There'll be plenty to comfort me: no end of footmen, coachmen, gardeners; an acre of 'em to choose from, proper men, not like this lot.'

'Finn Collins is all right.'

'Except for the Aunt – she won't let go of him so easily. And sure, who in her right mind would fancy bedding down with him, while she's sitting up in that chair all night like Dooley's ghost? Your da's right, Tessa, you need a good marriage, and you'll not get it here!'

It was but two weeks to the Long Dance and Tessa had made her way, against a smokey-grey sky and warm summer drizzle, to the

200

cave. 'They've got to have a lick of fresh grass,' she had said with pretended reluctance, reaching for her crook. And so she stood at the mouth of the cave, high on the ridge. The valley below was blotted out by mist. Exhilarated by the climb, her face glowed with anticipation at seeing Finn. She reflected on the easy relationship that had evolved out of the talking, dancing, laughing; now they could touch hands, when the dance dictated, without embarrassment.

She did not like getting there first, for anxiety gnawed at her heart, lest his aunt had somehow discovered their secret. Oh, the states she often got into, thinking the Aunt had discovered another awful way of preventing him from coming. But then the goats would prick up their ears, the plovers would cry out in annoyance, and there he would be, running up the hillside with wild energy, moving with the grace and suppleness of a great cat.

Her thoughts of Finn refused to go beyond the Long Dance, because after that what reason would there be for them to meet? If only the practices could go on for ever and ever. Yet she said nothing of this longing to him; unlike Marie Jane she did not want to push herself, for fear of spoiling what was already there. Finn had told her of his desire for an aim in life, and this confidence strengthened the bond between them. The question uppermost in Tessa's mind now was what would happen when this particular 'aim' was fulfilled? But on this her mind refused to dwell.

He was there! He came forward to greet her, the fine rain silvering his thick hair, drops of moisture on his long black eyelashes. They looked at each other, drinking in as much as they could absorb in so short a time, not knowing what to make of it and uncertain what to do about it; of late, there seemed to be an unspoken pact against silence or inactivity.

'I thought you might not come,' she laughed, as he reached out for her hands and swung her inside the cave. 'I thought to meself, he's forgotten, or he's fallen asleep and being lazy!'

'Lazy!' he spluttered. 'And all these hours, all these afternoons I put in at the Bog!' He nodded his head to where he had thrown the spade.

Tessa called the first dance.

'Marie Jane said a lot of the practices have been rained off, down there.'

'They have so, but sure to God, Tess, what's a drop o' water? They won't melt! She's right, though, there's been a lot of it. Jasus, what a summer! Ach, you should hear the old 'uns talking of the rains they had in time past, when folk up here never felt dry ground beneath their feet all year! And how the strength of it could flatten a fella to the ground. Oh, and the river; will I tell you now, that it flooded trout to their very doors!'

Despite rain-soaked clothes they jigged, reeled, tapped and twirled with unflagging energy. The dance was the thing. When in each other's company the desire to perfect it was paramount. But when alone, each recalled not the dance or the discussion, but the looks, the graceful movement, the sweet surprise of unexpected touch. Each smile, look and frown was recalled, mulled over and dissected for secret meanings; both dreaming of what could be . . .

While Tessa made her way past the nearer shore of Ennabrugh, singing to keep the goats together – for the young ones could stray in the mist – Frank Kildare was in conversation with her father. Perched on the corner of the square table and swinging a buckled, gaitered leg, he approached the subject that was nearer to his heart than the actual purpose of the call.

'Have you ever considered your daughter going into service in the house?'

Riley's bushy eyebrows shot up. 'Sure to God, Mr Kildare, I've never given it a thought.'

'You might try giving it some, now, Mr Riley. May be you've not given it any consideration because the opportunity was not put to you. Your daughter herself must be aware of the possibility because I've put a word in Lady Fitzcarron's ear regarding O'Malley's girl. O'Malley thinks it's a good move.'

'Ach, he would and all. But listen, Mr Kildare, Teresa and me, we're quiet in our ways; we don't go in for all the talk and blarney like a good many. And you saw how Teresa was about going down to those practices. I could've sworn she'd snatch the offer up like her bloody goats snatch at me spuds, given the chance. So,' he moved his chair back from the hearth, 'even though I might give it some of that consideration you're talking about, it'll make no difference if she doesn't want to go – with or without O'Malley's girl. There's nothing I can do, short of taking me belt to her.'

'Wasn't her mother in service?' Kildare knew she had been, yet hoped the question would be productive in some way.

Riley's fingers moved uneasily to the buckle of Timothy Thomas's belt . . . His thoughts wavered. Teresa Donnelly had got with child through being in service. True, she and Timothy Thomas were set for marriage, but it had not worked out, and he had finished up in his grave and she'd gone wandering with Clancy's crew. He suddenly recoiled from any hint of consideration.

'She was so,' he answered the question. 'And like a lady herself, she was; tall, but not strong like the girleen. And so clever she was with the reading and writing, and the fine words.' He stopped, the recollection proving too painful. 'Anyways, Mr Kildare, Teresa will be down with the goats soon.' He glanced at the window and got up to set the kettle on the stones. 'She'll be glad of some tay, the damp and drizzling day it's been. You're welcome to put it to her yourself.'

'But will you back me up if she agrees?'

'You young fellas are all the same, Mr Kildare, too wild and anxious to be settling things. Shall we wait to see what she says herself?'

Kildare sighed. He stood down from his perch on the corner of the table, unfastened the belt and buttons of his Norfolk jacket and went to the window. It was so tiny, and placed so low in the wall, that he had to stoop to see through it, and all he could see was softly falling rain against a background of feathery mist.

What a desolate place to build a cabin, he thought. Why, in the name of the Almighty God, were people content to live like this? As for Riley, I might as well not be here. Look at him, reaching for his leather; making footwear for his daughter, no doubt. A memory flashed across the rain and mist . . . Tessa's feet, stained brown with peat, but strong and beautiful. She had been putting on her shoes to be witness for Murphy's girl and he had felt the urge to stretch out a hand, to touch her feet. He had since called himself all kinds of a fool.

Had he been a fool to take on this clearance? He thought it would be an easy if unenviable task, but he had been wrong. Stooping, hands on the low window ledge, eyes on the now blotted out landscape, he realised the task was still far from easy, but it was a challenge, and time was on his side. Not only time, but also the priest and the

Humane Society . . . Frank Kildare straightened his back. He was proud of his cunning. A word dropped here and there, pointing out to the visiting priests and the Christian Brothers the dreadful moral dangers which beset these isolated communities . . . Intermarriage, incest. Anyone with half an eye, he had pointed out, could see that the Byrnes – all six of 'em – were 'short upstairs', harmless, but God alone knew what they in their mixed up ways got up to! And God may not be pleased that His children were being allowed to continue in this state.

He had drawn the attention of the Health Authorities to the Grogans who were constantly puddled on poteen and to Kevin Connor's brother, the one they called 'Tommy Two-mouth' because of his cleft palate. Infant mortality was rife – they only had to look in the graveyard. And, although there were not above three dozen children, many were deformed with rickets, bowlegs, squints. Even O'Malley's youngest had a curved spine, and the lads, Dion and Pat, were as thin as laths. As for education, he had pointed out to the authorities in Rohira, there had been no teacher in Ennan since Pat Feeney had been marched off eight years ago. Mona Donal's enforced marriage to Kevin Connor had produced a baby that, according to gossip, appeared to be deaf. Moreover, there were not enough marriageable men for the girls. What chance had the six Duggan girls of marriage? Yes, he had done his investigations well, and O'Malley had been a hive of information.

But O'Malley could also put the screws on. God Almighty, was that man crafty! Saw through it all, he did. What was it worth to him, he had asked with that mild look from behind his spectacles, to help sow the seeds of discontent, to get the people to leave of their own free will? Not that O'Malley disagreed with Lord Fitzcarron; he had thought for some time there was no future for the valley. It was 1898; the nineteenth century was almost gone, and Ennan must go with it. The twentieth century should herald a new start for everyone – God, that man could go on!

So what price O'Malley's help? It had to be enlisted or he could, as head-man, lead a campaign of solidarity against his lordship, and where, thought Kildare, would that leave me? He had to hand it to O'Malley: for sheer cunning he had no equal. His terms? A gradual absorption of as many of the young people as wanted to go and work on the estate, starting with his own daughter, and not in the kitchen either! Kildare had begun this task with a determined detachment, but O'Malley had eroded most of that.

Then there was his involvement with Tessa Riley at Ennabrugh rescuing that bloody goat! How, and why, he became involved, the Lord God only knew, but now here he was waiting to persuade her to join Marie Jane. This original purpose for the visit had been to sound Riley out about the future. But Riley intended to stay. 'God love us, Mr Kildare,' he had said. 'Where else, in all the green of Ireland, would I fit in?' So, the old man was not for going. But time would tell, and there was still plenty of it. He had fixed in his mind to see the last of them off the soil by the end of November and certainly by the eighth of December, by fair means or foul. His thin lips curved into a mischievous smile at the irony of the date. The eighth of December, by tradition, was the day farming and country communities went into the big towns for their Christmas provisions. He doubted whether this community had ever heard of the custom, but this year any that were left would join the rest of the country folk on a pilgrimage, not to the shops, but to the workhouse!

The mist had absorbed the daylight earlier than usual, and Riley stopped his fashioning of shoes to light the lamp. He's not said a word this past half hour, thought Kildare, wondering whether to be glad or sorry. How on earth could any young woman stand it?

Tessa saw the horse tethered at the gate. Aware that something was dangling from the saddle, and not wanting to see whatever it was, she averted her eyes. Leading the goats to what passed as their outhouse, she swore heartily at his intrusion. She feared him a little less now it was clear he was not seeking retribution for loss of the gun, but the sight of the horse always sent a lurch to her stomach. The lurch today reminded her she was hungry and thirsty, and needed a big cup of strong, hot tea.

At first, the contrast between dancing with Finn on the ridge and descending to find Kildare was too much to face. She stayed with the goats for a while until common sense took over. He had seen her arrive, and if he hadn't seen her, the noise of the goats was indication enough, so nothing was to be gained by lurking in the outhouse.

Hearing his daughter's return, Riley chanced to raise his head in time to see Frank Kildare fasten his coat and pull it straight. He pursed his lips and lowered his attention to the leather on his last. So, that was the way of it, Kildare was still interested. He had thought

Teresa's refusal to go down to the practices had put him off. His heart swelled; he knew there'd be a good suitor for his girl, he always knew deep down that she'd catch the eye of a gentleman. He made up his mind there and then on a point that had been bothering him while he cut the leather for Teresa's shoes. Even if she fancied going with Marie Jane for a maid in the Fitzcarron household, he would not let her. For once out of his sight and protection, Tessa would be within easy reach of Kildare. And gentleman though he was, if he wanted Teresa the 'walking out' would go on from this cabin, from the valley, and in public. That way lay the wedding ring. Not that he thought for a moment that Frank Kildare was or would be dishonourable, but it was best to be on the safe side.

Kildare's hazel eyes, keen in his hunter's face, were the first thing Tessa was aware of as she entered the door. Hand on the latch, she instinctively swept into the cabin, thought Frank Kildare, with as much style as Lady Fitzcarron! Her sodden skirts and homespun blouse clung to the lines of her body and the rain had moulded her hair to the shape of her head. Her total disregard for the elements captured his imagination. Such wild, natural beauty, it seemed to him, was crying out to be caught and tamed.

Moving to the hearth, she stretched her hands towards the fire. 'Have you finished your business with me da, mister . . .' She paused and added 'Kildare?'

'I have so,' he replied with energy. 'But there's something else.'

'Is there, now?'

He knew before he formulated the question what the answer would be, yet he felt constrained to ask, knowing the answer she gave would annoy him.

'Would you be interested in going into dacent service in the Fitzcarron household? O'Malley's girl will be going when there's a place, and it's likely to be soon.'

Riley could tell what his daughter's answer would be, and caught up in the elation of scheming, felt it safe to show Kildare he was still an ally. 'Will you not think about it, Teresa?'

'No, Da, I will not think about it.'

'May I be asking you why not? What can you possibly have against going into service at so fine a place?' Kildare amazed himself. 'May I!' he thought. Me asking, 'May I?' – and she nothing but a peasant's daughter! God Almighty help me, I must be mad!

'It's not the service,' she said looking over the brim of the big cracked cup. Thoughts of Finn came unbidden, but what could she say – what was there to say? Her feelings were still too precious, too personal. Besides, for her da, Finn had nothing to offer Proud Riley's daughter!

'It's the killing, the hunting and the dreadful shoots they have. Even Lady Fitzcarron goes shooting. I've seen them from the distance drinking cups of wine, shouting and yelling and striding about with bloody great guns to blow the heads off the harmless birds you reared and who trusted you – and then boasting about how many you bagged. And all the setting of traps for the wild things, and you and the keepers riding about with their poor corpses dangling from your saddles. That's why I'm not going.'

He stared at her in total amazement as she stood by the fire with clouds of steam rising from her wet clothes. Her voice echoed from Ennabrugh on that wild February day. 'I don't want the goat killed, mister,' she had said. 'Either by that great stinkin' Bog or your shotgun. I won't have any bloodshed, do you hear?' He had heard. He was hearing again.

'Teresa,' Riley said, not wanting her to lose her chance altogether. 'Remember your manners girl.'

'He wanted to know why, Da, and I've told him.' Then to Kildare. 'Are you satisfied now, mister?'

No, he thought, by God I'm not satisfied! He wanted to be annoyed, to hold something against her, to pay her back for not being more responsive to his overtures. Annoyed, put out, angry; any of these emotions he had been prepared to feel, but he had not expected to be astonished, amazed, and totally set back. It was as though he were floundering in the Bog again.

Somehow he extricated himself from the turmoil created by Proud Riley's daughter. Outside he swore at the darkness. It had closed in early, being the sort of day it was. Too late to find the path over Ennabrugh, now. He was more likely to end up in a bog-hole. He would have to stay over at Flavell's. Christ Almighty, he thought, recalling the lengths he had gone to keep Murphy's girl there on a trumped up charge, to enable him re-establish some contact with a ragamuffin young woman who wore calico drawers! It's off me head I must be. He urged the horse on. God Almighty, Kildare, you're a fool! Hanging about a godforsaken cabin like a stable lad!

It was the fact that he'd been left sprawling that had set him going; he did not like being got the better of. When he had first come across her that day, seduction had been uppermost in his mind. Most of the colleens here and about, and almost certainly the pretty Marie Jane, would not have said no to a joke, a kiss, a caress leading to a playful tussle on a sheltered patch of warm bracken. No woman had turned him down yet, so he had never doubted his ability to persuade a passing fancy. But Tessa was proving to be more than a passing fancy. He had jettisoned the seduction scheme long since, but had not yet fathomed what drove him on to pursue her. For some obscure reason he wanted to ingratiate himself with her. Refusal had damaged his pride. But if she were resident at Fitzcarron House she would see the respect in which he was held, the power he wielded, the power that could see her and her da in the workhouse come the eighth of December.

He felt the hares jolting against his leg and for the first time it irritated him. What the divil did she expect him to do with 'em? God, what crass stupidity! Her father was as bad; he ought to have made her enter service for her own good! And to think he'd got himself involved in the Long Dance – schemed to get her there – and she had flung it back at him. That was the end of it. No more Tessa Riley.

CHAPTER TWELVE

To Tessa and Finn, the two remaining weeks to the Long Dance passed as swiftly as 'Jackson's Reel'; they concentrated their efforts and she was too full of it, too excited, to concern herself with the gamekeeper or moves to the Fitzcarron estate.

On the actual day she almost fell down the loft ladder in her eagerness to see if the weather was dry. The mist hung over the ridge like a canopy, but there was no sign of rain. Her father had set the kettle on the stones and she could hear him refilling the water buckets outside. Her eyes sparkled and her heart jigged with happiness; already she was humming the tunes. A great feeling of community spirit enveloped her as she stood in her nightgown at the window. All the others down below would be up and preparing themselves – and Marie Jane would be in a turmoil about her clothes and her hair!

The Gaelic League and all the folk from town would have set out on their way up, some on foot, some in wagons, others on horseback. Hawkers would be coming up too, along with all kinds of vendors, musicians, umbrella sellers and pickpockets.

Struggling into her brown working skirt, she gave a wry smile; the Jarvey men would be doing a great trade today. Finn said all their donkeys had been hired to bring up the duckboards for the spectators in case the day was wet underfoot.

Soon she, too, was outside, swilling, washing down the flanks, milking and tethering the goats. Back inside to tea, griddle bread and cheese, and finally she climbed into the loft to titivate. The chores had all been accomplished without a word between herself and her father. They had worked and eaten in easy silence. The subject of the Long Dance had never been broached but it was understood they would go down together. Riley, although the gamekeeper appeared to be out of the running, still had hopes of finding a good husband for his daughter; and although Tessa resented the idea of everyone knowing she was being 'hawked', the attendant delights were too attractive to put her off. And of course, this year would be different. She and Finn would astonish them all!

While she was in the loft, her father, stripped to his dirty grey drawers, sluiced cold water from the barrel over his head and body. The water was icy against the clammy summer morning. He shook the drops from his ragged hair, seized a piece of hessian and rubbed his wiry body vigorously until he was in a splendid glow.

Tessa mourned the loss of her peacock-blue gown. It was still stuffed in the corner of the loft where she had thrown it, unable as yet to bring herself to the task of salvaging any of it. The gown reminded her of Kate Murphy. She often thought of her and wished her well with Martin Jarvey; he was a nice fella, and would make Kate the best of husbands. Her thoughts brought a smile to her face; he would have had the hell of a time with Marie Jane!

Choice of clothes was not difficult for Tessa. She was now down to two best skirts: the white cotton which O'Malley had bought for her some two years ago, and the fine black woollen one. She decided on the white cotton, for it was the lightest in weight and the skirt swung nicely. Then she chose the blue gingham blouse which matched the colour of her eyes, and had sleeves which showed off her forearms. Enjoying her titivating, Tessa brushed her hair with long, even strokes and wished for a better hair ribbon than the white sliver of cheese muslin. There was the black velvet, but it would not do for summertime. The little shoulder shawl with tassels was lifted from the hook in case it turned chilly when the sun had gone in – if ever it came out! The new leather pumps had been finished just in time, and she slipped them on her bare feet. Feeling suitably preened, Tessa eased herself down the ladder.

Proud Riley stood with thumb hitched in Timothy Thomas's belt, and his 'other' cap on his still damp hair. He wore a clean shirt and corduroy trousers instead of the winter moleskins. He waited now with all the pride of a man about to give his daughter in marriage.

Unhampered by sacks and packs and kettles, as they had been for the Fair, the two set off down the hillside toward the valley. Although the canopy of cloud blotted out the view of the mountains for the visitors, that same canopy acted as a sounding board for the excited voices below. Tessa's sharp ears caught every sound. Her heart beat faster with eager curiosity. The voices were town voices, clipped and careful of usage. The Gaelic League folk would already be roping in the young men from the town to help set up the bunting and flags. The young men and lads of the valley – the two Duggans, Finn, Kevin Connor, old and young Jams, Moira Muldoon's brothers and O'Malley's eldest boys – made themselves scarce. They were shy of coming out before the direct and distinctly curious glances of strangers, so they lurked in hut and cabin until the valley was crowded and the barrels of ale settled after the journey.

They were getting in sight of folk now. What a picture! What a difference all the bustle made! People and horsedrawn vans and vehicles jostled with donkeys and carts. Flags and bunting hung limply on or between poles. A banner on which the words 'Ennan Long Dance 1898' were printed in red letters stretched across from O'Malley's wall. A few wooden chairs stood here and there like stunted trees, and still people swarmed in through the narrow entrance by the Aunt Hanratty's cabin. All these people! She never knew there were so many in the world!

Unlike her father, Tessa did not entertain any hopes of meeting a future husband; the very idea filled her with anxiety lest she be separated from Finn. Their lives seemed to be linked and anyone else would be an intrusion in her heart – but there could not possibly be anyone else!

So they had conspired at their practices to pretend they had not seen or danced with each other; it was their secret to be kept at all costs. Any leakage of the deception would jeopardise any future plans. There were no young men down here could equal Finn Collins, and for the first time in her life Tessa felt definite stirrings of rebellion. Why, in God's name, had she to 'make a good marriage', as her da put it? Marriage with Finn would suit her fine – despite his aunt. Marriage! Mother of God, what was she thinking of? He hadn't even kissed her yet. In any case, unlike Marie Jane, Tessa had not the temperament to take a kiss lightly, and so was loathe to start something which might complicate her life, especially with her da being what he was. And so her puzzled thoughts brought them to where the track broadened out to the valley floor.

Riley, who had led the way, lest his daughter's pumps got stuck in soft pockets of peat, noticed uneasily how the grass, although growing on the hillside, was not to be seen in the valley. He had heard Tessa comment on this, but until Mr Kildare had started

211

talking about the state of the ground, he had paid no attention. Not that it would make any difference to him. He was born in Ennan and would die in Ennan.

Waiting for her friend, Marie Jane had found herself a position by the Gaelic League banner. She wore a gown of pink with sleeves puffed above the elbow, and the hem of it was printed with roses. Her ringlets gleamed, her eyes shone, and her whole being radiated pleasure at the admiring glances which came her way. The older men thought her fine-looking and the younger 'a stunner'. Marie Jane was holding court, and enjoying every minute of it.

On catching sight of the Rileys she flung her pose to the winds and hurried, or, rather, skipped prettily, towards them. Slipping her arm through Tessa's, she said primly, 'Good morning to ye, Mr Riley. Sure it's not a bad day for the Dance, don't you think? And aren't they already all here? Oh, and have you seen the pipers?'

Never sure what to make of such volubility, Riley did not reply, but his manner was such that Marie Jane did not take offence. 'Will ye go in and take a drop with me da, Mr Riley? While Tessa and me take a stroll about? He said I was to be sure to ask you.'

'Sure, I'll be all right, Da,' Tessa assured. 'These are proper people up from the town, not tinker scum.'

Riley glanced at all the town folk, at the women wearing fine coats and hats, the men with walking sticks and chains across their waistcoats, and nodded assent. He was pleased his daughter could feel at ease among these people. Not so, himself; like the valley lads in hiding, he scuttled off to the safety of O'Malley's cabin.

'You said you'd come! Oh, it's glad I am he brought you down. I've been racked in case he changed his mind. Oh, glory, glory, Tessa, you look wonderful in your blue and white; the ribbon shows off your hair, and the blue matches your eyes. Isn't it just like the Fair? Us parading about like Lord Fitzcarron's paycocks – and every bit as grand!' She paused for breath and was off again. 'Oh, I'm putting it on, as they say in town,' she swaggered, 'for when I go into service. Oh, and I've got the best news. Frank's been to see me da this morning. I'm going for a maid next week!'

'But you can't!' Tessa stared in dismay. 'Surely they've not found you a place already. Oh, Marie Jane, you can't go and leave me.'

'Come with me then! The two of us would be as happy as pigs in muck. Oh, and another thing,' Marie Jane's voice took on an edge of pride. 'I can tell the time.'

'What do you mean?'

'Ach, Tessa, you don't know anything!' teased her friend. 'In the big houses and down in Rohira, people have to do things to time. They've not all day, like us. Me da bought me a clock; he didn't want his daughter to be as ignorant as the pigs now, did he? When I came out it was nine o'clock, and a short while ago it was half-past eleven. Everyone in civilisation has clocks.' She smiled and sighed happily. 'So, you see, even if I can't read and write, I can tell the time.'

'Will you teach me? C'mon, show me the clock.'

'In case you change your mind, and come into service with me?'

Tess shook her head, and related the incident of Kildare's visit and how she had refused to take up his offer.

'You can always change your mind, Tessa,' Marie Jane said archly. 'When life's all as black as a bog-hole, and the winter rain starts trickling down the wall, and you're stuck up there in the wind and snow with no one but your da to look at, and no one at all to talk to – '

'Oh, yes!' broke in Tessa. 'While you're chinwagging with Kildare and her ladyship and half the county beside!'

'Me da's going to ask yours if you can walk with me to the house, else sure to God I'd get lost on Ennabrugh. And it's too far to walk down the ten miles to Rohira and approach it from the road. You will walk with me, won't ye?'

'If me feet have recovered,' Tessa teased. 'They were sore for days after the last Long Dance.'

'And you're in for another surprise. Wait till you see Finn Collins!'

'Why? What in the name o' God's happened?'

'Nothing's "happened", as you put it! I can see this is a case of "absence makes the heart grow fonder". Sure, there's nothing like it for kindling the very fires of passion!'

'Away with ye! What am I going to be surprised at then, about Finn?' she asked wonderingly. 'Or is this just one of your games and there's nothing to it, at all?'

'There is so. Listen while I tell you. He got me da to get him some clothes off the old Jew, with his wrestling money. Oh, and he does look the paycock! He's got a white shirt and some black breeches. He tried 'em on; not in front of me very eyes, you understand! Oh, an' Tessa, the sight of him's enough to make your mouth water. The white shows up his dark looks, the shirt sleeves are full and the neck stays open to show some of his chest. Oh, and Tessa, the black breeches fit his rump something marvellous; you can imagine it, can't you, from the wrestling. He looked really handsome. I mean, he is, but in those old corduroys and that checked pig-shirt . . . well, they do nothing for him. The only thing that spoiled it was those bloody great boots he wears with the split in them! Sure, he'll never get any dacent footwear this side o' the Connemara Mountains with the size of his feet!' She gave Tessa a nudge. 'He's done it to impress you. He knows you always look like a woman regal born, as he puts it. But, I'll tell you this. He intends to dance with you. Said if your da wouldn't bring you down, you'd come yourself. But all the valley knew Proud Riley wouldn't let a Long Dance go by without eyeing up the form. I'm not supposed to tell you this, but me da had to get you a bottle of Guinness as well – a little present – ' Another nudge. 'Things are looking up, Tessa!'

'I don't know about that . . .' Tessa stood on her toes and looked down the valley in the direction of the Aunt's cabin. 'We'll never find him in this crowd, but he's not a fella you'd easily miss . . .'

Silence came between the two as their attention was captured by the goings on of the people up for the day. The fat men, the thin. The jolly man in white apron and cap. The quack putting up his rostrum. Black-bearded men drinking ale and wiping bushy whiskers with the backs of their hands. The pompous and the proud. Young women on the arms of young men; young women who wanted to be and tried not to show it. Matronly women, their rotund and well-corsetted figures presenting a solid front of respectability. And all who passed wore well-made clothes and proper shoes. Such nobility – as it seemed to the crofters – such style and elegance seemed eminently desirable, yet hopelessly unattainable.

The officials, easily recognised by the conglomeration of gold chains, medals, rosettes and harassed expressions they presented, were trying hard to mould the crowd into order. Before the dancing could start, the President of the Gaelic Preservation Society felt the need to address the assembly in Gaelic while in truly Gaelic surroundings, but he was not aware that the residents and half the visitors had not thought it necessary to preserve their native tongue.

Bored with the bouts of inflamed and unintelligible oratory, Tessa and Marie Jane wandered off to look at the stalls and booths which were springing up like mushrooms. Barrels of ale, brown and vast, stood at strategic points, their tops littered with jugs, basins, bowls and tin cups. Men in white aprons sold bread: gingerbread, currant bread, soda bread. Children wearing stockings, shoes and coats played at catching gaily-coloured balls; others played at catching each other! Two priests stood conferring, the brims of their wide hats almost touching, their cloaks flowing behind them in the light wind. The Society for Total Abstinence, with an eye to the huge brown barrels, hurriedly handed out tracts while people were still sober enough to read them. Little groups sat on blankets by huge wicker picnic baskets. Others had arranged themselves on stools, carts or on the edges of the many platforms.

Tessa stared at the procession of faces, but Finn's was not among them. She began to feel uneasy. What had happened? Why was he not here in the finery Marie Jane had described? The thought of dancing without him filled her with dismay. The joy, the anticipation, was slowly draining out of her limbs. She couldn't – wouldn't – dance without him, not after all these weeks of practising.

The speeches continued. A member of the Gaelic League then got to his feet and, when he sat down, Father Donaghue felt constrained to commit the proceedings to the Almighty, to be followed by Sister Bernadette with a few words; and all the while O'Malley charged up and down taking bets with his most disarming smile. Not only was he taking the odds on which dancers would hold out the longest, but also which fiddler would stay the course.

'I can't see Finn anywhere,' said Tessa, still looking.

'He'll turn up.' There was a pleasant sighing sound to Marie Jane's voice, and turning round Tessa saw the reason for it: the gamekeeper had arrived. At least, thought Tessa charitably, one of us will be suited.

A man with a gold chain about his neck got to his feet and fired a starting pistol for attention. He bade all the dancers gather to the middle of the valley floor, and the fiddlers to tune up. Kildare was still some way off so the two young women stayed together. They exchanged worried glances about Finn. The starting pistol – the signal of the Long Dance to begin – shattered their thoughts. And then he was there! Before them! Tessa blinked and looked twice.

Marie Jane's jaw almost dropped open. Finn observed these glances and the observation did nothing to make him feel better.

'Was I not expecting you to be the fine paycock?' flashed Marie Jane as the fiddles began with an eightsome reel. 'What the divil's happened to your fine clothes?'

Finn glanced disparagingly down at his old corduroys and pig-shirt. 'It's a long story,' he said ruefully.

'Oh,' Marie Jane pouted her lips. 'Come on then, tell us!' She was about to say more but he passed to another partner. Tessa, attracting her friend's attention, indicated by a shake of her head that the subject was not to be pursued. What did it matter if he was in his old clothes? Besides, she and Finn had discussed strategy, and part of it was to save breath. Tessa was happy now. His presence was enough. To know he was there, that he would be there to the end, was all the knowledge she needed to set her mind soaring and her feet flying. He caught her smile gratefully; it warmed him and wrapped itself about his heart, binding up the hurt, covering the disappointment, the anxiety of the last few hours.

He had gone confidently to his aunt's cabin yesterday, anticipation of the Long Dance flooding his soul. It had shone in his face, his eyes, as he carefully draped the breeches and shirt on the only other chair in the cabin.

It was then she launched into her terrible tirade. The rocking chair contributed with its crack-and-grind . . . crack-and-grind. Her hoarse, crow-like voice clawed at the air . . . about the pig which had died . . . the one which was left.

O'Malley's words had flashed across his mind 'Are you still skivvying for the Aunt, then?' He had thought of his parents and how he owed it to them to speak up and break free. He had spoken up and declared his intention of attending the Long Dance. He had waited for a threat, but it never came. On reflection, he might have known she had taken his stand too quietly. Victory, however fleeting, did not usually come his way. But then, he did not have a suspicious mind. As O'Malley had said, he was 'too soft on the sentiments'.

So he had gone to sleep looking at his new clothes, imagining Tessa's surprise when she saw him in his finery – him in finery! Marie Jane had been impressed, and that was a good enough sign.

Waking with the dawn, Finn had stretched his full length out on the rushes; he had yawned and waited for the morning light to gather in the small window. The Long Dance! Glory, it was the day of the Long Dance! He turned his head slowly, to savour again the sight of his new clothes.

They were not there. The chair on which he had left them was empty. He sat up. Surely in the name o' God he had put them on that chair. Leaping up, he pulled on his corduroys and, still bare to the waist, he looked again, but in vain. His clothes had vanished with the night.

The Aunt's chair had begun to rock. She was sitting still and upright, as though asleep, but he knew she was watching his every move, observing with malicious pleasure his distracted searching, not that there was much to search. The shelf, the cupboard? The only other place was the locker by the Aunt's chair in which she kept the bread.

They're in the locker, he had thought. She's got 'em in that bloody locker! Hidden 'em to stop me going to the Dance! It wouldn't have done any good to ask for them, merely given her the pleasure of refusal and another chance to get at him. Momentarily stunned, he remembered O'Malley's advice – his brain was littered with these marvellous fragments – 'Make some tay', O'Malley always said. 'You'll get a better view of your problem over a cup of tay.' So he made it, and all the time his stomach had churned with anxiety as to how he could get the clothes from the locker. He couldn't go to the Long Dance in working clothes unfragrant as the pigs themselves, not with all those town folk there. And Tess would be in her best . . .

He had finished the tea and was vaguely disappointed when O'Malley's prediction had not come to pass. He had leaned forward to put the empty cup on the hearthstone. His heart had stopped. He could scarcely believe his eyes. The clothes were not in the locker. For there, smouldering beneath the glowing turf, was one small piece – the remains – of his lovely black breeches, and a pearl button from the shirt.

She had burned them! While he had been asleep she had deliberately taken them from the chair and put them on the fire! For one wild moment he felt capable of hitherto unthinkable things.

All the past paraded before him; the cursing of his parents, the

217

continual labour, the continual hunger, and the countless humiliations. The parade passed and he focused on the gaunt black figure.

As he stood up from hearth, slowly, filled with anger and hatred, he had not known himself. It was as though he had been standing to one side, observing this person who now had all the urge to kill surging through the power of his muscled arms, his hands, his racing heart. He had been beyond fear of being cursed, beyond rational thought. He had taken a step toward the rocking chair, one stride, one reaching out, one breaking of that . . .

The observer who had been standing to one side suddenly disappeared. Finn was on his own. He slowly drew back, sweating. Snatching up the old shirt he had run out. There had been a great silence out there, a soothing silence, as though the world had stopped and he could lean his bare back against the cold cabin wall and recover.

He felt as though he had killed his aunt, and although he hadn't he knew he could have done. He had wanted to. To know he had been capable of such desperate emotions set him shaking, and in no mood for civilised society. As he had recovered, the importance of the Long Dance dwindled. He could not go without even a clean shirt, and with a drooping heart he silently mourned the loss of his new clothes.

And then the reassuring familiarity of labour presented itself. The huge grey and pink pig, hearing someone astir, began to thrash about the sty. He swore at it savagely, but the action had restored a sense of perspective. The effort involved in fetching water for washing down pig, sty and compound released the rest of his anger. He fed the pig and eyed it anxiously for any signs of sickness.

'Just keep going, will you,' he had addressed it. 'Or she'll have you, from ears to trotters, from bladder to brains; mashed and rendered down you'll be, like she rendered me new clothes.' Usually cheerful, he would have waved or shouted 'Fine morning' to the steady stream of people passing by a short way off on their way up the glen. But he ignored them all and went on with his tasks with averted head. He had not been impervious, though, to the sounds of the valley . . . a skirl of pipes; great shouts of communal laughter; a burst of oratory; applause. The wind brought them all down, whispering . . . soothing . . . tempting . . . and then with a hint of urgency. Time, and the Long Dance, would wait for no man!

Snatching at the shirt he vaulted over the wall and, buttoning it as he ran, he had arrived in time for the starting pistol.

And that was how Tessa saw him, his strength and eagerness shining through, his skin aglow with exertion, his curls tousled, eyes bright beneath the dark fringe of alluring lashes; uncomplicated and free, and with a smile, a special smile, a secret smile just for her. But she could tell something had happened with the Aunt and for that reason had warned Marie Jane not to pursue the question of the clothes.

There were some two hundred participants in the Ennan Long Dance of 1898 and as many spectators. Although a picnic atmosphere prevailed, the occasion was known to have a serious side. In the past, the hilarity and effort had caused quite a few to drop dead. Others had been thrown into fits, made lame or come on with a stroke; but nothing impaired the rapture, the enthusiasm, of the start.

The dances were a mixture and at the whim of the musicians, causing great fun at the rapid change of sets. The ancient custom was now overlaid with rules, one being that the tempo should be alternated, to prevent bribery of the fiddlers resulting in an unfair advantage to certain parties.

And so it began. The dancers were at once into the mood; stomping and gasping they whirled and twirled into a rapid change of partners. One of these changes brought Tessa face to face with Frank Kildare. He knew he was light on his feet, but with Tessa as a partner, he felt clumsy, though even that knowledge could not spoil his pleasure. Arms linked, round they went and, joining hands, galloped down the set to wild clapping. Kildare was exuberant: she was his partner for these few minutes, his alone.

The spirit of the dance was in Tessa and there was no place for resentment. She took him as he was. Out of his usual clothes he seemed like any other man. But considering the men of the valley – Finn apart – she conceded him to be a little better than the rest. In tweed trousers, braces and white shirt he looked fine enough . . . thickening about the waist, but Marie Jane liked a 'well-fleshed' man, and Frank Kildare was certainly that. He danced as he walked, with the smooth movements of a hunter. She concluded that even Marie Jane would have her work cut out with such a catch.

Kildare wanted to speak, to make some comment, but feared to interrupt the pleasure of the dance. He was intensely aware of the strength of her hands, her supple waist; she was as fleet as a deer, and as innocent and transparent. Knowing he could not keep up the crazy pace for long, he still tried to manoeuvre himself into another set with Tessa, but he had reckoned without the caprice of the fiddlers. When he expected a reel it was a jig, or a foursome turned out to be an eightsome.

Marie Jane was more perceptive and recognised the opening strains of each tune early enough to get herself to dance with, or opposite, the gamekeeper. She was grateful to him for getting her into service, and the open gratitude he found enchanting. Always susceptible to a pretty woman, he enjoyed her readiness to flirt, her response to the squeeze of his hand, the tightening of his arm about her waist; and the pressure of her breasts against his chest as they closed together for a whirl. After a while, he gave up trying to stay close to Tessa and enjoyed instead an amusing game with Marie Jane, trying to get together, and pulling wry faces at each other when they did not succeed.

As each hour passed the President of the local Gaelic League Society – gold chains across his paunch and a presidential one about his neck – scraped back his chair on the platform, lifted a megaphone to his mouth and yelled out both the time and the number of dancers left in the arena. At one o'clock those who were taking part solely for the fun and the occasion had worked up sufficient appetite to open up their picnic baskets or packages and start on the ale. Consequently, about a hundred were left.

Proud Riley kept himself with O'Malley and his own people. He had no time for strangers, yet he hoped his daughter would have 'struck it up' with the fair young man, obviously a clerk; or the tall one with white gloves; him with the red face who had brought the ale up; or the elderly man who treated her with real deference – even Kildare, but he had noticed the gamekeeper now danced more often with O'Malley's girl. He sighed and drank deeply from the tin mug. All this speculation and hoping was proving too much for him. If Teresa did not land herself a young man from the town, he would have to spend another year on tenterhooks! What was the matter with young fellas today? Why the divil couldn't they win a young woman's heart and get on with it? Not everyone was like himself.

Look at O'Malley; not much more than twenty when he went to the altar.

'Ladies and gentleman, it's pleased I am to inform you that it's two of the clock and there are now precisely fifty people on their feet!'

'Tess . . .' said Finn as he came nearer. 'Do you remember me telling you about Guinness, the black stuff in bottles with a label on for you to read?' He felt like a man of the world out to impress his lady.

'I do so.' She recalled his enthusiasm from his trip into town that time the miller had dropped dead.

'I asked O'Malley to fetch a couple up with me wrestling money. Mrs O'Malley's keeping them safe – for when we win!' Fool, he thought suddenly. I should have left me new clothes there, too.

Tessa expressed both surprise and pleasure, taking care not to let slip that Marie Jane had already told her. 'We'll need it at this rate. I've a thirst already!' She recalled herself and Marie Jane conspiring not to drink too much: 'You can lose precious time by going for a pee.'

'Not only that, but everyone knows where you're going!'

'I'm sweating like a pig already,' Finn said.

'It's all right for men, they can take their shirts off!'

He grinned. 'I'm leaving that treat till later!'

'Competition's still good. Can you see Marie Jane?'

'Dropped at the last dance.'

'And the keeper?'

'The one before that.'

'Marie Jane's got her eye on him, you know.'

'It serves him right!'

The sun had come out briefly, as though to give its blessing to so energetic an event. Marie Jane had suggested a walk to 'sort out their legs'. Kildare knew what she meant. Their departure from among the spectators went unnoticed as the dancers who had given up now swelled the number to four hundred.

'I'll race you to the trees!' Marie Jane cried daringly, and setting off towards the hillside, she shouted. 'Give me a bit of a start!'

He had intended to. Her dainty shoes would not get her far, and when she went down – as they always did – he wanted her to go down out of sight. But they did not get her beyond the worn out grass.

'Race you!' he echoed, looking down at her and laughing. 'You're scarcely under starter's orders!'

She waited until he had sat down before saying coyly, 'Had we not better be getting back, then?'

'Better to watch from here, don't you think?'

'You're sweating.' She ran her finger along his forehead.

'It's not with the exertion, either.'

'And what would it be, then, that's fetching you out all in a sweat?'

'Could be your pretty eyes.' He reached out, his knuckles brushing her neck, to touch a ringlet. 'Or, your dancing curls.'

'Not me dancing feet, Mr Kildare?' She raised herself up from her elbow and wiggled her toes.

'Those, too.' But it was not her feet which had grabbed his attention, so much as the daring display of rounded bosom as she had leaned forward. And not so much that, he realised, but the fact of her having loosened the neckline somehow! My God, he thought, the little minx!

'Why,' he drew closer to ask, 'won't you call me Frank?'

'I really don't know, Mr Kildare.' Marie Jane admonished herself seriously; sure, you'll burn in hell, she thought, for haven't you been calling him Frank to Tessa most of the time!

'I'd better warn you though.' His hazel eyes dwelt on her. 'Any woman who calls me Frank always gets kissed. So, 'tis up to you, Miss O'Malley!'

Marie Jane wallowed in this delightful quandary; should she, or should she not?

'Let me tell you, though.' He decided to make it easier for her. 'It might be an idea to get used to my name; after all we'll be seeing something of each other at Fitzcarron House.'

'Oh.' She rounded her mouth and, feeling he had offered her a way of acceptance that was not too forward, she said on a low sigh, 'Frank.'

His instinct told him this young lady was in the bag, but would be bagged in her own sweet way. There was no hurry; her eyes, bold and mischievous, told him she wanted to play. Sitting on the ground, they leaned forward, and his lips touched hers warmly, gently titillating. Their eyes met; met, and held. She should have looked away, over his shoulder to the crowd beyond, at the trees further up, anything. Her face flushed, her heart pounded. Her caution was lost in the recklessness of her passion. Her hands moved up to his shoulders and beneath his shirt she felt not the scrawny muscle of the mountainy men, but flesh, firm, warm flesh. She felt the smoothness of his neck, the arch of it, the beginnings of the hairline, and then she was pulling his head down, narrowing the gap between their lips, her mouth seeking his with a passion that was both unexpected and demanding.

Frank Kildare could not believe it. Was there no end to the surprises these people had in store? With a tinkle of a laugh, she met his astounded gaze. It went to her head. Her mind whirled like the wings of a dozen partridges. She had only to play her cards right and he would be hers.

She knew his eyes were on her throat, her breasts, the next thing would be the pressure of his hand there. In her previous games, the temptation to touch had been too great for hot, eager lads and their ears had been cuffed. But this, she realised with a catch of her breath, was different. He was not a hot eager youth. He was a grown man of thirty.

Touching his lips with her forefinger she reprimanded him playfully. 'In the name of the good God, Frank, you'll have to do better than that!'

The fiddles, the shouts from the distance which had been replaced by the hammering of her heart, were now becoming audible. She was up, on her feet, and making towards the dance. Her senses were enhanced and heightened. Marie Jane felt herself to be suddenly more mature, full-grown, desired. Was he annoyed? What did she care if he was? In the game of love they always came round. He had caught her up, was beside her. Hazel eyes agleam, thin lips smiling.

'I will do,' he said.

'Do what?' She knew what he meant, but it was all part of the game.

He grabbed her waist, and she let out a little stifled scream; he squeezed and let go to whisper in her ear. 'I will do better next time. But,' he wagged a finger, 'remember, you asked for it!'

The President was on his feet again. 'Ladies and Gentlemen. It is now four of the clock and there are but ten left in the dance! Let's give them a hand! Encourage them! Cheer them on!'

223

Finn and Tessa were the last remaining two from Ennan. The other dancers were regular competitors at dancing functions. One was the gardener from Lord Fitzcarron's estate who had won last year. Then there were two clerks, both members of the Gaelic League, from Bray and Sligo; a farmer and his wife from over the other side of Rohira; one of the pipers from St Joseph's looking very grand in kilt and thick stockings; a young girl who was the niece of Father Donaghue; and Old Paddy, a tall, thin, straight man who had appeared every year since anyone could remember. He was always the fifth from the last to drop out, never dropping out willingly. Paddy's method was to fall senseless to the ground, recovering with a glass of ale thrown in his face and another one being placed in his hand.

By this time the ale had gone, apart from Paddy's which was saved especially, and the shiftless now began their rounds, moving like wraiths, offering poteen at exorbitant prices and hoping they would not approach an 'excise' in disguise. The dancers had moved further along the valley because the ground was becoming churned up with so many trampling feet.

Tessa and Finn had discarded their shoes and their feet felt light and free; the chill of the earth was refreshing, and a soft rain had began to fall. To the competitors it was welcome, except to Father Donaghue's niece who, suddenly chilled, ran off to the shelter of her uncle's serge cape. The spectators set up a groan.

'Ach, will you look at the rain!'

'At least it's kept off until now.'

'Has it set in?'

'Will you look at the clouds! Mother of God, it's set in for a week!'

Umbrellas shot up like overgrown mushrooms; topcoats, macintoshes and capes were donned; tarpaulins were raised to double as shelters; some crouched beneath carts, and the rest got wet.

Proud Riley, watching with O'Malley, did not know what to make of his daughter's expertise, for her barefooted grace was openly commented on. Nor did he know what to make of young Collins, who looked set to share her victory.

The rain refreshed Tessa; she was thankful, for her mouth was dry and her throat felt shrivelled. But the very rain which was good for her soaked the piper's heavy kilt, and he limped off to sporting cheers for so great an effort.

These last hours drew the best out of Finn. At times his mind had wandered to the health of the grey and pink pig . . . his aunt . . . his new clothes smouldering while he had slept. But, now, on the last lap he was buoyant.

In contrast to Finn, the two clerks were not so much dancing as hopping about like magpies. One hopped on the wrong ankle and sprained it; another took the cramp and was helped to the side. Only the farmer and his wife from the other side of Rohira were left to battle it out with the two from Ennan. The music grew wilder as the dance reached its climax, the fiddlers responding to the excitement of the audience. Cheers again . . . for the farmer's wife being carried off by her family. Tessa was now the only female between two men. The farmer was a lot more experienced, but the other two had youth on their side, and determination . . . to go on . . . to the end. Energy was now flagging, feet were heavier, breath shorter; craving fluid, they strove to keep up the pace.

The farmer's skin had turned from red to purple, his eyes began to bulge, his lips crack. He began to stagger. The crowd cheered. Excitement ran high. Riley felt her heart would burst with pride, and wished her mother could have seen her now. Marie Jane, not caring about being wet and bedraggled, forgot the parlourmaid decorum she had been practising and, cupping her hands to her mouth, yelled support. 'Keep it up, Tessa, Finn. For the love of God, keep moving!'

Frank Kildare watched with narrowed eyes the sweating body of the half-naked barefooted young man. He instinctively pulled in his stomach, feeling all of his thirty years. He looked to be what he obviously was, honest, upright and strong, yet with the bright look of a boy. Was this not the young fella who had wiped the floor with Mick Murphy?

'Marie Jane?'

Startled, and having forgotten in the excitement about the gamekeeper at her side, she looked up.

'Is there,' Kildare nodded towards the dancers, 'is there anything between those two? You know, sweethearts?'

Always quick to keep her friend's secret she shook her head emphatically. 'Her da's out for a good marriage. None of the valley fellas would ever dare.'

'Does she not fancy . . . anyone?'

'Never gets the chance; he never lets her down here since that swine Mick Murphy tried it on. If her da thought she'd find anyone from Ennan he'd have her in a convent, sharpish. And she thinks too much of the old fella to go against him. But she's the great girleen, Frank. Who'd think she'd been dancing for over six hours!'

'The farmer doesn't look so good,' commented Kildare. His eyes were no longer narrow; his enquiries about Collins had resulted in a lighter heart. The fiddlers now turned wilder . . . faster . . . as if wearying of it all and ready to make an end. Tessa and Finn could scarcely hear the music for the pounding of their hearts. The crowd was silent now. The dancers, all three, seemed to be moving as in a trance.

'Oh! Oh!'

The great roar summoned Tessa's numbed mind back to the present. The farmer was down. Carried off. The music stopped. The fiddlers declared themselves exhausted.

'They've won!' yelled Marie Jane, and leaving the gamekeeper ran to hug her friend. Amid the tumult of noise, the skirling of pipes and the outbursts of song, O'Malley conducted the stumbling figures to the platform, where gentlemen congratulated the victors from under their umbrellas and ladies poured glasses of water. The water was another of the rules. Six years before, a man had downed poteen on an empty and dehydrated stomach, and had gone into a raving fit and died before nightfall. Garlands of summer flowers from the town were placed about both their necks, and while they sat wet, mud-stained, red-faced and speechless, they marvelled that water tasted so good. All the talk of honour, history, ancient custom and fortitude passed over their heads unheeded.

Still standing where Marie Jane had left him, Kildare felt piqued to be so easily forgotten by a young slip of a thing who, only a short while before, had kissed him with a maturity beyond her years. He, who never failed with women, always had them at his beck and call, was being given the brushoff! He had no doubt that her brushoff was momentary, but that he was on the receiving end did not go down well.

Although the rain had soaked through his shirt and breeches, it was warm rain and he did not mind. So, hands in pockets, Kildare prowled about the gathering, observing, assessing, amusing himself at the antics of a bearded photographer tying to settle the tripod of his camera on the churned-up earth. He had photographed the huts, the hovels, the platform, the committee and the crowd. He had developed a splitting headache; his three-piece suit was soaked; his fine kid boots were utterly ruined, and he wanted nothing more than to get his equipment onto the pony and trap and get home to put his feet in a bowl of mustard and hot water. Make the most of it, Kildare thought; this'll be the last Long Dance in Ennan, or my name's not Frank Kildare!

Everyone was making the most of it. Members of the Gaelic League, anxious for snippets of folk lore, had their heads together with two of the Duggan girls, Gypo Kelly and Pat O'Malley, who, for sixpence each, were willing to provide such details.

'Oh, that was in the old days, you understand,' he heard Larkin say. Of course it was, thought Kildare in amusement. If the town folks are so gullible, they deserve to be fleeced!

'Blue butterflies!' echoed a naturalist. 'And bog orchids?'

Dion O'Malley nodded. He knew just the place. 'Will you be a good lad, then and take me? There's a sixpence for you.'

Kildare heard the soft, silver tone of O'Malley himself. God, no show without Punch!

'And will I tell you, now, that in 1650 the Great Bog went on the march.'

'It never did?'

'God strike me dead if I tell a word of a lie . . .'

And Kevin Connor was at it, making a good show of recoiling in horror when asked to take a party up to Ennabrugh. 'Miles and miles of bloody great bog,' he echoed. 'Sure, it's the most desolate sight in the green of Ireland . . .'

'But you can take us? You know the way?'

Kevin hesitated until a sharp-eyed man with binoculars about his neck suggested a 'whip round' to make it worth his while – then Kevin was on his way.

The rain did not dampen any spirits; they had set out to enjoy themselves and wanted to take advantage of this golden opportunity to see it all. Those not of an enquiring mind held their own little gatherings of dancing, singing or just drinking.

Kildare stopped to watch the photographing of the winners: bedraggled they looked, their heads peering incongruously above the garland of flowers about their necks. Never having been photographed before, never even having seen the equipment, they stared uneasily at it wondering why the man kept putting his head beneath a black cloth.

'Look this way, please!' yelled the photographer. They looked. 'Thank you!' He sighed, and with a mustard footbath in mind, prepared to go.

The winning pair were toasted by friends and strangers alike. The latter, wanting to experience a 'proper hooley', yelled for music. 'Will you tune the fiddle?'

'A flute! Mother o' God, is there no flute?'

There had not been a flute since Riley's.

'What, no flute? No bloody flute?'

Young Duggan sprang up to save the day with his accordion. His sisters, all eight, laughingly seized a male each and hands joined and feet flew in a kind of recklessness which drew others into its spell. All joined in, the old and the young, swinging, arming, footing it and hooching with wild yells of laughter. Martin Jarvey's father, who could drink a bottle of whisky and still walk a straight line, challenged all comers.

Finn and Tessa, under cover of all this, had sneaked into O'Malley's cabin, where Mrs O'Malley rubbed their feet with green oil. 'Works wonders with Jarvey's donkeys!' And then she produced the two bottle of Guinness with a flourish. 'You can sit awhile,' she said. 'But not too long, or you'll have your da after you, Tessa.'

Finn reached for his garland and gave it to Mrs O'Malley. 'Will you take this,' he said, his voice a little croaky with emotion. She hesitated. 'Go on,' he urged. 'Me ma, God rest her soul, she'd like you to have it, and so would I. You're an angel, Mrs O'Malley.'

She looked from one tired but jubilant face to the other. A choking sensation filled her throat. No one, not even himself, had ever given her so much as a daisy. They watched her carry the flowers gently to the other end of the cabin.

'Sure, that was nice of you, Finn. And it was nice of you to buy this Guinness. Oh, glory!' Tessa exclaimed. 'Just look at the reading on the label!' Then, while he opened the bottles, she remarked casually. 'It was a pity you didn't leave your new clothes here as well.' She saw the cloud cover his face immediately, and swore at herself for reminding him of the Aunt. Who wanted to think of her on this, their very own night?

'I was a fool, Tess. I've called meself all kinds of a fool since.' He stared at the two opened bottles. 'I could have killed her, Tess; I reached out and, God forgive me, murder was in my heart.'

'Try not to think about it. I was a gobbeen to remind you.'

He raised grateful eyes. The cloud lifted. 'I've forgotten already!' He began to pour the Guinness into cups.

'Finn!' she cried out. 'Stop! The top's coming over!'

'Froth,' he explained loftily. 'They call it "a good head" in the pubs.'

'You should keep your eyes on the bottle!'

'Oh, Mother o' God, it's terrible difficult with a girleen like yourself sitting so near.' Both heads turned toward the end of the cabin. Mrs O'Malley was still there. Tessa drank the Guinness eagerly.

'Do you like it?'

'It's just like you said – drinking velvet!'

'That's what they said in the pub. You've a moustache of froth. No, don't wipe it, let me.' His finger traced the creamy smudge. His eyes were so intense that she knew if Mrs O'Malley had not been there he would have kissed her. He wanted more than anything to kiss it from her lips. Instead, he kissed his froth covered finger. Today they had shared so much; but it was not enough. He replenished her cup and his own.

'To civilisation!'

'You sound just like Martin Jarvey!'

He immediately felt good, for hadn't Martin been the boyo? 'I've started hoping, Tess, that you and me will go down to civilisation one day.'

She did not know what to say. How could they? If he was reckoning without his aunt – and he ought to, wicked old witch that she was – she could not reckon without her da. As if to confirm her thoughts, Mrs O'Malley's thin figure was with them in a trice. 'C'mon, move, for the love of God! Your da's after you and as drunk as a lord he is.'

Tessa thrust the empty bottle toward Mrs O'Malley. 'Will you hide it from me da? I'll take it up when I go. I want to keep it for ever, like me ma kept her hat and muff.'

Riley entered the cabin and staggered up to them. He leaned forward and wagged his finger beneath Mrs O'Malley's nose. 'It's a disappointed man y'see before you . . .'

'And why is that?'

'Dancin' with a clerk my daughter was. Every inch a clerk that young fella was. And the one in white gloves . . .' He turned to Tessa. 'Sure, you hardly spoke a word to him, and followin' you about he was.'

'Da, will you sit down before you fall?'

'Y'see, Mrs O'Malley. She knows she's wronged her da so she's changing the subject!'

'God Almighty, I've not heard him talk so much for years!'

'Those men were being polite, Da. Just because a fella passes the time o' day, it doesn't meant he wants to marry me!'

'And why shouldn't he want to marry my daughter?' he demanded of Mrs O'Malley. 'Sure, she's the finest colleen this side o' the Connemara mountains . . .'

'I'm going outside,' said Tess. 'I'd rather be singing than listening to him!'

As she went out they were singing the chorus of the 'Rambling Candy Man', and from sheer exuberance of spirits Tessa joined in a duet with Flowery Nolan the travelling street singer, thinking the others would join in too. Realising they hadn't, she clamped a hand to her mouth, but Nolan encouraged her to continue singing with him. No one knew Tessa had a good singing voice, except Finn; she had not recognised its quality, but Flowery Nolan was adamant.

'Give us a song on your own?' he suggested. 'Sure, you'll never be short of a penny on the streets while you can sing like that. C'mon, give us a song?'

'I don't know so many,' she stammered.

'Give us what first comes to mind.'

Purposely not looking a Finn, who had made his escape shortly after her, she began to sing 'The Lovely Lad of My Dreams' and with each note she grew more confident.

> 'I wake from my dreams of thee
> In the first sweet sleep of the night,
> When your vision haunts me so,
> And the stars in your eyes are bright.
> I wake from my dreams of thee,
> With heaven in my heart it seems.
> Oh, how I love you so,
> Lovely lad of my dreams.'

She sang with a lilting, yet resonant voice, which rang with the feeling of those who live in wild country. Finn listened avidly to every word, and entertained reckless thoughts of real houses with an upstairs he had seen in the town.

'You kept that close, Tess,' said Marie Jane sharply, consumed with one of her little jealousies. 'Not satisfied with winning the Long Dance, you join up with Flowery Nolan.'

'Must have been the Guinness set me up; I didn't know I had it in me.'

'And when you knew, you couldn't stop!'

'I've got to have something,' Tessa protested. 'It isn't me that's going off to the grand life.'

'At least Finn did buy you Guinness; but, well, Frank's not at all free with his money.'

'Give him time,' Tessa said soothingly to her friend. 'And think on that being all you give him. Remember, he's a grown fella, not one of the lads.'

Marie Jane was glad of the semi-darkness, for her face had suddenly gone scarlet; she could not bring herself to disclose her passionate adventure, and its sequel.

While Mrs O'Malley had been applying donkey oil to Tessa's sore feet, she had been luring Frank Kildare to the shadows behind the deserted platform. She had only intended to carry on the teasing of the afternoon, and had not been prepared for his intoxicating kiss or the hardness of his embrace. She had felt the hard firm flesh of his thighs through her pink skirts, and the urge to give some kind of response had rapidly mounted.

'I told you I could do better,' he had laughed softly. He must have heard her sharp intake of breath when he caressed her bosom for, lifting her chin, he had challenged, 'You asked for it?'

She could have stopped there and then, but her lowered eyes gave assent. His fingers had expertly unfastened the buttons of her gown. Her face burned, heart hammered, and her eyes closed as she felt herself exposed to the damp summer air. She had removed her shift since this afternoon, and he knew it. No one had ever touched her naked breasts before. The feel of his warm hands sent the blood racing to her head and she'd felt so weak she had been compelled to lean against him. Her mind had whirled apace with his fondling. 'Oh, God and all the angels forgive me,' she had sighed inwardly, for whatever happened next would be what she had most desired. Oh, this was love, with a real man.

She could scare believe her ears when he had whispered 'No more ... Not here, it isn't safe.' He had buttoned up her gown. 'What if the President of the Gaelic Preservation Society came back for his umbrella?' Plummeting down to earth more quickly than ever before, she turned her head and there on the platform was a large black umbrella. The sight of it brought an explosion of laughter to their lips, easing a situation that could have been embarrassing for her. Marie Jane was not yet used to carrying the memory of the adventure ... her standing there in front of a man with her breasts bare to the winds, and he the first person to see her so. She felt as though she had lost something. It must feel like this to lose your virginity ... She sighed, not sure whether to be glad or remorseful.

The Rileys stayed the night at O'Malley's cabin. Tessa's feet had been too sore to cover the distance back and her father too drunk. He dropped on the rushes by O'Malley's wall and remained there until Tessa threw water on his face and head. She told him it was dawn and that she was going up to milk the goats.

With the tasselled shawl on her shoulders, and bare feet – for they were still too swollen for the pumps – she put the garland of flowers about her neck, clutched the empty Guinness bottle and, waving her hand to the shiftless who were scavenging, set off up the hillside.

She and Marie Jane had spent the night drinking tea. They had discussed the Long Dance, the gossip, the future, Marie Jane's future, and Tessa had admired the clock and learned to tell the time. Neither could have slept; Marie Jane for thinking about Frank Kildare and how her next encounter with him would be on the estate, with no left behind umbrellas to put him off his stride and Tessa for wondering what had happened to Finn. After singing 'The Lovely Lad of My Dreams' she had not seen him. When would she? The prospect looked as bleak as Ennabrugh in winter.

Finn, after hearing Tessa sing, had faded away into the shadows. He could not bear to walk away from her. After so much sharing, so much laughter, parting would be agony. It would be better to slink away, to mingle with those going down past the Aunt's cabin, whilst

232

the torches glimmered and glowed, leaping about like jack-o'-lanterns on the Great Bog of a midsummer night.

The Great Bog, he thought, bitterly. The Great bloody Bog! It's swallowed me ma and da, and now it's got me in its grip. If it wasn't there, he reasoned, I wouldn't be here; Ennan would not be here. It gave them peat and rushes. Little offerings to sustain basic life, to placate them into staying on, for where could anyone live as cheaply as this? And now Ennabrugh was in a mood. It was holding so much water, due to the rainfall, that peat would not form. Even Proud Riley, who knew it well, was worried. The turves should have been cut in May, turned and dried out all summer – Almighty God, that was a joke, summer! – then come September it would all have to be brought down. At least Jarvey would do a good trade hiring the donkeys.

As for his 'penal servitude' to his aunt, which O'Malley was always on about, he had as much chance of cutting that as he had of cutting turf on Ennabrugh. He had very little money, and still less after buying the new clothes. He had not enough money to support a flea, still less himself.

In the company of the revellers, Finn had reached the Aunt's cabin sooner than expected. He moved away from the human company. He was alone in the shadow of the compound. A quiet terror began to tease his fast beating heart. The pig! He had forgotten about it! Was it dead? If it was, what terror awaited him? The cabin was in darkness. He heard a noise. He listened. It was the pig snoring! Marvellous! Sure, it had not sickened, it had not died! Oh, the lovely beautiful beast! His feet were too tender to vault, so he climbed over the wall. So pleased was he to see the animal alive, and to be sure it stayed that way, he curled up beside it, his back to the great snoring snout. It had not had the evening washdown, but he did not mind. It was better than facing the Aunt in the hours of darkness.

CHAPTER THIRTEEN

Every Sunday, the priest came up to the tiny stone chapel to say Mass. Not that Tessa attended regularly; 'because of the distance', Riley told Father Donaghue. But everyone else knew different.

On the Sunday following the Long Dance, Tessa was allowed down, for after Mass she was to accompany her friend along the length of Ennabrugh and across the ridge to Fitzcarron House.

Proud Riley, still railing against fate for not coming up with a 'good marriage', had no fears for his daughter's wellbeing on this occasion, for no strangers dared wander about such a treacherous place.

To give her daughter a good sendoff Mrs O'Malley had made a dinner of chicken and potato broth. In the chapel she had lit a candle for the moral safety of Marie Jane, and hoped her husband knew what he was doing, getting a nature like hers into service, and so far from home. He had convinced her that the money Marie Jane earned would help with extras for Little Annie, and wasn't Dion constantly outgrowing Pat's handed-down clothes? Yes, by Almighty God, Mrs O'Malley now thought, it's time the girl served some purpose.

With all her clothes in a battered suitcase and a flat hat perched on her ringlets, Marie Jane was ready. Her parents would have liked to see her a little less eager to be gone, a few tears, or merely a crumpling of the red lips. But Marie Jane, eager for freedom, had no thought of pretence or artifice on this occasion. There was nothing hypocritical about her filial affections and going away did not alter anything.

The eldest boys stood with hands in pockets and grinned. None of the family had gone away before, and they stood there uncertain, aloof from the procedure. Bridget, who had not forgotten the incident of the tinker's pinafore at the Fair, sidled towards her mother's skirts. Tim, with his sturdy, infant charm and a perception beyond his years, did not actually look pleased in case he got a cuff from his mother, but in his large brown eyes, so angelically lifted,

Marie Jane recognised his awareness that with her leaving he would now be packed off with his elder brothers, and not his elder sister. Marie Jane did not resent this. A tacit understanding now passed between the two. She stooped to put her arms about Little Annie who began to cry, for Marie Jane was the only beautiful thing in her life.

'God bless you, Little Annie,' Marie Jane whispered. 'Don't cry, now. I'm only going to get you something nice. Goodbye to you, Ma! It was the finest dinner you gave us.' She kissed her mother on the cheek and felt embarrassed. Her mother's thin, harassed body could no more unbend at this moment than could Marie Jane.

'C'mon,' said her father, stepping forward from the line in which the family had arranged itself. 'Sure, I'll walk a little way with you then.' He smiled at his family. They were all aware he was saving the situation and breathed little sighs of relief. The solemnity had now changed to laughter and frenzied waving of hands as the three left the compound.

Mrs O'Malley ushered Little Annie inside, thankful that her husband had spared her the spectacle of an emotional parting with his favourite child. Their farewell would take place at the end of the valley with Tessa walking on a few paces; himself would return with the tears scarce dry on his face. And this night would be the first night in years that the rafters had not echoed with the talk, the jokes, the arguments between the two.

It was as she had presumed and, O'Malley gone, the two young women continued the journey amicably.

'Oh, by the grace o' God, it's a dry day, Tessa, not much wind either. At least I'll not arrive looking as though I've been pulled through a hedge backwards!' She indicated the sun as it appeared from behind a great column of cloud. 'And it doesn't look as though it'll rain.'

'You'll not get wet, but you might get sweaty with the heat!' teased Tessa. 'Carrying that awkward case.'

'Would you like me to carry me stuff in a sack?'

'It would have been easier!'

Marie Jane trudged doggedly on, lifting her head occasionally, her eyes scanning the sky for any tell-tale signs of rain. Even though the suitcase was heavy and awkward and banged her knees, she would willingly carry it twice as far to get away from the godforsaken valley and this terrible Bog. There it lay alongside them as they walked, snaking this way or curving that. Hot and panting under great bulks of brassy cloud, as it had before time began. And over the eternity of decay hung the sweet stifling odour of ripeness. Marie Jane shivered, despite the warmth. The earth beneath her feet now felt soft, a constant reminder of the danger beneath, of how they, too, could so easily become part of the eternal decay. She hurried after Tessa, following her closely along the narrow path. Her heart was pounding rapidly, partly from hurrying and partly from fear of the ghastly solitude. Marie Jane hated silence and solitude; it seemed unnatural to one who had always been surrounded by people talking, crying, joking, dogs barking and chickens clucking. Here everything was trapped in silence, including themselves, for conversation, like the path, had ran out. Even in the full heat of summer it was eerie up here, full of ghosts. There was not a dwelling in sight. Not a plume of smoke, no birds, no sign of life except themselves.

'Can you see the house, Tessa?' she called out and was immediately cheered at the sound of her own voice. 'We've been at it for hours – '

'So, you're reckoning in hours now!'

'What else? It's as it should be.'

'No, I can't see the house yet for the hills. C'mon, now, hitch your skirts; we've got to climb up out of this and then you'll be able to see the gates.' Tessa knew it would work, for had her father not used the same ploy on herself many a time. Marie Jane, eager to see the gates, soon caught up.

A little while later they stood on the rise looking at the great iron gates, the narrow spikes tipped with gold. The Fitzcarron crest did not now appear as boldly emblazoned as in her childhood and Tessa recalled her father's warning about trespassers.

Marie Jane sucked in her breath. 'Mother of God, it's like the gates of paradise. Oh, to think I'm going to work in there!'

'Well, let's get on. I'll only come as far as the gates.'

Marie Jane stopped. 'Now, why are you doing that?' she demanded. 'It's not friendly to desert me on the last lap.'

Tessa knew it would be useless to try and convey the horror of the childhood experience, memories of which were now flooding back. Marie Jane had never understood; she never would.

'You have a reason for entering,' Marie Jane said.

'Look how quickly they collared Kate Murphy!'

'This is different. We could be two maids instead of one so far as the outside staff know.'

'Staff?'

'Yes. That's what anyone working on the estate is called. Frank says it all the time. I,' she said importantly, 'am staff.'

Tessa considered for a moment and, not liking the thought of desertion, agreed to accompany her friend to the kitchen.

The gates on the Ennabrugh side were rarely used and it needed their combined strength to push one open far enough for them to enter. Getting through the gates without incident was a relief to Tessa, but Marie Jane remained amazed at it all.

Neither had ever seen such great leafy trees and fat bulky bushes. Like criminals they crept along by banks of late rhododendrons and suddenly, following the bend, Fitzcarron House stood square in front of them.

They looked at each other in a kind of dazed fulfilment, as though a great mission had been accomplished. Tessa felt a touch of pride, for she at least had seen it from a distance, and Marie Jane felt she had reached the promised land.

Fitzcarron House, in comparison with other Irish country houses, was small. Grey-stoned, it stood squat and square. The front door was reached by impressive steps and was flanked by two pillars, the base of each smudged with swirls of olive-green lichen. The uniform sash windows, like pairs of great eyes, looked out loftily onto the world, and caught the awed glances of the two young women.

'We'd better get round the back,' said Tessa, in a hushed voice. She had become conscious of the many windows and was frightened of being taken for a trespasser, like Kate Murphy had been. 'It's as quiet as the bloody grave, this, Marie Jane,' whispered Tessa as they approached the back. 'You're sure he said today, this week?'

Marie Jane dumped her case down and joined the silence. They looked all around. The place seemed deserted. Stumps of dried grass shot up from between cobbles. Traces of horse manure dried hard in the sun and wisps of straw had been pushed by the light wind against the wall where they remained. The upper halves of two stable doors yawned open and a stray hen stalked about in melancholy silence.

'At least Frank could have been on the lookout for us,' declared Marie Jane, and almost at once her anxious tone turned to one of relief. 'Talk o' the divil! Look who's here!'

Frank Kildare had opened a door and, after pausing for a moment, made his way toward them. He had noticed their approach some time ago, for it was Sunday afternoon and nothing stirred in Fitzcarron House until tea. He had been sitting before the kitchen fire, arms folded, feet on fender, when Mrs Quail, the cook-housekeeper had descended on him.

'Will you get your arse off that chair and keep a lookout for the colleen you've wished upon me – and by the good God, I hope she's a worker. I don't give a tinker's cuss if she limps, squints, or has a hump on her back – '

'Now, Mrs Quail, would I be getting you a maid that wasn't fit to present to her ladyship?'

'God Almighty, 'tis one of them,' Mrs Quail had yawned, and adjourned to the chair in the butler's pantry. It was his afternoon off, so she flung a muslin over her head, to keep off the flies, and immediately faded into a post-luncheon nap.

He had sat a while longer, before going to look from the windows. The silence between Sunday lunch and tea always bored him. Although allowed to take his meals in the kitchen with the rest of the staff he did not always take advantage, but today was different. He had, therefore, ample time to observe the two young women, and their surprise and timidity. O'Malley's girl was certainly a looker, he thought, and if she was anything like her father, would avoid as much work as possible and yet retain her popularity. Perhaps her coming would encourage others – Tessa perhaps. With an impatient sigh he wished they would all come to the estate and leave the valley to Lord Fitzcarron's sheep. The crofters would provide cheap labour. If Mrs Quail had got a girl from Rohira, she would have wanted twice as much money. Of course, they'd have to teach Marie Jane, but she was quick and eager to please, and without fancy ideas about 'time to herself' and what was her 'due', or notions about certain duties 'not being her place'. The harangues he had heard over that one!

'You've taken your time,' he smiled, drawing nearer.

'Am I too late?'

'By the time you've put your things down,' he said easily, 'Mrs

238

Quail's table will be full of as much cake and tay as you've ever laid eyes on.'

'Can Tessa stay for a cup of tay, Frank? Sure, she's an awful long way to go back.'

He turned his hunting eyes on Tessa. 'And why not, indeed.'

'So there she is!' yelled Mrs Quail from the doorway. 'For God Almighty's sake, there's two of them! You said there was only one!'

He explained, and the two girls walked to the kitchen close together, Marie Jane's case bumping against her knees.

'Me name's Marie Jane O'Malley,' she said proudly. 'And I've come to work, if you please, Mrs Quail.'

Tessa's eyes rounded at the sight of her friend going down almost on one knee, as they did in church. And no wonder. Mrs Quail was a ramrod of a figure in a long white apron, and from beneath the apron poked the largest feet Tessa had ever seen. Jet black hair was scraped up from a small forehead into a bun on the top of her head. Mrs Quail's face was crumpled like dough which had failed to rise, and from the dough emerged a short straight nose, and to give that air of absolute authority, stern, staring black eyes. No wonder Marie Jane went down on one knee! This woman could be God!

'You'd better come in, then, the two of yous. Sit yourselves down at the table.'

The large kitchen was warm, despite doors and windows being open. The two friends perched on the bench indicated and, as if by magic, other servants appeared, pouring in through the various doors leading off the kitchen. Some clattered down short stairs, others clambered up steps from the cellar beneath. Through one of the open doors, leading into the dark belly of the house, Tessa caught a glimpse of great mahogany surfaces gleaming like the Bog after rain, and behind them a long window and crimson curtains to the floor. She swallowed in amazement. What a tale to tell Finn. He must have felt something like this when he went to Rohira with O'Malley. That is, she thought dully, if I ever see Finn again. Mrs Quail was talking, addressing a sandy-haired girl with freckles on her nose, commissioning her to 'show Marie Jane the ropes after tea'.

'And mind you behave yourself properly. You seem to be a dacent enough young woman, and we're a dacent household here – below stairs at least – ' she added, with an arch look at Kildare, who was taking his tea with the men on another bench. 'You'll have to work hard, you will. It's not all black and white aprons and serving tea . . .'

Marie Jane listened respectfully, and with dismay, to the catalogue of tasks included in her work. She had not thought to soil her hands with the cleaning of grates and making of fires; the latter was always done by her father at home. The fetching of coals and beating of carpets was also unexpected. Gas lights and mantels she had no experience of, but intended to learn. At least, she thought, it's not kitchen stuff, or chambermaid duties.

Tessa, having recovered from the initial shock of civilised life, sipped her tea and eyed all the pans and platters hanging on the whitewashed walls. On long shelves stood piles of plates, cups, saucers, tureens and jugs. She had never seen so many in her entire life, still less at one sighting. As for instruments, there were ladles, knives, cleavers, and saws. Sacks of potatoes lined the corner, boxes of salt adorned the walls and great fire irons gleamed on the hearth.

The floor was flagged, and the fire, flanked by two huge ovens, was as long as the loft in which she slept. Great kettles simmered, flies buzzed comfortably, and great wedges of cake were consumed, washed down by equally large cups of tea, dispensed out of an urn by Mrs Quail.

By the time an urchin of a lad had taken all the cups to the scullery, Marie Jane had already been absorbed into her new life, and as Tessa stood to take her leave, the long way home suddenly seemed onerous. There had been no time to say goodbye to Marie Jane, for the sandy-haired Veronica had taken her immediately after tea to 'show her the ropes'. No one took any notice of Tessa as she left.

It was cooler now and, as though refreshed by the tea, the big house was coming alive. There was movement in the stable. The trap had been taken away. She walked quickly to the side of the house, and pushed the gates. They had been stiff enough before but now they would not part even an inch. She swore and pulled again.

Apart from climbing over the top, there was only one thing to do and that was go back to the stables, where perhaps one of the lads would be about to open the gates. Not that she wanted to retrace her steps, but taking courage from thoughts of her friend's sheer bravery in facing her new life, Tessa went back to the yard. It was not lack of courage which made her hesitate, but fear of confronting Kildare again.

But there he was, walking across the yard. Suddenly familiarity seemed all in so intimidating a place, and she approached him. 'Mister?'

He turned and affected surprise. She couldn't know that he had wedged a stone in the heavy hinges and had been hopping about the yard like a magpie ever since, awaiting developments. How many times had he seen women doing just the same thing, loitering, hesitating, hoping to see or encounter himself!

Kildare smiled when she had related the problem. 'Ach, let me tell you something, especially if you're counting on coming to see your friend again some time –' He paused, and touched her elbow briefly to direct her past the stables. The brief contact sent a perceptible current of pleasure right through his body; for a moment he was taken aback, then he continued. 'The side gates through which you came are not used much nowadays. But, the gates at the back of the house are always open for the coming and going of traffic – carts, horses, vans, tradesmen, even the odd motorcar. You must use those.'

'Thanks . . . mister.' And grateful for the advice she added his name, '. . . Kildare.' He noticed the pause, and was satisfied. They had reached the back gates which stood permanently open, reclining rustily against squat grey pillars.

'I'm going a little that way meself, on his lordship's business to Flavell's cottage.'

He felt her watching his quick fingers adjusting the girth, slipping on the bridle. He hesitated before asking casually 'Would you care to ride?'

Tessa continued to walk slowly away. 'Thank ye all the same, mister – '

'Tessa!' He interrupted the refusal, bringing to her attention the empty saddle. A faint smile twisted the corners of his thin lips, and even as she looked to him for some explanation, the smile travelled to lighten and warm the cold hazel of his eyes.

But Tessa's silence unnerved him. She was not making it easier for him as clumsily he tried to explain what he had done, how he had deliberately given up the trappings of his work. 'Can ye not see how I've left behind the game – the animals – and the "bloody great shotgun" . . . ?' He fought down a desire to shake her by the shoulders as she stood there, the distance between them clear in her eyes. He

241

wanted to shout at her, force her to realise what it meant for him, a gamekeeper, to be without his gun and the evidence of his quarry; force her to realise what it had cost him as a man to take such a revealing step.

He stood there, arms stiff at his sides lest he put thoughts into action. For a moment nothing was said, until Tessa, unable to counter such an intense gaze, ventured to fill the silence. 'Is it the trapping you've given up?'

Instinctively irritation rose in his throat; her refusal to understand his gesture seemed wilful and he began to put her right. 'The laying of traps – the control of game – they're a necessary part of life on an estate. I take my orders from Lord Fitzcarron . . .' But a kind of despair began to well up inside him as he realised the gulf that lay between them. He could not look at her. Such open, mobile features, so incapable of dissemblance, would be too painful to behold. And he knew that he was responsible for their faded brightness.

A lifetime of flirting, conquest and artifice made Kildare ill-equipped for Tessa Riley. He suddenly wished she was more like Marie Jane: ringlets, giggles, encouragements and cold shoulders – these he understood. He had made an effort to accommodate this young woman's whim, and when he had indicated the empty saddle, he had for a fleeting moment felt a joyous anticipation of her reaction. He had felt capable of tenderness, had wanted to indulge her, to have her recognise the effort he had made. He had felt something deeper than mere disappointment, something more akin to anguish, that the experience of tender indulgence had been so short lived. For a moment, a wild, stupid moment, he had displayed a dangerous vulnerablity; thank God she was not sophisticated enough to comprehend it. And what a day for complications – it was so damned hot. Christ Almighty, he thought impatiently, Jesus Almighty Christ. May God forgive me blaspheming tongue, and preserve me from the vagaries of women!

Tessa remained silent, refusing to be drawn into the keeper's snare, anxious to relive in her thoughts the times she had shared with Finn. The eight days since the Long Dance seemed an eternity. Did they seem so to Finn too? Thoughts of Finn gradually pushed aside the present. He must feel the same way she did, else why would he have spent his wrestling money on Guinness for the two of them? But had the Long Dance only been a step for him, just something for him to aim at, like O'Malley had said, and would he now be moving on?

So they walked, each alone in the company of their uncomfortable thoughts. He led the horse, torn between an urge to gallop off and a desire to linger, hoping for some development to redeem the day. This was no companionable silence, no bond of easy comradeship. Both were uneasy, yet feared conversation would be no improvement. It had been on the tip of his tongue to suggest they shared the saddle, or even that she ride, for it was ridiculous for them to walk! But another refusal would fray his patience, and he would either do or say something he would regret.

Tessa set the pace, a brisk pace, partly to cover the distance as quickly as possible, partly to cover the uneasiness she felt in this man's presence. Part of the uneasiness was, she knew, due to embarrassment at the memory of him holding up her skirts by this very Bog. He was probably not thinking of it at all, but she could never forget. The very idea of those quick hazel eyes darting about her legs, her thighs, her calico drawers, added to the flush of her already overheated face.

Kildare was conscious of her full stride, head high and shoulders back. The very strength of her intrigued him. The motion of her arms swinging easily to and fro, the thrust of her boots, the lilt of her skirts, from these he derived a pleasant satisfaction, a reward for the irritations of the day. Dressed for riding, he was far too hot; he possessed the finesse of a stalker, not the capacity for footslogging.

Besides, Ennabrugh was no place to be when the weather was hot. It was no place to be at all, he thought, but in the heat . . .

His eyes, shaded by the peak of the deerstalker, expertly surveyed the landscape. Nothing caught his attention, nothing moved . . . and despite the heat there was no softening of the harsh outlook. No splendour of summer here. Why, in the name of all the blessed saints, he wondered, were the crofters and the shiftless content to put up with it? The only sounds were the noises of Ennabrugh itself, the faint subterranean bubbling as the gasses below fermented, occasionally erupting on the surface with a plop. Like every other mortal within living distance, he had no liking for this treacherous wasteland, but the knowledge of it was one thing, at least, he had in common with Proud Riley's daughter. And the way things were going, he thought, it would be the only thing!

Flavell's cottage would soon be in sight and the realisation brought to Kildare a sense of urgency – and inadequacy. For Tessa the nearness to Flavell's brought relief – oh, such a relief. It even freed her thoughts and loosened her tongue. It was Marie Jane she should be thinking of – Marie Jane who thought so much of this man at her side.

'It seems only yesterday,' she reflected, almost as though they had chatted amicably for hours, 'that we were all out searching for Kate Murphy, not knowing that you had her at Flavell's.'

Ah, this was more like it! 'And did she not go off with young Jarvey?'

'She did so.'

'A good lad, young Jarvey. Got his head screwed on right, leaving like he did. I've told you before, Tessa, there's no future for places like this. Like the Long Dance it's an antiquity, a thing of the past. Marie Jane, now, she's the wise one, too.'

Tessa glanced sideways. 'You'll look to her, won't you? For all her clever ways she's only young, not used to civilisation, or . . .'

'Or, what, now?'

Tessa refused to be drawn on that point but seizing the opportunity, the nearness of Flavell's making her reckless, she asked. 'You seem . . . well, as though you liked her . . .'

'And who wouldn't?'

'I mean as though she were – special.'

'She is special, don't you think?' He, too, was refusing to be drawn.

'Yes, I do. Her da worships the ground she walks on, you'll have noticed. She's expecting so much of going into service. I don't want her to be disappointed, that's all.'

'Whatever else Marie Jane will be, she'll not be disappointed with life at Fitzcarron House.' He stopped at the path which led off to the steward's cottage. 'Tessa,' he said earnestly, 'try and get over this unfortunate attitude of yours. Believe it or not, guns and traps are a necessary part of life.'

'Not mine, mister!' The words came out stiff and staccato, stunning him with their impact. Her summer blue eyes darkened. 'I don't hold with none of it!' Then on a calmer note. 'You will look to Marie Jane?' Before he could reply she had swung off and away, a sense of liberation in every movement.

For one who earned his living by craft and the pitting of wits, he had not managed at all well. But he had patience; lots of it. The very nature of his calling demanded it. His turn would come again, of that he was sure.

Feeling a great sense of freedom, almost escape, Tessa set off on the last three miles home. The ridge would soon be in sight. The ridge . . . the cave. Their cave, where they had sheltered and practised and talked, and where they had got to know each other and discovered what a delight it was to be together. The tremors lest he didn't arrive, lest the Aunt had discovered. She hurried, beckoned by the wild urge to be on more familiar ground. Her heart began to thump against her ribs. The ridge was in sight, that great edge of mountainy outcrop that separated them from the Fitzcarron estate. Beyond the ridge was her world, which she knew and understood. The uncertainty of new people and their ways was not for her.

Tessa was beyond the more dangerous part of Ennabrugh, where the path was more defined and where Finn dug the Aunt's turf, when she saw him running easily towards her. She could tell it was him. There was no mistaking the grace of movement and fleetness of foot. Not knowing why, she broke into a run herself, escaping from what was behind, eager and anxious for what was ahead. Coming nearer, he waved his hand. She waved back, and laughed out of sheer exuberance. Marie Jane was forgotten; Fitzcarron House, the gamekeeper, nothing mattered except that she cover the ground between herself and Finn as soon as possible.

Hot, sweating, breathless, and with a stitch beneath her ribs, she ran straight into his arms as though it was the most natural thing in the world. He caught her and swung her round as they covered each other with quick, random kisses of welcome and reunion.

'I had to come,' he gasped. 'I thought I'd never see you again.'

'I looked for you later on at the Long Dance – '

'Ah, I couldn't face parting with you.'

'Finn, it's the darling man, y'are . . .'

Now silent with relief, Tessa became aware of not only her own heartbeat, but his. Her blue gingham echoed with it. His shirt was open almost to the waist and her breasts could feel the warmth of his naked flesh. She drew a short breath and lifted her hot, flushed face to the adoring scrutiny of his deep blue eyes, eyes which reminded her of the velvety wings of the blue butterflies of Ennabrugh, and looking into the soulful depths she saw a longing to match her own. She was ready for her first kiss . . . her first proper kiss.

Tessa moved her fingers along his shoulders and felt the muscles ripple beneath her touch. The pressure of his big hands across her back transmitted the current which was carrying her along on a wave of mounting emotion. She sighed and quivered; he bent his head, softening his mouth on hers. The tantalising caress sent her arms about his neck, her fingers winding his black curls. Oh, Mother o' God, she sighed, how often have I wanted to touch his hair. They pulled away momentarily, and looked at each other with all the wonder of newly created beings. With a love-light, a shy eager smile, a sigh which dissolved into another kiss, deeper, longer, more satisfying. Reality faded into the magic world of love where images swirled and hearts met, breath mingled and bodies strove to be one. Before they submerged altogether into this enchanted world they had so suddenly created, Tessa pulled away.

'Oh, Holy Mother,' she breathed, pressing her hands against the bare flesh at the neck of his shirt. 'Will I tell you I've gone all weak at the knees!'

'I've gone all weak in the head!'

'I'll never make it to me da's.'

'And who in heaven's name cares!'

His arms went about her again, gathering her softness against his muscled body. There was a passion in the embrace which both pleased and startled her, and something in the resulting kiss which stirred her in a curious way which defied analysis. This time they drew apart slowly, held by the mutual astonishment of aroused emotions. Not wanting to break the spell too soon, Finn put his arm about her waist and they continued the journey to Ennabrugh. It was coming on dusk and jack-o'-lanterns – lean phosphorous fingers of light – leapt and danced on the surface, like weird sprites.

'I don't like to see 'em,' Tessa shuddered.

His arm tightened protectively. 'Don't look, then,' he laughed. 'It's only the gasses, y'know.'

'I don't like them, just the same.'

'Do you think Marie Jane will make out at Fitzcarron House?' he asked, to take her mind off the activity of the Bog.

'Did you ever know her not to make out? Her da always says that if she fell in the privy, she'd come out smelling of roses! She's set her sights on the gamekeeper, you know. That's what worries me.'

'But does it worry him?'

There was something comforting in his infectious laugh. He did not often have the opportunity to laugh, but when he did, it was with a sense of hilarity. 'I reckon Martin's well out of it,' he continued. 'Marie Jane gave him a real rough ride, the boyo never knew whether he was in favour or out!'

'If Kildare does love her –' Tessa, realising she had said the word 'love' and that for the moment it was significant to her, gave Finn a sidelong glance. But his mind was still on Martin's rough ride, thinking on all the amusing memories. 'I plucked up me courage and asked him to look to her –' She stopped to give Finn a dig in the ribs with her elbow. 'Will you stop your giggling an' listen!' And so she related all the afternoon's events with as much pride as he had shown over his visit to Rohira.

At the sight of the first spiral of smoke, the two pulled apart. They were within sight of Proud Riley's cabin up the hill and, at the end of the valley, the Aunt's cabin. Finn stopped to pick up the peat-cutter from behind a boulder. The sight of home brought a sudden volubility. Plans had to be laid. Strategies and deceits be put into action. Time must be found to talk – often. Urgency overtook them. There was so much to say, to discuss; so little time. And so much care to be exercised.

'Finn,' said Tessa in an awed voice. 'Me da mustn't find out about us. I don't know what he'd do, but it would be something to separate us.'

And if the Aunt finds out, thought Finn, she'll put the mockers on us both. It doesn't matter for me, but God prevent her from harming Tess.

'The cave!'

'When?'

'Whenever you take the goats.'

'How will you know I'm there?'

'I'll look out for you. Do you remember Marie Jane telling you how I watched you walk the ridge?'

She nodded. 'How will you get away from the Aunt?'

His eyes held a twinkle. 'The turf needs turning regular now, doesn't it? I mean, haven't I been at it all day!'

'She'll be expecting the best turf in the valley.'

247

'You ought to see it, Tess. It's a mess, but sure your da will have said how it's dripping wet. God knows what we'll do for fuel . . . O'Malley's right, you know; in the eyes of the town folk, we're peasants. You've only got to see the way they look at us at the Long Dance – "curiosities", I heard someone say.

'Ach, Tess, if only you could set your eyes on Rohira, see your ma's grave and the grand church of St Joseph's where you were christened. And all the wonders: shops with windows, people dressed in fine hats and coats. Houses with an upstairs to them. Will I tell you about the pubs, warm with fires, and Guinness out of long handled pumps.' He drew in a great sigh which expanded his chest several inches. 'That's the place to be, Tess.'

'It sounds right enough,' she said practically. 'And sure I'd like nothing better than to see it, but for the love of God how can any of us go with no money!'

He lapsed into silence, defeated by the obvious. The silence between them became prolonged as they entered the valley. Depression at parting was deepened by the sight of the shacks and shanties of the shiftless, the potato patches full of weeds and thistles, and the smell of dank earth. The Grogans were arguing, and Kevin Connor's father, already maudlin drunk, was singing 'The Last Rose of Summer.' Someone was hammering, a donkey brayed, a child wailed.

'Will I see you in the cave, then?'

'I'll have a lot to do with the goats, being away all day. Shall we say two days?'

'Two days! Oh, tomorrow, Tess! Listen, if it's fine, I'll use the weather as an excuse to get to the peat, and I'll be there, thinking of you, of us.'

'I'll try,' she said helplessly. 'I'm awful glad you came to meet me.' Not risking another look at his solemn face she turned away, towards the isolated cabin of the hillside.

As darkness cloaked the mountain community of Ennabrugh, and one by one the glimmers of light in tiny square windows disappeared, the jack-o'-lanterns on the Great Bog became more numerous, springing up, flashing, dancing, cavorting in their summer ritual.

248

In times past Proud Riley had brought his neighbours up to witness this fascinating phenonemon, but no one was interested anymore. He reflected, as he lay on his bed, hands behind shaggy head, that people's outlook had changed. All they thought about now was getting, buying and selling; and apart from the shiftless, most, although not actually stirring themselves, were talking – and how they could talk – of going down to the town, if . . . Yes, if, the big IF . . . If work could be found . . . If they could get lodgings . . . If they could only do this or that . . . As soon as any kind of calamity occurred the talk would be all about 'going down'. No one was content anymore. Young Jarvey had gone with Murphy, and now look at O'Malley's girl – and him glad to have her placed!

Could Riley have seen O'Malley's girl just then, he would have had to admit that she had made a move in the right direction. The tiny attic she shared with the sandy-haired Veronica and Ruby Moy exceeded her expectations. They shared a chest of drawers, on the top of which she placed her clock, and they had a drawer each; and there was a round mirror on the marble top of the washstand.

In the darkness her eyes picked out the long white apron over a chair. Sleep, despite the long walk, was kept at bay by the thought of all the new faces she had seen and the names she had to remember. There were those you called 'sir' or 'ma'am', or just Mrs, like Mrs Quail; no one was ever addressed as just 'mister', like Tessa addressed Frank. And having seen Frank at the long table at tea and supper, flanked by a half a dozen young men of varying degrees of handsomeness, she was now rapidly giving credence to Tessa's view that Frank Kildare, at the age of thirty, was getting on a bit! She wriggled her feet against the white sheets. Oh, she thought, if only Tessa could see me now!

And across the Bog, over the phosphorescent fingers of light, at the end of the valley, the Aunt Hanratty sat uneasily in the high-backed rocking chair. Her uneasiness stemmed from all the talk being put about by O'Malley of the community of Ennan being finished. Having never been out of her own compound since bringing her nephew into it, news came to her as she stood in the doorway of the cabin. People would stop for a few words, not caring to incur her displeasure. And so she had been told of how O'Malley's girl had gone up to the Fitzcarron House. Who would be next, she wondered. It was rumoured that O'Malley himself was thinking about it, and once he had gone, the rest would follow. Except for that good-for-nothing nephew asleep on the bed behind her. He was not going to leave. He had yet to work out the penance for the evildoing of his parents.

Finn Collins, she swore by God Almighty, was going nowhere. He and she would live on here, the only two left. Purgatory would be sweet compared to the fear she knew would be his, for without the interference of the O'Malleys and Jarveys and events like the Fair and the Long Dance, his only company would be herself. She knew he was afraid of the powers they said she had. Malevolent mirth brought a twitch to her dry lips.

Unconscious of the evil thoughts about him, eyes closed beneath a fringe of thick lashes, Finn slept stretched out on his back, one arm flung over his black curls; he inhaled and exhaled deeply, smoothly. Sleep ironed out of his brow the fear of his aunt. His last thought had been of Tess in his arms, her finger on his chin – a dimple, she had said, and he had blushed, thinking it was only girls had dimples, like Tess's. And tomorrow . . . tomorrow . . . Tess in his arms . . .

CHAPTER FOURTEEN

Finn, being the first to arrive, waited in and about the cave, alternating between excitement and despair. Then, sitting down in a patch of sun, he leant against the wall and thought of his sweetheart.

If Tess did not come today he did not know how he would bear the disappointment. She must come. She must find a way to escape from that silent old fella. What would she do, he wondered, without Marie Jane; her da wouldn't let her come down to any of the other young women of her own age, nor would he let them go up to the cabin. Poor Tess, she was in almost as bad a position as himself.

Tessa had approached the cave quietly and was standing watching him, admiring the view of his relaxed body. So far as she was concerned the future, far from looking bleak, could not be better, for did it not include Finn? She observed the curve of his thigh as she sat with knees to chin, the length of leg in dusty corduroys. Shirt sleeves were rolled tightly above the bulging biceps, and his smooth brown arms made her want to run her fingers along their surface, to caress the muscle and recognise the strength there to crush her willing body to his own.

It seemed years since she and Marie Jane had met him and Martin Jarvey by the chapel. He had looked so grand in himself that Martin in his new jacket had never got a look in and Marie Jane had been momentarily jealous. Yes, it seemed years ago, instead of only four months. Would she ever forget the sight of him? Of course, she had seen him when she and Marie Jane had gone to Aunt's with the excuse of borrowing a kettle. But outside the chapel, without the servility of the pig-apron, freedom had shone in him. With all the gawkiness of youth gone, he wore the grace of manhood easily, in an untrammelled, unfettered way, though God alone knew he was as imprisoned as herself.

His black curls gleamed in the sliver of sun, showing up the line of his jaw. He was lean and lithe; too lean really, Tessa thought, an' him being such a big fella. Scarce a picking on him; it was all muscle through a lifetime of digging, and pigging, fetching and carrying for the old witch of an aunt.

What had Marie Jane said at the wrestling? 'Brought up on spuds and brawn'. By comparison, her diet of goat's milk and cheese, griddle bread and soda bread, and broth made from dried goat's meat, seemed sumptuous. As for what Marie Jane would be eating – those great wedges of crumbly sweet cake, and that just to keep them going between their midday dinner and evening supper! Mother of God, it scarce seemed fair. She made a mental note to bring some food next time she came, and suddenly happier about his welfare, her spirits soared to exuberance.

'Got you!' She pounced into the cave.

'Lord save us, Tess!' he exclaimed, leaping to his feet and laughing at being caught out. 'You scared the living daylights out of me!'

She threw her crook down beside his peat-cutter and wagged a finger at him. 'And time, too. You needed something to shake you out of the mulligrubs!'

She began to sing the tune of a jig they had practised and immediately he was in her mood and out of the Aunt's shadow. Like jack-o'-lanterns on Ennabrugh, their feet flashed and danced as they cavorted in a ritual of their own making. The simplicity of the dance, the lightness of touch . . . fingers, arms, hands; the nearness as they swung each other round to let go and split apart, to side step – it was all so tantalising.

His eyes feasted on the swirl of her brown goat-skirt as though it were the finest silk; on the sprightliness and vitality of her movements. She seemed like a cascade of shining particles which were coming all together, just for him.

And Tessa's gaze, devoid of artifice, openly admired his 'dancing legs', the shapeliness of his body, the supple movements, and the lightness of foot in so big a man.

Their eyes met and lingered some half a dozen times, until the ritual, burning itself out, fused their glances and sent them panting for breath into each others arms. At first their embrace was close and still and silent. They held each other tightly, not feeling anything except the joy of being clasped together against the world, against her father and his aunt. This was their own private world into which no one else had access. A shared world, and such contact was a new experience for both, for neither had brother or sister to share a touch or emotion.

'Tess,' he eventually breathed into her hair. ''Tis the darling girl you are – an' the ravishing way you have with ye! I can scarce believe we're here, like this.'

'Like what?' she teased, feeling like Marie Jane, and happy with it.

'Will I tell you, now?' He stared down at her in blissful bewilderment. 'Sure, I can't believe me luck; that I'm standing here with the finest colleen in the green of Ireland next to me heart. And that we've been dancing about like jack-o'-lanterns. And that I'm supposed to be turning the peat, and you tending the goats!'

'At least I'm truthful,' she said with mock primness. 'The goats are out there, cropping the grass, sunning themselves, and waiting patiently.'

'They'll have to wait a lot longer . . .' He kissed her upturned lips, softly, teasingly. They held each other, closer and tighter, kissing and smiling in the rapture of first love. Impervious to the sweat and heat engendered by the jig, the odour of her goat-skirt and the grime on his peat-stained hands, they leaned against the wall of the cave and continued to look at one another with sheer pleasure and delight. For a long time they did not talk at all, until her fingers strayed to his thick curls and the nape of his neck where the flesh rose from his collar.

'Tess?' he said wonderingly. 'What are we going to do? I don't think I can live without the sight of you, without seeing you, every day.'

'Every day!' She pulled away, a shade of alarm in her voice. 'Now, will you listen Finn, darling man that y'are . . .' She felt all of a sudden to be the elder of the two, the more practical, responsible. 'We mustn't do anything to make my da or your aunt suspicious – '

'But, Tess we've got to see – '

'Will you listen?' She broke from his arms and sat down on the ground, patting the place beside with her hand. 'If you start going off to the Bog every day, staying away for hours, a thing you've never done before, she's going to suspect you're up to something. And as for me da, I bring the goats out two or sometimes three times a week in the summer, and I'm not risking more or he'll stop me coming out at all. We've to be thankful for what we've got. Now that we are . . .' She hesitated, uncertain of what words to use. She did not want to say 'in love' like they did in books, because he had not mentioned the word. Neither could she say they had 'an understanding', because they hadn't, and somehow, unlike Marie Jane, she did not want to rush anything. She finally settled on 'Now that we've got to know each other a bit – ' there, she had chosen the right words ' – it'd be enough to set the angels in heaven stamping their golden feet if anything got in the way of us seeing each other again. It could happen. I don't know what lengths me da would go to, and I'm not anxious to find out!'

'Yes,' he said, surprisingly compliant. 'I suppose you're right. But you will come up those two or three times?'

'Try and keep me away.'

'But what are we going to do about the future?'

'We'll think of something – I'm good at that.' She paused and a frown furrowed her wide forehead. 'Do you reckon there's any truth in the talk that's going round about leaving the valley?'

'The priest says people with children ought to go, because of the disease and all of that. You know, the rickets and the croup, as well as the bow legs, and the summer sickness. I think O'Malley's serious; he's not "all talk" this time. Anyways, his wife is bothered about Little Annie; they think another winter up here could kill her, and there's enough little O'Malleys in the graveyard already.'

Tessa's furrow deepened. 'But, if Mr O'Malley goes down, Finn, life up here will be finished. Apart from him dealing with Flavell and the keeper, he's brought the flour since the miller dropped dead. Who could we trust to bring supplies up?'

He shrugged his broad shoulders. 'The shiftless are out of the running for a start. Jams hasn't the strength. No one'd trust Gypo Kelly with their money, or Kevin Connor. The Jarveys might, but they'd charge for the hire of the donkey and cart! Old Duggan hasn't the breath and Young Duggan's talking of going down with O'Malley for good. Your da won't set foot in town, and that leaves only me who's trustworthy. I could go,' he added confidently. 'I'd have a word with the Jarveys; they'd have to loan me a donkey – or starve.' He touched her arm. 'By the time I see you again O'Malley may have talked them all into going down. He'd be a fine one to get your da to move, or even the Aunt.'

'I don't see what all the rush is about, Finn.'

'But,' he insisted, 'would you like to go, to get away from Ennan?'

She nodded. 'If you went, yes.' She gave a quick glance outside. 'Sun's off the cave. Time to go.' She reached for her crook. He stood up and gathered her into his arms.

'The day after tomorrow, then?'

''Tis so,' she murmured softly. Their parting kiss was long, and deep and unhurried. Parting added a depth of passionate despair, and with a fast-beating heart she broke away and hurried down without a backward glance.

Tessa and Finn continued to meet in the cave on the ridge. But the weather was never as it had been on their first assignation. It turned unkind and rained with a malevolent insistence, as though there were purpose in each downpour, a kind of punishment. To venture out with the goats in such weather was asking for trouble, so there were times when Finn sat alone, and Tessa longed to be with him.

By now she knew herself to be in love with Finn. Without a doubt, he was her life, her very soul. Their secret joy made light of his servitude and her solitariness; parting was becoming an agony. Farewells would be said two and three times before they could tear themselves apart.

'Roll on the next two days . . .' he would sigh.

'We're wishing our lives away, but I don't care . . .' She caressed his face, tracing his eyes, his nose, and then, 'Kiss me again . . .'

'Will you think of me tonight?' he asked huskily. 'When ye light the lamp.'

'I think of nothing else . . .' She sighed and sought his lips.

'Tess?'

'Yes?'

'Tess, I love you; oh, I love you, girleen.'

She laid her head against his chest. 'I thought you'd never say it! I love you an' all, Finn. I not only love you, but I care for you, I worry about you, and I pray for your safety on me knees, before the Sacred Heart on the dresser.'

While sitting together she wanted to cradle his head against her breast, to brush her lips against his curls, but felt she was not yet ready.

'I didn't know love would be like this,' he smiled down at her, and the blue of his eyes deepened until she had to get up and check the goats had not wandered off.

So, they talked and danced and sometimes Tessa sang a love song which made him blush. They revelled in the splendour of newly discovered love, of their youth, their bodies, and their plans for a future which made the present more bearable.

The attitude of his aunt made Tessa anxious at times, and yet she need not have worried, for his growing love and need for freedom to express that love were making him more aware and more resentful of his aunt's manipulation. He was determined to break loose – but the time had to be right.

Who, thought Tessa tenderly on such occasions, could wish ill upon so easy-going a temperament. 'Soft on the sentiments' was O'Malley's description. There was no merit or virtue allotted to Finn because of this. It was a natural element in his character of which he was quite unaware, and in this very unawareness lay his charm.

'And now,' he would exclaim, 'now, Tess, I know what the stars are for, why the moon is made of silver, and why I can suddenly talk like a lover.'

A shadow fell across the door of the outhouse. Tessa glanced idly up from milking the goat. Standing there was Frank Kildare.

'A letter from your friend,' he said guardedly, not sure whether her astonished glance was in his favour or not. He withdrew the letter from his breast pocket, and leaned forward, extending his hand to bridge the gap between them. It was still warm from contact with his body. She shivered.

'I have taken one to her family, already.' He felt an explanation was necessary. 'I had business with O'Malley himself.'

Tessa nodded. She suddenly felt guilty that her world now revolved about Finn Collins, to the exclusion of all else, even her best friend.

'How is Marie Jane?' she asked, stuffing the letter in the pocket of her skirts. 'Is she . . . happy?'

'As the day is long.'

'Thanks for looking to her – '

He laughed, a short brisk laugh. 'There was no need. Marie Jane,

256

it appears, has everyone "looking to her", as you say . . .' His hazel eyes feasted on this picture of her. Legs spread wide beneath the memorable skirts, sleeves rolled above the elbow, the sag of her blouse as she leaned forward to continue the milking showing the swan-like neck and a hint of more . . . Catching the way of his glance, she jerked herself upright on the three-legged stool. He noticed her consternation, and felt that at least it was better than indifference.

His explanations in bringing this letter to the cabin were still clouding about his head and this new wave of interest he was experiencing left him bewildered. Since O'Malley's little tease of a daughter had slapped his face and left a red mark which caused him acute embarrassment, his interest in young, inexperienced women had undergone a change. And if the truth were told the scheme to clear the valley for sheep was proving more irksome than he had at first thought. At the Long Dance he had gathered there would be a slight but steady migration. But no, nothing. No one had moved, except young Jarvey and Marie Jane. Ach, he thought despairingly, they were all talk these crofters. Talk, talk, and still more bloody talk! And apart from everything else, he was still smarting from yesterday's interview with Lord Fitzcarron. What a day that had been.

'And how is the clearance scheme, Kildare?' his lordship had asked. 'Anywhere near completion?'

'No . . .' he had stammered. 'No, my lord. But there's a lot of talk and excitement about it, and O'Malley himself will be moving down soon. That should set 'em off. They'll be lost without him.'

'Good God, man! It's damned slow you are. How many has the estate absorbed?'

'One, sir.'

'One? Good heavens, Kildare!'

'There's a couple of months yet, sir. The valley will be cleared before the winter sets in, as you requested.'

'It needs to be done sooner. The end of October.'

But he had stood his ground. 'Please be patient, Lord Fitzcarron. These things have to be done quietly, my lord, and with due care, especially if I am to avoid making your interests known.'

His lordship had digested this last remark and, choosing to ignore the veiled threat, had repeated the ultimatum.

Not caring to dwell on it further, Kildare brought himself back to the present. 'I've business with your father. Is he about?'

'Somewheres,' came the careless reply. It turned him on his heel directly, and no sooner had he gone than Tessa took the letter from her pocket and marvelled at it. A real letter. She had never had one before, and Marie Jane had never written one before. It was in a pink envelope and addressed to herself in hesitant black lettering. Really, it was a shame to spoil it by opening the flap! Carefully she unfastened it and, taking out a piece of pink paper, began to read.

'My dearest Tessa,' She smiled at the blots of ink, the crossing out of some words and the altering of others and her heart warmed at the memory of writing lessons in the loft. 'I like it here,' Marie Jane had written, 'and they are all very kindly. I see Lady Fitzcarron often and she is very beautiful and wears lovely clothes the like of which my eyes have never seen. They are teaching me to talk like Frank Kildare does. People think better of you if you tone it down like Mrs Quail says. I am not to swear or be blasphemous, you could do all this easily. I am not yet ready for my duties, but learning. You were right about a certain person being too old for me. I thought you would like to know this. There are five young men here and they are all fighting over me. I hope you will change your mind and come to Fitzcarron House.' Then as though the strain of decorum had been too much, she added, 'Dear Tessa, do come for we would be as happy as pigs in muck. Your loving friend, Marie Jane O'Malley.'

Inside the cabin, Frank Kildare sat on the edge of the square table, leg swinging, and his hand on the thigh of the other.

'I've ridden over with a letter from O'Malley's girl' he explained.

'Have you now? 'Twas a long ride for so small a thing' said Riley.

'There are other considerations . . .'

'And what do you mean by that?'

'Mainly your daughter.'

'Teresa?' Proud Riley's eyes looked up fiercely. He was standing before the fire, a thumb hooked in Timothy Thomas's belt and a cup of cold tea in the other hand.

'I think you've had an idea for some time that I hold her in high regard — '

'High regard? What the divil does that mean? I'm a simple fella, Mr Kildare; will you talk so I can understand you?'

'I will so. 'Tis the proud man you are, Mr Riley, with so fine a cabin and a handsome young woman to grace your hearth. So, I'm asking if you've any objections to me paying attentions to Tessa?'

'Attentions? To what end, Mr Kildare, to what end, eh?'

Kildare looked into the shrewd eyes, at the fingers which had strayed from the safety of the belt to scrub the fluffy sidewhiskers.

'Marriage,' he said.

'Marriage?' The wise old eyes held the gaze of the younger man.

Riley kept his elation 'close' as they said, but his heart thumped madly beneath the goatskin jerkin. A good marriage, at last! For Teresa Donnelly's daughter – his daughter, for he looked upon her as nothing else, never even considering her as Timothy Thomas's girl. And now, at last, this fine man was interested enough to ask about marriage.

'Marriage,' he repeated. 'There's a thought,' he said at length, and added. 'Have you spoken to Teresa?'

Kildare shook his coppery head, and Riley felt flattered. Surely, this was the honourable way of doing things, the way a gentleman would go about it, getting the father's permission first. Yes, he liked it. It made him feel important – as indeed on this occasion he was. 'Has she any idea that ye hold her in this "high regard", or that you want to "pay your attentions", as you call it?'

Kildare shook his head.

Riley pursed his lips thoughtfully. 'As you know, Mr Kildare, Teresa can be a strange girleen at times, I mean . . .' He assumed a man-to-man attitude. 'Does a fella ever really know how a woman's mind works?'

'That's why I wanted to get it straight with yourself. At least knowing you're agreeable is one hurdle over. Shall we . . .' Kildare paused long enough for the 'we' to sink in, 'tread softly?'

Riley nodded; indeed this was the best way. 'Would you like a drop o' poteen the while?' He reached for the five-noggin bottle from the black oak dresser, and unhooked two cups and, trying to conceal his pleasure, poured the poteen. Passing a cup to Kildare, he hesitated and gulped down his drink. He had been going to say 'Your livelihood's against ye,' but he swallowed the poteen instead. Mustn't spoil the girl's chances before the game begins. As he had said, women's minds were not the easiest of things, and she could change it. But if she liked a fella, surely his trade wouldn't matter? 'And the second thing you came about?' he prompted.

'It's bordering on the same subject, in a way.' Kildare watched the flies buzzing in a shaft of sunlight, with an odd sense of detachment. Mother o' God, he thought irritably, what am I doing here? Parleying and treading softly with an illiterate crofter . . . tempting him, enticing him, currying favour with him? It's this damned clearance that's getting on my nerves, he thought, and then became angry with himself. Nerves! Me! God help me, what a state to be in! And, now here I am, discussing marriage!

'There's one way in which Tessa could be persuaded to go into service on the estate.'

'Is there, now?'

Kildare took a deep breath and exhaled slowly. 'Yes. I think she would come if you, also, would come with her.' The silence was immediately charged. It was so intense even the flies stopped their buzzing as if to listen. Feeling he had to fill the gap quickly and constructively or else lose the initiative, Kildare began his 'enticements'. 'Let me tell you now that his lordship is not duty bound, or legally bound, to offer any of you anything. But, to certain crofters, such as yourself, he is making a most generous offer. The estate is always in need of good peat-men that know what they're doing. I caught one of the younger fellas the other week actually tampering with the crust at the edge. We need men of experience. If you came, there would be a cottage for you . . . so, as you're a solitary soul, Mr Riley, you could still keep to yourself, as you do now. And Tessa would live with you, as she does now.' He paused to try and gauge if his scheme was getting a good reception. The old man was giving nothing away, so he continued. 'If you were to live nearer, it would be easier for me to pay my attentions to your daughter in a more informal way.'

'Informal?' Riley seized on the word.

'You know . . .' Kildare felt on unsure ground. 'Not as pointed . . . as obvious.'

'You said you were thinking o' marriage, of courting her, walking her out.'

'I am. I am. But how can I do it at this distance? I've only found her in now by chance, and I must have called on you some half a dozen times. A woman needs courting gradually.' Sweet Jesus, he thought, this old fella bristles up like a hedgehog. He continued with a quiet air bordering on desperation. 'Both you and she would receive wages and perquisites . . .' The sharp look of enquiry encouraged him to expound. 'Perquisites are extras. A fowl at Christmas, fuel, good clothes the family have no use for, fruit in summer and vegetables, fish – anything surplus to the requirements of the house is shared among the workers. And the estate is nearer the town from the other side, as I'm sure you know . . .'

'Stop!' said Riley. 'The answer is no, Mr Kildare. They'll not drag me from this cabin until the rats are gnawing at me toes! I built this place for Teresa's mother. Here I've lived, and here I'm going to bloody well die!' He calmed himself to add, ' 'Tis more than satisfied I am with life here – '

'I know, I know. But is Tessa?' It was a random shot, but he could see it had scored.

The words had taken Riley back over the years to the anxiety he had felt about Teresa's mother . . . He remembered the Long Dances of the past, and how he had been afraid his wife would follow them down to Rohira. That look she had when the dancers and spectators were going down, as though poised for flight and yet too laden, her soul too heavy to take off. He recalled how, for days after, she had wandered to the front window, and then the side, and out into the compound and back into the cabin again. All the old fears at her restlessness now erupted, causing him to break into a sweat. Out of gratitude she had stayed with him, but by the time he, unable to bear the appeal in her restless eyes any longer, had promised to take her down, to find her and the child lodgings, it had been too late. She had died in his arms. And yet . . . the old man clutched at straws. It cannot be like that with his daughter, for had she not refused to go with Marie Jane? Or was she, like her mother, staying with him out of gratitude? Consideration of this filled him with a dread alarm that needed time for him to comprehend.

Kildare got off the table, went over to the five-noggin bottle and filled Riley's cup. 'Drink it, and think over his lordship's very generous proposal – these offers do not come thick and fast. And if you want to stay here until the rats are at your toes, ask yourself whether your daughter does.' He stood before Riley, sliding the deerstalker through his fingers. 'I take it I am at liberty to call again?'

But the old man was still in a daze. The past had hit him with a blow he could not easily shake off. Outside, Tessa was talking softly to Kildare's horse, her back towards the cabin. She would have noticed, Kildare thought happily, the empty saddle. There were no dead creatures to vex her.

He stood behind her, silently watching her strong capable hands stroking the horse's jaw. What a waste, he thought! Her fingers entangled themselves in the long black mane and he watched, fascinated, unable to take his eyes from her. In his imagination, he had moved towards her so that although in reality he had not yet touched her, already his arms were about her waist and his head, so plagued with this clearance scheme and confused with newly discovered emotions, had buried itself in the curve of her shoulder. He pulled himself together. He knew, and knew a thousand times, he meant nothing to her at all. Why did he bother? If he lived to be as old as the hills, sure he'd never know. But hope, there was always hope, and with her father's help and a bit of luck, he might yet be in at the kill. God help me, he thought, suddenly and acutely grieved, she's never given me a chance!

Tessa gave the horse a final stroke, a final word and, thinking to look through the window to see if the gamekeeper was any nearer leaving, turned straight into him. Caught off guard, his arms closed about her to stop them both reeling backward with the impact. The earthy, domineering masculinity of him took her by surprise.

'Mother of God!' she exclaimed with a stifled scream. 'Sure I thought you were the divil himself; fancy standing there in the half-light with never a word!'

He smiled, showing his strong white teeth and feeling suddenly exhilarated. 'I seem to make a habit of startling you, I'm sorry. But, no.' The perfectly arched eyebrows rose, the coppery head went to one side. 'No, I'm not the devil, not anymore.'

She made to stand back and realised he was keeping his hold of her. She could feel the buckle of the belted jacket against her stomach, the buttons of his breast pockets pressing into her, and his hands. Oh, Lord save me, those freckled fingers were about her back. The look in her blue-grey eyes, now saucer-wide with embarrassment, was full of alarm. For Tessa had seen a light in the cold hazel of his eyes and a softening of the hunter's face. She struggled to be free. He released her at once, and to settle her alarm remarked, as casually as was possible after holding her in his arms, 'You read your letter?'

'Yes, and thank you for fetching it.'

'If you write a reply I can call for it when I'm up this way.'

'Will you?' she asked, suddenly aware how much she missed Marie Jane.

'I will so.' He put a foot in the stirrup and mounted the horse. Silhouetted against the sky, his head slightly bent, he nodded and urged the horse out of the compound. Like a lover turning for a last look of his sweetheart, he risked a backward glance and wished he hadn't. She had moved away inside, no doubt glad he had gone.

'What did he want, Da? I thought he'd never go!'

'He wants us to go and work on the estate.'

'You said no?'

His eyes, the colour of peat, lit up at her quick response. 'I told him we'd think about it.'

'We?'

'He means both of us,' he said guardedly. 'Would ye not care to go with me and all? He said they're always after experienced peat-cutters. Would you believe it, Teresa, they found some young fool tampering with the crust of Ennabrugh! Anyways, there'd be perquis . . . oh, something of the sort . . .' He regarded her wonderingly. She was stronger than her mother. Teresa Donnelly would not have shepherded goats, nor returned from a day out with 'em with roses in her cheeks and a light about her. 'What do you think? Do you want to give up the goats and be the grand house maid?'

'No Da!' Panic fluttered about her heart. She could not, would not, leave Finn. 'Da?' she asked curiously, 'Is it yourself that'd fancy working on the estate?'

'You can't teach an old dog new tricks, Teresa. Them fancy ways are not for the likes of your da. I told him straight, I did. That I'll not leave this blessed place until the rats are gnawing at me toes. I built this cabin for your ma, God rest her soul. She died here and I'll die under the same roof!'

'Do you think there's any truth in this idea of Mr O'Malley's, that we can't go on as a community anymore?'

The shaggy head nodded. 'God forbid, but he could be right. There's been so much rain the peat won't form into turf. Without peat, Teresa, without fuel, what'll we do? Almighty God,' he breathed. 'If only I'd known the summer was going to turn out so wet, sure I wouldn't have sold a single piece to Spider Murphy's scurvy lot.'

'Is it so bad, Da?'

'I've a bit to one side, so maybe we'll get by if the winter isn't too hard. But there won't be any for the others. The Duggans, and young Collins, and one or two more who dig on the light side, only dig for the season, not for stock like meself, so they'll be without.'

'What will they do?'

'If they don't get a chance to work on the estate, they will have to go down with the rest. Holy Mother, can you imagine the shiftless in civilisation? The Grogans always fighting; the Byrnes, all six of 'em, "short upstairs"; and Kevin Connor's da always maudlin drunk and threatening to do away with himself! Borrowing, scrounging, drinking; the people of the town will wonder what's hit 'em! No one will give them work, they'll have to chance their arm on the streets begging, or go to the workhouse.'

'Workhouse?' Tessa frowned. 'Sure I've not heard about that before; what is it, Da?' The very word seemed to be loaded with overtones, and her father's manner indicated something to be afraid of. She, who never had need to ask questions of her father, was now curious about this new word in their vocabulary.

He scratched the top of his cap and watched his daughter sit down opposite him. He was uneasy in face-to-face confrontations; settling down to talk had never been his strong point, and he never knew where it would all lead to, especially with Teresa.

'When me and your ma took you down to St. Joseph's to be christened, there was a big barn of a house on the hill beyond the church. The stone was black and the house was surrounded by a six-foot wall. "That's the workhouse," she told me, for she was terrible feared when your real da died that she might have to go in there herself. "Charity house," she said it was called, and sometimes the "poor house", but "there's scant charity within those walls," she said. And she talked of it with such fear in her blessed voice that I was mortal sorry I'd asked. And sure to God, Teresa, I never thought the shadow of that fear would ever darken the threshold of this cabin.'

'It hasn't Da,' she pointed out quickly, alarmed at his sombre mood. 'Such places are only for the likes of the shiftless, unless they're too shiftless to call upon this . . . charity.'

'Sure, they'd starve in the streets first. It's called the "work-house", Teresa, because you've got to work bloody hard for the very cup of gruel and crust they give you!'

The silence which followed was filled with a vague kind of apprehension on her father's part. Not altogether understanding why, Tessa drew a deep breath and said lightly, 'But that doesn't bother us, Da. We're all right with the peat for this year. We don't even have to take up this offer to work on the estate, and if the worse came to the worse it would be better than . . . Ach, forget about such a place as the workhouse.'

Proud Riley regarded his daughter from beneath bushy eyebrows with a questioning expression. Now that Kildare had unwittingly reminded him of her mother's situation he could never be sure that history was not to repeat itself.

'Sure I've forgotten already,' he came back to her comment, and added casually, so as not to put her back up, 'Lord Fitzcarron hasn't made so good an offer to anyone else, yet. Though why he should bother, the good God only knows. It was dacent of Kildare to have come all the way round Ennabrugh to bring you the letter, wasn't it now?'

She hesitated before answering, giving herself a moment to enjoy the warmth brought about by the mention of the letter. Marie Jane's enterprise conjured up the memory of the large kitchen at Fitzcarron House, the benches and tables, the young men, and Mrs Quail with her strict eyes and big feet. She could just imagine Marie Jane speaking 'proper' and queening it in her 'black and white' . . . 'Yes, it was dacent,' she said at length, and got up to set the kettle on the fire.

Her father, encouraged by the admission, added, 'He said he'd call again for the answer, like.' She did not speak so he prompted a reply. 'Will ye be writing an answer, then?'

'I will so, and I'll leave it on the dresser in case I'm out with the goats.'

This was not at all what he or the gamekeeper had had in mind. The probability of her absence alarmed him, and his thought processes not being geared for speed, it took him some time to formulate what he thought to be a guarded comment. 'You'll not mind if he waits till you come back?'

'God bless you, Da!' She laughed, and reached for the piece of hessian to remove the kettle. 'Why would he want to wait for me? What difference does it make to the letter?'

'Him riding over and all of that, and you not being here to give your thanks: where's your manners, girl?'

'But I don't know when he's coming, do I? And why should he wait,' insisted Tessa, 'all day perhaps, for me to say me thanks? Surely you can do it for me? God save us, Da, it was him said he'd come. I didn't ask. And he won't be coming especially; he'll most likely call at O'Malley's place to collect their letter.'

As she poured the tea, her father gave up. He could cope no longer and, defeated by the logic of all she said, he retreated into his familiar silence. That very silence caused Tessa to wonder at the real reason behind the previous volubility. Such lengthy conversations between her and her father were by no means usual. It all stemmed, of course, from the gamekeeper's visit, offering him work on the estate, unsettling him and making him think of the workhouse!

So, she reflected as she sipped her tea, Marie Jane's given Kildare the brushoff. That was a relief, for she was better with fellas nearer her own age. Perhaps she had discovered her beloved Frank was not the marrying kind, or, as she had said before, was not free enough with his money. And Marie Jane was not a one to waste her time on unproductive schemes!

Eager to answer her very first letter, Tessa scurried up to the loft. A few sheets of note paper were among her prize possessions but never having had need of an envelope she had none and so decided to use Marie Jane's, sticking the flap down with her father's shoe glue. Resting the paper on one of O'Malley's magazines, pencil poised, she prepared the letter. 'My dear Marie Jane, I was glad to get your letter and am happy to know that you are doing well . . .' She paused and wondered what to write next. She waited, appalled at how little there actually was to relate. Nothing ever changed, and for safety's sake she could not mention Finn and the strategies they employed in meeting. She had not been down to the valley since taking Marie Jane to Fitzcarron House. None of the young women, not even Una Kelly, the brave one, would risk coming up to the cabin. What else could be said? The goats . . . the rain . . . the failing peat? Marie Jane knew all that; she had escaped from it, and anything Tessa could write would only serve to highlight the hopelessness of life in Ennan.

Crumpling up the paper she hurled both it and the pencil to join the peacock-blue gown – a relic of Ennan Fair, still crushed in the corner of the loft. In comparison, Marie Jane's life seemed to possess all the hustling roar and excitement of the Fair and Long Dance rolled into one. Whereas she and Finn, Una and Peggy, and all the others had to wait until St Patrick's Day, when the tinkers – and heaven knew who the next lot would be – got itching feet and took to the road, calling at Ennan on their march east in search of employment. She noticed the Guinness bottle, and drifted off into a daydream of every word, every touch shared with Finn in the O'Malleys' cabin while Mrs O'Malley had stood guard and been moved to tears when Finn gave her his wreath of flowers. At the time, victory and winning and the pleasure of achievement had seemed everything; she had felt like a queen. Her glance rested mournfully on the empty bottle, the spoiled gown. She pulled her knees up to her chin and stayed like that for a long time.

CHAPTER FIFTEEN

Over the next three days the summer rain fell with a light but monotonous obstinancy. Ennabrugh was invisible, the hills blotted out with mist. The goats stayed in the outhouse and Tessa in the cabin. She dared not go out for fear of raising suspicion, but her heart ached for a sight of Finn. The rain coming immediately after her melancholy bout with the letter, she had not been able to shake off her sad mood. If only she could see Finn, everything would change from grey to a shining yellow or a warm rose colour. What made it all worse was the knowledge of him being up there, waiting. The peat was a good enough excuse for him to get out, and if her father had not been in the cabin she would have been up to the ridge like the 'greased lightning' Finn often joked about, even though it would mean getting soaked to the skin.

The only ease she got from the overwhelming silence, which she was now finding hard to bear, was to think of Finn; to imagine herself in his arms, running her fingers through his wet curls, to feel the rise and fall of his chest, the thumping of his heart against her own. She leaned on the window ledge and stared out through the mist, trying to recapture something of the passion they shared, the magical way he had of tempting and teasing her emotions until she felt the weakness at her knees.

Then, eager for a change of scene, she prowled to the side window, and through the incessant rain her imagination saw him standing in the mouth of the cave. A thrill of pride ran through her as she pictured his physique, his handsome dark looks; the rain-drenched shirt clinging to the manly curves of his chest, the times they had clung together, their bodies soaked with rain, hair flattened to their heads, clothes clinging to mould their bodies, sharing rainy kisses and the feel of warm skin through the fabric of their shirts.

When it all became too much to bear she went out on the pretext of attending to the outhouse, but out in the compound she held up her flushed face to the rain. It was cool and refreshing, coursing down her cheeks, her throat, finding its way down between the valley of her breasts as if to assuage the fire burning in her longing heart.

This parading to and fro, in and out, was anxiously viewed by her father with an ever-growing anxiety. Instead of the brown-haired, rosy-cheeked daughter, he saw the tall, slender figure of his wife . . . saw the cabin as a cage . . . the windows as bars. He felt helpless. He did not know what to do, what to say.

The following morning Tessa ran to the front window. 'Da!' she yelled. 'The rain's stopped! Thank God, it's stopped!' And thinking immediately of getting up to the ridge, added, 'The goats will be ready for a bit of pasture.'

Her father looked towards the window and sighed deeply with a great and immense relief. Had he been the laughing kind of man, he would have chortled with relief that her window-gazing was merely due to her anxiety over the goats being cooped up!

His nights had been wakeful and tormented, filled with visions of the past. The burden of responsibility had all but crushed him. Lying on his bed, hearing her restless turning in the loft, he had thought the fires of purgatory would be sweet in comparison. And now the rain had stopped! She was no longer wandering about, and the purgatorial fires receded. At least, he thought, as he silently made the first tea of the day, worrying about Teresa stopped him from worrying about the peat.

Not at all put out by her father's lack of comment, Tessa's eyes feasted on the distant outcrop of rocks which led to the ridge. The curtain of mist had lifted, swept away by a gracious southerly wind.

'Da!' her voice sharpened. 'Someone's coming up from the valley.' Who could it be? Who would dare? She glanced at her father. Riley's mood of great and intense relief underwent a sudden change. Bristling visibly at the unwanted disturbance of his privacy, he stood up from the table, hooking his thumb beligerently in Timothy Thomas's belt. He did not ask who it was. Being a man of few words he waited until she told him.

'It looks like it's O'Malley's eldest. I can tell his spindly legs a mile off. Yes, it's Pat. Oh, Da?' she said, turning to her tea at the table. 'What can it mean? What can be fetching him up here?' Crossing to the dresser, she unhooked another cup. 'He'll be ready for some tay after his climb.' Watching his progress from the window she opened the door as he arrived.

Pale-skinned and freckled, boots wet and slimy, Pat entered the cabin and peered about to get his bearings. He had need of spectacles but no one recognised the need. Indoors he would peer at things, screwing up his face in an attempt to focus, then to cover his embarrassment he would laugh. His parents presumed this to be a mannerism which, like his clothes, he would outgrow altogether.

Pat stood by the hearth, absorbing the warmth, his clothes, dampened by the morning air, steamed gently. He screwed up his face, being unsure of how Riley would receive him, and focused in Tessa's direction.

Sensing his uncertainty, and knowing how the O'Malleys regarded her father's reticence, as well as the timidity which affected all invaders, she made it easier for him. 'What the divil is it, Pat? What's brought you up here so early in the day?'

'Me da's sent a message for both of yous. You've got to come down this very afternoon – '

'You can tell your da – ' cut in Proud Riley.

'Mr Kildare's called this meeting . . .' Pat continued as though he had not heard, as though he were deaf as well as half-blind. The gamekeeper's name at once stemmed Riley's flow of refusal. 'Mr Flavell came to tell us and said you should be told, but what with the rain and all – '

'Don't mention it,' she laughed, pleased at having someone to laugh with. 'I thought it'd never stop! But, what's this, Pat, about a special meeting? You must have some idea. Why have we to go?'

'Everyone's to go.'

'Everyone?' She thought of Finn and was immediately racked with indecision. Would Finn be at the meeting or would he be up at the cave? Should she go down or up? Some judicious fishing was necessary to find out. 'Do you mean the shiftless as well?' she prompted. 'The Byrnes, Tommy Two-Mouth, Kevin Connor's da, the Aunt Hanratty? Everyone?'

Pat nodded his fair head eagerly. His mother had told him to impress upon Tess that Finn Collins would be there, but not to arouse Riley's suspicions, and all the way up he had been troubled as to how to go about it.

'Not the Aunt!' he exclaimed. 'She's never left her cabin since she went into it. But her, you know, her nephew . . . Now what the divil is his name?'

Ach, thought Tessa, inwardly bubbling over with merriment, 'tis the terrible dissembler you are! May God forgive such convincing artifice in one so young!

'Finn,' he announced. 'That's it. He'll be there instead of the Aunt. 'Tis terrible important,' he nodded gravely. 'About the valley. Anyways, the keeper has something to tell us and he didn't want you to miss out.'

'Hmm. What do you think, Da?' She pursed her lips and forced a touch of reluctance into the question. It wouldn't do to be too eager. She sensed also that her father had some regard for Kildare and was pleased at being singled out in the general summons; she therefore added another touch of reluctance. 'But what about the goats? They've not been out for days.'

'Tomorrow won't disappear, girl.' And to Pat, 'Ye can tell your da we'll be down.'

Both Pat's and Tessa's purposes having been achieved, she, wanting the pleasure of company to last a little longer, began to talk about Marie Jane's letter.

'Me da reckons she's well out of the valley,' he said. 'I mean, you went with her, Tessa, to Fitzcarron House, so you know all about it and how fine a place it is, and how well she's settled. The cabin's not the same without her, though; at least not for me da.' He began to giggle. 'Eh, Tessa, can y'ever imagine, can y'ever think of our Marie Jane, all prim and proper? No swearing, she said in her letter, and no "blaspheming". Christ Almighty, I don't even know what it is, never mind not do it!'

While cleaning and feeding the goats, Tessa promised them and herself an outing. 'We'll go tomorrow if this rain keeps off. We'll go up to the cave by the ridge.' She moved among them, stroking a white flank, a velvety nose, a bony back. 'You'll like that, won't ye? A lick of fresh grass, a taste of sulphur on the way . . .'

Having washed, she hurried to the loft, and struggling out of her goat clothes viewed with dismay her diminishing stock of skirts. The loss of the peacock-blue gown had been a disaster. The white skirt, after the rigours of the Long Dance, could no longer be called white, and awaited dyeing when she could get round to gathering the lichens and mosses. So, it would have to be the black wool left from the Long Dance last year. I should have found time to go scavenging this year, she thought. But the atmosphere had been different; she'd felt emotionally satisfied after winning with Finn, and the evening's talk and Guinness, then the all night chinwag with Marie Jane . . . Scavenging would have been an anticlimax, an unfitting end to so glorious a night. So, away she had gone, hugging the empty Guinness bottle and her wreath of flowers, waving nonchalantly to the shiftless, who'd had the field to themselves this year. The black skirt and blue gingham, it seemed, were the only presentable clothes – and black wasn't really fitting for a summer day . . .

Soon they were off, her father in front. Each step down was taking her nearer to Finn. The import or the outcome of the meeting meant nothing to her other than as a means of seeing Finn. It was only three days since she had seen him, but to a young woman in love it felt like a lifetime.

In silence they passed the trees, and once passed, the view of the valley opened up. Voices in various states of speculative comment buzzed to meet them. Proud Riley observed the full turn-out; all of Ennan was there, except for the Aunt and other old ones. He frowned and wondered. He, too, cared not for the import or the outcome. It meant nothing to him. He would never leave the cabin, but any opportunity to put the keeper in his daughter's sight, or company, was to be seized.

The day was humid after the rain, the earth soft, the flies many. The Rileys walked solemnly toward the gathering, past the potato patches grown high with thistles, the shacks and shanties of the shiftless. Young O'Malley had been right; everyone was here: Father Donaghue in clerical cloak and wide-brimmed hat, despite the warm southerly wind; the shiftless had segregated themselves to one side; the Grogans were not quarrelling but united against the common foe; Kevin Connor, flushed with embarrassment, had crossed the divide to stop his father, already drunk, from entertaining everyone with a maudlin choice of sentimental ballads; Flavell was limping about.

If Tessa had not missed Marie Jane before, she did now. Every time she had entered the valley, Marie Jane had been there, waiting, running up to her, eager to re-establish their friendship, to slip her hand in Tessa's. Despite being with her father, the approach was now a lonely one. Peggy Jams saw her, yelled out and waved, but it was not the same. Those outside O'Malley's cabin turned their heads to acknowledge the Rileys; now they were here the scene was set and ready.

But where was Finn? Her former indecision began to niggle. She should have gone to the cave! He was no doubt there, waiting – but she had taken notice of Pat! But, no, Pat had not got it wrong. It would be the Aunt's fault. Her heart sank, and then rose in anger against Shena Hanratty.

'Silence! Quiet, if you please!' The gamekeeper, standing on the wall of O'Malley's compound, held up his hands. Tessa turned to where he and Flavell had positioned themselves. Flavell was leaning against the wall to rest his foot. There, next to Pat O'Malley, stood Finn.

He had seen her across the crowd, but had not walked over because she was with her father. Her eyes reached out to him. Her anxiety lifted like the mist from Ennabrugh. Her heart danced like the jack-o'-lanterns. Nothing had happened to him. He was free of the Aunt. But why, she asked herself, had he not chosen to go up to the cave? It would have been a God-sent opportunity: the Aunt would have thought him at the meeting, and she could have insisted on taking the goats . . .

The attention of all her neighbours was focused on Frank Kildare. 'I want to impress upon you all,' he was saying, 'that life in this valley is over, ended, finished . . .' He cut short a growl of dissent at once. 'The peat has failed! Sure as I'm standing here before Almighty God, I'm telling you the truth. If you don't believe me, if you don't take my word, ask Mr Riley. He will vouch for the truth of it. If anyone knows the peat, 'tis himself. Afterwards!' he yelled as half a dozen incredulous voices besieged Proud Riley. 'As if that were not enough, there are no potatoes. Mr Riley, the best spud grower hereabouts will vouch for that, too, if the evidence of your own eyes is not enough.' He indicated the patches overgrown with thistles.

'There's been bad years before. We didn't need to be dragged from our hearthstones to hear you tell us that!'

'Sure to God, I recall the times we never went dryshod in a year!'

'C'mon, Mr Kildare; tell us news, not history!'

'Will you listen?' Frank Kildare's patience was wearing thin. 'The state of the soil all those years ago was a damn sight better than it is now! And Ennabrugh, the Great Bog itself, was in a different phase, for this is the first year – and you must admit I'm right – that you've not had turf to burn.'

'So, why fetch us out?'

'What are you going to do?' he asked. ' 'Tis no good waiting until you've burned your last and hoping for heaven to perform a miracle! The answer is to face facts, the truth. Ennan is finished. It can't sustain human life. We are heading for the twentieth century; you cannot live for ever in the Dark Ages. You've all been living easy off the earth.'

'We've been hand-to-mouth for years!'

'I know, I know. But can't you get it into your thick skulls that there'll be nothing in your hands to put into your mouths! Of course,' he modified his tone, 'there are those who have never done a hand's turn in years, and of course,' he added with scant patience, 'there are others who are industrious, but, no matter how industrious you are, if there is no peat you will not survive the winter!' He continued to harangue his audience and to get more and more irate at their passive reaction to the devastating news. Their way of living up here had ended and they couldn't give a damn!

'Has anyone anything to say? Good God, d'you think I would have taken the trouble to gather you all together, to put myself and steward Flavell out, if your position was not serious? And not one of you so much as asks a bloody question!'

Tessa, standing by her father, watched Finn watching the gamekeeper, listening avidly to every word. If she wasn't going to get a chance to speak to Finn at least she could look!

'Easy, now, Mr Kildare . . .' O'Malley looked up from his position sitting on the wall. 'Will I say a word or two meself? I think you're rubbing them up the wrong way.'

'Feel free! See if you can drum sense into your fellow crofters. There has to be an understanding that they'll go down or come to the estate. Something definite.'

'Will you calm yourself, Mr Kildare; get yerself down here, out of their sight. Leave them to me.'

The gamekeeper stood down and O'Malley stood up. Frank Kildare's hawk-like eyes began at once to seek out the troublemakers, but they got no further than Tessa. Not so much her as the young man to whom her glance was directed. He recalled the height, the physique, and that it had been Collins who had wiped the floor with

274

Mick Murphy at the Fair. Oh, and had he not suspected as much when he saw them together at the Long Dance? Hadn't he even asked Marie Jane, and she, the little devil, had spun him so convincing a yarn that he had put the matter out of his mind.

He caught the smile which passed over all the heads and felt a stab of pain to realise it was a lover's look if there ever was one. And, somehow, he felt cheated. As O'Malley's discourse flowed by unheeded, he realised with a shock that her having a sweetheart made no difference to how he felt towards her. He was not giving up. He could no more give up the thought of her than he could fly, and he would not rest until she looked at him with so ardent a glance as she bestowed on Collins. Oh, such a look of love, a warm, embracing, encircling look, not a teasing or flirtatious look. He was tired of those. It had been in his mind, with her father's help, and by great patience and kindliness, to woo her, to make her trust him, love him. He saw, too, how all his actions from the rescuing of that bloody goat from Ennabrugh onwards had been directed toward her. He took a good look at Finn. At his weather-fresh face, so open a face, with his dark looks and curls and deep blue eyes. What people would call 'a fine young fella', well-formed, strong and smiling, guileless too. Questions now began to buzz inside his copper-thatched head. Obviously Proud Riley was not aware of his daughter being involved in a clandestine affair. No one knew. It appeared to be a secret. The question was, should it remain so?

Kildare's attention gradually returned to the tall, thin figure in stetson and spectacles, but O'Malley was not getting far. Objections, a babel of them, cluttered the air.

'We're not leaving!'

'We were born here and we'll die here!'

'You've never said a truer word!' answered Flavell.

O'Malley began to realise that they had lived with the idea for too long to take the present trouble seriously. By all the saints, they'd prick up their ears at what he now had to tell them. Holding up his hands, O'Malley played his last card.

'Will I tell you, now, that another month will see me and my family down in Rohira.' An audible gasp went up; merely a gasp, everyone was too astounded to comment. 'If I cannot survive up here, how can any of you? Why not come down with me? There's no reason on God's own earth why we cannot all go down. There'll be places for many of you. The Jarveys will do a good trade; townfolk'll be fighting to hire their donkeys. There's always work for strong honest hands, and the young women will find places in shops. There's tea shops, coffee houses, pubs, no end of cleaning work . . .' On and on he went with his glowing account, all of it in the most general of terms. 'And what's more,' he continued, 'we can still all be together in nearby streets. For those who have no fancy for the town, Lord Fitzcarron's estate will provide employment. What more could you want than money in your pockets and a roof over your heads? I've had a letter from our Marie Jane, already in service there. She eats three good meals a day, more than me in a week. They provide her with gown and apron, and she earns money as well.'

'Why's his lordship doing all this, O'Malley?' interrupted Gypo Kelly. 'Sure, he's never done anything for us in the past; why's he falling over himself to get us all a roof over our heads and provide us with work? Ask yourself that, O'Malley. It's well enough you telling us this has failed and that's failed, but we've had bad times before and got through it all. His lordship's got an axe to grind, or Kelly's not my name.'

'Have I an axe to grind, Gypo?'

'Who knows!' he laughed. 'You're a wily devil, O'Malley! Only the Almighty knows what's going on under that big hat of yours – and He's not saying a word!'

'Why not come down with me? Because as sure as God's in His heaven, O'Malley's going down. You see,' he added solemnly. 'This life isn't so good for Little Annie, not for any of the children – '

'How about the old ones?' shouted Grogan, who admitted to seventy, and all of those years shiftless. 'We can't work; we've no money. His lordship won't give his charity to us will he? You won't have us with you in your little house. You know where we'll end up once we leave here, O'Malley, don't ye? The workhouse. They'll have to carry me an' herself out of this valley. We'd rather take a chance on the mercy of God. And we'll not be the only ones to stay! Proud Riley won't leave his cabin and the Aunt Hanratty will die before moving an inch!'

And so the meeting went on and on. Exasperated beyond anything he ever remembered, and unable to stand the shilly-shallying any longer, Kildare rode off in a temper, leaving Flavell and O'Malley to salvage any kind of decision. But no decision emerged from all the talk, and Tessa returned with her father to the cabin without having exchanged a word with Finn.

The following day Tessa woke early. From the moment of opening her eyes, Finn filled her mind, and for the very first time in her life she wondered what it would be like to wake every morning and see him lying there at her side.

The implication of this thought took her breath away and brought a flush to her cheeks. She lay there in a turmoil. Her heart could scarce have beaten faster if he had in reality been there. God forgive me, she thought. What's come over me? Afraid to stay lest she fall into more sinful thoughts, she pulled on the goat-skirt and striped working blouse and padded barefoot down the ladder.

Her father had set the kettle and was out. Thank God! She needed time to recover slowly from her thoughts, and somehow the idea of Finn lying beside her in the loft did not seem as abandoned now she was dressed and sitting at a table.

With hands that trembled a little, she wet the tea and began to drink it slowly. Did Finn ever wake up and wish she was there beside him? Immediately the thought was overshadowed by the Aunt. Marie Jane had been right when she said no young woman could possibly share the cabin with his aunt.

Sweethearting was one thing, but to wake up wishing your fella was there beside you was another thing altogether! It was as well thoughts were invisible or her da would have her in a convent sharpish! A thousand questions buzzed about her head like flies. Questions of love . . . Well, she hesitated, reaching for the correct word . . . what she really meant was marriage.

Having been brought up with the idea of one day making 'a good marriage', she had come to look upon the word in a detached manner. All the things her father had warned her about, the odd sayings like 'only give through the wedding ring', came back to her. Of course, she had always known from the girls' talk behind O'Malley's cabin that certain lads could be 'after you for one thing'! She shuddered at the unbidden memory of Mick Murphy's attack and the public airing of it. If anyone was aware of 'base desires', as the priest put it, she was.

But this marvellous feeling, the loving she had for Finn Collins, was neither calculated nor base, and if Finn did not love her enough to marry her, then she would never wake up and find him there beside her. Mary Mother o' Jasus, she sighed over the second cup of tea, and wiggled her bare toes. Her thoughts were levelling out now and she was curious to know what Finn made of the meeting yesterday. Her father had not referred to it, but if he could hold out for this year with his present stock of turf, could she? Living in a deserted valley with no Fair or Long Dance, no O'Malleys, Jams or anyone? And Finn, what was he going to do? Work for him could be found on the estate, but it would not be far enough from the Aunt's curses. She put an end to such thoughts. Better get moving; there's the milking and the swilling down. Then she'd have to wash herself, brush her hair; at least try and look the best she could in these clothes, for to wear anything other would arouse her father's suspicion. Pulling on the stout shoes relegated her waking thoughts to the level of daydreams. Daydreams, God preserve me! And with Marie Jane in mind she took up the buckets. The clang of them set the goats in a frenzy of bleating and whinnying.

'All right, ye spalpeens!' she yelled, pushing back her yet unbrushed hair. 'I'm coming, I'm coming!'

It was just past noon when Tessa called out. 'I'm going with the goats then, Da.'

'Take your crook and shawl, girl.'

'Don't I always? But 'tis too warm to be trailing the shawl.'

'It could rain.'

'I'll risk it!'

And once out of the cabin, crook in hand, goats in front, her heart soared. Oh, the freedom, the blessed, joyful freedom of being out on her own after being cooped up by the offensive rain! She lifted her head and rolled up her sleeves to receive the warmth of the sun. The soft, whispering wind swished the folds of her skirts against her bare legs. The thin, washed out grasses tickled her ankles and all nature was friendly to her. Even Ennabrugh seemed kind. Every plant, every moss and lichen, caught her eye. Damselflies, burnished by the sudden warmth and tethered by desire, hovered lovingly over clumps of graceful pink and white bogbean.

After some half-hour's walk she paused and breathed a pleasant sigh of thankfulness for everything about her, for so enchanting a day. Mother o' God, the last three of rain had been the divil's own!

Glancing up at the rock formations on the ridge from which she took her bearings, Tessa shepherded the goats, touching their flanks with the crook, to the upward path. Not that it was much of a path; even on the slopes the lush green patches meant soft earth. Once near the top it was all safe, but the patchy bit on the way up warranted care. Not that the goats needed shepherding; the fresh grasses called, the shelter of the rocks, the mountainy crevices, the warmth of the sun. With quick little bleats and whinnies of anticipation, they obediently scrambled or trotted, according to age.

Tessa, lifting her skirts, clambered up and up, pausing for breath and envying the sure-footedness of the goats. She shaded her eyes and scanned the tops, hoping Finn would be there. But then, he always came the other way lest some sure-sighted person from below saw two figures striding the ridge. If her da ever found out, sure it would be the end of everything, especially after Mick Murphy. Thoughts of his mean and vengeful attack upon her occasionally came to mind, but hers was not the temperament to dwell on tinker scum. All her thoughts and efforts centred on Finn Collins, like the damselflies on the bogbean. Immediately, with that untamed part of her nature, she consigned Mick Murphy to the flames of hell, with the earnest and intense hope that he would burn there for ever.

The goats would be the first to know whether Finn was at the cave but, as if to tease, they held onto their knowledge. And even if Finn was there, he sometimes acted the fool and hid, or pounced out to startle her into his arms. The way now curved to become hidden from the valley. Her heart beat faster. Oh, there he was. He had removed his boots and placed them inside the cave, for the sweat of the ascent was still upon them, and he stood there, barefooted.

She gazed at him: he looked marvellous, with his natural proud bearing graceful and free, not decorated with dead animals like the gamekeeper. The air of freedom about him fascinated her, it struck a response from deep within her nature. She recognised yet another bond, and felt the old weakness nudging at her knees.

'Tess!' he reached out. 'I thought you weren't coming!'

'And I thought you might not be here!'

She was in his arms, smothered with quick, breath-catching kisses.

'Finn,' she breathed happily. 'This is where I feel I belong.' And trying to fold her arms about his back, she began to laugh. 'Holy Mary, I'm still clutching the crook!' They released each other and laughed together, sweetly and with a sudden shyness. She placed the crook by the peat-cutter and looked for somewhere to sit, ignoring with an odd, yet exciting reluctance the pile of rushes to the side of the cave. Rushes on which they had collapsed laughing and winded after practising for the Long Dance; rushes which she now wished to avoid. There was always, of course, the grass outside the mouth of the cave. She felt the warmth of Finn's hand on her arm drawing her to sit beside him.

'It's cooler inside,' he said and led her to the rushes. Avoiding his glance she smoothed the folds of her skirts. Her face was burning. He was right, it was cooler here. She slipped off her shoes and the cold, damp earth of the cave was soothing to the soles of her peat-browned feet.

'What did you make of the meeting yesterday?' she asked in a matter-of-fact tone, a tone she would not have believed possible ten minutes before.

'O'Malley's right, and Kildare's right,' he answered in the same vein. ''Tis only a matter of time, Tess.' He shook his head. 'I don't understand them; Duggan and Kelly are offered work on the estate and they're shillyshallying about it! If only you and me were free of the Aunt and your da; if only we had some money, we'd be down like greased lightning, wouldn't we, Tess?'

He had began to think of himself and Tess as 'we'. He was used to it, but to Tessa it sounded wonderful. Had he really said 'we'?

'Even when I get away from the Aunt , what about your da, Tess? I can't see him considering marriage with me as a good one.'

'Finn, what is it you're meaning? You've not talked of marriage before.'

He ran a hand distractedly through the raven-black curls and the blue of his eyes darkened. 'It usually happens to people in love; it happened to your ma and da, and to mine.' His words had conjured up in both their minds the fate of Tony and Moll Collins. 'God alone knows what I'm on about, Tess; forget it. Sometimes I think what's the use with all the cards stacked against us? Then I get to thinking I couldn't possibly ask a lovely young colleen like yourself to leave your da's marvellous cabin for anything I could offer; but it always ends up with me thinking we've got a chance. I've lain well into the night dreaming of the day I'll tell the Aunt to go to hell; dreaming of the money I'll earn – for us, Tess.'

She did not answer. His words about marriage had tied in with her waking thoughts that very morning, thoughts of waking up to see him lying there beside her. But he, not aware of this, took her silence to be an acceptance of the uncertainty of their situation.

'I woke up thinking about you, Finn,' she said softly. 'Do you ever do that?

'Always – and then I wonder what I thought of before I met you! Seriously though, I did think of taking up Kildare's offer of work on the estate, only it's too near the Aunt. I'd have to get right away from her – that was me da's mistake. Another idea I had was to join the army.'

'No, Finn!' she exclaimed in alarm. 'I couldn't go on without the thought of seeing you, knowing you were here, in Ennan.'

'But I'd get the Queen's shilling to start with. And perhaps your da would think marriage to a soldier was not too bad a thing . . .' He looked reproachfully toward the split boots standing to attention by the mouth of the cave. 'They give you a new pair of boots, and I could fancy meself in a red tunic!'

'I fancy you just as you are!'

His gaze returned from the boots to his own feet, and hers peeping from beneath the goat-skirt. He recalled with a thrill of pleasure how she had looked at their second meeting by the chapel. He had not even noticed Marie Jane or her clothes. Tess had looked like a queen in the peacock-blue gown. And a right mess the search for Kate Murphy had made of it! When he got some money he would buy her a new one, and a Connemara shawl to keep her shoulders warm.

She followed his look to their feet, unshod and bare. In the silence of the cave these unlikely objects became an absorbing focal point. His feet were big, broad and dusty; hers were small, browned with sun and peat, the skin smooth and the nails pink and shiny. Both became inexplicably animated and very much aware of the intimacy the sight aroused, yet neither wanted to define, even if they could, the emotions which engulfed them.

Tessa's old striped blouse seemed to echo with the thumping of her heart. She closed her eyes and sat there, still as the statuette of Our Lady, a curious aching churning away within her.

Finn saw her eyelids close slowly and the slight tremble of her lips. His foot moved toward hers and brushed it, then began to caress her toes, the raised arch, her ankle. Their eyes met. His foot moved against her leg; he felt the warmth of her skirts on his naked feet. Tessa raised a hand to his shoulder. She could not utter a word. Speech had gone. Her hand came down to his unbuttoned shirt. 'Tess, oh, Tess,' he murmured. 'I can't tell you how much I love you . . .'

The blue depth of his eyes glittered with something she did not understand. Each wondered at the alarming emotion which was tugging at their hearts; they wondered what to do about it; tried to comprehend the enormity of it. But these things defied comprehension. Unable to bear the suspense any longer she opened her eyes and met Finn's adoring gaze so full of yearning, of a desire that spiralled to match her own. Unprepared for so chaotic an emotion, panic took over. He saw the alarm written across her face and released her at once.

'Tess, what is it?'

'Nothing!' she gasped. ''Tis nothing, Finn!' She leapt up and bounded out of the cave, and would have set off down except she had forgotten her crook and shoes.

'Oh, Holy Mother,' she gasped, sinking down by a rock. 'Oh, blessed St Teresa, what shall I do?' She knew what she wanted to do, but all the tenets of church and hearth were against it. 'The wedding ring' her da was always on about. 'The sins of the flesh' the church was always on about. What had they to do with this? One day she and Finn would have a wedding ring. Her mind, suddenly lucid, struggled with the fear of her father. Struggled, and lost. Love was here and now. What did a ring matter?

Her burning face would not be cooled, her heart would not be stilled. What a furious thing love was. Furious, and strange. Only this morning she had wanted him beside her for ever, with all that entailed, and now she was running away. No, not running away. Unable to sit any longer she began to pace up and down between the rocks trying to think coherently, but could not. All that came into her mind was the look in Finn's eyes, the ache in her heart. How could she sleep tonight, or ever again with all this turmoil, all this fire raging as though her immortal soul was aflame for her lover? For Finn! Another panic took over. What if he had gone down? What if he thought she did not care – and she did! God, how she cared! She turned to hurry back – he was there, hurrying to meet her.

Arms about each other, they made their way back to the cave.

Two solitary figures on top of the world in an Eden of their own. An Eden which was no garden, but a wilderness of mountainy outcrop above the dark waste of Ennabrugh. But the hard landscape was sofened by lovers' words.

'You're the only colleen, Tess, in all the world for me. I don't care anything about the world or what's in it, just so long as you'll always be there . . .'

They entered the cave, arms still about each other. Tessa turned to him, lifting her head, offering her lips to be kissed in the heart-hammering way which blinded her senses to everything except the expression of her love. He led her from the sunny entrance of the cave to the more subdued light of the interior, and then towards the rushes. It was like a dream, being propelled slowly and yet surely to something which was both sensuously alluring and a little frightening.

The atmosphere of the interior was cool to their fevered emotions. She moved away from him slightly and he let her go, yet still held her by the brilliance of his gaze. Tessa's breathing quickened. This was the moment she had dreamed of at night in her loft. Finn lying by her side, touching her, easing off her clothes, caressing her breasts.

His hands were at the waist of her skirt. The homespun material was heavy, it dropped about her feet with a muffled sound which faintly startled her. She sat down quickly as if to recover from the shock and to hold onto the faded underskirt's drawstrings. Never being a one to rush things, unlike Marie Jane, she had to get used to the idea of undressing in his presence.

'Tess,' his voice came over soft and teasing in the semidarkness. 'What a lovely mixture of modesty and minx you are! There's just the two of us, alone on top of the world, like the Celtic lovers of old. Here we are, whispering like a couple o' horse thieves, when all I want to do . . . is to love you, Tess.'

Her blouse had joined the goat skirt on the ground but her shift was still on. Not that it impeded in any way the thrill aroused by his touch. He heard the sharp intake of breath, felt her heart bumping and fluttering beneath his possessive hands. Her arms reached up about his neck and, sighing with the sheer pleasure of anticipatory passion, she pulled him down on top of her.

The rushes prickled her midriff where the underskirt began and the shift ended. She did not care. Had it been a bed of nails she would scarcely have noticed. The warmth of their kisses, the moans, the sighs, the endearments muffled and sweet, all added to the urgent passion which young love could no longer resist. Despite being encumbered by her underskirt and his shirt, their love was given, exchanged, and fulfilled; sweetly, silently and urgently.

They lay together for a few moments, saying nothing, contemplating the whirlwind they had just experienced. Tessa recalled more information from the back of O'Malley's cabin. Mona Donal, who had seemed to know everything, had said making love for the first time was painful, it drew blood and men were rough. But Tessa had experienced none of this.

After a little while of holding close, her emotions were rekindled when Finn sat up and tore off his restricting shirt. Her exploring hands swept over his body. Her fingers dwelt on and stroked the corded muscles of his shoulders and upper arms which stood out, erect and hard. She recalled her admiration of his figure when he was wrestling. Ah, sweet Jasus, never did she think to have that handsome physique all to herself. Never did she expect to feel such a total sense of excitement, of conspiracy, as they prepared to repeat the thrilling experience, giving themselves more time to appreciate each other. Oh, Holy Mother, she thought to herself, I can scarcely bear the pleasure of it. Did people die of happiness, she wondered; the thought, far from chilling, urged her on. There was nothing to lose, for to die like this would be to gain paradise straight away. The fires of purgatory were nothing compared to the flames which threatened to ravage her entire being. Finn was absolutely naked, and she, for the stupid reason of modesty, was not. It now became a matter of paramount importance that she, too, should be as he was. Her shift, the last vestige of modesty, now became like a millstone lying heavily on her breast.

'Let me . . .' he murmured huskily, as she struggled to a sitting position to remove it. She liked him taking it off for her, the brushing of his knuckles, the sweet surprise of accidental touch . . . the warmth of the rushes, the semidarkness. And the subdued light added a mystical dimension, as though their love-rite was something special, to be experienced by the soul as well as the senses.

The shift removed she leaned her back against his chest and sighed her pleasure as the abrasive touch of his big rough hands gratified her spiralling senses. A vitality greater than their own rushed through them, they were helpless in its toils, slaves bound to a force older than the Celtic mythology. Thrilled in every nerve, trembling under the hand of merciless passion, he laid her back and, as the rushes yielded to her weight, so she yielded herself again to her first love, her hero, her lover. She wanted to hang on to that moment, stay together for ever, but even as it arrived, Tessa knew that mere mortals could not possibly endure such rare delight, so intense a pleasure. A little later, when they could bear to ease their grasp of each other, he kissed her tenderly, held her gently, and both vowed undying love. To stay with each other until death. But death was a long way off in the summer of 1898.

The days that followed were so like a golden dream that it took Tessa all her time to keep herself anchored to reality. Alone in the loft she lived over again and again every exquisite detail of the loving experience shared with Finn, impatient for the hours to pass until she could see him, hold him, love him again.

When day dawned she wanted to sing, to dance, to talk about anything and everything to the goats, to her father, to the very stones. But she did none of these things; she reserved all her excess emotion for Finn. Sexual fulfilment added a poise and almost instant maturity. She felt herself to be truly a woman at last. Peggy Jams, Una Kelly, all the other young women, were not of the least interest now. They would seem childish and juvenile. She thought of Marie Jane and no longer wished her back in Ennan.

Finn, in turn, was equally affected. She was the first, the only love of his life. The equal passion they had shared made him even more protective toward her. In the Aunt's cabin he lived in agony lest she detect any signs. He constantly racked his brains for a way out. Tessa was still against him going to enlist. In the aftermath of passion they lay on their little altar and planned schemes, but not with the old enthusiasm. In the light of their newly discovered love everything else paled into insignificance. His aunt, her father, O'Malley's plans, the gamekeeper's plans, the failure of the peat, even Marie Jane – nothing seemed important anymore.

On the last day of August, the sun having gone from the mouth of the cave altogether, Tessa and Finn lay in each other's arms, covered with her shawl, happily replete, and having the usual difficulty in bringing themselves to go their separate ways.

Tessa brushed her lips against his shoulder and sighed. 'I've been thinking, Finn, we can't go on sharing our love like this . . .'

'Do you mean with the summer passing, the cold and all?'

'I mean,' she said shyly, 'look what happened to Mona Donal. She had to marry Kevin Connor, didn't she?'

'Oh, God save us!' He raised himself to a sitting position and tucked the shawl to her side.

'Yes, God save us!' she smiled. 'We've got to think of this, Finn. No matter how much we want each other, it would be tempting Providence. If anything like that were to happen to us, love, there'd be hell to pay. Me da would kill me, I'm sure – '

'Tess,' he admonished. 'Don't be saying such things. But you're right.' He was suddenly alarmed. 'I never gave it a thought,' he grinned bashfully. 'You go to a fella's head, Tess. You still love me?'

'As me own life. Honest to the good God, I love you, but we really must put our minds to getting away, so we can be together all the time,' and in the same breath added helplessly, 'I can't just leave me da, I can't just go off without a word, he'd never lift his head up again.'

'What do you think if I came up to see him, man-to-man, like . . .' The eagerness died out of his voice. He could imagine what Proud Riley would say, or rather, ask. 'Where will she live?' he would ask. 'Have you any dacent money? Proud Riley's daughter,' he would say, 'is not leaving this cabin – which I built for her mother, God rest her soul – unless it be for something much better.'

Tessa caught the drift of his thoughts. 'We'll find a way, Finn. We'll have to, for I can't live without you and what I'll do when the bad weather stops us from getting out, the blessed God only knows.'

He had moved from the rushes and Tessa suspended her anxiety to watch him dress: the muscles on his back rippling as he struggled into the faded shirt, his lean hips and the moulded strength of his haunches disappearing into the corduroys.

Having respect for her modesty he busied himself while she dressed, moving across to his boots, pulling them on, tucking the ends of his trousers into the tops, standing in the mouth of the cave. These moments saddened him. Heaven was coming to an end. Paradise was closing its doors, shutting down, like the shops in Rohira at dusk.

CHAPTER SIXTEEN

The summer was short on Ennabrugh, and no sooner had August gone than the gilded clouds of autumn started to gather on the high ground. The clouds were gathering too, about Riley's cabin. The gamekeeper had called to collect Tessa's letter for Marie Jane. There was no letter, Riley told him; she was not writing one, and was now out with the goats. He had gone away with his shoulders hunched and a thoughtful frown on his hunter's face.

'What do you think of Mr Kildare?' asked her father while pouring his bedtime poteen. 'I wish you would make yourself agreeable to him.'

'I thought I was agreeable, Da.'

'I suppose I'd better tell you, girl.'

'Tell me what?'

'He asked me if I'd any objection to him . . . courting you, walking out. He wants to wed you, Teresa!' he exclaimed with a flourish. 'I always knew some well-set-up young man would carry you off to better things. I've told you often enough how I swore over your mother's grave that you'd make a good marriage, and now it's happening.' His voice took an uptilt. 'And I can't tell you, girleen, how pleased and proud it makes your old da.'

Tessa was kneeling by the hearthstones applying some of O'Malley's fat mixture to keep the wet out of her shoes. Despite the heat from the fire, she went cold.

'Jasus, Mary and Joseph,' she breathed. Her throat was suddenly restricted; it was a small voice which continued. 'You didn't say I would?'

Riley's heart sank a little. What had Kildare said? 'Shall we tread softly . . .' 'I told him I was agreeable, but the last word depends on yourself. You can be a headstrong colleen when you've got it on you, Teresa, but it'd more than please me if you'd give him a chance. There'll be nothing as good . . .'

Tessa applied more fat mixture, head down to avoid her father's eyes in which there would be either hope or reproach – or both. So that was the way of it, she thought, and lots of little incidents in the past concerning Kildare fell into place, the last being the trouble he'd gone to over Marie Jane's letter. I've not given him any encouragement either, she thought. And what about Marie Jane? Had he been stringing her along to get at me? A good thing she's dropped him. Marriage! And I don't even like him! She began to panic, her head began to whirl.

'He'll be a good husband to you.' Riley poured himself more poteen. 'Thinks a lot of you, and he's a good man, Teresa. And will I tell you now, he's the only man that can take you away from Ennan. God love you, 'tis a chance any girl would jump at! I thought he was taken with O'Malley's girl, but it appears I was wrong.'

'He's a keeper, Da,' she protested, knowing it wasn't the full truth. 'I can't be doing with dead creatures about, and him talking about killing things, and fetching stags down. Killing things is his job!'

'He's so taken with you, he'll not let you see the dead creatures; he doesn't sport them on his saddle anymore because of you – '

'He still traps and shoots, doesn't he? He's still got blood on his hands!'

'It'll be like it is here,' he soothed. 'When I've got to kill one of the goats, 'tis done while you're out.' He stared at her bent head, his peat-brown eyes puzzled, his face wearing a look of utter incredulity. It was not in him to talk overlong. He had not the gift of the gab, like O'Malley, nor the reasoning powers of his daughter, or her mother before her. It was obvious Teresa was not even giving the gamekeeper a chance; she was putting up arguments, and he did not know what to do.

'Don't you like him?' he asked at length.

It was on Tessa's lips to be easy on her father, to say she thought Frank Kildare was 'well enough' or 'a dacent fella' or something of the kind, but she knew he would seize on the slight hope and build on it. It was kinder to impress the truth on him from the outset.

'No, Da,' she answered flatly. 'I do not like him.'

Had she said she did not like the Blessed Virgin Mary or the Holy Ghost, he could not have been more shocked. Worse, despite his slight misgivings and 'treading softly', her forthright answer to his question left him without hope . . . disillusioned, disappointed and crushed. He knew she could be headstrong, and recalled her refusal of the gamekeeper's offer to escort her to the Long Dance practices – God, he'd had no idea. Refusal and disobedience had never come into their relationship, and now this second refusal . . .

He felt for the chair, pawing at the back of it like a blind man. He sank down heavily. In the lamplight, his face seemed to have shrunk into the shelter of the frieze of whiskers. Tessa, as much in a state of shock as her father, stopped greasing her shoes, wiped her hands on the hessian and sat on the chair opposite him.

'Are you all right, Da?' There was an anxious edge to her voice. Always a cocky little figure, head high and thumb in belt, one foot placed before the other, proud and defiant of the world; the sight of him crumpled in his chair filled her with concern.

If he had raved and shouted like Una Kelly's da, or took his belt to her like Mona Donal's, refusing to do as he wished would have been a lot easier. The conduct of other fathers – apart from Marie Jane's – brought to memory a lifetime of the gruff, if silent, kindness and consideration of this man, who was not even her real da.

'Give him a chance, Teresa. You'll get to like him. Will I tell you now,' he said softly and hesitantly, 'that your ma, God rest her soul, well . . . she didn't . . . couldn't . . .' He paused, and in that short time felt very old and tired and more inadequate than ever. How, in the name o' God, he thought, can I find the right words to make her see sense, set her on the right path, this daughter of Teresa Donnelly's, this clear-eyed creature sitting opposite? 'Your ma, God rest her soul,' he said again, 'married me because I wanted her to.' The words stumbled from stiff lips. 'She married me to give you a roof over your head and a name, and a father. She could not bring herself to . . .' The memory, even all those years later, was too hurtful for him to formulate the word 'love', the love he had so much wanted and the love his wife had so wanted to give. He could not bear to utter the word and sought frantically for a different one, '. . . to care for me because of your real da. She couldn't help it – even though he was lying in his grave at St Joseph's. Can't you see what I'm getting at?'

He felt a spasm of that special, unique pain caused by the memory of the woman he had worshipped. He saw her daughter as a superior being, and he loved her with a peculiar, private love for which he had never been able to find language or outlet. There was no look, gesture, or tone of voice which could give expression to it, and his incapacity to express it made him afraid. He envied O'Malley. He envied everyone who could talk freely and without constraint. His wandering mind came back to the worried, pale blur of a face before him, to the summer blue eyes which gazed with such a luminous intensity.

'It seems to me, Da,' she pointed out, simply and without rancour, yet with all the frankness of youth, 'that what you're getting at is you want me to marry a man I don't . . . like . . . just because me ma did.'

'She would want you to marry him. She wanted better things for you, and I promised, God help me, I swore on your parents' grave . . .' He heard her murmur something, looked and saw her shivering. Helplessly he blundered on. He had to. This was his daughter's chance, the opportunity he had dreamed of. And he wanted so much to be relieved of so great a responsibility. As he talked, another thought came to torture him. If, and God forbid, they had to leave Ennan and go down into the town, what would happen to Teresa there? Towns were full of fellas like that knacker's bastard Mick Murphy. Oh, she must, Teresa must, see sense and marry Kildare. It was the only way . . .

'I know you only want the best for me, Da, but – '

'Sleep on it,' he said quickly, anything to delay a further refusal. He reached for another cup and poured her some poteen. 'Think about it.' He looked at her helplessly, like Little Annie used to look at Marie Jane. 'Think of your old da, Teresa. How can I face him – how could I throw such a good offer back at him?'

'You wouldn't have to,' came the quiet reply. 'Sure, I'll tell him myself.' She sipped the poteen with a hollow sense of detachment, as though she had stumbled into some mysterious ceremonial transaction, some sacrificial rite, and was being conveyed . . .

'I shall pray for you, girl.' His voice cut into her detachment. 'I shall pray to St Teresa, to the Holy Mother, and Christ Himself.'

He scraped back the chair and moved away with a crumbling slowness. All her life she had witnessed the before bed observance of her father's prayers. He always knelt by the upright chair, no stooping forward, no leaning on elbows like the shiftless at Mass, and after crossing himself folded his hands and prayed silently. Now the sight of her father at his prayers was full of portent. He was invoking the aid of heaven to get her to marry the gamekeeper! Not wanting to be there when he finished, she downed the rest of the poteen and quickly ascended the ladder to her loft.

Tessa did not lie down. Sleep! Would she ever sleep again? Leaning against the end of the loft, knees hugged to chin, her bewildered thoughts whirred together like the wings of a dozen partridges. This was the time of night to which she always looked forward, the reflective time between reality and dreams, Finn's time. But now thoughts of Finn had to vie with the awful situation of the gamekeeper, and how to manage her father.

Of course, the plain answer was a definite, flat, outright 'no'. But, such an answer posed the question would a man of the gamekeeper's temperament, used to bringing down his quarry, take no for an answer? But I've not encouraged him; in fact, if anyone's had the brushoff, it's him! How could he possibly think I would be interested in the bloody goings on in his life? Another thing, too, was as sure as hell fire; she would not tell any of this to Finn – not yet. Not until it was all over and both Kildare and her da realised nothing would come of their 'good marriage'. Wait till Marie Jane heard. 'Oh,' she would say, forming her red lips, 'Ye kept all that close, Tessa!'

It was much later when she heard her father's snores ascending to the rafters. She struggled out of her skirt and into her nightgown, a little smile tugging at her lips. Proud Riley and his daughter were putting heaven in a quandary this night. He had assailed the ears of all the saints, the Mother of God, and Christ Himself to persuade his daughter to become the gamekeeper's wife; and she would now pray to those selfsame ears to be delivered from such an awful fate! Whether they heard or not was a matter of indifference, for nothing . . . nothing . . . nothing . . . would ever induce her to marry Frank Kildare.

Marie Jane, unaware of her friend's secret meetings with Finn, of their love consummated on the altar of the cave, of Frank Kildare's confessed passion, performed her first household duties with pride and pleasure. She still adopted a teasing attitude to Frank, but only to cover the embarrassment of her previous amorous adventures with him.

She was not vexed with Tessa for not answering her letter, for her father had called while down in Rohira on business and assured her that everything was the same. Mrs Quail had made him a parcel of cooked meats, crumbly cake, and a pot of curd for Little Annie. Marie Jane had painted so glowing a picture of her father that the strict housekeeper readily fell victim to the charm of the O'Malley tongue.

Marie Jane was also not aware that her father's visit had not been solely on her account, much as he loved her and had been delighted to take his dinner with her at the kitchen table. The main reason for his visit was an interview with Lord Fitzcarron. For his part in the clearance, O'Malley had just obtained the key to one of the houses Finn Collins had admired in Rohira.

He had come to tender his thanks and announce the date of his departure. 'Give me a week, your lordship, Mr Kildare, Mr Flavell; just a week and I'll leave Ennan for good, taking most of them with me. Those that are left will be up to you, Mr Kildare, to 'tice onto the estate.'

When O'Malley, hat in hand, had gone, followed by Flavell, Lord Fitzcarron turned his full pale eyes towards the gamekeeper. He did not utter a word, but Kildare read impatience and a smattering of doubt in the glance. O'Malley, plausible fella that he was, had done his part in good time. He and his family would be on their way in a week, followed, he hoped, by all the rest, like the Pied Piper with all the rats scurrying after him! Mother of God, what a thought! In the pale eyes he had read something which was no laughing matter. If anyone was left in Ennan by the end of October, he would lose his position.

As he left the estate office, where the interview had taken place, something else occurred to Kildare to add to his unease. Supposing, just supposing, O'Malley persuaded the Rileys to follow him down to Rohira? Despite all the talk of rats gnawing at his toes it was just possible that O'Malley, with his persuasive tongue, could get him to change his mind. The alarming part of all of this was that Tessa would go with her father, and once the old man saw the possibility of marriage for his daughter with clerks and shopkeepers, his own offer would not seem as good. And what about Collins? Somehow, despite the lover's look he had witnessed, he had not taken the sweethearting seriously. Her father knew nothing about it, he pursed his lips, so there was not much danger, not at least while they all remained in Ennan. The girl could not marry without parental consent, but once in the town, she could elope, run off.

Kildare had not heard of the situation or the history behind Finn

Collins' relationship with his aunt, or that the young man was penniless, or he might not have been so disturbed.

The following day, Kildare saddled his horse and rode over to Ennan, ostensibly to see how the crofters had taken the news of O'Malley's deadline, and also how many were likely to go with him, though heaven alone knew where they'd go once down! Then, he would need to find out how many he would have to chivvy, bribe or force into coming onto the estate.

His real reason was to see Tessa Riley.

He heard the noise before he reached the valley; the excited yells and shouts of alarm and anger. 'What in the name o' God's going on?' he muttered seeing a number of horsedrawn conveyances at the far end by the Aunt Hanratty's cabin. He groaned as the realisation dawned. The Health Authorities were up! Someone had set them onto the valley! He dismounted quickly and tethered the horse to O'Malley's compound gate. 'O'Malley!' he shouted at the door. Nobody was in, not even Little Annie. Frowning, he strode off in search of information.

Never had he seen such confusion. Some people were running into their cabins, others were running out. Some stood in clusters listening to Gypo Kelly shouting and protesting. A tumbled and disorderly mixture of young, old, and shiftless stood wide-eyed, as wondering as himself. Where the devil was O'Malley? Where the bloody hell was he? He took off his deerstalker and wiped his forehead with the back of his hand.

His face sharpened with dismay as he recognised Father Donaghue. Oh, Holy Mother, no! He looked at the turmoil as though in a preposterous dream. Murray from the Board of Education stomped about, paunchy and red-faced and followed by little runts of clerks making rapid notes in little books.

Diet, livestock, potatoes, numbers of children per family . . . Words came thick and fast. Convulsions, croup, cholera, miscarriages, still births . . . Crofters dodged the questions as they would hailstones; some ran for cover, some were caught. Dalmainy from the Health Authority, renowned for his loss of patience, was reduced to shouting hysterically as he lunged forward to collar the O'Malleys and the Jams boys. And over all, Kevin Connor's father, maudlin drunk, treated them all to an afternoon version of the 'The Last Rose of Summer'.

The Byrnes, all six, stood open-mouthed and vacant-eyed; they needed no catching and fell prey to Dalmainy at once, and then stood to be photographed by fussy men with tottering tripods. The young, never having seen long white coats before, stared in sheer fright at Dr Mahoney and his four assistants, supposing them at first, judging by their predatory movements, to be some weird version of Dooley's ghost. They watched goggle-eyed as these emissaries from the Board of Health loaded samples of earth and peat into little glass tubes, then took to their heels as the white coats divided to seize wriggling children who supposed the weighing and measuring of themselves had something to do with the glass phials. The Duggan girls, on the other hand, were delighted at the interest shown in their respective teeth. Never, it seemed, had they come across an entire family of ten whose teeth were all in an advanced state of decay. A stout, thick-thighed officer of some kind went from group to group demanding cooperation from uncooperative parents.

'God love us!' declared Frank Kildare as Seamus Brady of the *Irish News* approached him. 'What the hell are you doing here?'

Seamus pushed his hat to the back of his head. 'Remember calling at the office way back in spring, and the talk came round to places like this?'

Kildare did remember. He thought he had been smart; it had been part of his plan to drop a word in that ear and the other, never dreaming they would all join forces. He had not approached them in a rampant campaigning manner. 'I do so. But God preserve us, Seamus, can't a fella say anything on the quiet without the press making a shenanigan of it! Was all this necessary? Half of them are terrified to death of the white coats and the little black bags of tricks. What the divil do you hope to gain by it all?'

'Will ye calm yourself, Kildare? You were the first to say that clearing this valley would be doing God's work.'

'Don't for heaven's sake quote me on that,' groaned Frank, already seeing his job disappearing before his eyes. 'And if I did say it, I didn't mean that all hell should be let loose!'

'What did you expect? That the authorities would come up piecemeal? Damn that for a policy. If they don't all come up at once, they run the risk of these mountain folk taking to the hills, having been warned the first time. Everyone's being asked their opinion – '

'An' they're too damned scared to give it! You might at least have let me know . . . Father Donaghue, someone. Just to come up like this – '

'You've done 'em a good turn, Frank, having that word with us. They'll thank you for it.'

'Like hell they will!'

As Seamus went off to speak to one of the photographers, Frank Kildare returned to O'Malley's cabin. He was still not in. He looked about; even the hens were flustered. The valley seemed to be overrun with strangers. He groaned, just the very thing he had wanted to avoid. All of them are here, he thought, even the Guardian of the workhouse! He strained his neck to look about.

Was that . . . ? It was. Yes, Riley himself. So, they got him down – must have used dynamite! He felt a touch, a hand on his sleeve. The rush of blood to his heart told him whose hand it was.

Shortly after Tessa had left the cabin to keep her tryst with Finn, one of the O'Malley boys had run up for Riley. They were being driven out! Everyone must rally to the defence! While the two descended, Tessa and Finn, hearing all the shouting, had been drawn from their first embrace. They saw the vehicles arrive and the influx of strangers. Alarmed and curious, they set off down at once, to arrive at different places in order to avert suspicion – not that they would be noticed in the pandemonium. They, like everyone else, stood about in a state of bewilderment, observing the antics and the strange equipment of civilisation. Occasionally, they would look at each other from a distance, each seeming to know instinctively where the other was. Tessa had seen the gamekeeper arrive and had waited until he was alone.

'Can I talk to you for a minute?'

'You can so.' He smiled.

She felt self-conscious, and began to wonder if she was doing the right thing, but the longer she left the situation untackled, the more difficult it would eventually become. Taking confidence from the crowd, the noise, she launched out.

'It's about you coming to see me da about our keeping company and marriage.'

Her eyes were lifted to his, uncertainly.

'Tessa,' he indicated the people milling about. 'This is no place for a private conversation.'

She saw that, despite his words, he was worshipping her. She swallowed. Her throat was dry. 'I don't want a private conversation, Mr Kildare. Me da told me, last night, about your . . . proposition, and I wouldn't like you to be wasting your time thinking about me.' She paused, a little frightened, yet wanting to put everything in a clear, defined light.

'I want to be thinking about you. I think of nothing else.'

'It . . . it's no use.'

'No use? Why?'

She looked about, seeking a little support from a friendly face, and was confronted by the vacant stare of the youngest Byrne. She looked down at her fumbling hands. Her attention was back with the keeper. 'For the same reason I don't want to work at Fitzcarron House. 'Tis a man of blood y'are, Mr Kildare,' she added, not unkindly or briskly. 'I couldn't be doing with it.'

'A man of blood? What nonsense is this, Tessa? I've got a job to do. O'Malley wrings the necks of the chickens. Your da kills the goats when they're past their prime, I'm no more a man of blood than they are.'

'You are so! They don't go out with guns to shoot them and they don't set traps to catch them! I know you've got a job to do, but I keep telling you that I couldn't even live under the same roof as a gun, still less keep company with a fella that uses one!'

'Your da said you'd get used to it,' he said stiffly. 'He gave me to understand – '

'I don't know what he gave you to understand, mister, but I wanted ye to hear the truth from meself; that's all.'

He watched her walk away, with a mixture of admiration for her frankness and a bitter despair. That was all he needed. Rejection on top of all this bloody mess. He stared after her, not caring who saw or noticed. He had not known until just now that his love for her was so very certain – and now that he knew, she had told him that he was beyond her.

He felt alone and deserted. People swarmed about him but he knew them not. She had been frightened, he mused, too frightened to tell me when we were alone. That would have been the civilised way to do it, but these people were not civilised, and what he was doing here like some stupid lovesick swain, God alone knew!

His keen eyes swept the heads, the hats, scarves, caps . . . Yes! That head taller than the others . . . the raven-black curls. Ach, a regular Adonis he was. Might have known he would be where she was. The cold fingers of jealousy began to touch him. He caught the lift of the young man's head, the seeking eyes. He made himself watch. He'd seen her! Oh, 'twas a look of love all right. Such a look could only be recognised and interpreted by those in love, like himself. Tessa had probably, by now, forgotten all about him in the joy of that fleeting glance. Did they ever talk about him, he wondered, or laugh at the idea of a hunting man being deprived of his prey; oh, not that they'd laugh spitefully or maliciously, but with that selfish, indifferent confidence of lovers.

Seamus Brady was back. 'Cheer up, old man,' he quipped. 'It may never happen, as they say.'

'That's just what's bothering me.'

'It's all going to be cleared, y'know.'

'What is?'

'The valley is going to be cleared! You're not listening, man. 'Tis a bit pale you are round the gills. What's up? Had a skinful last night? They've got till the month-end to make arrangements, and then the carts will be up to transport any that are left – and to fire the cabins.'

He caught Kildare's look. 'It is clearance policy to fire it all, otherwise someone'll creep back and start it all over again! Keep your eyes on the *Irish News* if you want to keep informed! Tell me this, what's your interest in Ennan?'

'My interest?' he repeated, his eyes on the distant figure of Tessa. 'Friendly,' he murmured.

'You! Friendly? That'll be the day!'

'Damn you, Brady,' he said. 'I've got a fella to see. O'Malley?' he called. 'How the divil did all this come about?'

O'Malley made a play of defending himself. 'Wasn't any of my doing, but his lordship is not going to like it! What was it he said? No radical press asking questions?'

'You can hardly call the *Irish News* a radical press.'

'But that's not all, Mr Kildare.'

'What the devil d'ye mean?'

'Did you not hear the last bout of bother?'

'I heard the general noise, but Brady took my mind off it.'

'Well, you know how I had got some o' them eating out of me hand, so to speak, with me talk of going down, and all o' that – '

'Yes, yes,' he said irritably.

O'Malley shrugged his slim shoulders. 'All this has put them off.'

'Off what, for God's sake?'

'Off going down. What else? All the Duggans were going to come with me, and the Kellys, but now no one will stir an inch, not now they've seen all this. The polis with the wagon outside of the Hanratty cabin, all the little tubes and white coats, measuring sticks and weighing scales, bottles of this, and black bags full of instruments of torture. Old Duggan overheard one of the boyos telling how they would fire the cabins, so you can imagine they're not for going down at all – nor for going on the estate. And, would you believe it?' he said, eyes twinkling behind his spectacles. 'It was Proud Riley set them off! Rich, isn't it? A fella that scarce says two words together in public – or private if it comes to that – and he just happens to say 'em at the right time! "They'll not drag me from my cabin," he says, "till the rats are gnawing at me toes! Here I've lived and here I'll bloody well die!" But he was vicious and vehement. There's something gnawing at Riley already – the rats aren't waiting till he's dead! They listened to him as though he were the Pope giving utterance; and didn't they cheer him and back him up! Ah, merciful God, ye should have seen old Murray, from the Education; the veins on his red face stood out like sinews in raw meat! He stamped about and started with the threats. Well, that did it. Kelly accused him of "fighting talk" and the little runts of clerks called us savages. Dalmainy defended us and a fistfight between them was stopped by Dr Mahoney. All the little bottles and phials and samples were trampled on and smashed to smithereens.' He hunched his shoulders. 'And that's how it's gone on. Even Father Donaghue couldn't do a thing.' He nodded toward the Hanratty cabin where the vehicles were standing. 'They're going down now, but they'll be back in a month with warrants and polis – all the paraphernalia of a clearance.'

'You're still going down?' Behind the question lay the silent wish that O'Malley would stay until the final débâcle.

'I am so.' O'Malley's smile seemed to be gilded with satisfaction and hope for the future. It was not his fault the scheme had gone awry. He had got the darling little house for his family and, by God, they were going to it. 'There's many a slip 'twixt cup and lip', and

O'Malley was not a one to slip. 'There's one thing puzzles me, Mr Kildare.'

'Only one? 'Tis the fortunate fella, y'are.'

'How did all these people get wind of the situation? Everything was going quietly . . .' He shook his fair head sadly. 'Sure, 'tis enough to make all the angels in heaven stamp their golden feet.'

The days following the 'visitation' found Riley in a flurry of impatience and desperation. Give her time, he told himself; give the colleen time. And then he pondered on Kildare. If he's half the fella I think he is, he won't take no for an answer. After all, Teresa was only going on eighteen; time was all she needed; time to reflect, to consider.

Tessa did indeed need time. Time to be with Finn. They snatched greedily at the hours, and had met twice since the 'visitation'. In their mountainy cavern they talked as lovers talk, kissed as lovers kiss. And then, thinking of sin and circumstances, they stopped short of the fulfilment they had shared but twice, and resolved yet again to break their domestic ties and set out on their own.

Autumn came early to Ennabrugh. There were no trees to scatter russet coloured leaves over its surface. No soft whispering winds to fan the drying stacks of rushes. Nothing but the ethereal mist, eddies of it, whirling, swirling and curling. And overhead the lonely cry of the plover mourning the loss of summer days. The Great Bog observed with impatience the enactment of this ritual, and from beneath its black surface came mumbles of displeasure.

If Proud Riley was giving his daughter time to consider, she too was giving him time to reflect. She knew his moods by the type of silence which emanated from him, and this silence was a heavy one. She did not like to see him so burdened and did not want to be the cause of it, but the alternative was unthinkable. A couple of days, she thought, and by the time O'Malley leaves he'll be his old self. But the days passed, and he was not his old self at all.

While the celestial stamping of golden feet was in progress, Aloysius O'Malley prepared to vacate his cabin and move down to Rohira. Everyone, shiftless as well, were invited to the 'well-wishing', an old custom adopted many years ago from the visiting tinkers.

Riley, despite his unhappiness, would not miss so important an occasion. O'Malley had been his good friend, his only friend. He recalled their conversation as they had stood together watching Spider Murphy leading the tribe of tinkers along the ridge. So much had happened since then, so much . . . so much.

Tessa, hopeful of feasting her eyes on Finn, hurried to the loft, to struggle out of her goat clothes and into the black woollen skirt and blue gingham blouse. Tying her hair with the black velvet ribbon and seizing the little shoulder shawl with tassels, she was quickly down the ladder to where her father was waiting.

She had expected to see him as he always had been when they went down together, standing impatiently by the door, grumbling about titivating, a thumb hooked in Timothy Thomas's belt, and one foot before the other for a speedy takeoff. But, he had not even washed or put on a clean shirt; neither did he grumble about titivating. She saw the reproach still smouldering in his peat-brown eyes, and felt torn.

Merciful God, she thought as they left the cabin, have I to sacrifice meself to bring his old jauntiness back? Would he be his old self to see me marrying a man I didn't love? How could he? Mr O'Malley would never put Marie Jane in such a position. Ennan won't be the same without them, she thought bleakly.

That she had not missed Marie Jane more was due to the blossoming love between herself and Finn. Still blossoming, she thought, and look 'tis autumn, already – where the divil did the summer go? It did not seem so long since she and Marie Jane had sweated in the hot sun going to Fitzcarron House, and now they were enveloped in mist! The tops of the mountains were cut off by it – but she did not mind, really. It was rather like the curtain Marie Jane had put round the bed on which she slept to make her own 'private room'. Their cave was up there, curtained off, waiting.

Following her father's gnomish figure, Tessa refused to dwell on the slowness of his gait, or the way he stooped forward, his shoulders burdened not by spuds, but the crumbling of his plans for her future. She had never regarded him as an old man, for after all, he was only O'Malley's age and not old in the sense the Grogans's or the Duggans's fathers were; but now a stranger would put him in their class at once. Instead of the usual air of good-natured indifference, their progress was accompanied by a thick mist of reproach.

Tessa passed the clump of trees, the scene of many a quick change of clothes; but all that was gone, and she did not need a strategy for going down the hill anymore, only for going up! She hoped Finn would be at the well-wishing. If anyone was glad to see the back of the O'Malleys it would be the Aunt Hanratty.

Having set foot in the valley, Tessa's gaze quickly travelled among the red heads of the Duggans, the fair ones of the O'Malley brood, the hoary heads of the old, the close-cropped of the young, the bald, the caps and scarves – ah, she breathed in contentedly – the raven-black curls. And he had spotted her at once, for his eyes were upon her as she looked at him.

Her heart and step lightened; her father's reproaches slipped away as she greeted Peggy Jams and Una Kelly, gradually manoeuvering them towards Finn. Despite the poteen and O'Malley's infinite good humour, the hearts of some were not inclined to wish him well; despite the fact of his arrangements being made before the 'visitation', many regarded the move as desertion.

Martin Jarvey's father and uncle were supervising the loading of two donkey carts. Mrs O'Malley, with Little Annie, and Bridget – who was terrified of being left behind – clinging to her skirts, trundled to and fro with her cooking pots, bowls, blankets, and what was left of the peat. Pat stood about importantly, trying to impress Tiny Jams, Peggy's little sister, with a description of the job he had waiting in Rohira as lather boy in a barber's shop. Dion carried the first of the freshly killed fowl – nothing was to be left – by their long throats, reverently laying their corpses in a shallow zinc bath. Tim looked on solemnly.

Aloysius went the rounds with a five-noggin bottle, but his silver-tongued words of persuasion of what delights would be in store for any who were to come down with him fell on deaf ears. The mountainy men of Ennan were going to stick it out until the last; 'till the rats are gnawing at our toes!'

At the other end of the valley and over the ridge of mountains, Frank Kildare was making his way into the belly of Fitzcarron House, past the great gleaming mahogany surfaces and the long crimson curtains which Tessa had so wonderingly beheld on her visit, to the library where his lordship was awaiting him.

There had been a stag to bring down on the furthest side of the estate and he had busied himself over there so as not to be readily available when the *Irish News* arrived. Failure, he thought, has been my middle name of late. The bloody stag had been too far up on the high ground, and he still hadn't brought it down; Lord Fitzcarron would not like that either. He had failed, too, with Tessa Riley; and yet his heart still beat faster when he thought of her. He had to admit that his present consternation was due to his failure to set the clearance moving quietly and without undue attention. Undue attention! Mother of God, the world and his wife would be aware of it all when they opened their newspapers! With dismissal staring him in the face, he now stood before Lord Fitzcarron.

'You've been damned elusive these past few days, Kildare. After the stag, they said. Well, man, did you get it down?'

Kildare heard himself making excuses, excuses! This time six months ago, nothing would have got the better of him, stags, women, events . . . He waited for the explosion. Dismissal. His lordship stood up from his desk, and through a flow of words Kildare caught sight of the long face before him filled not with coldness or rage, but with satisfaction.

'A master stroke, Kildare! Why the devil did you not acquaint me with the facts at once instead of skulking up into the mountains like a heathen? You're not usually so modest a fella!' Hands thrust into the pocket of his velvet smoking jacket, Lord Fitzcarron moved nearer. 'So, if you wouldn't come to claim your reward I had to send for you, didn't I?'

'Reward?'

'I had Seamus Brady here, press interview and all, and I must say I cursed you roundly, until I began to put two and two together. From what he told me I could see how cleverly you had engineered it all. I've got to hand it to you, Kildare, you certainly know to set a snare and lay a trap, a trap the authorities walked right into. They're going to do it all for us! Clear the lot on humanitarian grounds. Now, tell me,' his lordship continued amiably, 'how would you like to enlarge your experience?'

'In what way, my lord?' Kildare tried to keep the tremor of relief out of his voice. He was not being dismissed!

'How would you like to become estate manager. How about that, eh, Kildare?'

'But, Jackson, the English fella, has managed the estate for years.'

'Too many years. He's getting too old he says, and I'm inclined to agree with him. The estate needs, apart from investment, fresh blood. You've been with me man and boy and I can't think of anyone already on the staff better placed to take over. You'll have to understudy with Jackson, and get to "know the ropes" as our good Mrs Q would say.' He always referred to herself in this abbreviated manner, a little familiarity that squeezed the last ounce of loyalty out of the stern-eyed housekeeper-cook.

'I've decided to promote Flavell from steward to your position of head gamekeeper – so long as he steers clear of his own traps!' Flavell's misadventure, which had caused his limp, always raised a smile. 'Now,' Lord Fitzcarron rubbed his hands together, pleased with the look of astonishment on the keen-eyed face before him. 'What do you say, Kildare? What do you say? Is the reward to your liking, or can I do something else for you?'

The reward was very much to his liking. His luck had changed.

CHAPTER SEVENTEEN

While Frank Kildare was on his way home considering the amazing good luck which had come his way, O'Malley, considering the same, was on his way out of the valley. The poteen had brought out the natural humour of his neighbours and, all rancour gone, they had wished him well to the very last drop.

The well-wishing procession wound its way along the valley floor. At the head of it walked the O'Malleys, each sporting a bundle on shoulder or in hand. Mrs O'Malley and the little girls wore their shawls and walked sedately; the elder boys darted about, filled with nervous excitement. Tim, who refused to carry anything but his bat, trotted along sturdily, confident of his ability to charm the new world to which he was going. The shiftless, never sure of their place on such occasions, played safe and brought up the rear.

Custom demanded a halt just before the sweep of the hill would take the O'Malleys from their sight. To follow meant passing the Aunt Hanratty's cabin. Tessa stayed with the Jams girls at the far side, away from Finn, who was with O'Malley and the two Duggan men at the head of the donkey carts.

Tessa shrank as they passed the cabin. At first she had wanted to take a good look at the cabin in which her lover lived when he was not with her. She wanted to look at the window out of which he often looked, at the compound wall over which he often jumped and behind which he tended the last great pink and grey pig. But she did none of this, for the Aunt was standing at the door. The sight of her nephew walking at the head of the procession had goaded her to raise a hand and shout hoarsely.

'Good bloody riddance, Aloysius O'Malley! 'Tis glad I am to see the back of your scheming head!' It had been on her tongue to damn him to eternity, to curse him for interfering between herself and her ~~ter, and then for influencing the nephew against her. But ~~how, even though his back was turned, the words would not ~~She was still at the door when the revellers turned back up the

304

glen. Her eyes narrowed when Finn walked past, his black hair in contrast to young Duggan's fiery mane. Her surge of anger was tempered. Make the most of it, gobbeen, she thought with scant charity; come the end of the month it'll be a different tale. No one is going to get me out of this valley alive – or you, either.

By the time the rest of the community returned an assortment of the shiftless had moved into the cabin recently vacated by O'Malley.

'Will ye look at that, now!'

'Merciful God! Will they be as quick in his grave!'

'The hearth wasn't even cold and they were in!'

'Too bloody lazy to rekindle the turf!'

But come month-end, they'd all be out.

But, as they all gathered together, the question was raised, who would know when the month ended? The consideration caused a temporary pause, and everyone looked blankly at everyone else. The passage of time was marked on a weekly basis by the tolling of the chapel bell and the arrival of the priest for Mass. But it was O'Malley who tolled it. And what about the flour, and tea and other provisions which he had taken upon himself to procure on their behalf? And, thought Tessa, there'll be no more papers or books to read!

Suddenly, everyone became over-voluble as to how much they had depended on O'Malley, and what in the name of all the saints would they do now?

'Ach, sure he had to go down,' they were saying, 'for Little Annie, God bless her.'

'And may the Holy Mother protect them.'

'And the fine fella he was!'

'Sure Ennan will never see his like again!'

A voice cut across the drunken eulogies. 'Tessa, Tessa Riley? Will ye come to your da!'

She looked up, alarmed. It was Duggan, but he was grinning in that lopsided way he had. 'Your da's legless,' he said. 'Legless as a crippled louse. Blind to the world, drunk as a lord. Sure, I've never seen him knock so much back in the all the time I've known him!'

Riley, unable to cope with his daughter's refusal of Frank Kildare, the loss of his only friend, and the threatened upheaval of his way of life, had sought oblivion.

'How you'll get him up there, heaven alone knows!'

Tessa's mind raced with a torrent of possibilities, none of which included how to get her father back home. The torrent ran so swiftly it overflowed to Finn who, catching hold of some of the possibilities, closed one blue eye in a mischievous wink.

'Would you like a hand with him?' he volunteered. 'Up to the cabin?'

'Let me think . . . No, we'd never get him up there, not without the use of his legs.' She turned to Duggan. 'Will you let him lie at your place until his head is sober?'

Daring thoughts flashed from Finn to Tessa. His were saying with your da down here, we can be up there. Her heart raced; the weakness came over her. We can be in my loft! I could wake up, she thought, on the morrow and see him there beside me . . . reach out to touch him. All her fears and anxieties about her father and the gamekeeper went to the four winds. It would transform her loft for ever to recall him having shared it!

And if all o' this is too risky, his glance told her, we could escape into the mist, to our cave.

A look from Tessa. What of the Aunt . . . when he didn't return?

He turned down the corners of his mouth, spread his hands, and shrugged his shoulders, indicating that the Aunt could go to hell.

They dared not risk leaving the valley and make off up to the cabin together for, drunk as most of them were, some would be sober enough to notice and anything that would jeopardise their relationship was to be avoided.

'I'll go up first,' she said quietly, her face bright with adventure, her eyes sparkling with hinted passion.

'It'll be dark soon, and I'll be up there like greased lightning. Don't worry Tess,' his voice softened to assure her. 'No one will see me leave.'

Tessa scrambled up the hillside with ungainly haste, not looking where she was going, her feet slipping and plunging into the soft pockets of peaty earth. Her feet might be stumbling, but her mind was alert and alive; she felt more alive than ever before.

A whole, entire night with Finn, not in the draughty cave but in her own blessed loft. 'Oh, Marie Jane,' she said softly. 'Wait till ye hear all me adventures! Finn and me, me and Finn!' How long would it be before darkness fell? She'd have time to wash, and she'd leave her hair loose and brush it until it was burnished and smooth, instead of tangled with wind and rain. What should she wear? Marie Jane had related how on occasions she had removed her shift to make her figure more alluring. Alluring? The word clanged about her head like the chapel bell. She directed her thoughts to making the assignation a memorable one. Bread, cheese, tea and poteen on the table . . . their feet on the hearth, the lamp hissing. Just the two of 'em . . . and afterwards . . . She caught her breath. Should she go up to the loft first and get herself ready, or should they enjoy the mutual pleasure of undressing each other by the fire? Her mind shied away from the latter, saving it for when they lived in one of the little houses Finn had told her about. It did not seem right; she couldn't be easy in front of her da's fire.

The loft was her own. It was warm up there . . . no cuthering under clothes and her shawl, holding onto each other, keeping close for warmth like in the draughty cave. Her eyes would be able to take their fill of his virile body, its curves, the muscled flesh, the hardness. He would look like a young god, like one of the Celtic warriors. Proud in her love, she recalled the wonderment of running her fingers over the bulged biceps of his arms, and thrilling – as she would again tonight – at the passion of him, the power, the sheer physical force of all that maleness at her whim, command and pleasure. She recalled the pleasurable tensions which tugged at their bodies, of the strange, fierce excitements which almost consumed them . . .

Her thoughts and fantasies brought her back to the cabin, and to the annoyed bleating of the full-uddered goat. Oh, the evening milking – God help us, it'd have to be done! Snatching up a clean bucket she ran, hitching up her black skirt, to the outhouse. Then back to the cabin, to lay fresh turf on the fire, set the kettle, brush her hair, roll her sleeves above the elbow, wash her hands and face. With every little duty performed her anticipation mounted. The very thought of having Finn to herself in a civilised manner, a bit like at Fitzcarron House, filled her with a kind of excited pride, and she understood what lay behind Marie Jane's aspirations, and why her friend could not stay in Ennan.

When she heard the door open her heart spiralled, and then plummeted when she realised that a sharp knock had preceded the opening. No one in Ennan would do that. Instantly disturbed she watched the door open fully. Frank Kildare stepped inside and closed it firmly behind him.

'Your father not at home, yet?' he asked, a little put out at her obvious disappointment.

She stared at him and shook her head. 'Mr O'Malley's gone down. We've been at his well-wishing . . .'

While the well-wishing had been in progress Frank Kildare, having left his lordship's presence, began to feel like a reprieved man. He had raced home to strip off his clothes, to wash and scrub and sluice himself with water. He emerged from the baptism feeling clean and new and committed. Changing his clothes, he had mounted his horse and galloped along the shore of Ennabrugh to Riley's cabin. Leaving the horse to graze, he surveyed the scene with uncertainty. It was not yet dark, so there was no lamp lit to indicate whether she was inside or still out with those blasted goats! Goats, he thought; destructive creatures . . . He stopped the thoughts; shooting was a thing of the past, now. He was free of all that. He felt altogether a different man. Would she see that, he wondered? Surely, she would be able to perceive that he was different, better, changed? He listened, hand on the compound gate, and still he was reasoning; if the old man was in he would ask her to take her shawl and come for a walk. He would ask her to take his arm. And if she was not in, he would wait pleasantly with Riley himself. His footsteps had set the goats whinnying – at least she was not with them. He hesitated another moment, to prolong a little longer the eager anticipation of whether she would be in or not.

And so he stood before her, wrestling with his emotions. He felt certain his news would make her happy – if only for the creatures' sake. He related his promotion to her astounded ears – but not, of course, the reason behind it – and ended with the same flourish she had observed outside Fitzcarron House when he had indicated the empty saddle.

'I stand before you a changed fella. See, I've even changed me field clothes and if you don't want me to, sure I'll never wear a Norfolk jacket or a deerstalker again!' His sharp eyes were alight under the shock of coppery dark hair. He was wearing the same clothes as at the Long Dance, tweed trousers, braces and a white full-sleeved shirt. The relating of how he was not 'a man of blood' anymore had brought back his exuberance.

'Is your father likely to be long?' he asked again, casting him in the role of an ally.

Tessa did not know whether to say her father would soon be back in case he decided to wait for him; on the other hand she did not want to say he would not be back in case he should still wait. Her mind was almost paralysed with anxiety, for if Finn arrived Kildare would guess the situation and might tell her father, or the Aunt. It was too awful a thought to contemplate.

'I . . . don't know at all, Mr Kildare.' She saw his eyes wander to the table; he would presume the food to be her father's supper. Her mind went again to the danger of Finn arriving. 'Is your horse tethered?' she asked in the hope that Finn would see it and be warned.

The coppery head shook. He had left it to graze at the back. Her heart sank again, for Finn would approach from the front. Then, with a little shock, she noticed the softening light in the cold hazel of his eyes, a gentling of the hunter's face – for it was still a hunter's face, whatever he said – and saw again, with heartsinking dismay, that worshipping look. He had not taken her refusal seriously. He was still bent on the idea of marrying her, taking her off to be not merely the head gamekeeper's wife, but wife of the manager of the Fitzcarron estate. The promotion would make her father more keen than ever, more insistent on the marriage. He would never, in a million years, understand how she could pass up so great an offer.

She merely murmured three short sentences, but he never stopped talking. 'I know your father's in complete agreement with my wishes, and despite our conversation when the "visitation" took place I'm sure you've not given me enough thought . . .' The words rushed from his lips, pouring into the air, into her head. 'And, now that my work does not involve stalking, or handling guns, or anything to distress you, I feel you might look upon me differently. Will you be my wife, Tessa? You're wasted here,' he told her. 'This sort of life is not for you. Just think of all the advantages . . . No, don't block my words out – ' he pleaded. 'Think of the advantages for your father: work, a cottage, respect. You will be near Marie Jane, and live in a proper house. You'll have position, Tessa. I can offer you all that –' Dare he say it? 'And more. I offer you love, Tessa. I've fallen in love with you. Ach, you needn't look so amazed. I know very well you don't feel the same way about me, but at least give me a chance, get to know me. Surely,' he paused. 'Surely, there is something about me that you . . .'

Her eyes stopped the rush of words. The look in their depths told him three things: that his love for her was agonisingly real; that he meant nothing to her at all; and that she would be glad when he went.

He stared at the sleeves of the blue gingham blouse, pushed up and revealing her forearms, round and slightly browned with the sun; his gaze then travelled to her bare feet, the lines of her body showing her to be on the very edge of maturity. She reminded him of a picture he had seen once. Not the whole picture – for he could not recall the looks of the subject, whether the woman had been dark or fair, old or young – just the detail stood out; the forearm, the bare feet on a flagged floor.

Had it meant death the next instant, he could not have prevented himself from his next action. The recollection of the oil painting had detached his mind from the look in her eyes, the furtive glance at the door. He put out a hand and touched a strand of her hair. He had never seen it tumbling about her shoulders like this; it gave her a softer, gentler, less robust look.

She remained motionless, expressionless, like an animal subjecting itself unwillingly to a caress. It meant nothing to her. Feeling rebuffed and humiliated, hardly knowing what he was doing, he stepped forward and took hold of her arm. In his intensity he gripped her more strongly than he had intended. Startled at the sudden move, she jerked back and lifted her other hand to push him away. He caught it like a bird in flight, and crumpling it in his palm kissed it and murmured her name.

He wanted to ask her to think, to consider his proposal. He wanted to persuade, to . . . beg. But something else was happening. He saw the terrible consternation in her face, the panic fluttering in her eyes; unknown to him his quick move had conjured up all the horror of Mick Murphy's attack. He saw her face, suddenly furious, close to his, her tongue, her teeth white against the pink cavern of her mouth. In desperation, she kicked out at him, hitting him on the shinbone with the side of her bare foot. He at once released her hand but drew her so tightly up against his body that she was in a deadlock.

He thought of all the helpless creatures he had caught . . . struggling, fluttering, beating their wings – the same look of mute appeal was in her eyes. With a groan he lowered his face into the thick brown hair, stared at the long strands of it against the white sleeve of his shirt. He let her go, and stood back, ashamed.

'I always seem to startle you,' he blurted out in reaction to the despair which was eating him. 'I didn't mean to. I'm sorry. I'm sorry!' She remained still. 'I meant you no harm. God knows I didn't. Say something?' he pleaded. 'You've scarce said a word. For the love of God, say something – anything. Do me at least the honour of another refusal!' He saw that look again, beyond him to the door. 'All right, I'll go!' he exclaimed irritably. 'If you find my presence so objectionable, I'll get out of your sight!' But still he stood there. 'I've given up all my former life, Tessa. Changed it for your sake. You made me change it by just being you – and having done all that, you just stand there, saying not a blind, bloody word! What's a fella to make of it all?'

Tessa eyed him warily and moved to light the lamp. It was becoming dusk. How long before Finn came up? She offered up a silent prayer that Finn would stay away a little longer. He had said he would wait until darkness; she prayed he would.

Kildare would not leave without an answer, that was for sure. But how many answers did he want, for heaven's sake? She had refused him once to his face and asked him not to bother her or her da again – and here he was! The flare of the lamp lit up her troubled face, illuminating the moulded structure of her high cheekbones, the elf-like chin, big blue-grey eyes, now as solemn as the brooding clouds over Ennabrugh. She's thinking about me, Kildare thought, his heart beginning to thump. Thank God . . . Oh, thank the blessed Mother – Tessa Riley is thinking about me!

Kildare was correct in his surmise. She was thinking about how she had been knocked off balance by the gamekeeper's hard and sudden embrace. Of course, she could now see he was no Mick Murphy, but at the time she had been terrified. Her thoughts had scattered in several directions and now in the lighting of the lamp she tried to collect herself.

Firstly, she must get out of this present mess; secondly, she couldn't help thinking what would happen if all her prayers were not answered and Finn came to complicate an already complicated situation; thirdly, she was already feeling some remorse on account of her father, for when he heard of Kildare's promotion he would become insistent again; and fourthly, she realised this refusal would have to be worded carefully for Kildare was a man of power and position, and of these she was, and always had been, afraid.

'It's very unfair of you to lay these things at my door, Mr Kildare. I never asked, hoped or wished you to change your way of life, to give up . . . well, what you have given up,' she said evenly, 'because of me. Besides,' she added with the innocent frankness of the young, 'you wouldn't have given any of it up if you hadn't been made manager.'

'I would! I would! And I have changed. I swear to you now, Tessa Riley, before the Almighty. I take this solemn oath. May God strike me dead if I kill another creature.'

The lamp hissed in the silence. A mature, profound understanding slowly dawned on Tessa. She saw in a flash that this was his last throw of the dice. She saw in his eyes, in the light they shed on her, that he was saying 'Now, *now*, you must give me a chance. I have found a way to get to you. I am giving it all up: guns, stalking, killing, hunting. Everything I've been brought up to, everything I've lived for until I saw you. This must go some way with you. This must remove what you have always objected to.'

She suddenly felt sorry for him.

'You could grow to love me,' he said softly, helplessly.

'I couldn't, Mr Kildare.' How could she tell him he was still a man of blood as far as she was concerned, despite his redemption, his oath. And after all that, how could she say that if he were the last man on earth she could not love him! 'I couldn't,' she repeated. 'And it'd be best if you didn't ask me or me da again – like I said at the visitation.'

The silence was awful. The kettle began to simmer and boil and splutter. Tessa, angry at it, swore and took it off the turf to the hearth. Kildare turned and left.

When he had gone Tessa remained motionless by the fire. She glanced at the window. It was dark already, and Finn would be up soon. Quick! Quick! She grabbed at the hairbrush and began brushing her hair, urgently and vigorously to remove all traces of those freckled fingers – from her mind as well as from her hair. Nothing was going to spoil this, her first night with Finn. First night! Would there be more? She began to tingle with the old sensation of excitement, and out of a sudden exuberance of spirit pirouetted round the table and right into Finn's arms. 'Jasus!' she shrieked.

'Sure, I didn't see ye come in!' Her body drew closer to his. 'I love ye, Finn. I didn't know how much until tonight.'

He led her to the fire and could feel her trembling. 'What's up, love?' he asked, his voice deepening with concern. 'Surely you didn't think I'd not come?'

'Oh, no. I knew you would. It's just the waiting – and the excitement!'

'C'mon, Tess, sit down. I'll get the poteen.' He reached for the bottle and cups. 'So, this is the dresser they're always on about?' He caught his breath with admiration. 'When people talk of your da, Tess, they always mention the dresser. Sure 'tis a fine thing, the like of which I've never seen before.'

'You ought to see what they've got at Fitzcarron House . . .' And so they talked, and he set the kettle to boil again. She stood up to reach for the bread and cheese, but he slid them along the table to her. They sat, side by side, eating, drinking and laughing in such domesticity that only added another dimension to their happiness. A happiness in which Frank Kildare, her father and Finn's aunt were forgotten.

'It's a grand cabin, Tess.' He whistled through his teeth, looking round at the two windows, the thick walls, the flags on the floor, and the dresser again. His glance went to her father's bed, and finally, for he had been avoiding it, to the loft with the ladder which would shortly lead him and Tess to paradise.

After a while, he banked up the fire and took off the split boots. Glances were exchanged, shy and playful. 'C'mon,' she giggled. 'Let's go up together. Mind your head, or you'll crack it on the rafter!'

With peals of laughter, sometimes muffled, sometimes subdued, with much teasing and fumbling, they struggled out of their clothes. 'I've often dreamed of waking up and finding you there beside me, Finn, and now my dreams have come true.'

'And may they all come true, girleen.'

'And all because O'Malley's gone down . . .'

'And your da got legless; it's not like him, Tess.'

She did not answer, for she guessed at the main reason for her father taking too much drink.

'I love your hair like this.' They were still sitting upright; he scooped up the luxurious hair and let it run through his fingers. 'And your skin's so soft.' There was not much light from the dampened down fire, but it was light enough to trace the contours of her limbs. Who needed sight when fingers could touch? Her body thrilled to the caress of his big hands. Their roughness delighted her senses. She leaned back against the end wall and gave herself up to the indescribable pleasure that was building up within.

She knew just how he would be looking at her, adoration written all over his face to make her feel like a goddess. His kisses were in her hair, her eyes, her lips, her body, bringing on that delicious weakness; a whisper of a sigh escaped her.

His wild energy set her desire for him into full blaze. The bed creaked and rustled as their youthful bodies entwined. Tessa lost her hold on reality; the loft whirled giddily beneath the demands of passion. She was swept along with him. She was his again and revelled in the bliss of such devastating fulfilment.

Both wanted to give urgently and, having given, to lie murmuring, whispering, and referring to the loft as their love nest. Later they playfully struggled and fought, she threatening to roll him off the edge, and he daring her to just try. Tessa, taking up the challenge, enjoyed the grappling with his naked body, until, suddenly, desire would flare and, high spirits over, they sank back, clasped in each others arms. Tessa woke with the dawn. She reached out to touch him, but he had gone.

Outside the rain fell, steadily and mournfully.

CHAPTER EIGHTEEN

When Riley returned later that morning he looked more drawn and haggard than ever. It made life no easier for Tessa to know she was the cause and yet, at the same time, she felt angry that it should be so.

'You've heard of Kildare's advancement?' he asked when she had set tea before him.

So, she thought, news has got round already. 'I have, so. He was here yesterday evening.' It was best to tell him. She saw his head lift in expectation.

'So?' he prompted.

'So nothing, Da.'

'You refused him again?'

'I did so, Da.'

He shook his head sadly, forlornly, like an old dog. 'It beats me. Why in God's name are you so pig-headed? An estate manager at your feet and you pass him over like the rind of an old cheese.'

'I've told you, Da. I don't love him!'

'Love,' he scoffed. ''Tis a dream, like the jack-o'-lanterns on Ennabrugh. What good did it do me? It's all this reading, filling your head full of fancy ideas. You can wait for ever for love. It fills your head when your blood is young and foolish, but wait till a few years pass . . .'

'I'm not going to talk about this anymore, Da. It's doing neither of us any good. My mind is made up for now and always. I will not make "a good marriage". I'm not a sack of spuds, a length of cloth, or a lump of cheese to be haggled over and bargained for. Yes,' she answered his shocked gaze. 'That's what you and the gamekeeper are doing, haggling over me, and I'm not having it.'

'You can't have everything you want in this life, Teresa.'

'I don't want "everything". I just don't want him! I don't ever want to see Frank Kildare again! Can you not understand me, Da!'

'Teresa . . . Teresa . . .' he said softly and unhappily. 'Does the memory of your ma, God rest her soul, not reach you? Do you not

315

think she'd want you to do well? I swore on her grave. And if you don't jump at such a marvellous chance I'll feel as though I've broken me word to her.' The peat-brown eyes avoided hers.

Unable to take upon herself anymore permutations of the question, she fled to the goats.

While washing flanks and udders, milking, swilling out and feeding the goats, she thought about her mother a great deal. If, and God forbid, if she were to take up Kildare's offer, she would be in the same situation as her mother had been, marrying one and loving the other. Only in her mother's case the other had been dead. How she must have loved him to mourn all that time . . . There was another difference, too; her mother had been pregnant. She couldn't have liked it much up here, coming from the town and service and all o' that. How could she, having experienced such style, have gone to live in the miserable dwelling where her father had been born and reared? Not that she had seen it, only the place where it had stood. O'Malley, describing it, had said it was so ramshackle that the shiftless had thought it grand!

Later that day, Tessa got out the little treasures her mother had left. She was sitting in the loft and had just finished stitching her mother's handkerchief to the place where Finn had rested his head. She fingered again the reticule, the little looking glass, the dainty muff . . . relics of the civilisation her mother had known.

Tessa's heart lifted, for the realisation came to her as slowly, easily and pleasantly as the dawn, that Teresa Donnelly's sacrifice would be in vain if she, her daughter, was to end up in the same kind of loveless marriage. Surely that was her mother's message to her? Of course it was! She was thrilled, happy and ecstatic; the lovely knowledge warmed her heart as she put the treasured things carefully away.

Tessa stretched herself over the place where Finn had lain, her face buried in the white lawn handkerchief. For the third time that week, as she stretched forward, a feeling of faintness overcame her.

She lay there as stiff and rigid as the poker on the hearth. At the back of her mind dwelt an uncertainty which she had tried all through the week to ignore. It had returned again, the fainting feeling. She, who had never fainted in her life! But now she was not ignoring it.

'Not that . . .' she groaned. 'Oh, merciful and everlasting God, not that.'

They had only made love twice apart from last night. Peggy Jams had said it could not happen straight away. But the longer Tessa thought, the more certain she became. With child like her mother had been. 'Oh, Blessed St Teresa, I can't! I can't!' she whispered fiercely, looking about the loft as though there were some means of escape. But there was no escape.

Despite her certainty about her condition, Tessa took to praying; not in her loft as usual, but kneeling on the flagged floor in an attitude of supplication before the Sacred Heart. She prayed and prayed again to the saint of her name that it would come right, that somewhere there was a ghastly mistake of nature. But another week passed and Tessa Riley knew that nature had not made any mistake.

She was pregnant. The awful fact stared her in the face. It would not go away. She and Finn had stopped making love, at least properly, when she had recalled that Mona Donal had had to marry Kevin Connor to 'absolve the sins of the flesh'. 'Oh, God save us!' Finn had exclaimed, raising himself on an elbow. 'Yes, God save us!' she had smiled. 'We've got to think of this. If anything like it were to happen to us, there'd be hell to pay. Me da would kill me, I'm sure.' But, even as they talked she had already conceived! She laid a hand on her stomach; in a few months it would be large and swollen with another being. 'Oh, God, Oh blessed Christ, what can I do?' It was there, inside her, yet she felt no different, apart from the faintness and having missed the curse. Marie Jane's words before the Fair came sharply into focus. 'You get married and what happens? You get round-bellied every year . . . when I think of the weddings I've danced at, and not twelve months later they've took to their graves with childbirth . . .' Dying did not worry her. She was strong and would not die. No, it wasn't that aspect which worried her, but her da. What he would do or say or feel?

Proud Riley had never been so worried, upset or miserable in his life. He had been given the impression that the clearance would not affect him and that he could go on fending for himself until he died. But at O'Malley's well-wishing he had heard that everyone had to leave, even if they had to be dragged screaming to the carts. His tired eyes looked lovingly about the cabin. Gypo Kelly had said they would fire it, fire all the cabins, all the huts and hovels. No wonder he had taken to the marvels of drink! What with Teresa refusing the grand marriage, and the cabin he'd built with his own hands to be fired – merciful God, what was the world coming to? It would be better to go on the estate, as Kildare had suggested, than into the workhouse, for where else was there? At least on the estate he'd have a position and honourable toil; but Teresa would not go, so what in Almighty God's name could be done?

'Tess?' said Finn when they met in the cave. 'Is there anything bothering you?' He held her at arms' length and smoothed the little furrow of care from her forehead.

'No,' she lied. 'Apart from the weather turning wet, and all this mist. How long I can use the goats as an excuse, I really don't know. I think me da would have wondered at me coming out today if the clearance hadn't been so much on his mind. He's worried to his very death since they told him the cabin would be fired with the rest.'

'Wouldn't you just think they'd let an old fella last out his days up there?'

'They call it progress, Finn. You'd think Kelly and the others would have spared him that bit of knowledge. Why make a point of telling him at the same time he was losing his old friend? Unthinking divils, they are! Couldn't pass up the opportunity of getting at him. Wait till I see Gypo Kelly!'

'That's right,' laughed Finn. 'A fighting mood suits you better than a worried one.' He looked at her with an enquiring lift of his dark eyebrows. 'You're not upset about us . . . being in the loft?'

'Will I tell you what I've done? I've sewn one of me ma's handkerchiefs – lovely it is an' all – just on the spot where your head slept. I think I must kiss the place some twenty times in the day – that's how upset I am! I wished you would have stayed until I woke up, though. Here's me dreaming of just such a thing and then you go off and leave me!'

'I couldn't have chanced meeting your da coming up! Or anyone seeing me going down, and them knowing your da had been out cold! I've to think of your reputation, Tess!'

Reputation, she thought wildly. Oh, Finn, you're not the only one thinking about it! What did they say? 'Many a true word spoken in jest.'

'Will you always love me?' Her anxiety drove her to seek reassurance.

'I can't help myself,' he said simply. 'You're a part of me life, Tess. My first, my only colleen . . .' His chin brushed the top of her hair as he held her in his arms, and through the mouth of the cave he saw the rain, a soft, grey curtain of it. 'I wonder what the month-end will bring . . . What'll happen to us? Oh, Tess, shall we make a run for it? Clear out quick and clean, find our way. Find work, the two of us. We're strong and not afraid of it.'

'I'd go Finn, sure I would, soon as look. Anyways, as Flowery Nolan said, I'd never be short of a penny while I could sing on the streets. But, I don't think I could leave me da – '

'Mother o' Jasus,' he said gruffly. 'What are ye thinking of, Tess? Proud Riley's daughter singing on the streets! I'd rather starve!'

'You could do as you please, Finn, but I'm not for starving!'

Tessa had decided not to tell him about the pregnancy, in case he ran off to do something desperate, like joining the army just to get money to be married; she couldn't bear the thought of him going away. There'd be no one left! Another reason crossed her mind – she had never imagined there would ever be so many reasons in her life! – but were she to tell Finn, he was so open and transparent his aunt would see something was afoot and winkle the news out of him. That would leave him at the terrible mercy of the old woman. He was already terrified of the Aunt cursing herself; how much more with a baby at stake? She had not yet got used to the idea of a baby, but whatever else, she didn't want it cursed.

Another thing; she did not want to be like Mona Donal, married to 'absolve the sins of the flesh'. So far as she was concerned, there had been no sin. Just love. She wanted to be absolutely certain Finn loved her for herself and that their marriage would be for no other reason. All the same, she thought practically, much as he loved her he had not asked her to marry him, to be his wife, like Kildare had. Unlike her mother, she would never marry to give this unborn child a name. Only the other day, she mused, I was thinking about me ma, an' all o' that – history repeating itself! Somehow the crisis of the clearance stemmed her fears. Fate, it seemed, would take a hand in all their destinies, rearrange their lives. And sure to God, she concluded her thoughts, anything would be better than Ennan.

She and Finn talked about little else now. How he would be rid of the Aunt if they took her off to the workhouse, and how he would be free of her evil mind. Free to go where he would . . . to take Tessa down to Rohira, to call on the O'Malleys, even Marie Jane.

But Tessa had reservations about her father, not that Finn knew of them.

'Once out of this place,' he said grandly. 'The world's me oyster – according to O'Malley.'

'What do you mean by that, Finn?' She gave him a sidelong glance as they settled on the rushes, his arm about her shoulders, her feet tucked beneath her skirts.

'It means you can go anywhere in the world.' He was in an expansive mood, and felt like Martin Jarvey.

'And where would you go?' This latest flight of fancy cheered her spirits.

'Us,' he corrected. 'Where would we go?' Tessa enjoyed his talk, all the more because she had so little of it; and he, never having an audience, gave his best performance on these occasions.

'Yes, us,' she prompted.

'Dublin.' Finn surprised himself as much as Tessa with this recent invention.

'And what would we be doing in that fair and noble city?'

'Going across,' he answered, pleased with the impression he was creating. He dared not look down at her yet, lest he be tempted to smile at the incredulity he felt sure was flooding her face.

'Across the sea? Where, for the love of God?'

'England. Doesn't cost as much as America. O'Malley and me heard the boyos talking when we were in the pub that time. Reckoned it was the place to be. A land flowing with milk and honey . . .'

The O'Malleys, she thought. How I wish they were living in their cabin instead of the shiftless. But would she, could she, have sought their advice? How often had she warned Marie Jane about the same kind of trouble she was now in!

Finn, looking down, smoothed away the little furrow again. Poor Tess, he thought, still worrying about her da and the clearance. Still, he had made her smile and taken her mind off it, if only for a short time. He felt the strangest satisfaction in comforting her. He wanted nothing else in all the world but to love and protect this brave and lovely young woman who strode across the hills like a Celtic goddess.

Tessa led the goats down the hillside in a thin, cold rain. She had tried not to show how worried she was over her condition, and was pleased with the attempt. Once the dreadful shock had worn off, pretence would be easier. Any bit of anxiety that had crept through her mask he, the darling fella he was, had put down to the clearance.

'If you need me at all,' he had said, fussing like O'Malley with Little Annie, 'put out your white scarf. Wedge it near this stone; for do I not look up to the ridge many times a day? You've got to look up to something with the old Aunt there! It'll trail in the wind, and if there's no mist I'll see it, and be up liked greased lightning!' She had laughed with him and they had kissed with rain-soaked lips.

Below the mist she looked out over the Great Bog of Ennabrugh. It didn't seem all that long since Finn and me watched the jack-o'-lanterns leaping about like weird sprites. With a bit of luck and the will of God, I won't be up here to see it in the winter months, when the rushes become hoary with frost and the ice tinkles in the reed beds, and the sky becomes heavy. Not that there was ever snow on Ennabrugh. The warmth created by the gasses below saw to that. There was never any whiteness, no purity, nothing of beauty in winter – only death and decay. For wasn't the Bog made up of those very things? It depended upon the process for its continuation . . . yes, she thought wryly; it'll be the only thing that does continue.

She shuddered, for the sight of the black Bog in the white winter landscape had always looked to her like a large, malevolent eye. She hurried away after the goats. The goats! Oh, merciful God. Come the clearance, what would happen to the goats, to the two little white kids, their brown-and-white mother, and the breakaway Billy? She had been so wrapped up with the discovery of being pregnant, the threatening attitude of the gamekeeper – no, he wasn't that anymore – the estate manager, and her da, that she had not thought of their fate. In a way she tried not to think of the future, yet after the Fair she had thought of nothing else. It was all so uncertain, so shadowy. The very lives of some forty or so of the community were at the whim and direction of the fat, paunchy men who had lined the platform at the Long Dance, bedecked with chains of office and medals.

The soft grey rain which Finn had seen curtaining the mouth of the cave continued to fall with a fanatical obstinancy for the next three days. It fell as straight as rods and with the rhythm of a beating hammer. Everything was blotted out by rain. Ennabrugh was invisible, the high ground smothered in great swathes of cloud. Relentless and determined, the rain defied Proud Riley and found all the weak spots of the cabin.

At first Tessa ran hither and thither with buckets and bowls to catch the drips coming through the joins of the thatched roof, but as the drips became rivulets, she gave up. 'God save us, Da! It'll put the fire out if it mounts the hearth!'

'We'll all be out by month-end,' came the doleful reply, 'so what does it matter? What does any of it matter?'

Tessa made no comment. Nothing she could say would alleviate his feelings. She thought of previous deluges and how he had regarded the elements as a kind of challenge, playing a game with them. 'You'll not get in here!' he used to say, jumping on a chair to plug up the leaks, and declaring with devilish glee. 'And you'll not get in there, either! I built this cabin to keep the likes of you out, I did!' And now look at him, she thought, lying there and not caring if it all fell in over his head.

Used as she was to his silent ways, this silence was too heavy and oppressive; added to which, the continual sound of rain, the hammer beats of it, the continual drip drip and the steady stream swilling across the floor, all served to dampen her spirits. She made tea and poured poteen, boiled potatoes and took them as offerings to her father, laying them before him as though to placate an angry deity.

Her only escape was with the goats, mucking out, laying fresh bedding for them. And all the time she talked softly and earnestly about things they could not possibly understand. The complicated world of human relationships. She stroked their rough coats and wished it was Finn's broad back she was touching; fondled their ears and wished it was his curls. While milking, she rested her head on their warm flanks and wished it was Finn's chest, wished she was lying up in her loft again with him, idly tracing with her finger the thin line of short black hair which led from the middle of his breast bone, over the taut muscles of his stomach and beyond . . . she smiled, for he was ticklish and when her fingers reached his bellybutton he squirmed and laughed and tried playfully to stop her.

'Oh, Finn,' she moaned softly against the flank. 'Oh, my darling, darling Finn.' And then with a little sob of despair, 'What'll happen? Oh, St Teresa, what'll happen?'

She went over again and again in her mind just how she would tell him about the baby. She would have to tell him sometime. And her da, he would have to know before it became obvious. There was plenty of time yet. But telling her da was the more worrying aspect of it.

All her wonderings and worries always resolved themselves into this new philosophy of her father's: 'By month-end we'll all be out.' The month-end referred to was, according to the calendar passed on by O'Malley, some ten days away. In a way, it was a relief to contemplate the idea that fate was going to decide everything, that those fat, paunchy men in their municipal offices somewhere were going to alter their lives for better or worse. Decisions were something new to the people of Ennan. Such things were never needed, but now she in particular had to fend them off as they came hurtling at her, one after the other.

No, she would not go and work on the Fitzcarron estate. No, she would not marry Frank Kildare. These first two major decisions had almost done for her da. But she had to stand by them. The third decision came to her at once. No, she would not tell Finn or her da about her condition until after the fateful month-end. By then, fate would have revealed her hand.

Ten days . . . she sighed. Not a lot could happen really; the authorities had not thought fit to enlighten the 'peasant community' as to where the carts would take them. Everyone thought the dreaded workhouse was the obvious place, but once down in civilisation, as Finn had said, 'the world was their oyster'. She sighed again, but on a smile this time. Him and his talk of Dublin, and boats, and going across! A touch of the O'Malleys there, to be sure!

By the third day the loft was too wet to sleep in. Tessa had removed her treasures to a dry place on top of the dresser, and was sleeping on the pile of rushes used for bedding the goats. Having become used to the endless sounds of dull thudding, the hammer beats of rain, the constant drip drip, she awoke with surprise and pleasure to silence . . . sheer silence! She leapt up and out to the cabin. 'It's stopped! The rain's stopped! Oh, Da, thank God! I'm amazed we've not been washed away!'

Her father was already up and had made the tea. ''Tis the authorities that wash people away,' he answered in the same doleful tone, 'Not the rain.' He reached for his coat and struggled into it.

'Where are ye going, Da?' she asked anxiously; for the last three days he had lain on his bed, a thing unheard of ever before.

'To the estate.'

'What are you going over there for? The ground will be dangerous after all the rain. Can you not put it off for a day or two?'

He shook his head grimly. 'I must go before the bloody rain starts up again.'

'Will I come with you, Da?' Her anxiety for him overcame her reluctance ever to set foot that way. Riley shook his shaggy head.

'What are you going for?'

'As O'Malley used to say, a small matter of business.' He fastened up his coat and went out.

Tessa sat down by the table and sipped her tea. Why would he not tell her the reason for going to the estate? He could only be going to see one person – Frank Kildare. But what about? Another glance through the window. She knew where she was going.

A little while after, she opened the door for the goats, and with shawl and crook made her way up to the cave, going carefully because of the treacherous state of the ground. She let out their arranged signal of the white scarf, watched it trail and then took shelter.

'I hope he sees it,' she told the two young goats who eyed the trailing scarf with curiosity. 'Keep a look out for him, will you? Keep a look out for Finn, eh? If it hadn't been for himself you'd not have had so many outings. But I think you know that, don't you, little spalpeens that y'are!'

Talking to the goats was, in a way, talking to herself, prattling away to stem the uneasiness her father's reticence had brought on. It seemed a long time waiting for Finn, and it was indeed some two hours before he had seen the signal and without a word of excuse to the Aunt set off along the valley floor and up the ridge from the distant side.

'Oh, Tess,' he murmured, holding her fiercely, his lips against her hair. 'These three days without a sight of ye have been the longest I've ever known! Are you all right?' he asked holding her away just a little. 'Sure, it was the divil of a downpour. Three days; I thought it'd never stop! And, do you know what, Tess?'

'No,' she laughed at the indignation of his tone, at his cheerful sociability.

'We've got the pig in the cabin with us! The Aunt's scared of it sickening in the damp and all that, and I've got the great brute lying there opposite me!'

'And I've had to sleep with the goats! It was the only dry place; the loft was soaking wet.'

'I didn't mind any of that, not even the pig, Tess. What I minded was not getting to see you. Wondering how you were getting on with your da, whether you were safe from the rain. It flattened old Grogan to the very earth, ye know. Retribution, they said it was. He was trying to help himself to the last of the Byrnes' turf; thought they wouldn't see him in the rain! And some of the huts of the shiftless collapsed like ninepins. But I was aiming to come up, just in case you'd convinced your da that the goats could do with . . . what d'ye call it? A lick o' fresh grass?'

'I didn't have to tell him anything . . .' And Tessa related her unease at her father's visit to Fitzcarron House. She did not tell him about Kildare's proposal of marriage. 'Still, I'm glad da's gone, in a way, or I wouldn't have got to see you . . .'

Yet, in her heart she remained uneasy.

CHAPTER NINETEEN

That evening, Tessa was drying the blankets by the hearth when her father returned.

'Thank God you're back, Da, what with the state of the ground an' all! You look a sight better than when you went out. The "bit of business" went well, I see.'

She set down his cup and turned to get the tea from the hearth.

'It did so; get yourself a cup.' She did as he asked and sat opposite him at the square table, the lamp hissing gently between them. 'It was Mr Kildare I went to see,' he said after a short silence. Her heart nearly stopped.

'Did you, Da?'

'I did so. I did so. You'll remember, girl, how a short time ago he made me a fine offer of work and somewhere to live, a cottage like Flavell's, only smaller, with an upstairs.'

She nodded apprehensively. 'But was the offer not made on the condition that I went with you?'

'It was so.'

'Do you mean you're going on your own, then?'

'That was not part of the deal, Teresa,' he said softly. 'I'm going and you are coming with me.'

Tessa put the cup down, her eyes large and frightened. 'No, Da, I'm not going to the estate. I'm not going with you.'

'You're coming with me, Teresa, and there's an end of it.'

'No Da, it isn't the end!'

Her father leapt up from the table so quickly the chair fell over. 'That's all I ever hear from ye, Teresa, "No, Da; I'm not going, Da; I'm not doing this, Da; I'm not doing that." Well, just let me tell you, girl, that this time you're going to do what your da says; what your da wants! You're still under age by a few years yet, and until you're twenty-one you'll do as I say, for a change!' He leaned over the table, hands on the edge of it, face flushed and eyes intense. 'In a few days the cabins'll be fired, the valley cleared and the workhouse'll stare

Proud Riley in the face. Yes, me, who they call Proud Riley, ending me days in the bloody workhouse! And when the manager of the Fitzcarron estate – manager no less – offers us both work and a roof over our heads, you say you're not going! What thanks is that for the past eighteen years? I promised your mother a dacent marriage to take you out of all of this. And now you want me to break that promise! Will I tell ye now, Teresa, neither Proud Riley nor his daughter is going to set foot inside the workhouse. And we're not going to stay here like gobbeens while they drag us out to the carts.'

Tessa stared. The echo of his raised voice sounded muffled against the damp walls. Never in her life had she heard him raise his voice to this pitch, and now she did not know what to make of it all. She had never seen him look so proud either – proud and as fierce as a fighting cock. He must have looked like this, she thought, when he had confronted Clancy over her mother.

'I was lying there,' he continued, 'watching the very water of heaven trickle down the walls I'd built, and I prayed to God Almighty, and the Mother of Christ Himself, that it should all be washed away, natural like, by the the hand o' God. And then it came to me, so clear, that if God was not doing us the honour, we'd leave in a civilised manner like O'Malley. They had a well-wishing for him, so they can hold one for Proud Riley and his daughter.'

Tessa said nothing. The words would not come. There were none to describe her tumultuous feelings. One aspect stood out starkly. Her father had fallen right into Kildare's trap. Once she and her da were employed on the estate and living in a tied dwelling, she would be at Kildare's mercy. For if she did not marry him willingly, she would not put it past him to force her into marriage by threats. Her father would not understand if she told him any of this. He saw no reason why she should not marry him and settle down. Tessa realised she was at a disadvantage because she had no alternative to offer. So far as her father was concerned the dreadful workhouse was before him. Who could really blame him for going to see Kildare, for accepting the only certain chance of escape?

If she were to tell him about her condition – and heaven alone knew where she would find the words – he would probably insist on her marrying Kildare to keep his promise to her mother. She refused to contemplate his reaction. If his hopes were crumbling because of her not wanting a good marriage, the fact of her pregnancy would be a death blow. He would consider himself to have failed in his promise to her parents. O Holy Mother, what a mess.

Another facet of this awful situation reared itself. She saw, too, as clearly as the tinker woman who had raised fourteen on the crystal, that were she to tell Kildare about her pregnancy, far from being put off, he would seize even this opportunity to make her his wife. He, like her da, would be only too glad to take on another man's child. It was her mother's story over again! Oh, Mother, she moaned to herself, oh Mother . . . But their situations were not the same. Her real father, Timothy Thomas, had died. Finn Collins was alive. He was down in the valley and she loved him, and him only.

She saw her father's lips move. He was talking, saying something, not shouting anymore.

'What did you say, Da?'

'Kildare's coming over tomorrow. He would have come today but the tracks are too wet for the carts – '

'Carts?'

'For the dresser, the table, your spinning wheel, pots and things–'

'Tomorrow? Oh, merciful God, Da, why so soon? Surely not tomorow?'

Great tears of absolute despair welled up and rolled slowly down her face. Big, heavy tears. Riley had never seen a woman cry, never seen his daughter in tears even as a child, and he felt sad to be the cause of it. But, heaven help him, what could he do?

''Tis all arranged, Teresa. It will all be for the best.'

Tessa's head sank into her hands, and there she sat, elbows on the table, sobbing softly, a picture of abject misery which twisted the old man's heart.

'Listen, Teresa,' he made an effort to stop the tears. 'We can take the goats . . . and Kildare sent for O'Malley's girl while I was in the office . . .' Yes, he would, thought Tessa blindly, he bloody well would. 'She came to tell me, in that fancy way of hers, how you'd like it, and that I was to tell you you'd not regret it. I scarce knew her – proper maid she is, with the same manner your mother had, God rest her soul . . .'

But Tessa was not listening. The word 'tomorrow' was tolling about her head, clanging from side to side like the chapel bell. Tears splashed onto the table and lay like the rain drops of last night. She felt trapped, like one of the Kildare's creatures; like a caged bird.

And still she sat, head in hands, immobile and bent. What could she do? In God's name, what could she do? Not hearing what her father had said – he had never talked so much in his life – she looked up in mute misery. Riley was not fierce anymore, but crumpled with tears like herself. 'It's a good offer,' he kept muttering. 'The best. We've got to go . . . we've got to go . . .'

She sat until he had swallowed the last of his poteen and thrown himself on the bed in the corner. She had not even been aware of him banking up the fire or taking the dry rushes from the hearth to spread in the loft for her.

'It's a long day tomorrow, girleen,' he muttered, not knowing what else to say. 'You'll get the things together, ready? 'Tis all for the best. You'll get used to a different way of life. And one day, girleen, you'll thank your old da . . .'

Tessa sat there for some time longer until her father was settled; until his accusing presence had disappeared into sleep. Even then she moved as in a dream, slowly, to turn down the wick of the lamp and climb ponderously into the loft. She spread the cover over the dry rushes and without undressing stretched herself out, a hand resting on the white lawn handkerchief where Finn's head had lain. Not that sleep would come, nor did she want it. Dry-eyed now, she stared into the darkness. She kept looking toward the square of window in the room below, waiting for the night to lighten. The even, rhythmic snores of her father became more insistent and intrusive, getting on her nerves, making her more impatient and irritable.

And so she lay until the thin finger of dawn beckond hesitantly. She was down the ladder in a trice, 'like greased lightning' – Finn's description always raised a smile, even though this time it was only a weak one. Still, it lifted her spirits. Shoes in hand, she grabbed the white muslin scarf and crept quickly out into the cold October morn.

She inhaled great lungfuls of fresh air and felt a tremendous relief to have left the terrible snores behind. Too perturbed and anxious to feel the cold, she slipped on the shoes which Marie Jane had referred to as 'boats' and started off up the ridge. The wind tugged at her hair. Good, there'd be no mist at the top to hide the signal of her white scarf. He must see it. He must, he must, even though it was so early. Thank God he had thought of this, for what else could she have done? She could scarce go to the Aunt Hanratty's cabin and ask for him! What if he did not see the signal? What if he wasn't looking? What if it was, indeed, too early? After all, it was only she who had been awake all night.

Clutching the coarse material of her goat-skirt and lifting it above her ankles, she scrambled up and up, slithering and slipping on the soft, rain-soaked ground. She stopped to catch her breath, to wonder if the earth was really trembling beneath her feet, and how long it would be before the rain poured afresh from the pewter-grey sky. The plaintive call of a plover echoed like a banshee, and Tessa shivered.

With a concentrated effort, stumbling and panting, she reached the top of the ridge. Before even stopping to rest and get back her breath, she wedged the scarf beneath the large stones and, watching it trail out into wind, prayed to St Teresa that Finn would see it.

Restless, and anxious already, even though she had only just put the scarf out, Tessa stood in the mouth of the cave. The wind blew her skirts flat against her legs, buffetted her body and tangled her hair. Yet she stood erect, head high, eyes searching for any movement below. But who would be out when it was not yet full dawn?

Only Frank Kildare. If he and the two underkeepers with the carts and horses were to be at the cabin by noon, they would surely have left Fitzcarron House by now. I hope the axle breaks, or a wheel comes off, or better still the cart gets stuck in a bog-hole . . . I hope the earth opens and swallows them up! She also hoped her father would sleep late after his long journey and the amount of poteen he had put away, for if he did not sleep he would be out looking for her. And she had not got any of their stuff together like he'd said. She was in no hurry to leave the place where she had been born.

Her eyes roamed over the mountainy terrain, seeking comfort, a little softness, a little green, a little lightening of the sky. But the dark clouds, jagged and heavy in the dawn light, stared bleakly back. She turned from the battering wind to the peace and shelter of the cave. Sinking down onto the pile of rushes which did service in turn as a seat, couch and altar, she closed her eyes and submitted herself to the torture of a whole series of 'ifs'.

Every now and again, Tessa hurried over to the mouth of the cave. The scarf was there, trailing. Oh, Finn, hurry, hurry. Where the divil are you? Then back to the rushes, to stare at the lichen-covered walls, hearing them echo . . . 'I'm terrible fond of ye, Finn Collins,' and he, being the lovely fella to talk to, was never more lovely than when he had answered 'I'm more than terrible fond of you, Tess; I love you . . . I love you.'

And the plans they had made, sitting or lying on these blessed rushes. Plans to escape, plans to elope like she had read in books; these stones had heard them all. But all their eagerly discussed schemes had eventually come to nothing. She could not bring herself to break with her da in so clandestine a manner. It would kill him, she had said, and him being so proud. Tessa wished now that she had broken with him, wished fervently that she was miles away from Ennan and the Fitzcarron estate.

Finn had had his reservations, too.

'If only I could get up the courage to leave the Aunt. Me, who can take on any number of knackers in a punch-up, I'm scared of an old woman putting the mockers – '

'Take no notice,' she always broke in quickly on such thoughts. 'No curse could harm you, you're too good a fella.'

'Me ma and da were "good", as you put it, but look what happened to them!'

'But they crossed her in love.'

'And doesn't everyone know she's taken it out on me ever since? Come the time when I cross her, she'll curse me all right, like she did me da. But, Tess, she must never find out about us, because in her crazy head she'd reckon it was you enticing me away from her, and I'll not have her put the mockers on you, Tess . . .'

And so the lichen-covered stones echoed their plans, plans which crumbled like cheese through lack of money and courage. At one time Finn had seriously thought of enlisting in the army. O'Malley had said the recruiting sergeant was in Rohira till the month-end.

'At least they give you a pair of dacent boots,' he had declared, ruefully looking down at the split in his own. 'And a uniform – Mother o' God, Tess, I could fancy meself in a scarlet sash!'

'I fancy you just as you are. Promise me you'll not go . . . Besides, what if me da married me off while you were gone!'

They had laughed. It had been a joke. There was an old saying, she thought bleakly – many a true word spoken in jest! Panic rose in her throat. What if he had already gone for a soldier? She presumed he had forgotten the idea since the clearance had come to the valley.

They had decided to wait and see, to put their lives into the hands of the men from the various Boards and Societies. But fate had overtaken her, with both the pregnancy and her father's decision. Oh, she had to see Finn today, before her da woke up – before Kildare came.

Pulling her knees up to her chin, she began to rock to and fro. What a terrible night it had been, and sure the dawn was the slowest that ever streaked the sky. And now, waiting here, every moment seemed like an age. If Finn did not hurry it would be too late. What would he do, she wondered. No one will know where me and me da have gone to, not straight away, that is. News would spread slowly and by clearance time would be common knowledge, but for the present they'd not be missed, except by Finn. And once she was on the estate there would not be time or excuse to come all this way back . . . Oh, it was all a mess, as rotten, as stinking a mess as the Great Bog of Ennabrugh itself!

Her thoughts now climbed on a roundabout of recriminations. I should have gone down to the valley and left a message with Peggy Jams, or tried to get a well-wishing together. Her father had mentioned it, but only in talk; there would not have been time. But she should have arranged one all the same, anything to delay the departure. And naturally Finn would have been present! Oh, Mother o' God, what a fool I was not to have thought of that before!

She hurried impatiently outside. It was now full daylight. The wail of a cock cut the air. But there was no sign of movement, of life, and the absence of it frustrated her. The length of scarf fluttering freely mocked her. 'Finn!' she yelled. 'The dawn's been and gone! Where are you, you lazy divil! Is it the poteen you've been at?' she demanded of the wind. 'Oh, why are you not out tending that bloody great pig! "Do I not look up to the hills many times in the day?" you said. Why are you not looking now? Why? Why?'

Shivering with cold and shock, and full of remorse for not having the foresight to adopt the well-wishing scheme, she left the cave and fluttering scarf. Tight sobs stuck in her throat, constricted by the cold. She felt herself to be the unhappiest young woman in all the green of Ireland. More unhappy, more miserable, more burdened than anyone else. She had come up in the certainty of Finn observing the signal, of him coming up so that they would take off together like the red kite, defying her da, his aunt, Frank Kildare, the clearance –

the world. And now, she was returning, because she was cold and hungry and numbed, and because Finn had not been looking to the hills like he had said.

Then out of the depths of this awful despair she clutched at the idea that it was not too late to set up the well-wishing. She could hurry down, grab her shawl, drink some hot tea and a drop of poteen – God Almighty, what would she not give for a drop to warm her bones – and appeal to her da's better nature, to the proud side of him, with the idea that she should race down and invite them all up to give Proud Riley the sendoff befitting his standing! That was it, play up to his pride. Surely, she would say, surely they were not skulking away like horse thieves! The new scheme gave her spirits a lift. The sobs gave way to a sigh of relief. She would see Finn, make sure he came if no one else did!

Finn Collins stretched himself out on his bed and yawned. His eyes focused on the small patch of window. Holy Mother, and was it the light of day already? The night seemed to have gone on wings. His ears picked up at once the crack-and-grind, crack-and-grind of his aunt's rocking chair. She was awake, he thought – if she ever slept! Inwardly he groaned. His nostrils twitched, he recognised the odour of the pig and remembered where the night had gone. He lay still, gathering himself, bracing himself; his morning ritual. This morning would be especially arduous. The third and last pig had shown signs of the sickness and the Aunt had not been for leaving it out. Finn had had to drag, push and urge the great brute within the door of the cabin, and with the natural perversity of pigs, it had flopped onto its side within a couple of feet of his bed and refused to move another inch.

'Will ye wake up, idle crayture that y'are!' The croak cut across his thoughts. 'Rouse yourself, for the love of God, and look to the pig!'

He swore. Sure, he hadn't been on his bed above a short while; still in his clothes he was . . . But the pig. The pig! Apprehension began to curdle his stomach.

'What's she like?' demanded the croak.

'Give me a chance to pull me boots on!'

'Ye don't need your boots to see.'

He did not answer. It was but a stride to where the great pink and grey creature lay on its side, taking up half the floor space. He prodded it with his toe. C'mon, he urged it silently. Look lively or she'll have you good and proper, from ears to trotters, bladder to brains.

It did not move, despite another prod. His apprehension grew. Reaching for the jug of cold tea he took a long swig of it, glancing the while at the heavy sky outside.

'Starting to rain again,' he muttered irritably. Tess wouldn't get out with the goats if it came on heavy. 'It does nothing else in this godforsaken valley. Ennan must be the wettest, most desolate place in all the green of Ireland. It needs clearing – wiping off the face of the earth – and the sooner the better!'

He was hungry – when was he not? – he needed bread to restore his humour, but he knew there would not be any until his aunt chose to unlock the cupboard at the side of her chair.

'Tis the crayture I asked you about, not the state of the weather or your belly.'

At the mention of his belly, his glance went down to the pig. 'I don't think it's moved all night. I reckon this is another ye can say a requiem for.'

'Don't you try to be funny with me! I know what you're up to. This is the third this year, and the last. Don't think I don't know what you're up to, killing them off to get your own back. To take some petty revenge.'

'Me? Killing the pigs off! You're talking crazy, you are so. Haven't I been up most of the night with the great snorting brute, wiping it down and dosing it up with drops of lime water, and me with never so much as a crust of bread past me lips – ' The injustice of her accusation astounded him. 'Is it my fault,' he turned to face her, 'if the fever's in the ground, the swill, the air, the very water? The earth's so dank and sour even the spuds and turnips refuse to grow! Ailing pigs, ailing children: if it isn't the summer sickness takes them, it's the winter croup. And rain, rain, and more bloody rain! Even the Bog's turned against us. No peat to speak of. There!' he felt strengthened and pleasantly surprised that it was her turn to look astounded. 'There, you didn't know that, did ye? I've done what I could but the peat's failed. The pigs have failed, everything's failed . . .'

He went down on his haunches to look more closely at the animal. The crack-and-grind of his aunt's chair denoting her displeasure at his eloquence went unheeded, for he was hearing again the soft, silver-tongued words of O'Malley. 'Still here?' he'd joked. 'Still skivvying for the Aunt? If she doesn't bring you down the weather will, standing up to your knees in peat, digging it for her to sell to the knackers! She's making a right trade out of you – and not a penny do you get! 'Tis penal servitude,' he had said. 'Penal bloody servitude!'

Not any more, thought Finn, with a sudden rush of fire through his veins. No, Aunt Hanratty, not any more. But first he had to make sure of the pig. He examined it critically: the huge flanks were not moving. That in itself pointed to death, but he had to be sure. He opened the mouth and there was no resistance. When he relaxed his hold the jaws flapped together limply. To be absolutely certain, he applied the last, the final test. In his experience pigs did not like their ears being blown into. If there was no objection, the creature was dead beyond recall. He blew into both ears, one after the other – twice. The white silken eyelashes never even blinked.

He stood up, his stomach churning, food forgotten. ''Tis dead all right.'

'Still skivvying for the Aunt?' The silver-tongued words flashed through his mind, followed by the prospect of the clearance, thoughts of Tess, of what he owed to his dead parents. All these elements suddenly came together to give him courage.

'And what's more, Aunt,' he said with calm dignity. 'You can bleed it and cut it up yourself.'

The rockers of the chair stopped grinding instantly. The old woman sat poker-stiff. 'Brave words,' she croaked. 'Brave words coming from a fool's mouth! Your head's been stuffed full of fancy ideas ever since you went to town with O'Malley. And because, by a fluke, ye floored Spider Murphy's lad at the Fair you think you're the big fella. Little good the prize money did you!' The memory of the handsome black breeches and his white full-sleeved shirt smouldering beneath the turves reminded him of how near he had been to killing the old crone who was sitting there, mocking him, goading him. She laughed with malevolent glee. 'Throwing your weight about looking for Murphy's girl! And the clearance meeting – oh, they couldn't hold that without you, could they! And it's drunk you were at O'Malley's well-wishing.'

Oh, if only you knew, he thought; sure, it wasn't poteen I was drunk with. No, I was hopeless, legless, weightless . . . sure to God

I was in heaven itself, with Tess Riley! 'Well-wishing,' she went on. 'Good bloody riddance to him! And there you were, acting the big fella again. Passing the very door at the head of Jarvey's donkeys – no show without Punch!' Her voice lowered. 'You're full of big ideas, but they'll get you nowhere. Such a fool as yourself is going nowhere, d'ye hear that?'

He closed his eyes against the goblin mirth. It was never easy standing up to the taunts, they had a way of dragging him down. They wouldn't drag him down this time. He held onto his courage and reached for his coat. Her next words stopped him dead.

'You're not only a fool, you've got a lying tongue in your head, as glib as your da before ye.' An insidious tone crept into the croak. She said with a deliberate slowness. 'And you can forget any ideas you've got about that young woman.'

He thought he had finished with his stomach, but it gave a great lurch, churned and twisted into a tight knot. His mind reeled. Was it true, after all, what people said about her being a witch? Did she really possess . . . powers? She had put the mockers on many an unfortunate soul – he knew that for sure – and the terrible bad luck had overtaken them. Did she really . . . but she must, or how in God's name did she know? His heart hammered in his ribs; the sound filled his ears and paralysed coherent thought. How long he remained in mid-step to his coat, he did not know. The crack-and-grind of the chair stirred him back to the terrible reality of his surroundings: the dim cabin, the black clad figure of his aunt, the red glow of the turf, and the dead pig. He eyed the door and wished he was through it. 'Tis only a stride, he told himself, and I'm rooted to the ground. Something held him there, anchored him, would not let him go until the Aunt Hanratty had finished with him, until she had delivered her next blow.

'If you've set your cap at Riley's girl . . .'

This time he did not reel beneath the shock. With the first he had shored up his defences. His thoughts became clearer. Holy Mother, he thought, I've been so careful. That's what he could not understand. He mustered up courage. 'Riley's girl! You must be mad. In fact y'are, to think I could set me cap at any girl. Me! What in the name of the good God could I offer? And me without a farthing to me name; you've seen to that. Sure, I've nothing to offer and not likely to have while I stay under this roof! Would any young woman

336

in her right mind jump at the chance of living in this cabin? Of kipping down with me here while you sit up all night in your chair, like Dooley's ghost? And if that wasn't bad enough, when the weather's wild ye bring in the pigs for company! Can you see Proud Riley, or any other da, letting his daughter in for that? Besides, it's well known he never lets her out of his sight.'

'And d'you know why he doesn't?' The Aunt leaned forward, her eyes maliciously bright. 'Because he's guarding her virtue. He wants her to better herself and he's afraid of her becoming second-hand like her mother before her. But what he doesn't know yet is that she's been seen with a fella up by the ridge.'

The chair stopped rocking. The words rumbled round Finn's head. How did she know? Was she just trying it on, laying a trap for him? Oh, he was no match for her, for all this cat-and-mouse stuff. He stood white-faced, staring at the pig.

'So . . .' The cunning undertone sent his head up with a jerk. 'So, that's the way of it. Ye *are* setting your cap at Tessa Riley, and you're jealous. Ye didn't know about her going on the ridge with this other fella, did ye?'

'Shut your mouth, woman! There's nothing in the way of anything. You've no right to talk about Tess like that!'

'So, 'tis "Tess", is it? Very familiar y'are. Listen to me, you great fool. I've every right to warn you. If she'll go up to the rocks with one fella, she'll go with another . . .' She went on and on, her voice hoarse and croaking, but Finn did not hear any of it. His thoughts were with Tessa, surrounding her, protecting her from the wrath of his aunt.

'Will you stop your shouting!' he yelled at her. 'There's only one fella Tess has been seen with, and that's me. Yes, you were right. I have set me cap at her. And I'm not staying here while you say bad things about her!'

Her voice rose above his, cackling and squeaking in its rage. 'You're as daft as your da before ye – taken in by a fancy face! You'd better think well before you leave this cabin that's sheltered you all these years.'

'I'm past thinking. I've made up me mind. I'm not even staying until the month-end. Nothing, not even the prayers of the Holy Mother herself could persuade me to stay another night under this unfragrant roof – '

He backed away. His aunt rose from the chair. She pushed herself forward and he raised a hand to ward off the expected blow. But it wasn't a blow. She was pointing the finger at him. 'If you leave the Aunt,' she said hoarsely, 'for the likes of Tessa Riley, I'll curse you as surely as I cursed both your father and mother before you. I'll put the mockers upon yourself as sure as you put them on my pigs!'

'How many times do I have to tell you, I didn't put the mockers on the bloody pigs. I wouldn't know how!'

'No, you wouldn't.' The raised hand quivered. 'You're too simple! But get this!' He tried to escape the words, but they lodged in his ears and filled his brain. 'You'll rue the day ye took up with her! D'ye hear me? Are ye listening to the Aunt Hanratty?' Her voice took on a rasp-like quality, the rough edge filled with menace.

'I lay this curse on Finn Collins as I did on his da and ma before him. Nothing will go right. Nothing but the bad luck will befall the fool that deserts the Aunt that raised him for a – '

Finn did not hear what she called Tessa for the rush of blood in his ears. He bent swiftly down and snatched up his jacket. His aunt's gaunt fingers clawed at his sleeves. 'Bad cess, and good riddance – good bloody riddance! A curse on ye, a curse . . . a curse . . .'

He turned toward the door and tripped on the body of the pig. He swore and balanced himself. Without a backward glance he was through the door, banging it behind him. Slamming it on the curse. Although terror filled his heart, there was relief that the curse had not included Tess. It may have done if he had lingered or stayed to argue – as though he would! God help him, what an escape! He suddenly felt calm and controlled. He had been cursed. She could do no more. She had no hold on him. The ultimate, the dreaded thing that had kept him on a leash for years had now taken place. It was over. He wondered why he had been so terrified!

He took in great lungfuls of air and turned his face to the rain; never had either been so welcome or tasted so sweet. He heard a noise. Putting his head to one side, he listened carefuly. What was it? Just below the level of the wind he was conscious of a low lumbering sound. And did the earth tremble beneath his feet? Was it thunder? He looked uneasily up the valley. The hills and heights were stark in the desolate early morning light. The clouds were scudding along on a chill wind. His eye caught sight of something fluttering on the outcrop. A bird? It was Tess's scarf – the signal. Their signal! What, he wondered uneasily, what could be wrong to have sent her up to the ridge at this time? He began to run, glad of the opportunity to stretch his legs, to kick off the scene with his aunt.

The stiff breeze blew through his hair and stung his face. He felt fresh and clean, and full of joyful surprise that he had finally made the break. O'Malley would be proud of him! He was proud of himself! Wait until Tess heard! Free! Free! He was as free as a – suddenly he stopped running and stood still. Something was wrong. He looked about uneasily like an animal sniffing the air for danger. His ears had caught that low rumbling sound again. Thunder? Surely not thunder on a cold October day like this? There was something wrong with the ground – it had definitely moved, trembled beneath him. There it was again! The strange low lumbering sound. He looked up the valley and continued to stare with uncomprehending eyes. 'God save us all,' he breathed as he crossed himself. 'Oh, God Almighty save us!'

There at the head of the valley was the most astounding sight ever to beset mortal eyes. The soft centre of the Great Bog of Ennabrugh had risen above the confines of its banks, like dough from a giant bread tin. Charged with the recent heavy rains, it was about to break loose. It remained poised for a moment, and then, even as he watched, with another dull, rumbling roar, the Bog began to flow.

CHAPTER TWENTY

Jerked into action by so awesome a spectacle, Finn raced along the valley, shouting, trying to raise the alarm. It was impossible to cover them all, to knock and hammer on every door. He pounded on the first he came to, not recognising or caring who lived there, just so long as they got up, opened the door and helped to tell the others. He ran to the next, yelling through cupped hands to make the sound carry above the wind.

'Duggan! Duggan – get up! Get up! Jams! Kelly! Donal! Connor, wake up! Wake up your da! Jarvey! Jarvey! Rouse the shiftless – oh, Blessed Mary, Mother of God, get 'em up! Get 'em up!'

No one appeared. No one came out to join him. Were they getting dressed, making tea? Mother o' God, they'd not live to drink it! Those who heard the roar and felt the earth tremble would think it was a storm, and turn over on their beds. No one looked out at so early an hour in bad weather. No one expected Finn Collins to be tearing along the glen like a madman. No one ever expected to be in the path of a bog on the march.

'Get up! Get up, all of yous!' He knew he was the only one who could save them, and they would not be saved. The black treacly flow of unformed peat was heading straight for Ennan. Still shouting and shrieking against the wind he struck off the level while he had the chance. All the time, his eyes were watchful of the great mass. It was moving slowly at first and then, when the contours of the ground allowed, faster.

'Tess!' he shouted as he neared the top. 'Tess?' He stumbled into the entrance of the cave. She was not there. Outside the white scarf still flapped wildly in the wind.

He called her name again and again, gasping in breathless panic. She was not up here! Oh, God save her, he thought, she's gone down for her da. Would she have seen it all, he wondered, as he had? Would she have stood here and watched it rise, and even felt beneath her feet the lumbering and thundering which he had heard from the

Aunt's cabin? Of course, they had all heard stories of bogs 'breaking loose' and 'going on the march', but these were regarded as tales of antiquity, like when it rained for a year and brought fish to the doors. No one ever expected these things to happen now.

He stood, unable to move, heart hammering, dry-mouthed and wide-eyed; totally unable to comprehend the awful catastrophe which was unfolding before him. The Great Bog of Ennabrugh, under whose shadow humanity had dwelt for years immemorial, had turned vengeful. The jack-o'-lanterns, the mists, the primordial remains, the clumps and stumps: the landmarks of centuries were on the move, parading before him like a grotesque peep show.

The thick cumbersome waterfall began to trickle, slowly at first, then, gathering momentum, poured steadily from its height down into the valley of Ennan. Sparing nothing and no one, it winkled out the limewashed cabins and huts, surrounding the walls and creeping in on its victims through every crack and crevice.

The sheds and shacks of the shiftless, like their owners, put up no resistance and collapsed at the first impact. The Byrnes, all six, were smothered while they slept, snuffed out like their smoking chimneys. The Grogans, too, were suffocated, never knowing what had happened.

The rest of the community were still not unduly alarmed. They had ignored the banging on their doors and the frenzied shouts of Finn Collins, thinking the clearance had come. It had been agreed to give the authorities as much trouble as possible, and no cooperation at all.

Gypo Kelly had been the first to see a sliver of black slime beneath his door. Thinking himself to be the victim of the slovenly ways of the shiftless, he had flung open the door to take them to task. The Bog poured in through the gap, the force of it knocking him down. Yelling to his wife and Una, he struggled to his feet. 'The door!' he cried. 'Help me with the bloody door!' But their frenzied attempts to close the door or block the entrance were futile. The muffled eagerness with which it encroached was more frightening than any noise. The weight of the slime, thick and coarse with formless, fibrous material, forced them back to the walls, the table, the rafters. Gypo tried to punch through the roof but the weight of the Bog on top prevented him. There was no escape and their prayers died on their lips.

The Bog had not yet reached the lower level of the valley. Jams and his family, roused by the screams of the Duggan girls, leapt from their beds and fled. The cries of alarm were added to by the Jarvey men. 'Get to the donkeys!' they shouted to the Connors. Mona shot a terrifed glance at Kevin struggling with the child in his arms and began to run. All eyes were on the five creatures tethered some seventy yards away, ears twitching, tails swishing anxiously. The sight of them, the hope of salvation stirred every heart and quickened the pace. First there, first served. The donkeys would make for high ground and safety . . . Ah, blessed safety! Never did seventy yards seem so far. On and on they stumbled, the Bog, tireless in its pursuit, catching at their heels.

Suddenly, the donkeys, crazed with the sense of menace, broke loose and bolted. Jarvey swore savagely and yelled after them. His voice trailed helplessly. Mona stumbled. Kevin stopped to lift her and fell too, with the child. Hearing it wailing and choking on the slime, the two of them desperately searched and dug. The cries stopped, and Kevin and Mona gave up, the Bog covering them like a blanket.

None of the others dared stop. Hope was now transferred to the Hanratty cabin at the end of the glen. What they would do when they got there was not clear, but it was a focal point; it was still standing. The Duggans, the Jamses and the Jarveys lurched toward it, the muffled roar of Ennabrugh in their ears.

'God save and help us . . . Christ and His blessed Mother . . .' Every breath was a prayer.

The Duggan girls, exhausted beyond endurance, slowly gave themselves into the cold embrace of their follower. Mrs Jams sank like a stone. Peggy, having lost the rest of her family, clung fiercely to her father. The lava-like flow, although on the level, was gathering momentum from the weight behind it. Young and Old Duggan, the Jarveys, and the two Jamses were not far from the Hanratty cabin, but all knew in their hearts that the Bog would be there before them.

The crack-and-grind of Shena Hanratty's chair stopped. She got up and listened to the unusual noise, the strange sound of her neighbours' voices. Glancing at the dead pig and cursing her nephew, her eyes narrowed. What was going on outside? She was not allowing anyone in her compound – just let them try! She opened the door. Ennabrugh was there, eagerly waiting to reunite her with her sister Moll and Tony Collins.

At the far side of the valley, Frank Kildare was on his way down when he realised something was happening. Instead of turning back while he still could, his desire to make sure Tessa Riley came to the Fitzcarron estate got the better of his judgement. He felt the earth trembling, saw with startled eyes the Bog poised to engulf him, and in an instant was swept down to his death.

Finn stared in helpless anguish as the figures in the valley below were swiftly overtaken. From this height he could not distinguish one from another, and did not want to. He would always remember them as they had been, alive and colourful in their various ways, not struggling hopelessly against death.

Mother o' God, why had no one opened their doors? Then he realised they had presumed the clearance was upon them. God rest their souls. They would never make things difficult for anyone ever again. Never dance, sing, play the fiddle, get drunk. The clearance had come all right – he shuddered. Ennan would be cleared for ever. What had he said to the Aunt? 'It ought to be wiped off the face of the earth and the sooner the better.' But he hadn't meant it to be like this! Oh, Christ Almighty, he had not meant it to be like this at all . . .

He lunged onwards, trying not to think of Riley's cabin being the first in Ennabrugh's wake, fear for Tess's safety giving him an extra impetus. He prayed she would not be there. Why had she not waited by the cave? To think that while he had been shillyshallying over that bloody pig she had been up here waiting for him . . . Anxiety, sharpened by a sudden fear of the Aunt's curse, made him run faster, stumbling over tussocks, sinking ankle deep in pockets of soft peat.

Finn made his way around to a point above Riley's cabin. From here he could see the river of peat flowing past, but saw that it might be possible to wade through its shallows to the cabin wall, lower here than in the front where the ground dropped towards the valley floor.

Memories of Tessa accompanied him as he ran. Himself punching a knacker's lad for making fun of her when she was little. Glimpses of her vitality, of how grand she had looked in a summer dress of cotton print O'Malley had bought from the old Jew. Beside Marie Jane, she had been innocently provocative, always different, set apart. Before the excise men took Pat Feeney, she had learned to read and write better than any. But the most precious recollection of all was Tessa in his arms, her soft warmth pressing against him, her generous lips beneath his own as they had sworn to love each other for ever. And over those memories fear cast its dark shadow . . . fear of the Aunt's curse . . . fear of life without Tessa . . . fear of finding so lovely a creature drowned in this stinking morass.

Finn felt as though it had taken him longer than he had ever thought possible to reach the high ground behind Riley's cabin. Looking down, he almost froze. The cabin, on the edge of the Bog's flow, was still there, but only just; the sliding tide of peat reached almost half way to its thatched roof.

He shouted. Nothing but the echo of his own voice broke the weird silence. He felt suddenly constricted by fear. Was he the only one alive? The only breathing soul in a valley of the dead? 'Oh, Jesus Christ, son of Mary,' he prayed, 'let me find her alive. St Teresa, let me find her living and breathing!'

Wading fiercely through the sucking river of peat, Finn reached the cabin wall and heaved himself up onto the eaves. He attacked the thatch with savage strength, tearing it away and hurling it into the Bog, which sucked it down hungrily, squelching and gurgling in the process. The Bog had covered the tables, chairs, hearth . . . the loft was empty – the ladder must have slipped, to be swallowed by the greedy Bog. Balancing precariously, he lowered himself down into the loft. Holding his breath, he looked down onto the dresser beneath. And then he saw her. She had climbed onto the fine piece of furniture for safety. Oh, she's the clever one, he thought, beside himself with the joy of finding her. Oh, darling girleen, thank the Holy Mother!

Up to her shoulders in the mire, Tessa was standing upright by sheer willpower. Her mind and body were numb. No longer could she think of Finn; even prayer was beyond her. Only dogged concentration remained. She must keep erect, must keep herself from keeling over, must keep her feet on the narrow shelf of the dresser, keep her chin from sinking onto her chest . . . keep alive.

'Tess? Tess!'

She heard the voice; it sounded distant, as though from another world. Her heart stirred. Memory shifted. She tried to answer, but her mouth and jaws were stiff with cold. She must answer, lest he go away thinking her dead. She felt dead.

344

'Tess? Can you hear me, Tess? Open your blessed eyes. It's Finn. I've come for ye. Oh, look at me, Tess; open your eyes!'

She was surprised to find her eyelids able to part. The sight of him, leaning over the edge of the loft, flooded her heart with hope. 'Finn . . . Finn!' The cry was faint, but the effort had been made, faculties had been set into motion.

'I'm here, Tess. I'll have you out o' there in no time at all. Keep your eyes open. Keep watching me. Do you understand?' He was shouting frantically, but was not aware of it.

Still leaning over, he stretched out his arms, wondering how to pull her off the dresser without both of them losing their balance and falling beneath the black surface, to remain there for ever.

'Try an' raise your arms, Tess,' Finn begged, as he lay flat on the loft floor, reaching down to her. And all the time he was calling out a wondrous mixture of encouragements, endearments, prayers and oaths.

She tried, and could not muster the strength. Then she felt the strong grasp on her shoulder, pulling her arms above the level of the Bog. Her fingers were too numb to clasp his hands. Her arms slipped back. She had not the strength to stop them sinking.

Finn swore. He was panicking now, and in his imagination he was fighting off not merely the encroaching Bog, but his aunt's curse. His parents had met their death in this same Ennabrugh; he owed it to them to survive. If he and Tess went under, the Aunt would win. By the Almighty God, she wasn't winning this time!

He tried with all his strength to pull her up again, but the moment he relaxed his hold to take another deep breath, the Bog sucked her back, unwilling to yield even a limb of its victim. The homespun skirt, which held water like a sponge, made the rescue more difficult. Tears of desperation gathered. The veins stood out on his face and arms. Chest heaving, he took great tearing breaths. The Aunt was not going to win. No curse was going to take Tess away from him.

'I'm going to get you out of this, I am!' His voice, hoarse with shouting, choked to a strangled gasp as, with a sheer frenzy of animal strength, he laboriously hauled her, slowly at first, from Ennabrugh's tenacious hold. Balancing himself, he pulled her up into the loft and over the eaves where she straggled and dangled helplessly like a big rag doll. With a last immense effort he slid over the wall.

Pulling her off the eaves and holding her tightly for a minute in his arms, he could feel the dead weight of her. She was weak and suffering from exposure, but he had to get her going.

'You must try to walk, Tess, I can't carry you. It's too thick and deep, and still on the move, still coming down. God help us, Tess, we've got to make for the hillside or we'll be taken down by the force of it. Are ye listening?' He addressed her closed eyes, her sinking head. She nodded weakly. He shook her shoulders roughly. 'Move! C'mon, girleen, for God's sake make the effort! It'll get your blood going, take some of the cold off you. See, I'm sticking tight to your hand, for if you stumbled and fell, sure to God I'd never find you. D' you hear me, Tess?'

She looked up at him, eyes glazed with terror, and nodded. Grateful for a response, he gripped her with his left hand and with his right made a swimming motion to part the black slime, to forge a way ahead. And so they pushed and inched their way carefully out of the path of the bog, until it became more shallow and the hillside took them out of its reach.

The fateful day closed in early. It was grey, and the lessening wind did nothing to stir the leaden weight of the clouds. After a slow and stumbling progress Finn considered they were far enough from danger to rest. Tessa collapsed with exhaustion, and he, scarcely able to go further, found a sheltered hollow where they slept.

'When I get some money, Tess,' he murmured before closing his eyes. 'I'm going to buy a Connemara shawl to keep you warm . . .'

The young keepers, who had set out with Frank Kildare but had remained with the cart, returned to Flavell's cottage and from there the news was hurried to Lord Fitzcarron. The Authorities would be up from the town at first light and the disaster would be reported in all the newspapers. Then the curious would follow; and the paunchy men who had lined the platform in the Long Dance would arrive in carts and carriages saying what a pity the clearance had not taken place sooner and saved the lives of an entire community.

Stiff and cold, Finn woke to the dawn and the sound of Tessa softly weeping for her father, rocking to and fro with bitter grief and guilt. Finn was content to let her mourn. His silence spoke more than words, and there they sat, arms about each other, on the wild moor. He stroked her mud-caked hair and smoothed away her tears with his forefinger.

'I should never have left the cabin.' Her voice was broken with sobbing. 'I left him this morning lying by the fire, drunk with poteen as though he'd never wake. Oh Finn! I had to get to him, and I tried to reach him, but it had covered him like a shroud. If I'd been there and not on the ridge I could have – '

'Ye couldn't Tess. Ye'd have been overcome – like all the others.'

'I could have done something – warned him. Oh, I could have tried to save him!'

Tears welled afresh, spilling out and rolling in hot rivulets down her peat-stained face. Her father had often said, while polishing the silver buckle of his belt, 'When I'm dead, Teresa, ye must keep this belt in the blessed memory of your real da.' 'Away with ye,' she had laughed. 'You're realer to me than him.'

And standing there beside his body, the tide of Ennabrugh rising higher, she knew the belt was buried with the man, she did not remove the belt. If he was to be buried like this, beneath the peat he had spent his life working on, he would be buried wearing the belt her mother had given him as a wedding present, and which he had been proud to wear. It would be a companion to the silver flute he had returned to the Bog after her mother's death all those years ago.

Her mind now whirled with dreadful remorse. Was she being punished for having sinned and not made confession of it? Although they had no resident priest in Ennan, if she had been repentant, she could have made arrangements to see him. But terror of being found out had been her uppermost emotion; terror and not sorrow. How could she have told her father she was pregnant? Proud Riley would never have lived it down – and now he was dead. And he wouldn't have been if she hadn't left him; if she hadn't been worried to death about the ramifications of her pregnancy, and Kildare and his carts –

Oh, Kildare! He, too, with the young keepers who'd come to take their stuff, all would have been overtaken. In her anguish she had wished their axles broken, their wheels to be caught in bog-holes, and the earth to open and·swallow them up. I didn't mean it! she cried out in her heart. Oh, God forgive me, sure I didn't mean it!

She looked up at Finn and gathered strength from his presence. He had told her about the Aunt, the curse; and, in a low voice, what he had said about Ennan, that it needed clearing off the face of the earth and the sooner the better. He, too, had not meant it. Poor Finn. The bright, free look had deserted him. He looked older. His eyes – the colour of the blue butterflies which lived a brief summer on Ennabrugh – were sombre, his jaw was set, and his mouth, usually generous to smile and quick to whistle, was grim.

'Why did you leave the cabin, Tess?' His question brought her back to her troubles with a jolt. 'Sure, an' never did I expect to see your scarf floating in the wind so early.'

Tessa swallowed hard. Not for her very life could she tell him about the baby here and now. It was not the time or the place. He would be rash and promise to marry her so as not to add to her bereavement, and Tessa Riley wanted to be married for her own sake, not merely to give their child a name.

'Why?' he persisted. 'Why were you up there, Tess?'

She thought quickly. 'It was me da, you see . . .' She told him of her father's arrangement with Frank Kildare and how the carts would be up at noon, and that that was the reason she had gone to the ridge and let out the signal. 'That's why I wanted to see you. I didn't know what to do . . .' It was the truth, God help her; in this world of falsehood, it was the truth. And in making her decision to delay telling of the baby until a more auspicious time, she somehow felt stronger, more in charge of herself and her affairs.

'Then I had this idea of getting up a well-wishing, just to delay things until I saw you and told you what was afoot.'

Their quick hurried bursts of conversation, interspersed with tearful laments for their dead neighbours and helpless comments about their own plight, filled the waking hours. In a kind of daze, ignoring hunger and cold, they talked to get the shock of it all out of their minds. Not that such sights could ever be totally erased.

'What will we do with ourselves?' Tessa's question hung in the morning air.

'We'll find something,' he answered.

'I suppose we could head back in that direction. The Authorities will still be . . . well, they'll still be there.'

'Is that what you really want, Tess?'

It seemed imperative to him that he put as much distance as

possible between himself and the place where his aunt had cursed him. Even though she was dead, he would feel safer away. Yet, for Tess's sake, he would go back, if that was what she wanted.

But, was it what she wanted? If – and God forbid – Finn did not want to get married, she did not doubt her capacity to work for the child and raise it herself. But life for a young unmarried woman with a child had other aspects to it. Men thought you were 'easy', and women regarded you with suspicion. The baby would be branded a bastard from birth, and if they took her to the workhouse it would be branded a 'charity bastard'. It would be the butt of jokes from other children and the object of speculation as to who the father was. If there was any shame or hardship in the future, she would endure it where nobody knew her. Yes, she owed it to her dead da's memory to take any chance of getting away from the mountainy country and its peat-bogs.

She and Finn would be presumed dead and Proud Riley's good name would be left intact. They, too, like Marie Jane, would embark on a new life, and when they were settled she would write and tell her of their survival.

Finn had always recognised a certain indefinable quality about Tessa – 'like a woman regal born' was his definition – but never had the quality shone through so much as now, when caked in black bog slime, she drew herself up, and with a sudden uptilt of chin, said, 'No, I don't want to go back. But, what else is there?'

'You could marry me, Tess, when we get out of this.'

She cast him a glance as though she had not heard properly.

'I can't be going on without you, without us getting married. Say you will, Tess? I nearly lost you and it made me realise how much you mean to me.'

'It's only because of all o' this you're saying that – '

'I love you,' he said simply. 'I want to be, not only your fella, your lover, but your husband.'

She hesitated. 'There's something you have to know. I'm going to have a baby.' She blurted it out, too weary and cold to bother wrapping it up; abandoning all the pretty speeches she had planned, all the fancy words to coddle the crucial statement. 'That's the reason, or part of it, why I felt so desperate to set the signal on the ridge. With Kildare coming, and all of that, I had to see ye; I didn't know which way to turn.'

'Tess, ye should have told me straight away!' He caught her by the waist and swung her round in a frenzy of delight. 'To think you've been keeping it to yourself all these weeks!'

'I thought that you, being soft on the sentiment, as Mr O'Malley used to say, you'd marry me just to do the right thing.' She threw him another glance, candid and straight. 'You don't have to marry me. I love you too much to hold you to the asking.'

'And I love you too much to let you go, ever.' He took her hands. 'I'm still waiting for an answer.'

'Yes. Yes, I'll marry ye,' she replied on a sigh of contentment.

'But, Tess,' his voice was suddenly loaded with concern. 'This changes things. We should go back to the Authorities while there's a chance. We could never walk to Rohira without warmth and food. Once they've gone down, it will be terrible risky. It's well enough to take chances when there are only the two o' us to consider . . .' He stopped talking to follow her glance.

Straggling figures had appeared on the distant skyline: a raggle-taggle procession of beshawled women like hooded crows and ragged children frolicking like hares.

'Tinkers!'

They both stared as if it was a mirage.

'It could be Spider Murphy returning to the winter quarters.'

'Or a tribe like the Clancys!'

'Keep your eyes on 'em, Tess. If they've got a caravan it's the Murphys!'

'But, Finn!' she exclaimed in alarm. 'Sure to God I'd rather die out here than throw meself on the mercy of that divil, Mick.'

'As if I'd let you do that, Tess. He was banished, remember? Tinkers don't go back on their word!' He pointed ahead. 'Look! God save us, I can't believe it!'

The barrel-shaped silhouette which Tess never thought to see again appeared on the landscape, swinging seductively from side to side, leisurely drawn by a long-tailed pony.

'Finn, there's two of 'em! What do you make of it?'

'It'll be Martin Jarvey! Him and Kate! Did he not say it wouldn't be long before he got a van for Kate? No more tents and rigs for them. Isn't he just the boyo? If Martin's there, Mick must be well and truly gone like I said. And it wouldn't be a case of throwing yourself on their mercy, Tess. They owe you on account of Kate, and tinkers always repay a debt of honour. Besides, we can't do much else – we're starvin' on our feet, and like to catch our death if we stay out another night.'

'But Finn, we're as black as sweeps and smelly as goats. C'mon, let's find a pool to get some of it off!'

Laughing with sudden relief he followed her, and while they washed he kept his eye on the distant procession. 'We can spend a few days with them and then be off on our own way before the winter sets in.'

'What do you mean? On our way to where?'

'To Dublin,' he said, full of the purpose which Martin Jarvey had always inspired.

She straightened up. 'Did ye say Dublin?'

'I did so. I'm going to find work and get enough money for the fare over, like I've often talked about in the cave. See,' he teased. 'You thought it was all daydreams, like Marie Jane, didn't ye! O'Malley used to say that England was the land flowing with milk and honey. What d'ye say, Tess? Are we to join up with Martin and Kate?'

'Yes,' she replied quickly, looking round the bleak mountainy moorland. 'Sure, I've no fancy to spend another night out here.' She breathed deeply on a contented sigh. 'Honest, I never expected in all the world to set me eyes on Kate Murphy again!'

'And I'm scared to death of her ma.'

Tessa suddenly went serious. 'Finn, we'll have to tell Martin about his father and his uncle being drowned.'

'Don't worry, girleen; I'll tell him. Before we go to meet 'em, Tess, you did mean what you said about marrying me?'

'I did so, Finn Collins – and don't be wriggling out of it already!'

'Well, to show you I really mean it – marry me over the brush, like Kate and Martin. Spider will marry us with the tinker rites.'

'But tinker rites are not the church's rites. Being married over the brush isn't legal, Finn. To be married proper we'll have to find money for the priest and put banns in, and all o' that.'

'We'll have all o' that, as you put it, when we get to Dublin, but in the meantime, I'll give ye a bright scarf to wear on your hair, and we'll make sure our little 'un has got a proper da and name. Besides,' he added archly, 'there's no harm in making sure of you, is there!'

'Did I ever tell you,' she smiled, striding out with him. 'What a darlin' fella you are!'

As they walked toward the distant caravans, the Great Bog of Ennabrugh, having devoured a community, lay like a huge serpent, satiated and still.

Its greed had changed the landscape, enlarging and levelling the valley, opening it out to a greater wilderness over which a sinister silence was already settling. No plover or kite stayed to mourn the dead. Ennan was a forgotten corner of Ireland, and Ennabrugh, to whom a thousand years was as a day, settled to rest.